HEIRS OF AVALON

Book Three of the Children of Fire Series

Alica McKenna-Johnson

Risk your heart

Alica McKenna

I dedicate this book to you, the beautiful, unique, intelligent person who is reading these words right now. Without you I wouldn't have the strength to write and edit and revise over and over until I wanted to cry. Without your kind emails, happy tweets, sweet messages, and thoughtful reviews I wouldn't be an author. For those of you who cheered me on in my fanfic days, supported me as a baby author, and are now joining my writing journey I feel blessed by each and every one of you.

Chapter One

"Experience: that most brutal of teachers. But you learn, my God do you learn." ~ C.S. Lewis

Never, ever, offer to help a leprechaun pick up its spilled gold. Groaning, I stretched. My hand protested as the scabbed-over teeth marks pulled, and my stiff muscles resisted the movement. Blinking, I looked around the room wondering where I was. Rich cream-on-cream striped walls gave away no secrets, and the mirrored sliding door leading to what I assumed was the closet didn't look familiar either. Sitting up, I watched the cream cotton sheets and black satin comforter pool around my waist. Swanky, yet, still unfamiliar.

Scooting to the edge of the bed, I let my toes hover over the polished oak floors, where a pair of white slippers waited for me. I slid my feet into them and stood, my knees wobbling. What in the world was wrong with me? I shuffled towards a door, but the locks on it marked it an exit and not the bathroom I desperately needed. I looked around. In the center of the room stood a cream love seat with black throw pillows, facing a flat screen TV set on the wall a few feet from the front door. Black drapes with hints of sheer cream underneath covered one wall. An ornately carved desk and chair sat against the far wall, and next to it another door. I opened the door, and couldn't help but gasp at what I found. It was the largest hotel bathroom ever. The sink, counters, and bathtub were carved out of some pale tan stone flecked with white. Glass encased a separate shower stall, and finally, I found the toilet. Ooh, thank goodness.

After I freshened up it was time to figure out where I am. On the desk sat a full sized pad of stationery with Royal Garden Hotel, London, England, embossed across the top. I pulled open the thick, black satin drapes, and revealed sheer cream underneath. Beyond both of them I saw a park. Gray branches reached into the foggy December sky. I placed my hand on the cool glass, and saw where red scabs marred my light copper skin. Stupid leprechaun. I remembered opening a portal in Ireland, getting bitten, the walk-ins, and then rushing to the hotel. The rest of the Cirque du Feu Magique had gone ahead to Belfast. Most of them have no idea who we are or why we travel with them, except Michael the ringmaster and his daughter Nyota, our tech wizard.

Belfast had crashed through my empathic shields. I was too tired and weak to protect myself, and the pain trapped in the stones of the city overwhelmed me. The last thing I remembered was being stuffed onto a small plane with images of bombings and the screams of its victims flashing in my head.

I heard a soft knock on the door, then it opened. "I'm checking on her now, Gavin," said Anali. Her shoulder-length hair looked mussed from sleep, and her turquoise nightgown and robe glowed bright against the neutral colors of the room. She held a cell phone in her hand. "Oh. Good morning, Sapphire. Feeling better? Yes, Gavin, she's up. Well, I don't know how she feels, she hasn't answered yet. Well, perhaps if you spoke to her." Anali handed me the phone.

"Hi, Uncle Gavin," I said, my voice raspy.

"Sapphire, are you okay?" I held the phone away from my ear. "I am so sorry. I should have known."

Anali looked me over as she placed her hand on my forehead, then handed me a glass of water. "Are you okay?" she whispered.

I nodded then guzzled the water.

"Good. I'll go get changed and then come back and help you get ready," she said.

I nodded again and waited for a chance to speak. "Uncle Gavin, calm down, I'm okay now."

"You sound fine," he said his voice soft.

"I am fine. Ireland was lovely, except for the damn leprechaun. I had no idea I would react so strongly to Belfast."

"I should have known. You were tired, and we were all drained from opening that portal and running from walk-ins. My only thought was to catch up to the circus and Nyota. I knew she would have the dampening field set up in the hotel and we'd be safe, but then ..." Gavin's voice cracked.

"'Experience: that most brutal of teachers. But you learn, my God, do you learn.' C.S. Lewis said that."

Gavin chuckled. "One of the quotes from your mom's journal. So what did she have to say about experience?"

"We can do our best to read and prepare, but life will always be our greatest teacher. We will make mistakes, flounder, and sometimes fail. But as long as we learn from each experience, then it isn't bad or wasted. Try not to stress out about being prepared for everything—that is impossible. Just do your best and learn," I recited from memory.

"True," he sighed. "But still ..."

"Uncle Gavin, none of us thought I would tap into the tragedies that had happened in Belfast. It was too much and too new. I was unprepared to deal with it. Anyway, you got me out of there."

"I worried when you didn't wake up right away. Anali said you were fine."

"And she was right. Isn't she always right?" I teased.

Gavin huffed. "Yes, she is, but still you were asleep for over twenty-four hours. How do you feel now? What do you feel now?"

"My body's a bit stiff, but if I slept that long, I know why. My empathy isn't picking up on anything specific right now. But this hotel seems modern, and we are pretty high up."

"I thought that would help," Gavin sighed. "After the trouble you've had, I didn't want to put you in an older building. I hoped being higher up might help buffer anything that had seeped into the ground."

Gavin did this for me? We stayed in nice places, but this was insane, and I couldn't imagine how expensive. I ran my fingers over the silky drapes. He chose this place to help me?

"Can you feel anything at all?" he asked.

I closed my eyes and reached out to open up my empathy to the area. A gentle hum of old magic came from the garden. "If I open up, I can feel an ancient magic."

"You said the same thing about Ireland."

"Yes, but Ireland felt more mischievous. Not that the magic here is all serious, just a calmer playfulness. It's like magical beings have lived here for so long their powers are soaked into everything." I laughed. "I wouldn't be surprised if there was pixie dust in the soil, and fairies' tears in the water. It's everywhere."

"But it all feels safe?"

I took a deep breath allowing my empathy to stretch out. "There are dark beings here just as they are everywhere. Nothing feels overwhelming or sinister, and from my room I have to focus to feel even a faint shadow of magic. Thank you, Uncle Gavin."

"I'm glad I was able to make things easier for you." Gavin sighed, and I imagined him running a hand through his wild flame-red hair. "I have to go. Have fun with Anali. We'll be there tomorrow morning. Tonight's the last show."

"Tell everyone I said hi. Hey, what did you tell the circus people?"

"I told them you had a severe migraine and sometimes they can last for days, so I sent you and Anali ahead for the peace and quiet."

"They bought that?" I'd seen some of the circus performers rolling their eyes at the lame excuses we gave over the past year. Of course, if we came right out and said, "Hey—we are descendants of a Phoenix King and Queen. We'll be gone for a week while we open a portal to Akasha, return magical creatures to their home, and battle an ancient evil," I doubt that would go over very well either.

"As much as ever." Gavin answered. "They know they are paid well and given much better food and lodging than most circuses, so they put up with my eccentric ways. I need to go. Michael wants everyone at the gym in half an hour."

"All right. Have a good day."

"Bye, Sapphire, and stay safe."

"You too, Uncle Gavin."

Guilt trickled into my stomach, I felt bad for not being there for the show tonight, and for keeping Anali away. Even though we needed to disappear now and then, we did our best to make it to performances. Sighing, I opened the closet door. My clothes had been hung up or folded onto the shelves on the side. Anali must have gotten bored. I grabbed some clean underwear, socks, jeans, a tee shirt, and sweater and headed for the shower.

After trying all the different settings on the shower—rain being my favorite—I felt ready to face the day. Anali sat at the desk flipping through a guide book. "Feeling better?"

"Much," my stomach growled. "Well, except for being hungry."

Anali smiled, her brow crinkling around her red bindi. "That we can fix."

Luxury surrounded us. The décor was subtle and simple, but even I knew it was the best quality. The brass railings on the elevator didn't even have smudges or fingerprints on them. Anali's footsteps echoed on the black marble floor of the lobby.

Her pink cotton pants and tunic, trimmed with silver leaves and vines, were reflected in the marble's polished surface. Note to self: be careful when walking across this floor in a skirt.

My stomach growled again as we reached the restaurant. The gentleman seating us wore a crisp, dark gray suit. A moment later a woman in a white blouse and straight black skirt filled our glasses with water. "What can I get you this morning?"

"A pot of Oolong tea to share, and I think we'll have the continental breakfast," said Anali.

"Very good. I'll bring that right out."

Anali patted my hand. "You stay here. I'll bring you something."

"Okay." I sipped my water and watched the other guests, feeling very conspicuous in my simple outfit. I felt like I was sitting in a movie or fashion magazine. Well-groomed people ate with impeccable manners. Silk ties and scarves were in no danger of having anything spilled on them. Hair stayed put, possibly from gel and hairspray, but I suspected it was force of will that all should be perfect that kept many locks in their stylish dos. I ran my hair through my damp curls, and my fingers caught on a tangle.

Almost a year ago—had it only been a year?—on the morning of my fifteenth birthday, I woke up to find my brown hair had turned black with fire-red streaks. My dull gray green eyes had become pale peridot green with golden flecks, and my light brown skin had become a soft copper brown. I went from being another unwanted group home kid to Gavin's niece and the Jewel of Shamash and Aya, the Phoenix King and Queen, my direct ancestors. Here I sat in London, days away from my sixteenth birthday, and I still felt lost in a faerie tale. Of course today it seemed more like an episode of *Doctor Who* because of all the lovely British accents.

"Here you go." Anali handed me a plate filled with several pastries, a bowl of yogurt topped with muesli, and fresh fruit.

"There is also a selection of cheese and rolls if you want something more savory."

"Thanks, Anali, this looks great." I picked up a pastry and moaned when I tasted the filling of bittersweet chocolate and almonds. Instantly I felt better.

"Pardon me," said the server setting down a white tea set with hand-painted periwinkles and poured us each a cup of tea. "Can I get you anything else?"

"No, thank you," said Anali. She turned to me. "It's been two days since you've eaten, so make sure you eat slowly."

Stuffing the last bite of chocolate almond awesomeness into my mouth, I nodded and added honey to my tea. She was right. As much as I wanted to try my first scone, I needed to slow down before my stomach cramped. Instead, I watched as Anali covered her scone in clotted cream and lemon curd.

"So what should we do today?"

I shrugged and sipped my tea.

"Well, we can stay in and watch TV or read if you're tired. Or do touristy things. Or you could finally admit that you've grown and your clothes are too small, and go shopping."

I reached up to adjust my bra. Was I spilling out of it again?

Anali raised an eyebrow and took a sip of tea.

I sighed. "Okay, we can go shopping."

"Wonderful. I was looking in the guide book the hotel provided, and Knightsbridge isn't far. It has a lot of stores, including Harrods and Harvey Nichols, which are department stores. We also need to get you several formal outfits," Anali said stirring her yogurt and muesli.

"What, why? And what do you mean by formal?" Images of lacy frills and pinching shoes filled my mind.

"Well," Anali said, "Gavin received an invitation to a charity gala, your birthday is coming up, and my cousin is getting married while we are here."

"Oh. But why do I need something fancy to wear on my birthday?"

"Miu is making plans," Anali said.

I hoped that Anali was helping with those plans. I guess, I could, in theory, find a nice outfit and wear it to all the different events, right? Then I wouldn't need more than one uncomfortable outfit. I bit into the scone—it tasted like a lemon meringue pie only better.

"My cousin is having a traditional Indian wedding, and I was wondering if you wanted to wear a sari," Anali asked. "Most of the women there will be wearing one."

My forehead crinkled. Anali always looked so elegant when she wore a sari. I wasn't sure I could pull it off. I certainly didn't feel elegant. "The saris you wear are very pretty, and they look more comfortable than a lot of dresses. At least there won't be any ruffles."

"Okay, we'll find a sari shop, and I am sure we can find several dressy outfits for you without any ruffles."

We stood in front of the hotel while the doorman got us a cab. The air felt cold and the gray sky threatened rain. Frowning, I wrapped my scarf around my neck.

Anali bumped me with her shoulder. "Come on, it'll be fun. I never get you all to myself. And I promise we'll only buy things you like and that look good on you."

I smiled. "It does sound like a lot of fun. And I do need new clothes," I admitted as we got into the cab.

I kept my eyes closed while Anali talked about all the clothes I needed. Riding on the left side of the road freaked me out.

"Here we are, ladies," the cabbie said. I strained to understand his accent, a mix of cockney and Turkish.

Anali paid him, and we scooted out of the cab. Our shoes squeaked on the damp cobblestones. Red brick buildings loomed above us with the bottom floors trimmed in bright white paint obscured by the fog.

"Where do we start?"

Anali smiled and linked our arms together. "Let's start walking and see what catches our eye."

A lot caught Anali's eye, and soon I had bags from several stores with jeans, blouses, sweaters, and even a denim skirt.

"Oh, perfect." Anali grabbed my hand, jostling the bags I carried, and pulled me towards a bright pink shop. In the windows hung bras, panties, and lacy things that didn't look practical or comfortable at all.

"Why are we both going in there? I can wait out here."

Anali stopped and turned to look at me, her light brown eyes warm. "Sapphire, you're almost sixteen now, a young woman, and it's time you had beautiful things. When I was your age my mom took me shopping for adult clothes like this." Anali bit her lip. "Not that I'm your mom, or trying to be your mom."

I grabbed Anali's hand. "I know. It's fine. I guess I could look inside."

She smiled and began walking again. "You're a beautiful young woman, and while no boy should be seeing your underwear, you should feel sexy while wearing it."

I wasn't sure how underwear made you feel sexy but I followed along.

"Good morning ladies, how can I help you?" asked an elderly woman. Her gray hair was pulled up into a neat bun.

"My niece needs to be measured for new bras, she's grown quite a bit."

I looked down where I was yet again escaping my current bra.

"Ah yes, blossoming into womanhood are we? Come here, and we'll get started," she said pulling out a tape measure.

She hummed then sent me to the dressing room. "I'll bring you several different styles in your size, then we can look at colors and fabrics."

I undressed and groaned at the stack of bras she passed over the door. The first one barely covered anything, the second pushed what I had up like an offering, and the third wasn't bad but didn't have enough support. "I like this one." I lifted my arms up above my head and the fourth bra didn't shift. It covered everything, and I didn't look like I was advertising.

"Pass it over, dearie, and we'll get some more in that style for you to try on."

"Can't I just pick them out since I know it will fit?" I asked passing the bra over.

"Goodness no, you need to see the colors against your skin and feel the fabrics."

"Are you doing okay?" Anali whispered.

"Yes, but I'm not sure I understand the point."

"I didn't either at first. I'll set aside a white, black, and beige in cotton. It's always good to have the basics."

"Thanks Anali."

A mass of color was handed to me over the door. I was supposed to try all of these on? Picking up a pick cotton bra with little pink hearts, I set it in the 'no' pile.

I fastened the hooks on a navy-blue satin bra with white lace on the edge of the cup. The color shone against my light copper skin. Was this what Anali meant? I picked another bra to try on my body flushed with embarrassed excitement.

Opening the door with a bunch of bras draped over my arm, I sighed, grateful to be done.

"Are these the ones you want?" The sales lady asked taking the pile from me.

"Yes, there's a bunch more in the dressing room."

She waved her hand. "You leave those; I'll get them later. Now, the matching panties are over here. We have each style in several cuts. I'll put these up front while you're looking."

In the past I wore plain cotton underwear, but looking at the display, I found the ones that matched the bras I chose. Sticking to boy shorts and low cut briefs, I matched each bra. My pink cheeks weren't going away anytime soon.

"Those are so cute," Anali said, pointing to the dark purple boy shorts with light purple polka dots. "You should change into a new bra so you don't have to keep fiddling with yours the rest of the day."

"Here." The sales lady popped up holding out a white lace bra with dark green leaves embroidered on the straps. "I've already cut off the tags. We also have some lovely nightgowns and pajamas if you're interested. Can I take those?"

"Oh, thanks." Anali handed over a sheer nightgown and some lacy thing. I turned back to the dressing room to change, not interested in my aunt's choice of lingerie.

When I came out, I searched through the sheer gowns and little lace whatevers until I found some simple satin camisoles and shorts, and several sets of cotton tank tops and soft pajama bottoms.

"All done?" The woman asked folding each piece into crinkling pink tissue paper.

"Yes. Thank you for all your help."

"You're most welcome, dearie." She handed me two large shiny pink bags with the store's name in metallic silver across both sides.

Anali handed her a credit card as the sales woman told her the best way to wash her delicate things.

"I'm going to wait outside."

Anali smiled at me and nodded.

I stepped onto the street. The crisp air refreshed and cooled my poor cheeks. The sun had burnt off the fog. I looked down the ancient street lined with tall, red brick buildings with white trim. Their pointed spires reached for the sky. A small group of brownies slipped between two stones into a bakery while faeries danced along the evergreen wreaths and garlands hung on the store fronts. I thought about going over and saying hello when I felt someone staring at me. Turning, I saw a young man, who looked like a poster boy for England. He was at least six feet tall with short brown hair and bright blue eyes. A long scarf was knotted around his neck and hung down his chest. He glanced at the bag in my hands, gave me a cheeky grin, winked, and walked away.

And I am blushing again.

"Ready?" Anali asked, making me jump. "Lost in thought?" she giggled.

"I'm ready." I tucked the pink bags closest to me and placed others on the outside of them.

"Are you getting tired or hungry?"

My stomach was still full from breakfast. "I'm not hungry, but I could sit and get something to drink."

"Let's keep walking. I'm sure we'll find a tea shop."

"Sounds good." We paused to look at the window displays which caught our eye, enjoying the holiday themes.

"Sapphire," Anali squealed. "Look at this. Isn't it the cutest thing you've ever seen?"

I walked over to the store front window and saw the smallest cable knit sweater ever. "It's very cute."

Anali sighed. "I have to have it."

I followed her into the shop, feeling her emotions bouncing against my shields. Anali is normally calm, but right now longing, hope, happiness, and nervousness all bounced against me. What in the world was going on?

"Oh, look they have a bunch." Anali sorted through a rack of tiny sweaters, pulling out the tiniest cream-colored cable knit sweater.

"Is someone expecting a baby?" I thought her youngest nephew was two, and the family lived in tropical India. They wouldn't need such a thick sweater.

She held the sweater against her belly. "No, but it's so sweet I can't pass it up."

"We have some other things for a wee bairn," the man behind the counter said. "Everything is hand knitted by the good women of Scotland."

I looked through the sweaters while Anali cooed, yes cooed, over the baby stuff. I picked a white cable knit sweater and one of green cashmere that was the softest thing I had ever touched. Looking at the price tags, I flinched. I started to put them back, but they were so beautiful.

"Look," Anali said dangling a pair of knitted baby booties in front of me. "Oh, those sweaters are gorgeous."

"They are, and expensive."

"Oh pish, don't worry about it today. You're here to have fun." Anali smiled. "I'm going to get one, too. Will you hold these while I look?"

"Sure," I said, taking the booties, two baby sweaters, several hats, and a blanket.

"This one," Anali held up a pale blue cabled cardigan sweater. "Let me pay, and then we'll go get something to drink."

I blinked at the whirlwind of emotions coming from Anali and followed. Should I say something? No. She knows I'm empathetic. If she wanted to tell me what was going on, she would.

We found a café a block away. Pine boughs and glossy springs of holly decorated the selection of cakes and pastries displayed in the front window.

"What would you like?" Anali asked as she set down her bags, tucking them under the wooden cafe table.

I looked at the handwritten chalkboard menu. "A chai latte please."

"Okay. I'll be right back." Anali hummed to herself as she went to stand in line.

I watched as a woman handed a hot chocolate to a little girl, who I thought looked like she might be her daughter. The girl grinned, and her mom brushed a stray curl from her daughter's cheek with a soft smile.

Anali set down two steaming mugs and a plate of cookies. "Here we are."

"Thanks." My fingers wrapped around the mug, soaking in the warmth.

Anali smiled and tucked a lock of my hair behind my ear.

My stomach fluttered.

Chapter Two

"Always be a first-rate version of yourself, instead of a second-rate version of somebody else." ~ Judy Garland

"Always be a first-rate version of yourself, instead of a second-rate version of somebody else." ~ Judy Garland

Anali and I stumbled into the hotel, tripping over bags and giggling. The doorman followed in behind us, carrying even more bags.

"I'm glad to see you two have been having fun," Gavin said.

"Gavin, honey, when did you get here?" Anali dropped her bags and rushed into his arms. His irritation faded as he buried his face into her neck.

Using my feet I pushed the bags out of the walkway so they wouldn't get in the way. The doorman set the others next to us and signaled for a bellhop.

"We thought you weren't coming until tomorrow." Anali pulled back, smiling up at her husband.

Gavin rolled his eyes. "Apparently I was too anxious, and Michael threatened to drug me if I bounced one more time." Gavin pushed up onto the balls of his feet.

"Well, I'm so glad you're here. It's been ages since the three of us went out. Help us with our bags and give Sapphire and me a chance to rest and then we'll go get some dinner."

"The bellhop will take care of them. Do I have any money left?"

"Don't worry, dear. Once you've seen what I've bought, you won't care how much I've spent." Anali smiled and walked to the elevator.

Gavin cleared his throat and gathered up as many bags as possible, while he supervised the loading of the rest of the bags onto the bellhop's cart. "How are you feeling, Sapphire?"

"Good. I had a lot of fun today."

Gavin lifted up the bags and reached into his pocket for a tip. "It sure looks like it."

* * *

I sat back and soaked in the warmth of the centuries-old pub. I ran my finger over the dark wood table, smoothed from thousands of people sitting here and running their hands over the same space. Wisps of sadness, despair, and anger seeped through the warm blanket of friendship and happiness.

Gavin's face scrunched into a frown as he chewed. "Okay, that wasn't what I was expecting."

Anali giggled. "Gavin, a month ago we left Mexico. Why in the world would you order nachos and guacamole?"

"I had to know. The salsa is okay, maybe if I dump it on everything."

"Hey, what if I don't what want salsa on mine?" I said. We had decided to order several items and share them.

"Trust me," Gavin said dumping salsa and pickled jalapeno peppers on the nachos.

I shook my head and took a bite of fried fish. It was salty, crunchy, and greasy—three of the four basic food groups. I splashed some of the malt vinegar on a piece. My lips puckered, but I liked the contrast. "This is great, and I like the mushy peas."

Anali took a bit of the vegetarian fried fish, which was made from spiced, battered and fried halloumi cheese. "This is delicious," she said, dipping it into a curry sauce.

Gavin pulled the vegetable pie to him, giving up on the nachos. He hummed at the first bite and hunched over the plate as if he didn't want to share. So, of course, I stole a bite. Oh, yes, yummy. So far I was liking London a lot.

"Good evening folks," said a young woman with a thick Scottish brogue. Her short kilt swayed around her thighs. "We're the Water Nymphs and we'll be playin' for you tonight. Hope you enjoy it."

I watched as the others took the stage. I felt a low hum of magical energy around them. The other woman held a violin, which she plugged into an amp. Her kilt was cut in the same style but made from a different plaid. Three men joined them on stage, all wearing kilts of different plaids with tee shirts. One plugged in a guitar, another sat at the drum kit. The third sat near the edge of the stage and cradled a polished cello between his legs. His kilt slid, up showing a muscular thigh. I squinted— was there a bit of tattoo showing under the hem?

Deep haunting notes from the cello echoed through the pub. I shivered as they hit me. His head bent, and his long dark curls fell over the cello and his milk-white arms.

"I do love the cello," Anali sighed.

Gavin arched an eyebrow. "Should I be worried?" He grabbed a French fry, or chip, and dipped it in the ketchup.

"Oh, honey," Anali said patting his hand. "He is so pretty."

I snorted while Gavin placed a hand over his heart. "I can't believe your love for me is so fickle."

"You'll just have to try and win my affection back." Anali's brown eyes glittered with amusement.

Gavin grinned and held out his hand palm up. "Will you dance with me?"

"Always." Anali placed her hand in Gavin's and followed him to the dance floor. He led her to the side furthest from the sexy cellist.

I smiled watching them dance with their eyes focused on each other. As they danced closer, I looked away. Adults can be so embarrassing. I watched the band. It was a joyous mix of rock and Celtic sounds. Relaxing back into the chair I began slow, deep, five-count breathing with my eyes focused on the band. Inhale to the count of five, hold to the count of five, exhale to the count of five, hold to the count of five. As I did the meditative breathing, I gently opened up my empathy.

There—something wild and hungry was woven into the song. The singer swayed, making eye contact with the crowd. She was definitely magical. I didn't feel any desire to harm, yet I felt a desire—no, a need— to connect. The violinist danced, also intent on making eye contact with people. The audience lost themselves to the joyous music, giving adoration and desire freely. Watching the women, I saw them breathe deeply and felt their energy rise. They were feeding off the crowd, sipping from the energy they radiated.

I focused on the men. The guitarist and drummer seemed lost in the music, and I felt their happiness but they didn't seem to be feeding on the crowd. Turning, I saw the cellist staring at me. Somehow he knew what I was doing. I blushed but didn't look away. Dark stubble covered his square jaw, full lips quirked into a smile under a crooked Roman nose. I couldn't see the color of his eyes under his thick dark brows, but I felt the humor in them. Winking at me, he looked away smiling, at a woman leaning against the stage.

Taking a few deep breaths, I released the meditation and strengthened my protective bubble that kept other people's emotions from overwhelming me. I wasn't sure what kind of magical beings they were. They might even be part human as the strength of their energy was softer than normal. Either that or they hid their nature well. Whatever they were doing, it didn't seem harmful.

Anali and Gavin stumbled back to the table. I opened my mouth to tell them about the band being magical, but they both seemed so happy. If I told them, then Gavin would get all tense and paranoid. "Having fun?" I asked instead.

"Yes, and you?" Anali answered.

"I am. The music is great."

"They have CDs for sale. I'll get us some to remember our first night in London," Gavin said, hopping up.

Anali placed her hand on my arm. "If you start getting tired let us know."

"I'm fine," I said, then yawned.

Anali rolled her eyes. "Come on let's go."

* * *

Twisting my mom's ring on my finger, I looked at the door leading to Gavin and Anali's suite. I was ready for breakfast, but neither of them had come to wake me up yet. I assumed they were getting ready. But what if they weren't getting ready? What if they were busy? They had been all sweet and cuddly last night.

I looked at my ring. Dark blue sparkled like a piece of the evening sky, set in silver. The ring had been a gift from the Phoenix King Shamash over four thousand years ago to one of his children or grandchildren, no one knew. The set of copper, silver, and gold bangles I wore with magical creatures carved into them were also an ancient gift. As was the pendent which looked like someone had poured liquid gems of purple, green, and blue for the heart of the flame surrounded by flames of red, orange, and yellow. And while they connected me to Akasha, the dimension where Shamash and Aya, my many times great grandparents lived, they couldn't help me figure out if it was safe to knock on the door.

I decided not to risk embarrassment and headed for the elevator.

"Little Sister."

Smiling, I looked up. Kayin stood by the elevators looking regal, as always. My black and red hair makes me look like a wanna-be rock star, but Kayin's tight black curls looked studded with rubies. Add in his ebony skin, wide flat nose, large deep eyes, and tall lean muscular body, and he looks like royalty. I ran and leapt at him. "Big Brother, I missed you. When did you get in?"

He hugged me tight, and any tension left over melted away. Kayin had been helping me figure out my life since I had met him a year ago at the San Francisco Center for the Circus Arts. Newly changed with unknown and unwanted powers rushing through me made life difficult until I met Kayin. He made me feel safe.

"We got in an hour ago." Kayin's deep rich voice with its Zimbabwean accent rumbled through me. "I just got settled and was heading down to get some breakfast."

I let go of him as the elevator dinged. We stepped aside and said hello to a group of circus performers who got off. "How was the show?" I asked.

"It was good. You and Anali were missed. Are you okay now? You look better."

"Much better, thanks." We walked towards to restaurant and saw a sign saying Cirque du Feu Magique—Blue Banquet Room.

We walked down the hall as indicated and found Anali and Gavin speaking to the manager.

"I don't understand why we have been separated," Gavin said. "This wasn't requested."

"I understand sir, and please be assured this will not be charged to your account. I felt as performers you and your guest would prefer to be left alone during meals." The manager's posh accent and overly polite tone sounded nice, but I felt his anxiety and irritation. "I do hope I haven't overstepped my bounds, sir. I had hoped to insure not only your privacy but allow you and your guests to dress as informally for meals as you like."

Anali's mouth pursed and she grasped Gavin's arm. I guessed she could feel the truth behind his pretty words, too. "Gavin, I believe our normal dress isn't what one expects to see when dining at such a lovely hotel, this sounds like a good compromise."

I looked down at my new black yoga pants and long sleeved purple tee-shirt, certainly not what the other guests wore to breakfast yesterday morning.

Gavin huffed. His anger felt hot against my protective bubble, but he stuffed it down and nodded. "I expect our meal options will be the same."

The manager bowed his head. "Of course, sir. In fact, I have taken the liberty of having a continental buffet set up inside for your convenience, and a waitress will see to your needs. If there is nothing else?"

"No, thank you," Anali said, her voice sharp.

The manager inclined his head and walked away. As he passed me and Kayin, I felt his disgust. Jerk. Kayin stood taller, and I grasped his hand. While I didn't like the manager, I didn't take offense at his stupidity. My mom had left a journal with me when she sent me into a police station in San Francisco when I was five. For ten years it had been my only connection to her. I had memorized the quotes and lessons she had written down before hiding me and facing death at the hands of the Sons of Belial.

People's opinions of who you are shows more about them than about you. It doesn't matter if they like you, hate you, look down on you, or admire you. How they feel about you tells who they are not who you are. So take a deep breath, and be yourself. Don't allow the perceptions of others to make you change or pretend to be someone else. Not only will it make you miserable, but who else can you possibly be?

"So?" Gavin asked as we walked into the blue banquet room.

"He doesn't like us much," Anali said, sitting in the chair Gavin pulled out for her.

Gavin snorted. "I could figure that out for myself. Was everything okay?" Gavin asked the trampoline troupe as the passed us to leave.

They glanced at each other. "The food was good."

"But the waitress."

"She seemed a bit scared of us."

What? The three women and men that made up the troupe were the sweetest. All physically fit, but none of them huge or scary muscular. Why would she be scared of them?

"I'm sorry. I'll get this fixed," Gavin said.

One of the girls smiled. "It was nice being tucked away. We didn't have to worry about being too loud, or getting looks for wearing workout clothes."

"Are you headed to the gym?" I asked.

"Yes, it's a mile away— that should help us warm up and give our meal time to settle."

"Have fun, we'll see you there later," Kayin said.

I stood and headed to the buffet. Yes! Chocolate almond food of the gods was waiting for me. I snatched one of the pastries and put one on Kayin's plate while he was looking over the selection. I added some crusty bread, several cheeses and some yogurt and fruit to my plate.

"Good morning," said Miu. Her straight black hair was pulled into two high ponytails on either side of the back of her head. Where in the world did she find workout clothes with pink sequins on them? My eyes watered. It was too early in the day for that shade of pink. "Oh. I was hoping for hot food."

"Good morning, and you can order anything you want," I said.

"Great! So have you run into any magical beings yet?" Miu asked as she filled her plate with fresh fruit.

I thought about the band we saw last night, but decided to stay quiet. I doubted if I'd even see them again. "I saw some faeries and pixies yesterday while out shopping."

She cursed in Japanese, then Miu's thin glossy pink bottom lip stuck out. "You went shopping without me."

"I made her go," said Anali coming to my rescue. "Plus I knew we would be busy as soon as you all got here."

"True. We only have a few quiet days before we start performing. And Michael said something about performing at a party," Miu said.

What? I hadn't heard anything about this.

"Yes, we got asked to provide some entertainment at a charity event," Gavin said. "I asked Michael, and he was going to get a few volunteers."

"Michael is going to check if Taliesin can set up the silks for the party," said Sasha in his thick Russian accent, as he walked into the banquet hall. His red-streaked wheat-blond hair fell over his forehead in a messy GQ style. His blue-gray sweater enhanced his round gray eyes.

"Is this the party we were invited to?" I asked.

Anali nodded about to speak, when a waitress came in.

"Can I get you anything?" the young woman asked. She kept darting looks between us and the door, which she had left open. What in the world did these people think we would do?

"I'm fine," I said.

"Me too," added Anali.

"I'd like the kippers please," said Miu, always one to try fish of any kind.

"Of course." She wrote down her order, took the menu and stepped back. She tried to make it look like she was focusing on the others, but her nervousness showed.

After Sasha and Kayin ordered the girl was practically twitching. Gavin held his menu out his eyes hard as he stared at her. She whimpered a bit.

"I want the eggs Florentine. I also want a server who isn't afraid of us. You will not come back into this room."

The waitress squeaked out a, "Yes, sir," and fled the room. I hid my smile behind my glass of juice.

"So what is everyone up to this morning?"

"Training, I guess" I said looking at Kayin, Sasha, and Miu.

"Yes, I want to go through the routine again today," Kayin said.

"Do you want help?" Gavin asked.

"Yes, please. There a few poses I am finding challenging," Kayin said.

"Taliesin and I are going for a run in the park before practicing," said Sasha.

"Where is our cheerful little unicorn this morning?" I said.

Sasha rolled his eyes. "He fell into bed as soon as we got here and was sleeping when I left."

"Is he okay?" Anali asked.

"Yes. Some girls figured out where we were staying and came to our room late last night and we had a difficult time getting them to leave."

Taliesin having groupies? This wouldn't go over well at all.

"Good morning," said a young man with his back to us as he pushed open the door with a large tray balanced in his hands. "My name is Brandon, and I'll be your server this morning. Now who ordered the eggs Florentine?" He smiled brightly, his rough London accent was refreshing.

I looked up and met his bright blue eyes. The air shifted and sparked. His eyes widened, and he backed up. He shivered then smiled again, this time it didn't reach his eyes.

Gavin raised his hand. "Me."

"Wonderful, sir."

"What was that?" Kayin asked.

I kept my eyes on Brandon as he set Miu's breakfast down. "He's something magical, but I don't know what."

Taliesin walked into the room, his white hair loose and flowing around his shoulders. "Please, tell me there is coffee in here."

"Bloody hell," Brandon whispered, almost missing the table as he set down Kayin's plate.

"Is there a problem?" Gavin said his tone sharp.

"No, sir. Sorry about that," he served everyone else.

"So did you draw the short straw?" I asked.

Brandon cocked his head to the side. "Miss?"

"How did you get stuck serving us?"

"Oh, I volunteered. I normally just clear and set tables. So this is my chance to show the manager that I can do a good job as server."

"Why exactly is everyone freaking out about us?" Miu asked, cutting into her kippers.

Brandon went over to the door to make sure it was shut, then stepped closer to us. "Well, you see, Americans in general aren't regarded as quality guests. Add in the fact that you're circus performers and have people from other countries in your troupe, they're expecting you to be nothing more than common riff raff. Actually there is a betting pool about how you can afford to stay here."

"What are the choices?" I asked.

Brandon grinned. "Well, we have had drug dealers, white slave traders, and kinky prostitutes."

"Oh, my," Anali said her cheeks turning bright red.

Gavin grinned. "If you add cat burglar to the list, I'll start talking about jewels and museums and such."

"Gavin," Anali slapped his arm. "Shame on you."

He snorted. "What? If they're going to judge us like this I should get to have some fun with them."

"We could get some rope while we're out today," Kayin added.

"Children," muttered Taliesin, as he held on to his coffee cup for dear life.

"Oh, sir, can I get you anything to eat?" Brandon asked, smiling softly. His gaze seemed a bit unfocused as he stared at Taliesin.

I felt Brandon's excitement and something else, almost a reverence. Taliesin felt tired and grumpy.

"No, thanks. I'll just have coffee."

Anali cleared her throat. The rest of us looked away. You do not skip meals around Anali. A few months ago one of the contortionists collapsed, and we found out she had an eating disorder. Anali was horrified. I guess they don't have eating disorders in India. She bought a bunch of books and now watches what we eat.

Taliesin sighed and flipped open the menu. "I'll have poached eggs with sides of tomatoes and mushrooms."

"I'll have it right out." Brandon rushed out the door.

I opened my mouth to let them rest of the group know he wasn't fully human, when Miu spoke up. "Seems our waiter has a crush on you, Taliesin."

Taliesin glared over his cup of coffee.

I was about to say something as the door opened and more than half of the circus performers came in. The room echoed with happy chatting in three, no four different languages, giving me no opportunity to share my sense of Brandon's non-human nature.

Brandon returned and set Taliesin's plate in front of him, trying for a moment to make eye contact, but calls from the others drew his attention.

"Anali, are you okay?" Her face had gone pale with a greenish tint.

"There are too many different smells in here I think." She pushed back her chair.

I rushed over to her. "I'm done eating, why don't we go upstairs for a bit."

"Honey?" Gavin said taking her arm.

"I'm fine, you sit and finish eating." She patted his arm and opened the door.

His brow furrowed as he frowned. "I can finish it later."

"I'm feeling better already, honey. Please don't worry. I'll go get our jackets and we can head to the gym okay?"

"If you're sure," Gavin said but didn't sit.

"I can text you when we get up to the room," I said standing beside her.

Gavin sat. "Okay, I give up. I'll see you in a few minutes."

"I have to get my stuff too," Kayin said. Gavin gave him a grateful smile.

Anali took slow steps and deep breathes all the way up to the room.

"I'll get my jacket and meet you back here," Kayin said once we reached our floor.

"Okay," I said.

Anali opened the door and her stomach gurgled. She slapped her hand over her mouth. I held on and rushed her to the bathroom where she threw up. Was she sick? I held her hair and rubbed her back until she finished. "Are you okay?"

"Yes, give me a moment to brush my teeth."

"Okay, just holler if you need anything," I said and texted Gavin.

I screamed when the door burst opened a few minutes later, how did he get up here so fast?

"Where is she?" he asked as he ran to the bathroom door. "Anali, sweetheart are you okay?"

The door opened. Anali stepped out, tears running down her cheeks.

"Sweetheart, what is it? What wrong?"

Anali sniffed and wiped at her eyes. I stood there, not sure if I should leave or not. I wanted to know what was going on, but I wasn't sure if they remembered I was even in the room.

"I was hoping, but I didn't want to say anything. And I didn't feel anything so I thought it was going to be like last time." More tears fell from Anali's eyes. "But now I'm sick. And I checked and I have a mommy line on my tummy just like my mom and sisters did. And I think everything is going to be okay this time."

Gavin led Anali to the edge of the bed and had her sit. "I don't understand."

Anali's chin trembled. "I'm pregnant."

My jaw dropped as Gavin gathered his wife in his arms and held her tight while she cried. Their joy and fear wrapped around me, the intensity making it hard to breathe. I walked to the door. This was private. I shouldn't be here. I didn't belong here right now.

"I'm calling a midwife, you are to do nothing but rest until we know everything is fine."

Anali laughed as I shut the door.

Chapter Three

"People loving people doesn't scare me. It's people hating people, that scares me."~ Mom

I stared up at the white three-story building. "This can't be right, there is no way this is a dance studio."

Kayin looked at his phone. "It's the right address."

"Mum hurry up," hollered a little boy. "Class starts soon."

"Go ahead," said his mother, switching a baby wrapped in yellow from one arm to the other. "You know where your ballet class is."

The boy squeezed between Kayin and me, rushed up the stairs and slammed the door behind him. The glass panels rattled, and I held my breath waiting to see if they would break.

"Sorry about that," his mom said.

"No problem," I said stepping out of the way. We followed her into the building. The entranceway had worn gray-blue office carpet, and the walls were lined with cubbies for shoes. Above those hung wooden bars with hangers. On the inner door a sign: 'Take off outdoor shoes'.

The inside were polished wood dance floors. On both sides of the corridor were windows that covered the top half of the walls, allowing us to see into the rooms. In the left room the clowns were practicing, needing most of the room to move around.

"Here we are," Kayin pointed to a schedule taped to the door on the right. "We have thirty minutes to warm up before our turn. We're in the center."

"Well, come on." At one end of the large dance hall, a juggler was practicing his routine. He juggled the balls onto the floor instead of into the air as he walked down a set of stairs. A group of kids were sitting with their parents against the wall watching with wide eyes.

On the other end two women flipped into the air, landing onto poles held up on either end by two men who balanced them on their shoulders. The crowd gasped as the women landed on the poles, which bent under their weight. Another few bounces and the women flipped into the air and landed on the opposite poles. A few of the little girls screamed and hid in their faces in their hands. The moms gasped and clutched their children tighter. I understood. Russian Pole scared the crap out of me too.

My muscles ached as I began to warm up. It had been three days since I had done any exercise. I went through a series of yoga poses until I felt warm enough to move into deeper stretches.

"It's our turn. Are you sure you want to practice? You seem distracted," Kayin asked.

"Yes, I'm sorry. I'm fine." I said, shoving all my worries and fears down and focusing on the routine.

Kayin hit the play button, and our music filled the air. I focused on the slow, haunting cello as Kayin and I stepped onto a round platform. I let my shields open and tuned into Kayin, matching my breath to his. It had taken ages to be able to connect to Kayin while blocking out the emotions of people around us. I didn't want to get hit by the audience's emotions and lose my focus. Placing my hands in his, I exhaled stiffening my muscles as Kayin lifted me up over his head.

I kept my body firm as he moved me slowly to add drama and maintain balance. I moved into a handstand, balancing on his hands over his head.

"Mummy, oh, mummy, please can we stay, please," I heard a little girl ask.

Once in a handstand I open my legs into the splits. Three breaths here, holding myself steady, while Kayin turned in a circle. His arms didn't even shake as he knelt on the floor. I tapped into his calm control and centered myself into my breath as Kayin lay down on the floor while I continued to balance on his hands.

Gasps echoed in the air. Kayin and I haven't performed statue in front of a real audience yet, just other circus performers. I had to strengthen my shields as amazement, excitement, and envy flowed from the small group watching us.

I brought my legs together as Kayin lifted his legs up. Curling, I sat on the bottom of his feet. When we started practicing this routine, I blushed the entire time. We are in constant contact from when I first take his hand until we left the stage. At this point I think I have touched as much of Kayin as possible without risking pregnancy.

We'd always treated each other as brother and sister. The first time I slid down his body in time to the sultry cello music, I wondered how our relationship would change. Then Kayin giggled because the end of my braid tickled his side. And the awkwardness vanished in a moment.

As the final notes echoed over the room Kayin lowered me on top of him and we curled together on the floor.

Someone clapped and a bunch of others joined in.

"You guys looked amazing!" Shin said, stepping onto the stage with a long wooden pole slung over his shoulder. "Very sexy." He wiggled his thick black eyebrows.

My brow furrowed. Something was off—he felt a bit sad.

"Isn't that the idea?" I said sitting up, reaching into my bag. I grabbed my towel to wipe the sweat off my face.

Shin shrugged and opened a cap in the round platform to secure the pole into the floor.

"Little Sister," Kayin said. "You did very well."

Shin perked up, his sadness switching to hopefulness. I looked at him, but his thin black eyes focused on Kayin. Oh, well this was interesting.

"Thanks, Big Brother. I think my abs are finally strong enough to support me through the whole routine." I grabbed my water bottle and started pacing as I waited for my breathing to slow to normal. Gavin had drilled it into our heads that we should 'Never stop moving until you can breathe normally again.'

"Excuse me," a little girl tugged on my shirt. "How did you do that?"

"Oh, well," I began. "Lots and lots of practice. You have to be really strong, eat all your vegetables, and get plenty of sleep." Her mother smiled at me.

"I'm going to be strong like you some day," said a little boy staring up at Kayin.

"I bet you are. Can you show me how strong you are?" Kayin asked kneeling in front of him.

He scrunched his face and flexed his arms.

"Oh, yes, you are very strong. How old are you?" Kayin asked.

He puffed up his little chest and held out three fingers. "I'm four!"

"Such a strong young man," Kayin said. "I bet you are a big help to your mother and father."

He nodded his head.

"Are you going to teach classes?" another girl asked me. "Mum, I don't want to take stupid dance any more. I want to take her classes. But you hold the classes during my mom's yoga class, it makes her happier that way."

"I'm sorry," I said trying not to giggle. "We are just here for a few weeks."

"Look another one is starting! Can we watch, Miss. Williams, please? Daddy won't mind I'm sure."

"For a little bit." She sounded distracted. I looked back and saw that she was staring at Taliesin and Sasha who were in the middle of their silks routine. They twisted into the silks, each movement in sync with each other. Their bodies half wrapped in the black fabric, they paused then let go. The crowd gasped as they rolled, free-falling towards the floor. Little ones peeked through their fingers holding their breath as Sasha and Taliesin stopped mere inches from the floor. They clapped wildly as Taliesin and Sasha began to climb back up the silks.

"Do you mind if we stay and watch?" Kayin asked. "We should stretch out anyway."

"Of course it's okay." Kayin sat next to me while the Chinese pole performers warmed up for their set. I bent down and wrapped my hands around my calves.

A piano and guitar piece played. They began to bounce from one foot to another, while the music sounded in the background. The Chinese pole performers turned in a circle as they climbed up the poles. Kayin's eyes were glued to Shin, which I understood. Slowly Shin climbed the pole, pulling himself up using only his hands and keeping his taut body a foot away from the pole. It was very impressive, and the play of muscles under his tight shirt was something worth staring at.

"Kayin, you like him."

"Of course I like him, he's my friend."

I pursed my lips wondering if I should say something more. Shin obviously liked Kayin as more than just a friend, and it sure seemed as if Kayin felt the same way.

"This is brilliant," said a little boy sitting down next to me. Soon Kayin and I were surrounded by small children gasping as Shin and the other Chinese pole performers leapt in synch from one vertical pole to another.

While stretching I did my meditative breathing to strengthen my shields. Between Shin and Kayin lusting after each other, and our audience admiring the performers, I felt overwhelmed and in need of a shower.

I flinched when everyone started clapping at the end of the performance. Turning, I saw that the back wall was lined with adults, most of them in workout clothes.

Kayin stood when the music faded. "That was amazing, as always."

Shin grinned. "Thanks."

Both boys shifted nervously, their eyes darting back and forth.

"Kayin, are you ready? Shin, are you headed back to the hotel? You can walk with us," I said.

Shin ran his thick fingers through his black and blue bangs, letting them fall over the right side of his face. "No, I still need to practice the acrobatics routine."

"Okay, see you later then?" I said.

"Yes, we should be done in time for lunch." Shin waved as the first child brave enough to go up and ask him a question tugged on his shirt. Soon the performers were surrounded by kids. Looking at the other end of the gym, Sasha and Taliesin knelt on the floor surrounded by little girls and boys in ballet costumes. It was so cute. Picking up my bag I found my phone and took photos of our performers talking to the children.

Kayin sighed as he watched Shin lifting little kids onto the poles so they could try them.

"Come on, we're close to the park. Let's get lost for a while." I tugged on his arm and led him through the crowded hallway as another group stood outside the left room watching the German wheel practice. The German wheel looks like a thin, human-sized silver hamster wheel. The performer stands inside the wheel and uses the strength of his body to make it spin, turn, stop, and even revolve on its side like a coin before popping back up again.

"That is bloody brilliant," said a man as the performer began to flip in-between the two large rings. The air outside was cold and wet

The park was beautiful in a desolate kind of way. Trees, naked in the cold December wind, seemed to reach for the gloomy sky. Flowerbeds absorbed the decaying leaves, ensuring that next year's buds would blossom. Junipers shrubs brightened the dormant grass with dusky green needles.

We walked, and I waited for Kayin to start talking. Hey, I could be patient when I had to.

"You were brilliant," said a boy as he rode his bike past us.

"Yes," squealed a little girl. The streamers on her bike fluttered as she rode. Their dad nodded at us as he passed.

"Thank you," I said.

Kayin rubbed his hand over his face. I grabbed his other hand in mine for support.

"My dad sent me a letter; he wants me to come home. He was angry that I had been sent away. He remembered stories of people changing how they looked and having special powers. He'd never told my mother because she was from another tribe and was obsessed with demons." Kayin wiped his eyes. "He took my brother and sisters, left my mom, and married another woman. He was so mad. He tried to find me, but there was no trail to follow." Kayin reached up and tugged on his black and red hair.

I waited quietly. He wanted to say more— I could feel it.

"Liking the same sex is considered a white people's disease. Those who do are sent to a healer." Kayin stopped walking and looked up into the bare branches of an old oak tree. "I don't think I can risk losing my family again, not when I just got them back. They sent me letters, and there was a picture of all of them, including a new baby brother from his new wife."

"Would it not be okay for you to be gay? Is there a chance they would accept it? Accept you?"

"There have been gay couples who visited the nature preserve before. My father was always polite and never said anything rude, but then my father never speaks ill of people. I'm not sure how he'd feel about me, and what if he hated me, or rejected me?"

"I don't know, Kayin. But I hate the thought of you living your life without falling in love— and hiding who you are."

"I'll always have you, right?"

"Of course you have me. I will be by your side no matter what you choose, but Kayin, I hope you choose love and happiness."

Kayin smiled, but the sadness didn't leave his eyes.

My heart ached. I wanted to help Kayin, but didn't know where to start. We walked back to the hotel with my mom's words playing in my mind.

Love is an amazing thing, and never should be taken for granted. The love of a parent, friend, child, sibling, or romantic love. It's all beautiful and should be cherished. However, before you can accept love and freely love others, you must love yourself, even the parts you don't like, the parts that scare you, and the parts you wish you could change. Love is worth it, it's worth the risk, the heartache, and being that vulnerable. I hope you find love in your life and cherish it.

We were almost to the hotel when strong arms wrapped around me. "Bloody hell," I yelled, as I wriggled to get loose.

Shin laughed and let go. "You need to be more aware of your surroundings. Gavin asked me to teach you Hwa Rang Do to protect you from getting kidnapped. I feel like I'm failing."

Glaring, I shoved Shin. He didn't move. I wanted to tell him that I could feel the Sons of Belial and their walk-in minions coming, their unnaturalness made me ill. But Shin wasn't a Child of Fire and didn't know about the ancient magical evil that hunted mythical beings, including us.

"And really, Sapphire, you've only been here two days and already picking up British cuss words." He shook his head and tutted at me.

"You make it sound like it's a foreign language," I said, as we pushed through the revolving door.

"It is. Between their accent and slang, I hardly know what they're saying," Shin said. Was he pouting?

I rolled my eyes. "If you joined our British immersion marathon, you would be having an easier time."

"All you did was watch Dr. Who and some weird department store show."

"That's not all, we also watched some mysteries, and Miu made us watch everything Jane Austen. The point is we're all having an easier time understanding what people are saying."

"My favorite was Sherlock," Kayin said.

"Maybe I'll watch that one," Shin said with a smile. "But I don't like Dr. Who."

"I can't even look at you when you say stuff like that." I turned and walked towards the blue banquet room.

"But Sapphire," he whined, then wrapped an arm around my shoulder. "Don't let this little thing come between us."

"Little thing? Little thing? You walked out on David Tennant."

"He's hot, but I'm not that into science fiction."

I huffed and tried to pull away. Shin leaned in and began to nuzzle my neck. "But, baby."

"Stop it!" I giggled trying to push away as Kayin opened the door. "You brute, leave me alone."

"What exactly are you doing to my niece?" Gavin's voice was firm and a touch cold.

Anali waved to me, smiling as she sat at the table. She looked pale but a lot better.

Shin straightened up, clearing his throat. "Nothing, sir."

Gavin raised an eyebrow. "She's only fifteen."

"I'll be sixteen in a few days." Wow, that somehow sounded younger than fifteen.

Shin held his hands up and moved closer to Anali. It was always a good plan. If anyone could calm my uncle down, it was Anali. "Dude, Gavin, no way. We're just friends."

"And you're eighteen," Gavin said. "Far too old for her."

Anali and I rolled our eyes, ignoring the fact that he was twenty-eight when he married Anali who was eighteen at the time.

Anali sighed. Gavin turned his head so fast his wild fire red hair whipped around him. "Honey, are you okay?"

"Yes, dear, I'm fine," she said fluttering her hand. I bit my lip to keep from laughing. "But could I get a glass of water, with a slice of lemon?"

He smiled and the love and tenderness nearly overwhelmed me. "Of course. Anything."

Where the breakfast buffet had been this morning there was now an array of beverages and snacks. "Do you want anything, Kayin?" I asked.

"What kinds of juice do they have?"

"Um, orange, apple, pineapple and mango."

"Mango please," Kayin said.

"Me too, me too." Shin batted his eyes at me, his short lashes not helping his cause.

He could be such a brat. I sighed and poured three glasses of juice. I held my breath and walked back to the table. Success! I smiled as I gave them their juice—juice I had not spilled all over the floor.

Gavin chuckled. "It's cute how you can do an entire statue routine, balancing in challenging position in the air while Kayin holds you up, and yet you seem prouder of yourself for being able to carry three glasses a few feet."

Blushing, I picked up my glass. Rude!

"Hey guys, how was practice?" Miu asked.

"Good. What did you do this morning?" I replied.

Miu held up sparkling, cotton-candy pink nails. "I practiced my fan dance routine in the room. I'm going to start training in hula-hoop this afternoon."

"That's wonderful," Anali said. "I'm glad you've found something else you are interested in."

"Hello," Sasha, said as he walked in. Taliesin followed behind him.

"Did you escape your rabid fans?" I teased.

"Fans? Were people bothering you at the gym?" Gavin asked.

Taliesin sat down after pouring a glass of pineapple juice. "Sapphire is trying to be funny. A few young kids watched us practice and came up after."

I pulled out my phone. "I have pictures."

"Oh, that is so cute," Anali cooed as she looked through the photos. "I took a photography class in school, maybe I should start taking pictures again now that I can't perform."

"What?" "Why?" "Are you okay?" were all said at once.

Anali smiled and took Gavin's hand. "We have some news. I'm pregnant."

After a moment of stunned silence. Miu squealed, breaking everyone out of their stupor. I stayed back while the others offered hugs and handshakes and congratulations. Once it was clear, I gave them both a hug. "Congratulations."

"Kayin and Sapphire, we are going to have to ask you to take over for statue right away," Gavin said.

"Of course," I said, "She's pregnant—she can't do anything like that."

"Is everything okay?" Kayin asked. "Or is this an American thing? The women in my village kept working while pregnant."

Anali sighed, and I felt a soft cool sadness coming from her.

I strengthened my empathic bubble. There were too many emotions floating around here.

"I was pregnant during our first year of marriage, but had a miscarriage. We are being extra cautious, and I think everything is fine, I already have morning sickness. Last time I had none, and I have a mommy line."

"I am sure everything is just fine," I said.

"What's a mommy line?" Sasha asked.

"Some women get a dark line from their pubic bone to their belly button when they become pregnant. I guess it's a reaction to the hormones," Anali said.

Sasha frowned. "I'm sorry I asked."

"Are you going to keep traveling with the circus?" Shin asked.

My gut clenched as fear flooded me. I stared at the glass of juice. I would have taken a drink but my throat felt so tight I wasn't sure I could swallow.

"Of course. I already talked to Michael, and we will take six weeks off from touring, because Anali wants to be in India with her mom and sisters to have the baby," said Gavin. "But we plan on staying with the circus."

"As if we could leave you guys. We're family," Anali said, her eyes glistening with tears.

I forced a smile and did my best to keep my emotions to myself. Anali was also empathic, and I didn't want to ruin her happiness. I wrapped up my fear and worry in a cocoon of energy. I guess it worked, because Anali's smile never dimmed. While the others talked baby stuff, I replayed Gavin's words. *We plan on staying with the circus.* Plans can change, plans aren't certain. And because as the Jewel, I was the only one who can open the portal to Akasha, I would be staying with the circus no matter what they chose. And no matter how I tried, between the constant traveling and being hunted by the Sons of Belial, I couldn't fit a tiny helpless baby into the picture.

* * *

My muscles were warm after jump rope practice, and I slid from yoga pose to yoga pose as I waited for the others to be ready for Hwa Rrang Do practice. Shin took Gavin's request to train us seriously, and we practiced at least four times a week. I frequently wound up with bruises on my body and even more on my ego. Every time I thought I was getting better, Shin would teach us something new and I was lost again.

"That was a great flip you did during jump rope," Kayin said as he joined me.

"Thanks, they said if I can do it right three more times during practice I can do it during the show."

"All right, my little grasshoppers, time to get beat up," Shin said with an evil grin on his face. "Today we are going to continue to work on escape and evasion, focusing on bear hugs. Someone grabs you around the waist with the intention of taking you wherever they want to."

I shivered at the thought of one of the Sons of Belial ever grabbing me.

"You have seconds to react. Never, ever allow them to take you to a secondary location," Shin continued. "The first few minutes are the ones where the aggressor has the least amount of control. Whatever he tells you to do helps him, so always do the opposite." Shin pointed at me. "Come, my little warrior princess."

Sighing, I walked over to him willing my muscles to relax. I learned early on the more relaxed and the more you went with the move, the less it hurt. Shin stood in front of me.

"Wrap your arms around my waist," he said. Shin found that we all learned better if we had the move done to us first. "Most people find being this physically close to a stranger startling and will freeze. You will not. You will yell for help and then place one hand on the chin. You reach the other behind your attacker." Shin's palm covered my chin and his fingers wrapped around my braid. "My left hand is in her hair so I'll step back with my left foot. Pushing her chin to my right, I'll pull her hair towards me and down."

The rest of my body followed my head and soon I was on the floor, exhaling as I landed.

"From here you can either let go and run, or drop to your knees into the rib cage with your full body weight. That should crack, if not break, a few ribs." Shin helped me up. "Pair up and make sure you practice taking the person down in both directions."

"How do you pick a direction?" Miu asked as she stood in front of Sasha.

"The terrain," Shin said. "If there is a wall on one side of you, you'll need to go the other way. I know it seems easy in here, but done hard and fast, your opponent will hit the ground with a lot of force and hopefully be stunned for a few seconds."

"Kayin doesn't have any hair to grab," Taliesin said.

"Dig your fingers into his scalp, or reach around and grab an ear. If you need to make sure he won't be an issue again, reach around the head and grab him by the eye socket." Shin turned to me and wrapped his arms around my waist. Most days Anali joined us so Shin could watch and correct everyone while we were paired off. I guess I got lucky today.

I stared at his chin for a second took a deep breath and stepped back with my right foot. My right hand went to his chin, and my left reached around, and grabbed his long bangs, as the rest was cut too short to hold.

"Very nice, but which way are you twisting me?"

"This way," I said moving his head and realizing my feet were all wrong. Always, my feet were always wrong.

"Deep breath, and do it again."

Nodding, I repeated the move. Shin allowed me to move his body with the slightest pressure. And I had him on the floor.

He hopped up. "Good. Again."

I did it ten times to the left. Each time Shin would be a little bit harder to move.

"Okay, other side."

My mind went blank. What did he mean other side? I was supposed to twist him to the right? What? How? Where would my hands go?

"Sapphire, calm down. Start slow." His arms wrapped around me.

I reached up with my right hand wrapping it in his hair, my left palm on his chin, and stepped back first with my left foot, then changing to my right and tried to twist him to the left.

"Other way," he chuckled.

Seriously, why did changing directions short circuit my brain? I got Shin on the ground because he let me.

"Again."

After ten good moves. Shin went to help the others.

"I have a question," Miu said. "What happens if they are too tall to grab easily?"

Shin grinned. "Then you loosen them up first. Cup your hands and slam them over their ears, shove a finger in their eye. But, honestly, if someone big was going to grab you they would just pick you up." Shin scooped her up, her belly over his shoulder. "How would you get away?"

Miu hung limp. "Um. I could put my hands on the back of your head and slam my knee into your face?"

"Yes, you could, but what about this? Take your hand around my head and grab my chin then flip over the back of me. Throw all your weight into it and don't let go of my chin until your feet touch the ground. You risk him falling on you, but once your toes touch, do a forward roll and you should get away."

Miu bit her lip and nodded as she reached around, tucked her head, and flung her legs over Shin's shoulder. His head and shoulders came up, and he began to fall. Miu curled into a somersault and stood several feet away from Shin, who was lying on the floor.

"Perfect. You probably knocked the wind out of him and maybe even wrenched his neck," Shin said, getting up.

Kayin cleared his throat. "What if they have your arms pinned?"

"Ah, a volunteer for our next move."

Kayin stood in-front of Shin. "Grab me." Kayin's long arms wrapped around Shin pinning Shin's arms to his body.

"Any ideas?" Shin asked.

"A head butt," Sasha said.

"Yes, to loosen him up if needed but you risk getting cut by his teeth. You twist your hands so your thumbs are pointed towards your opponent, stick your thumbs out, and jam them into him." Kayin squealed and jumped back his hands covering his manhood.

Shin pressed his lips together trying to stifle a laugh. "If you're really lucky, that happens. The thumbs hit on either side of the pubic bone where the tendons run. This will hurt both men and women. They will jump away from you, then you ram your knee right between their legs."

Sasha, Kayin, and Taliesin all cringed and stepped away from Shin.

"Now if the person grabbing you is a professional, they might be wearing a cup. So after the knee strike, you're going to slam the heel of your foot onto their instep, hopefully crushing tendons and breaking bones. Their face will come forward, you will head butt them—aim for the nose if possible. Their head and shoulders will go back. Swing your arm under their shoulder, locking your hand over it. Step in front of them, put your hip into their stomach, and flip them over you. If necessary after the hand lock, go into a forward roll. This is good for those who still have their balance or if they're much bigger than you."

I blinked. Okay that was vicious, and I think I forgot a few steps already.

"Okay pair off and kill each other," Shin said.

Miu grabbed my arm. "I don't want to practice this one with the boys."

I nodded and turned to grab her.

"I guess you're stuck with me, Kayin," Shin said.

While I moved with Miu's gentle attack, I watched Kayin. He swallowed as he gazed down at Shin, he seemed frozen. Poor Kayin, he was confused enough already.

Shin licked his lips. "Kayin, you need to try and get away from me."

I held my breath for a second then Kayin began to move.

"Well, this isn't full of homo-erotic angst, is it?" Miu whispered.

I laughed. "I can't decide if I should try and rescue Kayin or hope this helps him make a decision."

Miu wrapped her arms around me. "He'll be fine. Now jab your thumbs into my crotch."

Chapter Four

"You are a lifesaver," Melusine said, smoothing her turquoise wool skirt as she stood. "When the other band canceled on me, something about the flu, anyway I wasn't sure what I was going to do. Then my personal assistant Miss Thurston heard you play in the pub last night, and now my problems have been solved. It would have been a disaster. I have royalty coming to this gala for the Marine Conservation Society. As it is, I need more items for the silent auction."

Ramsey laid his cello on the floor. "This is an amazing opportunity. Thank you for letting us audition. If you need more art pieces, I have friends who are artists. I can contact them if you like. What are the terms?"

Melusine walked over to him, adjusting a pale green silk scarf in her long dark hair. The silver sequins along the ends glittered in the light. Her lean curvaceous body swayed as she walked towards him. A smile curled her thin pink lips. Ramsey's eyes glazed over. She released a gentle wisp of power, and he shivered. "Are they like us? I feel an obligation to help our kind of people as much as possible. I will buy the pieces I like. I prefer an ocean theme." Reaching up, she touched the three ropes of pearls that hung around her neck. "I am also willing to have the artists at the cocktail hour, before the dinner to talk to people."

"That's good of you, and, yes, I can get you in touch with those like us." Ramsey said, his black eyes fixed on her sea-blue ones. "We would be willing to auction off a performance." His band mate huffed.

Melusine handed him a business card. "Wonderful. You are obviously my good luck charm. Please have them contact me. Email is fine, and if they send pictures of their work, that will make everything go much faster. Speaking of which, I have so much to do. Collins will show you out when you're done."

"Okay, and thanks again, Melusine," Ramsey said, shaking his head as she walked away from him.

Melusine's heels clicked on the parquet floor, and her personal assistant met her outside the doorway.

"Miss Thornton, you are a genius. They will be perfect for the gala, and they are quite powerful. I should be able to get a lot of magic out of them."

"Excellent. I have several gnomes for you to practice on."

"Shall we try the ritual again now? I am tired of being tied to that megalomaniac Cartazonon. I believe I have the incantation worked out."

"They are ready when you are," Miss Thornton said, checking her phone. "And you have two hours before your hair appointment."

"Perfect." Melusine walked up the stairs and into her bedroom, through her walk-in closet and into her ritual room. Kicking off her heels, she walked over to an old oak table and opened an iron cage. She grabbed one of the gnomes, tuning out their screams and cries as she went over the ritual in her mind.

"Shush," she said, sending a pulse of power into the small man. He stilled as she cradled him to her chest. Sitting in the center of a black pentacle painted on the floor, she began to chant in ancient Gaelic. Power built, crackling along her skin, and swirled around the whimpering gnome. She pulled him closer and began to rock to sooth him as she increased her chanting.

Melusine ignored the high pitched cries for mercy from the other gnomes. She didn't want his life, only his magic. She followed the ribbons of energy as they seeped into the gnome. There—in his heart a glowing ball which sent out ribbons of golden magic that wove through his body. Grasping the ball she tugged. The gnome kicked and clawed as she removed his magic.

"Hush, little one. It'll be over soon," Melusine cooed.

Magic filled her palm, hot and alive. Holding the gnome in one arm she brought the magic to her lips. She drank it, feeling it flow to her root chakra. Stolen warmth and power pulsed and swirled, then began to move up her chakras. It would take hours before the first drops of magic reached her crown and began to spread to her nervous system where her body would absorb it. Then she'd be able to use it.

Standing, she put the gnome back in the iron cage. The other gnomes held their now magic-depleted friend. His comatose body twitched, and whimpers escaped his chapped lips.

"Miss Thornton, please make sure they get food and water," Melusine said, her hands shaking.

Miss Thornton stepped into the room. "Of course."

"And I want to know how long he stays alive. I can't imagine a wholly magical being can survive without his magic for long. After all, removing the little bit of Phoenix magic from that singer last week caused her to become extremely ill."

"I did check on her," Miss Thornton said as she dumped apple slices into the cage. "She's depressed, not physically ill."

"How interesting. Keep tabs on her for me."

"I will. I put the paperwork for the new gallery on your desk. You should have enough time to go over it before Salvador arrives to do your hair."

Melusine smiled. "You are a gem; I couldn't survive without you, Miss Thornton."

"You're too kind. I also have a cappuccino waiting for you on your desk."

"Now you're spoiling me." Melusine walked back through the closet, her heart pounding at her success. After a thousand years of being bound in servitude in exchange for immortality, her freedom was within her grasp. Cartazonon was such a fool, he had little faith in Earth-based magic. Knowing she collected such 'archaic things' he'd even sent her the book of magic which would gain her freedom from him. He might be the leader of the Sons of Belial, but she was no longer following him. Her email chimed as she sat. Ramsey had been a busy boy—three emails already. Oh, yes, her freedom was very close indeed.

Chapter Five

My muscles quivered as I stretched after the power yoga/conditioning class taught by Michael, the manager/ringmaster for Cirque du Feu Magique. He might have gray mixed in his short brown hair and a receding hairline, but his stocky frame was pure muscle.

"Your dad is evil," I said.

Nyota laughed and unwrapped her dreadlocks from an orange cotton scarf. "I hear that a lot."

Kayin snorted as he rested his head against his shins, stretching out the backs of his legs.

"Saturday is our first performance," Michael announced, as he mopped the sweat off his golden skin with a towel. "If you need anything from me, help with choreography, costumes, makeup, or anything else, please let me know."

Michael said that every time we went to a new place. It made me smile. He's a great manager. Once he finished talking, the audience we'd attracted moved in. I was surprised at the number of people who watched. We were just working out this morning, nothing fancy.

"Hey, quick question. Do you guys feel anything when you're in the dampening field?" Nyota asked, twisting to get a deep stretch in her back. Her eyebrow ring glinted against her milk chocolate skin.

As our tech wizard, she had developed a way to block our Phoenix powers from being detected through some vibrational frequency thingy I didn't understand. I did know the field worked best when we weren't using our powers. In the past, it had prevented walk-ins and kept some of Cartazonon's generals from finding us.

"What do you mean?" Kayin asked, turning to face us as a group came closer. I wasn't sure if he'd done that on purpose, but I carefully avoided eye contact with them until we were done talking.

She sucked on her lip piercing while she thought. Sweat beaded on her skin. She didn't perform in the show, so I didn't know why she put herself through this hell. Groaning, I sat up. She looked right at me. I did my best to stay relaxed. Her eyes were so pale gray-blue they looked almost clear, and I always felt as if she could see right through me.

"Well, I'm a bit worried about how the dampening field might affect Anali or the baby. Do you feel more tired while in it? Do you get headaches? Loss of appetite?"

"I have never felt bad while in the field," Kayin answered.

"Nyota, you've asked all this before, and I do remember the stern lecture to tell you if I ever felt off in any way so you could make sure it wasn't the field," I said.

She sighed, and her shoulders relaxed. "Yes, I know. I'm just worried. It's a new technology and with the baby ..."

"I have an idea." I looked around the room. Circus performers mixed with dancers in a multitude of styles. None of the little kids were here yet, so who were all these people? School was still in session, so they had to be older. Sasha was basking in the attention of several women, if his puffed-out chest was anything to go by.

Taliesin leaned against the wall, his arms crossed. He was talking to the women and men around him. Taliesin smiled and tilted his head forward, allowing his white braid to fall over his shoulder. He looked at one of the women through his lashes and grinned. Another woman reached out and touched his arm to get his attention, and his body become rigid and tight. Okay, time to earn some good karma points. "Sasha, Taliesin, do you two have a moment?"

"Yes," Taliesin said walking away. The girls pouted, but their pique soon faded when they watched his butt as he walked towards us.

Sasha said goodbye and walked more calmly towards us, his bottom also under close inspection.

Once they were seated, I talked to them about the dampener. "Sasha, Nyota is worried about the effects the field might have on the baby. Would you try to Dream about it?"

"Da, but why don't do you ask? I know you dream of Akasha, too."

I shrugged. "I do sometimes, but your Phoenix gift is Dreaming, you remember so much more than I do."

He nodded, and his red-streaked, honey-brown hair covered his gray eyes. "Sure. I will try to focus on the baby and the field."

Nyota smiled. "Thank you. That will put my mind at ease. I'll see you guys later. My roommates are busy chatting with some guys, which means I can get into the shower first." She wove her way through the crowd, disappearing into the hallway.

"Sapphire, I did have a Dream last night," Sasha said. "It looked like a large castle doorway standing on a hill in a big field. No castle, no door, just the doorway. I wasn't going to mention it since I don't know any more than that, but since we were talking about Dreams . . ."

"Is it a portal?" Taliesin asked.

"I don't think so, but maybe it leads to the portal. There might be some connection," Sasha said.

"Have you tried using the crystal?" I asked, remembering how he found the faerie village in Peru by holding a crystal on a silver chain over a map.

"No, not yet," Sasha answered.

"Is there anything else?" I asked.

Sasha's thick brows pulled together as he frowned. "You are supposed to talk to a tree. But not any tree. That part isn't very clear."

Well, that's helpful. I'll start walking around talking to trees and see what happens. "It always takes a few nights in a new city before you settle enough for your Dreams to become clear again. Don't stress about it, just let me know when you find out something more."

Sasha nodded and smiled. "Da, you're right."

"Did you need me for something?" Taliesin asked.

Smiling, I shook my head. "No, I just thought you needed rescuing."

Kayin and Sasha chuckled.

"I don't mind answering questions, or even receiving compliments, but once they start touching me. . ." He shivered.

"I'm sorry." Being part unicorn, Taliesin was very sensitive to people's,—well, aura— for lack of a better word. He sees and feels how pure you are, and the less pure the more irritating that feels to him. He once described it like listening to a child play an out of tune violin. "I'll try and keep you away from them."

"Thanks," he said his tone was cold, but I felt his relief. Taliesin, our beautiful ice prince.

"I'm headed back to the hotel, want to come along?" I asked.

"Yes." Taliesin jumped up and held out his hand.

Okay, odd. I took it, and he didn't let go. Ah, I see: protection from the fangirls. I felt disappointment bouncing off my shields as we walked through the crowd.

Calls of *goodbye* and *see you later* to Taliesin, Sasha, and Kayin echoed as we bundled up and left. We huddled together, as if standing closer and hunching over would protect us from the icy drizzle.

"Wait up," Shin called out, running over and throwing an arm across my shoulders. "Are you guys ready for some fun this morning?"

This didn't sound good. "What are you talking about?"

"Today, after breakfast, we are going to do a real life escape and evade test," Shin answered as if that explained something.

Not good at all. "What?"

"We will go to a crowded area, I will grab you, and not only do you have to get out of the hold, you have to get back to the hotel before I can catch you," Shin answered. "It'll be fun."

His definition of fun was warped and evil.

"That does sound like lots of fun," Taliesin teased.

"I'm glad you think so, because I've drawn names and you'll be first," Shin said.

I sniggered. I guess Taliesin thought Shin was talking to me. HA!

"Tomorrow is Miu, next Sasha, then Sapphire, and last Kayin," Shin explained.

Wonderful. I would be doing an escape and evade test days before my first performance. With my luck, I'd fall and break something.

* * *

"Good morning, Miu," I said, drying my hair. She stood in front of the mirrored closet door, applying sparkling lavender eye shadow.

"Morning. I'd stay and chat, but I have hula-hoop practice in a minute." She rolled her thin almond-shaped light green eyes. "Gavin asked me to see if Anali was okay. I told him that even though my Phoenix gift is healing, I can't scan someone and figure out what their general state of health is." Miu adjusted the pink bows at the top of her braid. "Anyway as far as I can tell Anali is fine, but I recommended mint tea and nibbling on candied ginger. Oh, I am planning a big party the night before your birthday, so don't make any plans. If you don't have a clubbing outfit, we can go get one later this afternoon. Okay, I have to go. Have fun."

I blink as the door shut. Wow, okay, busy Miu equals frantic Miu. I tried not to imagine what Miu was concocting for my sixteenth birthday. I hadn't planned on doing anything big, but she had insisted. I stepped over the clothes she'd left on the floor and put my stuff away. Grabbing my purse, coat, and scarf, I headed down to breakfast.

In the hallway Gavin was talking to an older woman with ash blond hair. "Thank you so much for coming."

"You're welcome, and ring me if you need anything," she said, walking towards the elevator. A large blue tote bag hung over one shoulder.

"Thanks, I will," Gavin said. "Morning, Sapphire."

"Are you okay? Who was that woman?" He had dark circles under his eyes.

"Yes, I didn't sleep well." Gavin opened his room door. "Come on in. Anali is in the shower, so we can talk. That was the midwife, and she said everything seems fine, just really bad morning sickness. Probably worse due to stress and worry because of the miscarriage she had when we were first married."

I sat at the desk, while he plopped into a chair. "Anali mentioned the miscarriage yesterday, but she seemed okay."

Gavin smiled. "She was devastated at the time. Even knowing it wasn't her fault, she still blamed herself and cried for weeks." He shook his head. "It was awful. I finally flew her home, and we spent a month with her family. She needed her mom and sisters."

I blinked back tears. Poor Anali. "Is she okay now?"

"Physically, yes. When we talked about having a baby, of course I worried about traveling, the Sons of Belial, and the energy we deal with opening the portals, but I was also worried about another miscarriage. She's acting brave, but I know she's scared. I think the midwife helped a lot."

"Is there anything I can do?" I asked.

Gavin shook his head. "No, I just wanted you to understand what was happening and not to worry if you don't see us at meals. The different smells get to her."

"Okay." The shower turned off, and Gavin turned to look at the bathroom door. I stood up. "Tell Anali I said hello, and I hope she feels better."

Gavin opened the door to his room. "I will. Once things calm down we'll figure out what to do for your birthday."

"Don't worry …" I began.

"Gavin, can you come here? I feel a bit dizzy." He dashed to the bathroom. I left, not wanting to interrupt.

Poor Anali and Gavin. I wouldn't bother them with anything silly, they had enough to take care of right now.

* * *

I jumped as a shop door opened. Shin had taken me a few miles away from the hotel and told me to wonder around, and then he disappeared. My fingers twitched at every movement and sound as I waited for him to attack. I looked in the window at a short black dress with a drooping neckline that caught my attention. They had paired it with copper heels that laced up mid-calf. I bit my lip trying to decide how uncomfortable the shoes would be and whether they were cute enough to put up with any discomfort. Maybe I should try them on. No, what if I liked it and bought it and then Shin attacks and I dropped it? I can find it again. One last look and I started walking. Stepping off the curb, I kept my eyes on the ground hoping to avoid the puddles.

Arms reached out and pulled me into an alley and trapped me in a bear hug. I gasped as the arms tightened around me, pushing the air from my lungs and pressing my back against a strong chest. I squirmed trying to get free, but he was too strong. How do I get away? What do I do? My fingers gripped the dark arms wrapped around me tugging at them ineffectually.

A deep laughed rumbled through me. "Sapphire, why does this escape always send you into a panic? Calm down you know how to get out of it."

I sagged in his arms. "I'm fine when I know we're training, it's being snuck up on that freaks me out."

Shin picked me up keeping my arms pinned in the bear hug. "You need to be able to react quickly and sense when someone is about to attack you."

I rolled my eyes. I could feel the Sons of Belial coming for me, but purely human attackers were different. Of course, Shin knew nothing about my powers. He thought people had made threats and attempted to kidnap me, and that was the reason Gavin engaged him to teach me self-defense techniques. Looking down, I tried to remember what I was supposed to do in order to get away.

Shin rested his head on my shoulder his black and blue bangs hanging down. "Are you planning on trying to get away or should I just take you away and have my wicked way with you?"

I snorted. "Whatever."

Shin chuckled and began to walk. "Whatever, sounds good to me. If I make it to the end of the alley I win."

Damn it, I had to get away. Not that I was scared of Shin, but I knew from experience he considered this a bet. Last time I had to wash and fold all his clothes for a week. His workout clothes smelled so rank! And I swear he changed his outfit three or four times a day.

Okay, first I had to get my feet on the ground. Bringing my knees up as high as I could, I exhaled and shoved my body down. Only my toes touched the ground, but it was enough to push off of and fling my head back. The back of my head didn't make contact with his face, but Shin responded as if I had. His arms loosened as he brought a hand to his face.

I stepped to the left, pushing my arms out straight, then slammed my elbow into his stomach. Shin made a loud *oof* and bent forward as I brought my fist down as if to hit him in the balls. His hand was there for me to make contact with and he jerked and hunched forward. I brought my fist up to hit him in the nose, and he had his hand there ready for that, too. Shin doubled over and fell to the ground.

I turned to face him and backed away.

Shin smiled, his thin dark eyes twinkling. He waved a hand at me. "Good job. You might want to run now, because I will come after you. You hit like a wuss, so you have until the count of twenty. One Mississippi, two Mississippi . . ."

Growling, I turned and ran—well not ran as that wasn't safe. I knew running would cause people to stare, which would leave a trail for him to follow, and I couldn't outrun Shin. Sliding in between shoppers, I walked down the street, making turns randomly looking for something, though I wasn't sure what. Turning left, I came to a shop with a deep inset doorway. Several racks stood next to the door. If I squeezed myself into the shadowed corner, I could hide and make a plan.

I spun around, and not seeing Shin, I darted into the doorway. I pressed myself between a customer and the brick wall and into the few inches of shadow the space provided.

"Ach, lass, so sorry I was in your way, you know, standing here."

"I am so sorry," I said looking up into black eyes. Wait, I looked him over: wild dark curls, milk pale white skin, scruffy square jaw, crooked Roman nose, toned chest under a tight black tee shirt and leather jacket, Earth-toned plaid kilt, and Doc Martens. When I looked back up, one thin eyebrow was cocked and a smile curled his pink lips.

"I know you. I mean I remember you. The other night you played the cello in a pub."

"That I did. I remember you too." My legs quivered a bit. I'm sure it had to do with Shin hunting me and not this sexy Scottish accent.

"Why exactly are you hiding in this corner?"

"Oh, well. I'm being hunted." I peeked over his shoulder—no sign of Shin.

He stood taller and adjusted the black yoga bag slung across his back. "I've heard of monsters like that. They look like people but suck the magic and life out of you. Mum used to tell stories of them at bedtime when I'd been a naughty little pup. I'd thought they were stories to scare a wee bairn until I was seven and saw my older sister taken. That was eleven years ago, and I've never had the chance to get my revenge."

Guilt thudded into my stomach like icy rocks. "No, I mean, yes, people like that do exist, but I'm learning to avoid them. My friend is teaching me Hwa Rang Do, and today is a test. I'm so sorry about your sister and about upsetting you."

"So you're not in real danger?"

I bit my lip and shook my head. I wanted to look away in shame but I forced myself to meet his eyes.

"Now, lass, don't be looking at me like that. I'm glad you're learning to stay safe, and I assumed what you meant without asking, so no hard feeling. All right?" He turned and pretended to be looking at the rack of sunglasses. "What does he look like?"

I described Shin, while hunting for my phone. I had been careless and wasn't sure where I was. "Damn it, he stole my phone."

"Do you need to call someone?"

I shook my head. "No, but I'm supposed to get back to the hotel and I have no idea where that is."

He grinned and held out his hand. "My name is Ramsey McDaniel and I would be honored to be your escort this morning."

Feeling nothing but playfulness from him, I shook his hand. His energy felt cool and calm. "Sapphire Rayner. Thank you, but it might be cheating to get help."

"Please, a lass as pretty as you will always find a gentleman willing to come to her aid."

My cheeks heated up so quickly I was afraid little flames were dancing on them. "Well, thank you. I need to get to the Royal Garden Hotel."

"Very posh. Should I be calling you Lady Sapphire?" His eyes danced with amusement.

"I bet you think you're funny."

He grinned—a grin that promised equal amount of trouble and pleasure. "Now, M'lady, let me check to make sure the way is safe, and we shall sally forth to your palace."

I grinned. I tried not to, but I couldn't help myself.

He stepped out of the doorway and I heard Shin's voice. "Excuse me. Have you seen a young lady with long red-streaked black hair? She dropped her phone, and I'm trying to return it."

"I saw a wee lass going into that bookshop," Ramsey said quickly, thickening his accent.

"The bookstore?" Shin asked. See, he should have done our British immersion marathon.

"Och, aye," Ramsey said making his brogue even stronger.

"Um, thanks."

Ramsey reached his hand back to me while he watched Shin walk away. I stared at it for a moment before placing my hand into his. His skin was rough and cool and his long fingers wrapped around mine. We stood there for a moment until he tugged on my hand. "Okay he's inside the store."

"Can't he see out the window?"

"Naw. Old Mr. Peterson has so many books in there, the windows are blocked." He tilted his head to the side. "Come on, fair lady, let's get you home."

I rolled my eyes but let him lead me through the crowds.

"So why are you in London?" Ramsey asked.

I stopped watching his kilt swaying around his legs and looked up. "I'm with the Cirque du Feu Magique."

"Really, what do you do?" he asked, grinning at me again. My heart fluttered.

"I spin poi, walk on stilts, jump rope, and Kayin and I are now doing statue, which is like a balancing act." If Shin hadn't stolen my phone I could show him pictures. I wrapped my scarf tighter around my neck as a cold wind swept over us.

"Sounds brilliant."

"I ... um would you like to come? I can put you on the guest list." At least I assumed I could put him on a list of some kind somewhere. That's what people in movies said.

"I'd love to."

I ran a hand through my hair, my fingers getting caught in the wild curls. "Okay. I, um, our first show is Saturday night."

"What time? My band usually plays in the evenings," Ramsey asked.

"The shows start at seven and last about two hours. I can have two tickets waiting at will call so you can bring your girlfriend." I flinched. Oh that didn't sound stupid or like I was fishing for information in the most childish way possible. "Or friend, or whatever." Oh good. Classy quick save.

Ramsey chuckled, and a shiver ran through my body. Even his laugh had an accent. "Brilliant, thanks. Our gig Saturday night starts at ten, so I can come."

I sighed. "Great. I'll text Michael. Wait—I don't have my phone! Damn Shin."

He opened the small black leather bag with a silver Celtic knot clasp which hung around his hips. He saw me watching him and said, "It's called a sporran, and here is my card. You can call or text me when you know what's going on."

His card was pale blue with black lettering: Ramsey McDaniel, Cellist of The Water Nymphs, and his email and numbers. I tucked the card into my back pocket. "Thanks."

"We need to turn here."

Oh, this looked familiar—green awnings with white Christmas lights along the edges and a bakery advertising Christmas puddings. Their window was painted with a large flaming round cake. I looked around—there was my dress. I veered towards the store and slowed down.

"Everything okay, lass?"

"Oh, yes, of course," I said.

Ramsey stopped moving. "I have a mum and two sisters. Something has caught your eye. I'm guessing the sexy black dress."

"It's nice enough I guess," I said. "It probably wouldn't look good on me anyway. I have to get back to the hotel."

Ramsey looked at the dress, and then his black eyes turned to me and slowly looked me over. I held as still as possible but inside I was squirming. "You'd look very bonny in that, the shoes too."

My cold cheeks heated up so fast I became dizzy. "Maybe."

"Come on, let's go this way. We'll take side streets so it'll be harder to sneak up on us, then we can walk through the park."

"Sounds good." We walked in silence as I looked at the beautifully painted Victorian homes and felt a twinge of homesickness for San Francisco. I should really call Shante soon. I kicked some dead leaves as we walked into Kensington Park.

"Are you all right?" Ramsey asked. "You're frowning."

"Sorry, just thinking."

Ramsey dipped down and nudged his shoulder into mine. "'Bout what?"

"The past. A year ago I was living in San Francisco in a group home with a young girl named Shante," I explained. "She was five when I went to live with my uncle. I had promised her I would never leave her."

"Where is she now?"

"Gavin made sure she would be taken care of. My friend Taliesin, he tours with us—anyway his mom, Cordelia, became her mentor and recently adopted her," I said.

"So she's happy?"

"Yes, very, and Cordelia makes all our costumes for the circus, so we talk all the time."

"Why so unhappy then?" Ramsey asked. "You are walking on a cold but lovely day through historic Kensington Park, with a dashing man in a kilt."

"It is a lovely kilt, maybe I should get one. Do you think a plaid would look nice on me?"

Ramsey's eyes sparkled and his happiness bubbled against me. "You are obviously an uneducated American. While there are skirts in tartans, this is a kilt, and it is for men. And do you know how to tell the difference?"

Biting my lip to keep from laughing I shook my head.

"Well you see lass, if this were a skirt," he pulled at the brown and green tartan. "I'd be wearing pants under it."

I frowned for a minute, pants? And then my British immersion lessons kicked in, and my eyes widened as I flushed bright red. Pants mean underwear, he wasn't wearing …Eek! "Um, well, but, aren't you cold?"

"Are you offering to warm me up?"

"No!" I shrieked stuffing my hands into my coat pockets.

Ramsey held up his hands and stepped back. "Calm down, I'm only fooling. My sisters would beat me within an inch of my life if I mistreated a girl."

I sniffed and grinned. "I suppose you can be forgiven since it looks like you've gotten me to my hotel."

"Was there any doubt?"

I shook my head. "I feel like I've cheated. I'm so relaxed, and I haven't kept an eye out for Shin at all."

"You should have," Shin said.

Chapter Six

"The ends justify the means."

I jumped and screamed. Ramsey stepped in front of me. Shin raised an eyebrow and smiled. "I love that you found someone to help you once you realized I'd taken your phone. It would have been even better if you'd kept track of where you were. And you did fine, except for not watching for me, until you went down the quieter neighborhood streets and now into the park. I was openly following you for several blocks."

I stepped out from behind Ramsey. "Hey, Shin, Sorry. I guess this means I lose."

Shin cracked his knuckles. "Well, I don't have you, and the hotel isn't far."

I looked behind me. The Royal Garden Hotel was a gleaming tower of glass and metal. "True, it's only a block or so away but I can't outrun you."

"If your escort agrees to stand down, and if you hit me hard enough to make me let go, you might make it back," Shin said.

"No worries," Ramsey said stepping away.

"So what are the rules?" I asked.

"Still the same. You have to get to the hotel, but I won't make it easy." Shin pointed to a large tree about halfway to the hotel near the parking lot. "And if I get you to that tree I win."

I took a step back. "Okay, sounds good."

Shin changed, his eyes became cold, his smiled faded, and his face hardened. He lunged, grabbed my wrist and began to drag me down the path. My brain shut down. I grasped at his hand and pulled back. I couldn't remember what to do. I dug my heels into the ground, but Shin easily pulled me over the dead grass. Anger and aggression hit my shield like a hot wave, he'd never come at me like this before.

He chuckled, his grin evil. I shivered. "You are going to have to hand wash my laundry for a week, and I'm going to change my outfit four times a day."

Oh, gross. That is so not happening. I let my weight drop a bit. Shin tugged me harder to force me forward. I flung myself at him. Shin stumbled. I twisted my wrist pushing against his thumb, yanked out of his grip, and hit his hand away. Shoving him in the chest as hard as I could with both hands, I took three big steps back. I'd gotten away from Shin, but if I ran he would catch me. I moved into a fighting stance. "If I was under attack I would scream, drawing a crowd."

Shin nodded. "Good." Darting forward his foot came up. I moved to block the kick. Shin struck and twisted my arm behind my back. I could barely breathe as Shin tucked his shoulder under my chin. His arm snaked around my back, pressing my chest to his. Okay, we had not practiced this move. Shin began to walk, taking me with him.

"Sapphire?" Ramsey said.

I tried to say I was fine, but couldn't talk. I gave a thumbs up before focusing on Shin.

With my free hand, I grabbed his bangs and jerked his head back, stopping his movement. Bringing my knee up forced Shin to jump back just in time, so I hit him in the stomach instead of between his legs. Pressing my foot down onto his foot, I pinned it down and pushed. Shin's eyes widened. Because I pinned his foot, he couldn't get his balance and fell onto his back. I slammed my foot into the ground next to his knee indenting the soil.

Shin blinked then grinned. "A knee strike—that was a vicious move. I'm impressed. And pinning my foot—I didn't teach you that."

"I complained to Gavin about not being able to make you lose your balance, he taught me. So I win?"

"Oh yes. If you had hit my knee, I wouldn't be able to run as fast as you, if I could even run at all. Can you tell me where you would have hit me to take the knee out?" Shin asked as he stood up.

"The side," I said.

"Ah, Grasshopper, you get a gold star."

"That was brilliant." Ramsey came over to us. "My sisters are fierce, but I wish they could fight like that."

Heat filled my cheeks. "I've just started learning."

"True, but you were able to get away, and that's what matters. Come on, let's get to the hotel and get some lunch. I'm starving." Shin rubbed his flat belly.

"Oh, give me back my phone," I said.

Shin chuckled and handed me my phone. I texted Michael asking if Ramsey could be put on the list for Saturday night.

"I'm Shin Park by the way," he said holding out his hand.

"Ramsey McDaniel." A pale white hand clasped Shin's light amber brown one.

"Thanks for helping Sapphire. I wondered how she was going to get back to the hotel as lost as she was," Shin teased.

"Rude. I would have figured it out," I said, fake pouting.

"Of course you would have, lass," Ramsey said. "Now that the fun is over, I should be going. It was nice to meet you."

"You too, and thank you so much for your help. I'll text you once I know about Saturday," I said.

"Cheers, have a good afternoon." Ramsey turned and walked away.

Shin lay his arm across my shoulders. "I did have a lot of fun following you."

I elbowed Shin in the side. Watching Ramsey walk away, I agreed—his view had been lovely.

Shin's phone rang, and he cringed when he saw the caller ID. "I'll see you later. It's my mom, and then I have to go rehearse."

"See you later, tell her I say hi."

He nodded, answering the phone.

* * *

A group of jugglers left the blue banquet room tossing bean bags at one another and chatting in French. I guess separating us wasn't such a bad idea after all.

Shaking my head, I sat at an empty table. I chose new foods at the buffet they set up for us: cheddar and potato patties and vibrant red purple beetroot puree. Stirring in the pure white dollop of sour cream, I was amazed at the color it created.

"So, I have a wonderful plan," said Miu sitting next to me. She unwound the scarf from around her neck. "We'll go to a club—a lot of them have private rooms you can rent—we can find one that serves food, and we'll have cake, or cupcakes. It'll be great! And before we go, you are coming with me. My birthday gift to you is an experience."

"I found a great clubbing outfit this morning," I said taking a bite of the beetroot puree. Interestingly sweet and Earthy. Not my favorite food, but good.

"Can I take your order, Miss?" Brandon asked. His energy felt anxious, but not upset or scared, more like trying to contain excitement.

"Jasmine tea, and the buffet you've set up is fine," Miu said. Brandon nodded, his energy buzzing under his calm professional exterior.

"Brandon, could you recommend a club? Miu is plotting my birthday party."

Miu huffed. "Why do you make it sound like it's a bad thing?"

"Yes," Brandon said almost bursting with desire to tell us. "My family owns a club, well my aunt does, and my cousins work there. They have a second floor you can rent and they serve good pub grub."

"Wonderful, can I get the name and phone number?" Miu asked her pale green eyes sparkling with excitement.

He tore a page off his note pad. "Here. Tell them Brandon told you to call. They are the half of the family that actually like me, so dropping my name might help."

"Wonderful. See, Sapphire, your birthday is going to be awesome! Everything is falling perfectly into place," Miu said.

"What is awesome?" Taliesin asked. "Can I get a latte please?"

"Of course, anything else?" Brandon asked.

Taliesin looked at my plate. "No there seems to be plenty of options at the buffet."

"I'll be right back with your drinks."

"He likes you," Miu said to Taliesin with a smile before going to the far side of the room to call the club.

Taliesin groaned, running his hand through his white hair. It fluttered around his face and fell across his back.

"If it helps at all, Brandon is very confused as to why he feels drawn to you. I don't feel anything romantic or physical. I think the bit of magical being in him is reacting to you being a unicorn."

Taliesin tilted his head to the side while his eyes became unfocused, like he searched for something in his brain.

"Here you go," Brandon set the tea down by Miu's spot and latte in front of Taliesin.

Taliesin reached out and placed his hand on Brandon's arm and let a bit of his power lose. Cool, moonlight magic flowed around him. I sighed, as did Brandon. "Thank you Brandon."

"You're welcome," he grinned and left, his need for Taliesin's attention satisfied.

"That was nice of you," I said. "I don't think he even understands why he's so fixated on you."

Taliesin shrugged. "I've been working on controlling my powers and learning more about my magical nature. Anyway, he's a good person."

"Yes," yelled Miu. "The club sounds perfect; they'll even set up a full buffet. All I need to do is get Gavin to go check it out with me and pay for it. We have a show that night, so everything will be set up and ready for ten-thirty."

"Oh, by the way," Miu said as she went through the buffet. "Gavin and Anali said they plan on going on an outing at two. Well, Anali insisted. I made her an herbal tea that helped settle her stomach. If she can keep down some lunch, she wants to leave the hotel."

"Are they coming down for lunch?" I asked.

"No, the smells of so many different foods bother her stomach." Miu sat and poured herself a cup of tea inhaling the delicate flowery fragrance before taking a sip.

"Hello," Sasha said his cheeks flushed pink and his hair sweaty. He sat next to Taliesin.

"What have you been up to?"

"Trampoline. I watched them practice. A couple of the guys said they would teach me if I wanted. Apparently, I'm a natural," Sasha grinned and his cheeks pinked even more.

"I'm sure you are," I said. "After years of ballet, your balance and core strength are perfect for cirque acts."

Taliesin nodded. "I agree. You picked up silks very quickly."

Sasha inclined his head. "Thank you. I found you to be a very competent teacher."

"Do you know where Kayin is?" I asked.

"He wanted to shower before coming down to eat," Sasha said and went to the buffet.

"Gran, please," Brandon said, following an older woman through the door. He carried a large tray of food in his hand that threatened to tip in his hurry to keep up with her. She was tall and slender with bright blue eyes, gray hair pulled into a messy bun, and deep wrinkles in her white skin that spoke of a life filled with laughter and smiles.

"The cards told me you were coming," she said, patting a dark blue velvet bag and sat down next to me at the end of the table. "And I knew I had to come and do a reading for you. And you," she pointed at Taliesin, "are something special but I don't know what, yet."

"Please, Gran, you'll get me fired," Brandon said as he refilled several dishes in the buffet.

She waved her bony finger at him. "I have the sight, like my mother, and her mother, and her mother before her. You do, too, although you ignore it. And I know I need to be here and read the cards for them."

Brandon sighed.

"It's fine," I said. "Please don't worry."

"Bring me some tea, and you, dear children, call me Grandmother."

Brandon closed his eyes and his lips moved. I think he muttered a prayer, or maybe a curse.

Sasha arched an eyebrow at me as he sat down balancing a full plate, a bowl, and a steaming cup of coffee. He must like beets, as the bowl was full of them, the white sour cream melting into the mashed red-purple root.

"Now, dear, have you had your cards read before?" Grandmother spread a silk scarf that looked to be painted with watercolors in a variety of blues on the table.

"No ma'am," I said.

"That's fine." She unwrapped an old deck of cards from a square of turquoise silk. "First, I want you to look through the deck. Let your subconscious see the cards, then shuffle them until they feel full."

Okay, this was weird, but it seemed like a good idea to go along with her. I didn't feel anything bad from her. I held my hand over the cards, and their energy fizzed against my skin. These were old; her family had used them for generations.

These cards had told of fortunes, of true loves, betrayals, deaths, and destiny set into motion on several occasions.

I pulled my hand back. "I can't touch them, I'm sorry."

Grandmother took the deck and spread out the cards. Hand-drawn pictures in black ink of people in Renaissance-style clothing adorned thick, yellowed cards. Words in Latin were written on the bottom with Roman numerals on the top. "According to my grandfather, God rest his soul, one of our ancestors drew these," Grandmother said. She scooped them up and began to shuffle them, then laid them out face up.

"A very dynamic spread, lots of major arcana cards."

That didn't sound good at all.

Grandmother hummed as she looked over the eleven cards, her wrinkled fingers hovering above them. "The Moon shows a new force in your life. A new power that you have yet to encounter, something sinister, you need to be careful."

She pointed to the Chariot. "You have a purpose, you bring balance and bring people together to create a powerful unit." She tapped the Nine of Wands which lay half over The Chariot and Ten of Wands, above them. "You feel a lot of pressure, a lot of people are counting on you. You are strong enough to handle it. Inside of you is the strength and power to follow through in your future."

These cards lied; obviously, they were untrustworthy. I felt like a hot mess most of the time, barely holding myself together.

"In the past there was grief, pain, and hopelessness," she said pointing to the Five of Cups, then touched the Three of Swords. "Ahead of you lies sorrow, separation, maybe the end of a love affair."

Oh good, something to look forward too.

"But the fifth card, that which is unknown but supports you is Judgment, rebirth, acquiring purpose, and atonement for past sins." Grandmother frowned. "Perhaps a person."

"These cards here." She touched the Ace of Swords, the World, Ten of Cups, and the Star, which were in a row. "They balance out the darkness. They show a strong family, and love—possibly romantic love. You have a lot of strength and love to balance the darkness and danger. You feel like you're being pulled, unable to regain your balance. It's because you try and do too much by yourself. You need to let others help you."

I looked at Taliesin. He glanced up from the cards and smiled. Was he laughing at me or trying to tell me that he was someone I could lean on?

"The Ace of Swords and The Chariot as the signifier show how important your work is. You give life. You are vital, but without love, family, and support, you might crumble." Grandmother reached out and took my hands. Her skin was powder soft. I began to shake. Not good—not good! I felt her connection to the cards, her connection to her ancestors who could tap into the spiritual essence of the person they read for, making the messages from the cards more powerful and accurate. Magic whispered in Grandmother. It felt foreign and familiar at the same time. Flashes of Grandmother's life began to come to me: watching her dad milk a cow, her mom and aunt teaching her to communicate with devas, riding in a train, an explosion, blood, screaming.

"Sapphire." Cool moonlight energy flowed into me, and my throat ached. Had I been screaming? I opened my eyes. Taliesin's sky blue eyes filled my vision.

"I'm sorry," I whispered.

His brow furrowed. "Why?"

"You always seem to be the one calming me down when I freak out." I began to sit up. How did I get on the floor?

"I don't mind helping you." Taliesin held my hands and helped me into my chair. "You reacted badly to everyone else, it was odd."

Grandmother clutched Brandon, her blue eyes full of tears. "I'm so sorry, I didn't realize, I didn't know."

My hand shook as I took a drink of water. "It's okay, I'm okay."

"Hey, Gavin," Miu said into her phone.

"No!" I turned to her, a wave of dizziness crashing over me. I tried not to let it show. "Miu, no. I'm fine, and they have the baby to worry about," I whispered.

As my vision cleared I saw her frown, but she nodded. "I wanted to check and see how Anali is feeling. Are we still going on an adventure this afternoon?"

I fell back into the chair. Thank goodness she listened to me.

"Are you sure you're okay?" Grandmother asked.

"Yes. Some more water and the rest of my lunch, and I'll be fine." I forced a smile.

Taliesin grabbed his plate and moved to sit next to me. I reached for his hand under the table. He squeezed my fingers.

"Gavin said they would be ready by two." Miu reached out as if to touch me then pulled back. "Are you sure you're okay?"

"I'm fine, just got overloaded," I said.

"Grandmother, I'll call dad to come and get you, okay?" Brandon said.

She sat up, wisps of gray hair falling around her face. "I'm sorry I didn't realize touching you would hurt you, but I need to read for Taliesin."

"It's fine with me," Taliesin said, politely but I heard the weariness in his voice.

While she shuffled the cards, I took a deep breath and allowed Taliesin's soothing unicorn magic to flow around me. Wait, I could feel his power but not him. "You're blocking me. When did you learn to do that?"

"I've been practicing, but it's less blocking and more a barrier of magic."

Sasha grunted. "We should find out why you reacted so badly to everyone else."

"I agree," said Kayin. "I was scared, Little Sister."

"Big Brother, when did you get here?" I asked.

His brow furrowed. "When the screaming started."

"I'm fine now. Go, get something to eat and sit down."

Kayin frowned but went to the buffet, filled a plate and sat down next to me.

I squeezed Taliesin's hand and let go. I didn't want to tire him out. I should be fine now. Wait. Hadn't Sasha asked me a question? "I don't know why no one else could touch me, but I will try and figure it out, I promise."

Miu's fingers twitched. "May I?"

I held out a hand to her. She put her hand in mine, her fiery healing gift warming me almost to the point of being uncomfortable. "Other than being tired and your empathy being shattered, you're fine."

"See, I told you," I picked up my fork and began to eat. People always seem to think as long as you're eating, everything is good. It took focused effort to keep my hand from shaking.

"Young man, may I begin?" Grandmother asked.

Taliesin nodded, and she laid out the cards in the same pattern as before.

"You are strong, a warrior, you help people, help them balance their soul. But it bothers you because of the chaos and destruction it can bring." Her hands hovered over the three cards in the middle, Strength, Two of Swords, and The Tower.

Taliesin was as still and hard as a statue, his breath shallow and quick. What Grandmother said didn't make much sense to me, but it seemed to make a lot to Taliesin.

She touched the Queen of Cups. "Your mother is a strong woman who loves you very much, and you have grown from the foundation of love and acceptance she gave you."

It's true, Cordelia was wonderful. Taliesin nodded slightly.

"You are waiting for something bad to happen." She tapped the Nine of Wands at the top of the spread. "Your mind is always seeking the next challenge or threat, looking out for those who might deceive you. You feel burdened and weary. But don't worry, The Knight of Swords shows your inner strength. With your vigilance and insight, you will see what is coming, what hides within the darkness." She pointed to the Moon, which was upside down.

Taliesin frowned at the cards. I'd had the Moon in my reading too. So, yeah, attacked by unknown forces.

"Your future, not your near future, but what is building, what you are helping to create now is full of good possibilities. The Three of Cups shows great friends who come together to make a more powerful group. Maybe one will even become your lover." Grandmother grinned and winked at Taliesin whose cheeks pinked a little bit. She pointed to the King of Cups and the Magician. "You could become a great man. A man of power, skills, insight, and ability with a loving heart. But you worry you'll turn to darkness and let fear consume you, betraying those you love and hurting the innocent."

Taliesin stiffened next to me. I reached out and squeezed his hand. I wouldn't let him go dark, none of us would.

"You have the World before you. If you trust in your friends and yourself, you'll have a future full of possibilities, of travel, triumph, and hope." Grandmother sighed and sat back.

Taliesin stared at The Tower. The image on the card showed a crumbling stone tower on fire, with people falling off of it. "I don't want to cause such pain and destruction."

Grandmother shrugged. "Sometimes life needs to be shaken up. Sometimes we have to leave the safety of what we know, or perhaps suffer the consequences of our actions, which can be devastating. Often the ends justify the means."

"The ends justify the means is an easy way for bad people to justify doing what they want. For good people it serves as a warning. Will your actions today justify the outcome tomorrow? Will you be able to look at yourself in the mirror after what you have done? Will the good you do outweigh the pain you cause? Only you know what the right choice is, but I have faith that you'll make the right one, my darling."

Biting my lip, I turned to look at Taliesin. He looked like marble, and a tear slid down his cheek. Lacing my fingers through his I reminded him I was here. He didn't move, but his hand molded to mine.

Grandmother's stared at the cards, her blue eyes losing focus. "What am I missing?"

Taliesin cleared his throat. "It's okay, I understand."

Gasping, she looked up her eyes glowing. "Oh, I see you now."

For a second the star on Taliesin's forehead glowed blue-silver.

Blinking, she looked at the cards again. "Yes, it all makes since now."

A group of acrobats burst into the room, their bright, laughing voices cutting through the tension and gloom.

Grandmother smiled and gathered up her cards. "Remember the messages, Taliesin. They might not be clear now but they will be. Now Brandon dear, you get to work. I'll go see if the others would like a card reading; they look very interesting."

Brandon sighed and rubbed his hand over his face. "I am so sorry. I had no idea anything like this would happen. She just showed up, and told me to let her in. I can never say no to my Gran."

"It's fine." Taliesin let go of my hand. "I think they need to order lunch."

Brandon nodded and went to the other end of the table where his Grandmother entertained the acrobats.

"Well," said Miu. "That was a ball of suck."

I snorted. "Eloquent and tasteful."

"I try," she smiled. "Hey, it's almost one. Taliesin, did you want to …" she trailed off.

"Yes," he looked at his half full plate and sighed. "I don't think I can eat any more, let's go."

I thought about saying something, but I wasn't Taliesin's keeper. And after what happened, I wasn't hungry either.

* * *

After finishing my history report on Nicola Tesla, I scrolled through the list of assignments I needed to complete. The virtual academy Anali and Gavin signed us up for was intense.

Our schooling wasn't going to suffer just because we traveled the world on a magical beings rescue mission. Let's see, my choices were: conjugating French verbs, a geometry test, or reading a chapter in marine biology and taking the quiz. It all sounded like so much fun while sitting in my luxury hotel room in London. Placing my finger on the screen, I began to chant eenie, meenie, miny, moe to choose when someone knocked on my door.

"Hey Gavin," I said.

He smiled, his eyes calm and focused. "Are you ready?"

"Sure let me grab my things. Where are we going?" I texted Miu and asked if she needed anything from the room.

"Well, Anali would like to go to the British Museum, but you have a bad reaction to antiques." Gavin fluttered his hands at me.

"I don't mind going. I've been practicing, and my shields are stronger now." I ignored the fact that I hadn't been able to fully repair them since the encounter with Brandon's grandmother.

"There are large sections that are newer and many exits," Gavin said.

I smiled at Gavin's emotions tugging in different directions. "Gavin, I'll be fine. I'll be careful to not stare at or touch the displays, and I doubt anything too traumatic happened in the museum itself." My phone beeped, and I hunted through the piles of Miu's clothing to find the requested items. "If it'll make you feel better I'll stay next to Kayin the whole time, and he can keep an eye on me so you can be free to take care of Anali."

Gavin frowned. "I don't want you to feel ignored."

I rolled my eyes. Adults are so difficult. "Anali needs you right now; I might have an issue. These are different things. If it'll make you feel better, once Anali is feeling better, I'll demand you spend a day with me."

Gavin gave me a one-armed hug as we walked out the door. "You won't have to demand. I enjoy spending time with you. Both Anali and I feel bad that we haven't been around much, but thank you for understanding."

"Uncle Gavin, you worry too much. I understand the difference between someone needing attention and being ignored."

"That's because you're very mature," Anali said. I jumped a bit. I hadn't heard their door open. She looked pale and had bags under her eyes, but she smiled. The joy radiating from her felt like soda bubbles.

"Not really, just used to seeing kids losing it when I lived in group homes. Helping me with math wasn't as urgent as helping a kid who was hysterical over a missed visit." I smiled. "It's all about perspective." And I knew this was temporary and nothing to worry about.

Anali hugged me. "You are so special, thank you."

I hugged her back. I wasn't that special.

"Are we going?" Miu asked as she and Taliesin came down the hallway.

"Yes," Anali said, letting go. "I need to get out, even if I can only handle an hour or two."

Taliesin looked tired, but I felt his sense of accomplishment, while Miu felt pleased. What had they been up to? "Did you guys have a productive time together?" I asked."

Miu nodded, and her braids slid over her back. "Yes, very, and you?"

"I finished my history essay,"

"Guh. I still need to do that one," Miu said. "I've read everything, I just need to put it all together."

"I finished all my work for this semester," Taliesin said.

Anali patted his arm. "Good for you. I'm sure the others are almost done."

There was no mistaking the mom tone. Miu and I dutifully recited the assignments we needed to complete. Anali smiled, pleased with her little brood of chicks. I hoped Sasha and Kayin were also close to being finished.

* * *

I bit my lip as we walked up the steps to the British Museum's towering Greek revival building. The off-white stone looked old, and my stomach clenched as I watched ghosts of memories walk around: transparent women in dresses with bustles and men in top hats and tails, people in hard hats running in between rubble as bombs dropped from the sky. I saw these flickers of the past all the time. The emotions and memories seeped into the stone, brick, and wood of every building. I ignored them since few were strong enough for me to feel. It's like walking through movie images with no sound.

"It's beautiful," Kayin said standing next to me as we looked up at the columns and the gods and goddess carved into the building above them.

"Yes, very," I said.

"You okay?" Sasha asked.

I took a deep breath and stood straighter. "Yes, I'm fine."

He snorted, but I ignored him. It was just a building and with beautiful treasures inside. I wasn't going to let it overwhelm me.

The museum won, not because my empathy was overwhelmed but because I was. The beauty, the history, the power of seeing our ancestor's creations was awesome. Truly awesome, not the slang version of the word but such as to inspire awe. If I stared too long at an object, I could feel a tug as if it wanted to tell me the story of its life. When my powers were new I fell into the emotions trapped inside a Sumerian bottle and saw the bottle's 'life.' A few months ago in Peru, I walked into a square once used for human sacrifices and couldn't block the images or emotions seeped into the stones. So far I resisted the call of the different objects.

"Oh, look at this," Miu said her eyes focused on a display of samurai armor.

I shivered, it looked demonic. Images of the men who wore it overlaid each other inside the helmet, making the demonic image complete. Ghostly blood splatter appeared on the lacquered plates and polished metal helmets. Emotions swirled:

fear, strength, pride, pain, and triumph. The armor had a story to tell, and it called to me. Stepping back, I took a deep breath and turned to look at a painting, a woodblock of a man and women, and oh! I blushed at the racy wood block. The next one showed a girl combing her hair, wearing a blue kimono with white flowers. I stared at it for a long time while the others admired the samurai weapons.

"Are you alright?" Taliesin asked.

I smiled. "Are you guys on a schedule? I don't think the same person has asked if I'm okay twice in a row."

He smiled. "This way you can't get angry because one of us keeps bugging you."

"I'm fine. There is less emotion trapped in the woodblock, so I'm admiring it while the others finish. You can go back and look at the swords if you want."

"They are amazing works of art, but I can sense the pain they have caused. I'd rather look at this." Taliesin pointed to the next woodblock. Huge blue waves rocked two small fishing boats, half hidden behind frothing white caps. "The plaque says each color needed its own carved block."

"How did they fit it together so perfectly?" I asked. "Do you sense anything?"

Taliesin shook his head his white hair fluttered around his arms. "No. You?"

"A vague sense of peace and joy. I'm guessing that it's because the painting wasn't handled," I said.

"Do you need to sit down?" Gavin asked Anali. "The map shows a cafe close by."

Anali squeezed his arm which she had taken as soon as we left the cab and had not let go of. They looked so cute, his arm bent, hand on his stomach so she could hold onto him easily. "I'm a little thirsty, and the midwife said eating smaller amounts frequently should help with the nausea."

"Well, then, we shall have some refreshments," Gavin said.

They smiled so sweetly my teeth ached. I was so not sitting at the table with them. Adults are so embarrassing.

Gavin, Taliesin, and I watched the others to gush over the rooms which showed their countries' art and history. It felt odd not having anything to connect to. "Gavin, what am I?"

He looked away from the gold Russian icon displayed across from the cafe. "What?"

"Well, where do our ancestors come from? I don't know if I'm British, or German, or what." I twisted my mom's ring, watching the midnight blue strip set in silver sparkle like the night sky.

"Oh, yes, well," Gavin ran his fingers through his fire red hair. "Your father was English, Scottish, and French. And our side is German, Danish, and Swiss, I think. Of course you go back four thousand years, and originally we're from Babylon."

Yes, and a Phoenix King. "Thanks."

"You know your dad loved genealogy. I know he traced his family and our family back as far as he was able to."

"Maybe we can find his research," Anali offered.

"I can ask Preston to start looking," Gavin replied.

"You don't have too. It isn't that big a deal," I said.

"It's not a problem; he's probably bored anyway. And if you want to find out more about our family and who you are, then I will make that happen," Gavin said.

"Thanks, Uncle Gavin." I moved to look at a collection of Russian stacking dolls before things got too mushy.

The museum was about to close. We scattered to look at as much of the current exhibit as possible, despite the fact that we could come back over the next few weeks. I was looking at a display of Roman-era artifacts found in England. A pair of dragonesque brooches caught my attention. To me they looked like seahorses, the silver dull, and some of the blue and red enamel chipped. There was something about them, something different. A hint of Akasha, but it wasn't strong. Then I fell—no, not fell—was pulled into the piece. I still felt my body and heard the low hum of voices. I was shown the history of the brooches.

An elf lay dying. His whole village had been infected by something, no one knew what. They tried to contact Shamash, but were too weak. A little green deva came to him. Earth devas—each planet had them—little beings that helps things grow, nature spirits that were tied to the land.

"I think I can help," the deva said. "But it'll change you. Do you wish it?"

"Yes." He didn't want to die.

The deva smiled and her hands began to glow.

Ache was the next thing he knew. His whole body ached, his mouth went dry, and his neck itched. Rolling over he found a cup of water. His long fingers wrapped around the wood cup which hummed in greeting. The cool water seemed to sing and rejoice as it soothed his dry mouth. Reaching up to scratch his neck, his fingers touched his necklace: a simple silver chain from Akasha, a chain which now bothered him. It wasn't painful, but the power in it moved too fast and felt too strong.

Dressing in simple green tunic and leggings, he went to see how the others fared. Some chose to die, or were too sick for the devas to heal. The rest chose life and found themselves changed—they belonged to Earth now. Their soft magic tuned into the steady deep heartbeat of Earth. He missed the wild, strong, rhythm of Akasha. His necklace seemed to mock his lack of power.

He went to a human silversmith, careful to hide his ash-blond hair, as they had some silly superstition about it being evil. He had the necklace melted into Earth silver and made into images of water fairies with bright blue-and-red- lacquered scales. The silversmith thought they looked like dragons and asked if he could make the design for others. The elf didn't mind.

The elves mourned their loss, but over time learned to use their new powers and accept life as one of Earth's creatures. When the humans multiplied, they created a deep lake around their village. Some curious humans watched them and ran back to their villages with stories of magic, enchantments, and creatures of myth and legends. Others asked to learn to study how to be stewards to Mother Earth. They wanted to connect to her and not dominate and fight her.

The elf stood on the top of the hill looking over the village of stone houses and thatched roofs, lush fields, and at elves and people studying Earth's magic, while devas and fairies flew around them. His heart filled with joy and peace. Together they had created a new home: Avalon.

A hand took my elbow and warm Phoenix energy thrummed. Blinking, I took a shuddering breath. Wow, that was interesting.

"Sapphire, are you okay?" Kayin asked.

"Yes, fine," I shook my head black and red curls fluttering around my face. "I stared at that piece a little too long."

"Should we tell Gavin?" he asked.

"No, I'm not hurt, it wasn't anything scary or bad, and you know now, so you can keep an eye on me," I said.

"Time to go," Gavin called out as he helped Anali to her feet.

"See, we're leaving now—it won't happen again." I smiled. Kayin arched an eyebrow and stared at me. I held his gaze for a minute, but as usual his deep brown eyes demanded the truth. I squirmed, looked away, and sighed. "Big Brother, I should have been more careful, but if I hold onto you, I'll regain my focus and strengthen my protective bubble so my empathy isn't picking up everything."

He took my hand, his warm fingers wrapping around mine. "This is the second time you chose to keep things from your uncle, Little Sister. I do not like it."

I nodded. "I know, but neither thing could harm anyone, and with how Anali is feeling, I don't want to burden them right now."

"You are not a burden."

"I know." And I don't intend to become one.

Chapter Seven

Running my finger down the glossy image, I couldn't believe that it was me and Kayin. Michael arranged for a photographer to come and take photos of everyone during a dress rehearsal and make them into a new program. The make-up we wore to highlight our features made us look older and more severe. Of course we were both concentrating on not falling over, but you couldn't tell. We looked powerful, balancing against each other, defying gravity. We wore skin-tight red costumes, that showed far more skin than they covered, so my copper brown skin contrasted beautifully to his ebony.

I closed the program and peeked out into the theater. I could smell the popcorn and candy. Small children waved pink clouds of cotton candy close to their parent's faces. The clowns were beginning to come out and mess with the audience. The show would start in about fifteen minutes. Little faces lit up as they saw the clowns wearing their baggy, silly mismatched clothes. The male clowns wore dresses and tutus, and the girls wore ugly plaid sport coats and ties. Their hair was in silly, messy styles. Their make-up was strong, but not creepy clown make-up, thank goodness. They slinked through the aisles. Adults sitting in the front tried desperately to not make eye contact, not wanting to become the focus of the clowns' attentions. I searched the crowd. There! Ramsey had come. Sitting next to him was the pretty lead singer of the band. Oh, well, it's not like I was staying or could have an actual relationship with him. Sighing, I watched her fingers tame his wayward brown curl.

"Ready?" Kayin asked.

"Yes, just watching the crowd."

Kayin leaned over my shoulder to peek through the curtains. "They seem excited tonight."

The crowd burst into laughter as the clowns threw a bucket of confetti over a woman. "I think we are the ones who are excited. I hope I don't mess up on our first time performing statue."

"You'll be great," Kayin said. He placed his large hands on my shoulders and squeezed. "And remember what Michael says."

"Someone get me a coffee," I teased.

Kayin chuckled and shook his head.

"If I didn't have to go on right now," Michael said, his eyes sparkling. "I'd make both of you do push-ups for that comment. I believe the one saying Kayin was referring to is, 'have fun and do your best. The audience doesn't know the routine, so if you make a mistake, fake your way through it."

"Yes, Michael," we said, stepping aside so he could sneak through the audience while the clowns held the crowd's attention.

The house lights went out, and the audience gasped. Their excitement swirled through the air like autumn leaves dancing on the wind. I watched as a crowd of strangers, hundreds of strangers, become one. Their eyes widened as the Chinese pole performers walked onto the stage. Their costumes, which looked like multicolored ribbons, brought small smiles of delight. Watching the audience gasp, cry out, flinch, hold their breath and clap, I was able to tell exactly what the performers were doing. It was amazing to see all of these different people captured by the power and passion of the performers.

As the music faded, the audience released their collective breaths and clapped, coming out of the trance. I watched looks of admiration and envy, and several people were flushed with desire. This is magic, not the strange powers I woke up with almost a year ago, but being able to unite people, if only for a moment. This is true magic.

"Sapphire, we need to go queue up," Kayin said, tugging on my arm.

"Okay." I listened to the fast violin music begin, signaling the diabolo act. Would their performance of tossing a wooden hour glass figure between each other on thin ropes entrance the crowd in the same way? They were very skilled, it was difficult and took hours of practice, but would the audience be as enchanted, or were the feats of strength, of seeing the human body in all its glory what enchanted them?

"Have you seen Gavin and Anali?" Kayin asked as we waited in the back.

"No," I said as I stretched. "They said they would be here to see us, but they were going to nap first. Anali was really tired." I didn't expect them to come. I ignored the cold shard of sadness in my heart that accompanied the thought, but Anali wasn't feeling well, and I truly did understand. There would always be other shows.

Kayin nodded.

"Are you ready?" Sasha asked. He wore skin-tight leggings of blue and silver. His make-up had triangles of blue on his cheeks, making his GQ cheekbones look viciously sharp. The silver on his lips and eyes seemed to glow.

Sasha looked amazing, but Taliesin looked heartrendingly beautiful. Taliesin's mother Cordelia designed all the costumes, and these new ones made her son seem godlike. His white skin and hair glowed against the blue and silver. He looked as if he was bathed in moonlight with his unicorn nature exposed, glowing silver under the moon's gentle caress.

"Wow," I gasped. "You two look stunning."

Sasha grinned. "Yes, I do look very nice."

I rolled my eyes at Sasha, grateful for the distraction so I could catch my breath. I thought I was immune to beautiful people after traveling with the circus for so many months, but apparently my teenage hormones could still get the best of me. For once I was grateful for the thickness of the stage makeup that covered my blush.

"You two look great," Taliesin said, "The red complements both your skin colors, and makes the differences stand out. Very sensual."

"Thanks." It was nice of him to say so, but as I stood surrounded by these three breathtakingly perfect men, I felt very plain. Hopefully the costume and makeup would help the audience buy the illusion of my being as beautiful as Kayin.

The violin music faded and the diabolo girls bowed and waved to the audience, while the clowns ran about in their usual between-routine performance intended to distract the audience from set and prop changes. Kayin held out his hand, I took it, and we walked out on stage. Our breathing synchronized as we moved into place. I could feel the audience. My shield held, so I wasn't overwhelmed by them, but I felt it when we caught their full attention. The audience began to breathe as one, gasping and cheering as we amazed them with our strength and balance.

Kayin held up my hands, and I tightened my body, moving into a handstand above his head. Breath by breath, we moved into different balancing poses. Tightening my stomach, I held motionless as Kayin moved to the floor with me balanced above him on his shoulders. A wave of excited fear from the audience hit my shields. My body trembled, and I wrapped my arms around Kayin's chest to balance myself.

He froze, and I curled down. "Let's go to the floor together," I whispered.

"Yes." Kayin began to move again. I slid next to him on the floor then, in what I hoped was an artistic way, repositioned myself so we could get back into our routine.

Only a few beats later I was sitting on the soles of his feet, then we stretched out in opposite directions before he brought me back in, and we curled around each other as the cello music began to fade.

"I'm sorry," I whispered.

"You did great."

Now that I wasn't focused on the routine, I felt the audience's full force. Lust and envy licked at my shields. Later when we interacted with the audience, I would need to keep an eye on Kayin. If people were feeling like that about him, they must also look at Taliesin and Sasha that way. Maybe Miu would help me protect our boys.

The music stopped. A pause of silence, then the audience broke free of the spell and began to clap. We stood, bowed, then waved to the audience before walking off stage as the clowns ran on and began their routine again.

"Well done," Sasha said, slapping Kayin on the shoulder.

I smiled, my chest heaving and my body buzzing with excitement. We had done it. Our first statue, and we had done it. Okay one minor slip-up, but we managed to bring the routine back on track.

"Sapphire," Taliesin said, "you looked wonderful out there."

"Thanks, I wasn't sure I would be able to do it."

"You two practiced a lot. Of course you would be great," Sasha said.

"Okay. Sasha and Taliesin, you're ready?" Michael asked.

"Yes," they said.

"Great. After the clowns, it's the hula hoop, then you two." Michael pointed at me. "After silks is poi and stilts so you need to go and get into your next costume. Then we'll have intermission."

I smiled. At this point we had the schedule memorized, but Michael felt better saying it out loud and reminding everyone of what was to come. "I'll go get changed right now."

Because I was supportive in poi/stilts and jump-rope I added pieces to my costume but didn't have to change my make-up, which was lucky as this stuff is a pain to get on and off.

"Need a hand?" Shin asked.

"Yes, thank you." I took his hands, tucked my stilts against his feet and let him pull me up. The black-and-white striped skirt fell almost to the floor, hiding the aluminum stilts. "You guys were amazing, the crowd was entranced."

Shin grinned. "Thanks. I like the routine, and the new guys are a strong addition to the group." Reaching up, he adjusted the black-and-white polka dot vest I wore over the red top.

"Is my hat okay?" I touched the tiny top hat pinned in my hair, hoping I wouldn't mess it up while checking to see if it was messed up.

"It's perfect." Shin sighed. "So how is Kayin?"

I frowned. "Fine, he's around here somewhere. You could ask him yourself."

"He seems a bit nervous around me lately," Shin said.

"Oh, well, he's trying to figure things out."

Shin nodded.

"But I know he wouldn't want to lose your friendship. We're going to the pizza place afterward, you should come with us."

"I think everyone is going. Michael reserved half the restaurant and already ordered pizzas. But yes, I'd love to go with you guys."

My stomach growled at the thought of pizza, the heavy protein shake I'd drunk at five would get me through the show, but I would eat a disgusting amount of pizza later.

"So did your rescuer show up?" Shin asked.

"Yes, and he brought a very pretty woman with him."

"I'm sorry."

"It's fine. I mean, it's not like we could date or anything." Inside I was pouting, but on the outside—total fake maturity. Go me.

"No but what about having a torrid romance?"

"Really? Me in a torrid romance? Please." I rolled my eyes. The music changed. Looking out, I watched the hula hoop performer disappear as two silks fell from the ceiling.

The audience leaned forward in their seats when Sasha and Taliesin came into view. Many lifted fluttering hands over their hearts.

Moving in sync they climbed the silk, their bodies solid as they used only their arms. When they got over half way up, they stopped and began to twist in the silk. I had seen them do this before so I looked at the audience. They were enraptured, and gasped, eyes wide, as Taliesin and Sasha slid down the silks head first, stopping a few inches above the floor. Jumping to their feet, the audience clapped and roared their approval.

"They make me feel clumsy," Shin said. "I've seen them practice, but this is amazing."

I rolled my eyes and stepped back. I needed to queue up. "You're ridiculous. Yes, they're graceful and stunning, but so are you, Mr. Park."

Shin jerked his head, which would have tossed his bangs about dramatically if they hadn't been gelled to his head. "You speak only the truth, Sapphire. Thank you for setting me straight. I *am* magnificent."

I was surprised there was enough air in the theater to breathe with the size of the egos around here. Reaching down, I shoved his shoulder. He didn't move. Huffing, I left to queue up before Michael got mad at me.

* * *

Dodging the other performers backstage while wearing stilts is a special skill set. I made it back to my changing area and grabbed hold of a flimsy pole, saying a quick prayer before starting to lower myself to the ground.

"Wait, let me help." Gavin held out his hands.

I took them and let him help me to the ground. "Thanks, I didn't think you'd come."

"And miss your first statue performance, of course I came." Gavin lost his smile. "Did you really think ..."

"Sapphire, you were so beautiful," Anali interrupted, her arm linked in Kayin's. Her skin was pale still, but her amber brown eyes shone brightly. "And the two of you together, the skin color difference alone is erotic, but the way you moved, I was afraid your Uncle Gavin would have a heart attack."

Gavin blushed. "I knew it was just an act."

"Well, Little Sister, if we could fool your uncle, I'd say we did a good job," Kayin said.

And no one seemed to notice my mistake. I smiled and began undoing my stilts. "How are you feeling Anali?"

"Okay. We had a lovely nap, and made it here just in time."

"I was thinking of taking her back to the hotel so she can eat, then get to bed early," Gavin said, taking Anali's hand.

"Of course. I didn't expect you to come anyway, not with Anali so sick," I said. Really. What were they thinking coming here when she felt like this?

"Anali, are you feeling better?" Taliesin asked, handing out bottles of Recharge. "Michael asked me to pass out the drinks."

"Thanks," I said taking a deep drink, shivering as the cold sports drink chilled my hot body. It felt like air conditioning went off in my chest.

"Taliesin, you were stunning," Anali said. "Where is Sasha? I wanted to congratulate him, too. I swear several women near us were about to faint watching the two of you."

Taliesin rolled his eyes, but smiled. "I'm glad you liked, it but I doubt anyone was in danger of fainting."

"Why is someone fainting?" Sasha asked.

"Because the two of you are just stunning," Anali said and fluttered her eyelashes. I would have to move away soon, the teen boy egos were expanding quickly.

Sasha choked on his drink.

"Don't worry, you'll get used to it." Gavin said. "I can offer advice; it is a burden being this handsome." He tossed his hair and posed.

I groaned. Here we go.

"Gavin, my dear, how will you ever survive before we can perform again? Your poor ego will deflate without a constant supply of hot air."

"Anali, I'm wounded. Are you saying you won't spend this pregnancy telling me how wonderful I am?"

Anali giggled and then froze, her eyes lost focus, and her breath became shallow. What was happening? I reached towards her.

Gavin moved to support her to the floor. "Anali, breathe. It's a dizzy spell. It'll pass but you need to breathe."

Anali took a shuddering breath. "Okay, sorry. Everything just got fuzzy for a moment."

"No, worries I have you."

I hugged myself, how does someone go from vibrant to weak so fast? Was she really okay? I bit my lip, and watched Gavin.

"Gavin," Taliesin said, handing him one of the Recharge drinks.

"Thanks," Gavin said. "Anali, I have a drink for you, and then we are headed back to the hotel."

She took a sip and nodded. "Okay. I'm sorry."

"Nothing to be sorry about. The midwife said it could take a few weeks before your body settles down," Gavin reminded her.

Weeks? She was going to go through this for weeks? I was never getting pregnant.

Anali laid her head on Gavin's shoulder. "I hope it isn't this bad the whole time."

"It won't be," Gavin said, his voice firm as if he actually knew. "Feeling better?"

"Yes, but I feel silly," she said.

Gavin kissed her forehead. "No need, darling. Come on, let's go back to the hotel, order room service, and you can gush about how amazing I am."

Gavin stood and helped Anali up. I kept my eyes on Anali in case she felt faint again. Gavin wrapped an arm around her waist.

"Sorry for the drama," Anali said. "You were all wonderful and I'm so glad we got to see your first performance."

"Good night, Anali, take care of yourself," I said, reaching out to touch her. I drew back. I didn't want to upset the delicate balance Gavin had created.

We watched them walk away, all of us holding our breath until we couldn't see them.

"Poor Anali," Miu said.

I jumped. "Where did you come from?"

"I just finished getting ready." She was painted like a geisha, and wore a pale gray kimono with pink and white cherry blossoms on it. A paper fan dangled from one wrist.

"Can't you help her?" Sasha asked, his Russian accent thick.

His worry prickled against my shield.

"Not really," Miu said. "It's her and the baby coming together. Basically she has low blood sugar. The fear and worry because of the miscarriage isn't helping. As far as I can tell everything is fine with the baby, and the teas and ginger are helping her some. Her body will settle soon."

I hoped so. I didn't like seeing Anali so weak.

"Fifteen minutes," Nyota said as she walked by, her focus on some piece of equipment in her hands.

"I need to go get ready," Taliesin said.

"I'll go with you," Kayin said, and they walked off to change for their next routine.

"Sasha, were you able to Dream about the dampening field?" I asked.

"Da. I told Nyota this morning. There is no problem, Anali and the baby are safe," Sasha said before following the others to get changed.

"Good." At least we could continue to protect Anali and Gavin under the dampening field. I couldn't imagine what the Sons of Belial would do if they captured Anali while she was pregnant. I pulled on the baggy, blue overall shorts with bright yellow flowers, neon green knee high socks, and purple tennis shoes I wore for jump-rope. I didn't look at myself in the mirror. This outfit was not my favorite.

* * *

The show was over, and I was back in my statue costume, chugging a bottle of water before going out to meet the kids. I don't know why I always said kids. Just as many teens and adults came over to the tables where we would answer questions and sign programs as small children did. I guess I liked the kids better. It felt less weird signing programs for a child than an adult. Also, the children's emotions were easier to handle—simple admiration and excitement. I took several deep breaths and strengthened my empathic bubble, preparing myself for the onslaught of emotions.

"Ready?" I asked Kayin, who was also back in the skimpy statue outfit. Since we were background for the other acts, Michael wanted us in our statue costumes to help the audience remember us.

"I guess so."

"Are you headed up?" Miu asked, walking as quickly as the kimono would allow.

"Wait for us," Taliesin called out.

Sasha nodded. "Strength in numbers."

The smell of popcorn was stronger in the lobby, and stale yellow puffs crunched under our feet. We stood behind one of the tables Michael had set up. A few security guards were scattered about. Some of the other performers were already there signing programs, answering questions, and apparently giving out their phone numbers. I scowled at the acrobat who was leering at a giggling young woman. Michael must have seen it too, because he came up placing his hand on the acrobat's shoulder. Michael couldn't stop them from meeting later, but he didn't want the flirting to happen in front of other fans.

"Will you sign my program?" asked a little boy with a proper British accent. It was so cute I had to bite my cheek to keep from squealing.

"Of course." I picked up one the Sharpies off the table. "Did you enjoy the show?" I asked as I flipped to the page my picture was on.

"Oh, it was wonderful. I've begged and begged, but mummy and daddy said we can't come again." His lower lip stuck out in a pout.

"I'm glad you liked it that much. Maybe you can come the next time we are in London."

"I shall, thank you." He shifted, handing his program to Kayin, complaining about his parents once again. His mother stood behind him, shaking her head and trying not to laugh.

I signed several more programs and answered questions from kids. I was about to rescue Taliesin from a fan with a lot of cleavage and grasping hands when another program was set in front of me.

I looked up and blushed so hot I didn't think the make-up hid it.

"Hello, Sapphire," Ramsey said, his brogue sending a shiver down my spine.

"Hello, did you, um, did you enjoy the show?" Very smooth. Only I can go from circus superstar to babbling idiot in a second flat.

His gaze traveled over my body. "Oh, very much. I had no idea what you meant when you told me what you did. That was amazing."

"Thanks. Did you want me to sign this?" I pointed at the program.

"Oh, yes. I want proof that I know you." He grinned. His dark eyes sparkled.

I chuckled and opened to the right page. *Ramsey, thank you for rescuing me. I would have been lost without you. Sapphire*

He grinned. "Cheers! I have to go. I have a gig soon, and they will kill me if I'm late."

"I understand. Thanks for coming." I saw the lead singer waiting in the back of the crowd, texting someone. I sighed. She was very pretty.

"Oh—my cousin insisted that I tell you how much she enjoyed the show." Ramsey winked and walked away, his kilt swaying.

"Who was that?" Kayin whispered.

"I'll tell you later," I said as another program was set in front of me.

"That was the sexiest thing I have ever seen," said a breathy voice. I looked up and a handsome man was staring at Kayin, his hunger licking against my shields.

"Oh, thank you," Kayin said, his fingers twitching as he fumbled with the Sharpie.

Jealousy flowed around us and I looked over to see Shin glaring at the man, who didn't notice because he was staring at Kayin's abs. Where was Michael? I looked around, and the little kids were all gone. I guess the adult fans had waited. That was nice. Oh, there he was—keeping an eye on some of the other performers who would encourage the fans' attentions.

"I would love to learn some of those moves—do you offer private lessons?" the man said.

Wow, he was forward.

Kayin's brow furrowed. "I'm sorry we aren't offering classes right now. Did you want me to sign your program?"

"Sure."

Kayin signed it and smiled as he passed the program back. "I'm glad you enjoyed the show."

The man grinned and set a business card on the table. "Call me. I'd love to get to know you better." He licked his lips and walked away.

Kayin squeaked and looked at the card on the table. Shin's hand darted out and grabbed it. "You don't have pockets I'll hold that for you." His thin eyes narrowed, and he was staring at the man's back.

"Miss, I'm flattered, but no thank you," Taliesin said, removing her hand from his arm.

"See, I told you he'd like me better," said her friend.

"Excuse me. I'll be right back." Sinking into performance head space I sauntered over, letting my hips sway and wrapped my arms around Taliesin's waist. "Is everything alright?"

Taliesin sighed and wrapped an arm around me. "Yes, just meeting the fans. Are things okay with you? No one being rude?"

I laughed, it was cold. "Oh, honey, you are so sweet, but you are the one that has to worry about fans overstepping boundaries. It's one of the curses of being as lovely as you are." I glared at the girls who frowned at me and stomped off.

"Thank you," he said, not letting go.

I took a deep breath. Taliesin's anxiety scratched against me like sandpaper. "Do you need to go?"

He shook his head. "No, I just need a moment." Taliesin smiled as the next person asked for their program to be signed, but he didn't let me go.

* * *

The cold December air felt wonderful as we walked to the pizza place. I let the puffs of wind clean away the sticky residue of lust, envy, and longing that clung to my empathic bubble. I hadn't been a main performer before and hadn't been on the receiving end of so much admiration. I was grateful for the people who enjoyed our show, but I needed a shower, and to

ALICA MCKENNA-JOHNSON

get away from the groupies a few of the performers had encouraged to tag along.

My stomach growled as soon as the scent of pizza enveloped us. I found the first table with six chairs with a Cirque du Feu Magique sign on it and sat down. No room for lecherous groupies here, so sorry. The warm honey-colored table was already set with plates, water, bowls of olives, almonds, salads, and antipasto platters.

"So, I threw away eight cards with phone numbers on them," Shin said as he sat down.

Miu huffed. "I got eight, too."

Were they serious?

"Is it okay to throw them away?" Kayin asked pulling them out of his pocket. "I don't want to be rude."

"Do you want to call any of them?" I asked, taking some salad before handing it to Taliesin.

"No," Kayin said, handing me a bowl of green olives.

"Then, yes, throw them out," I said.

"Count them first," Shin said, taking a bunch of salami before handing the antipasto platter to Kayin.

Kayin frowned but counted. "Ten."

"I threw away twelve." Taliesin passed the salad to Sasha who frowned at it and passed it to Miu.

"Nine for me," Sasha said taking the olives.

I shook my head—that was crazy. I couldn't believe how bold people were. We could be crazy killers for all they knew. Who invites a stranger out with them? And let's be honest, they weren't asking to go for a cup of coffee. High-pitched giggles echoed around me. I guess there was your answer. Of course, I should be fair. She could be the psycho killer.

"So, Sapphire, how many cards did you get?" Shin asked.

I shook my head. "I don't know, not many—maybe one or two. The security guard grabbed them and threw them away."

"That can't be right?" Miu said.

"I'll just have to accept that I'm not as pretty as the rest of you."

Taliesin snorted. "Yeah right—it didn't have anything to do with the security guard standing behind you glaring at everyone."

I would have argued, but I had a mouthful of mozzarella cheese, tomato, and fresh basil. My eyes might have fluttered a bit, so yummy.

"Oh, I saw him," Shin said. "He was positioned like the others, so I didn't think he was there just for Sapphire, though."

"I would bet Gavin paid him," Taliesin said, popping an olive into his mouth.

The conversation stopped as servers came out offering up slices of different kinds of pizza. I was relieved. The topic had gotten ridiculous, but it was nice of them to come up with an excuse to explain why I didn't get as many phone numbers.

"So who was the guy in the skirt?" Kayin asked taking a bite of his third piece of pizza.

I blushed remembering Ramsey's explanation of the different between a skirt and a kilt, no underwear. "It's not a skirt, it's a kilt, and his name is Ramsey."

"He saved Sapphire," Shin offered.

"What?" Miu demanded.

"He didn't save me. He helped me find the hotel during Shin's test." I snagged another piece of pesto pizza as the waiter walked by.

"That's cheating." Sasha scowled at me, and it might have looked scary if he didn't have pizza sauce on his face.

Shin threw a napkin at him. "You have something," and swirled his finger indicating his mouth. "And it's not cheating to find someone to help with directions, or better still, walk with you. It can keep you safe because witnesses aren't good."

Sasha's gray blue eyes narrowed as he cleaned himself off.

"And he just happened to come to the show tonight?" Miu asked.

I shrugged. "I comped him two tickets to thank him for helping me. No big."

"Who was the girl he was with?" Shin asked.

"Um, he said it was his cousin."

"You asked him?" Taliesin frowned.

"No, he told me when I signed his program."

Miu leaned forward. "Are you going to see him again?"

"I doubt it." I mean we didn't have any plans to see each other again.

"You have his number, you could always call him." Shin grinned.

"This is ridiculous, let's talk about something else." I took a bite of my pizza. Really, I don't know why Ramsey was so interesting. And it's not like I'd ever see him again.

Chapter Eight

"Beauty is not in the face; beauty is a light in the heart." ~
Kahlil Gibran

Tucking my chin into my scarf, I questioned my brilliant idea to go for a walk. The park seemed sinister this morning. Dormant gray branches like fingers blended into a cold gray sky. Cold damp gusts of wind cut through my jeans and wound its way into the holes of my knitted scarf and sweater. I sighed and turned back to look at the hotel, but even its multiple floors of mirrored windows couldn't brighten the morning. I should go back. Wind whirled around me, and I wound up with a mouthful of black and red curls. There was nothing to do, well nothing I wanted to do, back at the hotel. I'd done the yoga/conditioning class this morning and eaten breakfast. There were no chocolate almond pastries this morning, which might be why I felt moody, and then everyone else took off to do something.

Taliesin and Miu had gone off, whispering to each other. Kayin, Shin, and Sasha left to go play on the trampoline. I had thought about joining them, but watching the trampoline artist made my stomach queasy. I assumed Gavin and Anali were taking it easy in their room. I sent a text letting them know I was going for a walk, but didn't get a reply. So my choices were limited to walking in the cold gray London or going back to the hotel to do homework.

You know, gray is an underrated color, it doesn't have to be gloomy. Gray kittens aren't gloomy; they are sweet and fuzzy. I kept walking. I smiled when I passed the ballet school with the Angelina Ballerina poster outside. Last night I had called Shante, time differences and post-performance adrenaline working in my favor. Shante loved her first grade teacher, but was excited about winter break. Taliesin's mom, Cordelia, had told her that since this was their first Christmas together as mother and daughter, it was going to be extra special. Shante sounded happy as she talked about her new pink room, all her new pink clothes, and pink shoes, and how much she loved living with Cordelia.

I needed to check with Gavin to make sure he mailed my package to Shante. He said he would, but still this Christmas was important and I didn't want anything to ruin it for her. Soon I found myself back on High Street, the Christmas lights trying to cut through the gray gloom. I was able to enjoy the holiday decorations as I walked along the street. I stopped at a display of Christmas ornaments. A lush evergreen was decorated with an assortment of crystal snowflakes, origami cranes, Santas from many different traditions, painted balls which reflected the lights, glowing silver bells, animals in bright wild colors, and so much more. Within minutes I had found a perfect ornament for everyone. I moved to go into the store and then stopped. What was the point? We didn't even have a tree.

Turning, I bumped into a solid wool-covered chest. "Oh, I am so sorry."

"Shin would be very disappointed," Ramsey teased.

My face heated up. "Well, it could be our secret."

"I suppose so." Ramsey's dark brown curls fluttered around his face in the wind. A blue scarf wound around his neck. Black jeans hugged his legs, yum. "So what are you doing? Not another test I hope."

"No, I just went for a walk. What about you? Why are you here?"

"Me and my mates are staying in a flat nearby." He adjusted the yoga bag slung across his chest.

"Are you going to yoga class?"

He smiled. "It looks like I found something better to do." He held out his arm. "Come on."

I placed my hand on his forearm, the dark gray pea coat he wore soft. "How did your gig go last night?"

"I barely managed it," he groaned.

"Why what happened?"

"I couldn't stop thinking about how sexy you looked last night. If I didn't know our songs by heart, I wouldn't have been able to play." His dark eyes sparkled. "I'm surprised your partner lets you out of his sight. What if someone snatched you up?"

I was in danger of veins exploding in my cheeks if he kept this up. "Kayin? We're like siblings. He calls me Little Sister."

"Brilliant, fancy a cuppa?"

"Um, sure?"

Ramsey laughed. "Would you like a cup of tea?"

Oh, yes, of course. I should have known that one. "A cup of tea sounds lovely."

We walked to a tea shop that I vaguely recognized—maybe it was the holiday decorations that made everything seem familiar. I looked over the pastries and clutched Ramsey's arm.

"Is everything okay?"

No, I shouted in my head—they have chocolate almond goodness… make that *one* chocolate almond goodness. There were four people in line ahead of us and what if one of them ordered it? "I'm fine; it's so nice and warm in here." I let go of his arm and took off my scarf.

"Okay." He didn't believe me.

I tried not to stare at the pastry, or glare at the others in front of us, but every time a server would reach into the case my stomach would clench. One would think I hadn't eaten an hour ago. I focused on my breathing as the man in front of us ordered. "A cup of coffee and a *pain au chocolat*, please."

"We only have chocolate and almond left sir," said the server.

He looked at MY pastry.

"No I'm not a fan of almond. I'll have a blueberry scone and clotted cream, please."

Yes, it was all mine! I smiled but forced myself to stand still.

"How can I help you?" asked the server.

"Go ahead, Sapphire." Ramsey offered.

"Thank you, may I have a tea and the chocolate almond pastry please." The server placed the food of the gods on a plate for me. *Do not snatch that plate up, try and look like a normal person.* I waited until Ramsey had ordered and followed him to a table by the window.

I cut a piece of pastry and put it in my mouth, humming in happiness.

Ramsey chuckled. "I take it you enjoy those?"

And I'm blushing again. "I love them, I'd never had them before coming to London."

"So where else have you traveled? You told me you lived in San Francisco."

"Yes. Well, we traveled all over the United States, went to South America, Central America, and Mexico before coming here."

Ramsey rested his chin on his hand. "That sounds amazing, I would love to travel and see the world. Do you have a favorite place?"

"Well, Machu Picchu, and Chichen Itza are both amazing, but London has been a lot of fun."

Ramsey grinned. "What have you enjoyed the most so far?"

I bit my lip and looked at Ramsey through my lashes. "Well, the British Museum, and meeting you."

His cheeks pinked and his eyes sparkled. "Is it because I'm so handsome, my sexy accent, or because of this..." Ramsey reached out and touched my hand, and let his power flow. Cool, deep, calm power washed over me. Flashes of seals swimming in the ocean, racing, the water flowing over their thick brown fur as they hunted large silver fish, invaded my mind.

Gasping, I pulled my hand away and resisted the urge to wipe my eyes. I knew I hadn't been in the water, but the images were so clear.

"I didn't realize you were that sensitive," he said.

"Sorry." I picked up my cup of tea and took a sip.

His brow furrowed. "What do you have to be sorry for? So, we've met four times now. Would you like to share what we are?"

"Oh, um, I didn't realize there was etiquette to meeting each other." And now I sound like a dork.

Ramsey sat back. "There isn't I suppose, at least nothing formal."

"So do we count to three and each shout out our magical side or something?" I asked trying to be teasing.

"I'm a selkie," he offered.

"Myths say you can come on land only once every seven years," I said.

"Yes, well, it made booty calls easier in the olden days. Men would come on shore, seduce a woman and then not have to worry about her looking for him again." Ramsey grinned.

"I suppose cell phones have ruined that."

"That and no one believes in selkies anymore."

The waitress came and refilled our tea.

I waited until she left, took a deep breath and said, "Phoenix."

He nodded. "That would explain the heat in your magic. I've met other Children of Fire, as you call yourselves. But you feel stronger than the others I've met."

Interesting, he didn't know I was the Jewel of the Phoenix King and Queen. Should I tell him? No, I don't want to be treated differently, not by him. And it could also be a safety issue right? I mean, Gavin doesn't like me letting people know who I am without his approval, so best to keep quiet. "So is that why you helped me the other day? Because I'm magical?"

Ramsey flashed that wicked grin, the one that promised trouble and fun all rolled into one. "Well, it's how I noticed you at the show. I felt it when you reached out to find out about us. I assume that is how I got your attention, that you felt me."

That and the glimpse of tattoo on your thigh. "I felt the singer and violinist feeding off the crowd."

He nodded "Yes, they're part siren. They don't hurt anyone."

"I figured that out. It's a wonderful way to incorporate your magic into the performance," I said.

"Their music calls to people."

"And the other three of you?" I asked.

The enticing grin came back. "Well, the flutist is from Pan's line and the drummer is my older brother."

"So let's see," I thought about what I knew of magical beings. "The flutist would also be able to entice and call to people."

"Well, to their more animal base emotions." Ramsey waggled his eyebrows. "And my brother and me?"

I tried to keep my lips from twitching. "Eye candy."

Ramsey laughed, and the sound sent shivers down my spine. He leaned towards me. "I refer to us as the raw sexual magnetism."

Okay, this blushing thing is getting boring. I jumped when my phone chirped, letting me know I had a text.

"Everything okay?" he chuckled.

"Stupid phone," I muttered checking the message. "It's my uncle reminding me that we have some event to go to tonight, and I need to be ready by six."

"What time is it now?"

"Eleven thirty. Do you have to go somewhere?"

He smiled. "Nope not for hours. You?"

I shook my head.

"Well, would you consider spending the afternoon with me?"

"Because we are both magical beings?" I teased.

"No, because we are both *hot* magical beings." Ramsey stood and held out his hand.

He thinks I'm hot? "So what should we do?"

"I know just the thing."

Ramsey didn't let go of my hand as we walked down the street. We stopped, and there in the window was the dress I had looked at the other day.

I glanced at him and he arched an eyebrow. I felt his amusement and a touch of challenge against my empathic shield.

I walked into the boutique and sneezed. The scent of fake roses filled the air. I was going to smell like this all day, yuck.

"Can I help you?" said a woman with short, spiked brown hair. She looked me over and raised an eyebrow. I guess my jeans and sweater weren't impressing her.

"Yes, I'd like to see the outfit in the window please."

She sniffed, handed me the dress and shoes, and led me to the changing room.

Ramsey lifted his nose into the air and flipped his hair back with his hands acting all snooty. Giggling, I went into the changing room.

I slid on the black dress—the neckline draped down lower than I expected. The dress fell along my curves and flowed out around my thighs. I sat on the small bench and slipped my feet into the copper shoes and laced the straps up my calves.

Standing I looked at myself in the mirror, the heels made my legs look longer and pushed my butt out. Was this sexy? Did I look sexy in this, and how can one tell? I thought of my mom's journal entry on being sexy:

I hope I am with you when you grow into a young woman, but your father has been having dreams, awful dreams and I fear I won't be there. So how can I help you as you try to express yourself, your beauty, and being sexy? Of course I want you to know that true sexiness comes from within, from being kind, courageous, intelligent, strong, and having self-respect. But I know when my mom said this to me as a young woman, I rolled my eyes. So here is a bit of more practical advice: wear what feels comfortable. If something is too tight or too revealing, it won't be sexy because your discomfort will come through. No matter what the media says or celebrities wear, remember exposed and sexy are two different things. If you're confused, go look at pictures of Marilyn Monroe, Audrey Hepburn, Greta Garbo, and Eartha Kitt.

I wished my mom was here now. I wiped my eyes and looked back in the mirror. The soft material hugged my body but didn't show my panty lines. The dropping neckline hinted, but didn't show anything. I liked it. I felt sexy and confident.

"Come out here and let me see," Ramsey said.

Would Ramsey agree?

Ramsey twirled his finger. I rolled my eyes and twirled. The light fabric swirled around my thighs. "Hen, you look really braw."

I flushed, I wasn't sure what he meant, but his desire felt warm and intense.

I looked into the mirror, smoothing the fabric over my waist and hips. "If you're sure, I'll get it."

"Very sure, hen. I'm very sure."

I ducked back into the dressing room, hiding my grin. I did I little happy dance before changing. I had to take several deep breaths to calm myself and not smile like a crazy person.

I walked over to the counter and handed her the dress and shoes. "I'll take these please."

The sales girl sniffed and rang them up and raised a challenging eyebrow at the amount. I smiled and handed her my credit card. Gavin had helped us get prepaid credit cards that would handle foreign currency so we wouldn't have to always worry about exchanging money and fluctuating rates. The sales girl smiled and wrapped everything up for me. "Have a good day."

"Thanks," I took the bag.

Once on the street, I turned to Ramsey. "Where to now?"

Ramsey tugged on the strap to his yoga bag. "Do you want to walk around? At some point I need to get my kilt, jacket, and waistcoat from the cleaners, but other than that I have no plans."

"Going somewhere fancy tonight?"

"Aye, there is this gig tonight, a big benefit party for a marine charity. We have to dress smart."

"Well, which way is the cleaners?" I asked.

Ramsey pointed to the left.

"Let's walk that way, and we can pick your stuff up. I wouldn't want you to be running late," I said, walking down the street.

"Cheers, anything to not have Solange yell at me. So what are you doing tonight?" Ramsey asked.

"My uncle got invited to some fancy party. It doesn't sound like a lot of fun to me."

"Maybe you'll be at the party I'm playing at."

I laughed. "I might be magical, but I can't create miracles."

Ramsey winked at me. "So seeing me again would be miraculous?"

"You wish." I looked at the window display of holiday themes antiques.

"I know if you showed up in that dress you just bought, I would think a miracle had happened." Ramsey leaned close to me and his curls fell over my shoulder.

Flushing, I walked to the next window full of cooking stuff—boring. I walked on. "I'm wearing a different dress tonight. My aunt helped me pick it out." The next window displayed antiques with fake pine boughs and ornaments scattered about. The faint pulse of Akasha vibrated through the window. "I need to go in here."

"What? Why?" Ramsey asked.

I turned leaned in close to him and whispered, "There's something magical in there."

"Okay," Ramsey opened the door, and a bell jingled. Warm air scented with old books, lemon oil, and tea enveloped us.

I took a breath and thinned my empathic shields, following the vibration to the glass display case. In the center, surrounded by antique jewelry, lay a solid necklace of braided silver. The ends were beautifully carved dragon heads about two inches apart. The eyes of the dragons were deep, clear blue. Definitely from Akasha. I felt it, but not from Shamash. Reaching up, I touched my fire pendant, a gift from Shamash to one of his children four thousand years ago. The thrum of Phoenix energy was clear in the pendant, but didn't come from the odd necklace. It also didn't feel like his brother Quetzalcoatl's energy, but I would have to check it against the gold cuff back at the hotel.

"Bloody hell," snapped Ramsey.

"What?" I asked. At the same time the salesman said, "Sir, please watch your language."

"The sporran," Ramsey said pointing to a round, gray fur bag. It reminded me of the cloth one he wore with his kilt. "It's made from a selkie's pelt."

"Oh, God, Ramsey." I stared at it. "Who would do such a thing?"

The bell chimed as a customer left, and the salesman came over to us. "Can I help you?" he said, disapproval evident in every perfectly pronounced syllable.

"I would like to purchase the necklace, please," I said. "And the bag."

He sniffed and made no move to unlock the case. "The torc and sporran are both quite old and valuable."

Ramsey's horror and pain wrapped around me, tightening as his breath became more shallow. "Would you like me to pay for them before you take them out of the case?" I snapped.

He blinked. "I'll bring them over to the counter so you can examine them."

"Thank you." I grabbed Ramsey's hand and went to the counter.

The salesman laid out a piece of black velvet and set the objects on top. I didn't look at the sporran, but Ramsey growled as he looked at it. I handed the man the credit card Gavin had given me for emergencies, my stomach rolling with nausea as the bill came to over a thousand pounds. I hoped he wouldn't be too upset. This felt like an emergency to me. The salesman ran my card, looking at me suspiciously until it cleared. Then he wrapped the torc and sporran in white tissue paper and into boxes to protect them.

I jumped as my phone rang. The sales man sniffed his disapproval. "Hey, Sasha."

"Where are you?" he snapped. "I looked for you all morning. I assumed I would bump into you by lunch, but no! This hasn't happened before, I didn't realize that my Dream was happening today. I mean I saw everyone else, so I assumed you were in your room. Where else would you be?"

"Sasha, calm down and tell me what's wrong?" My skin itched and my stomach felt like it was rolling.

"Are you shopping?" he snapped.

Oh, good a new crazy. The old crazy was getting boring. "I went for a walk, ran into a friend, and, yes, we are shopping. I did text people that I was leaving. I don't see ..."

"Shut-up, are you buying a solid necklace?"

"Yes."

My eyes widened as very foul and creative Russian curses echoed through the phone at the same time my stomach felt queasy and my skin began to itch. "You need to leave—now! Something is coming. I don't know what. In my Dream a black shadowy spirit came into the store, a walk-in I think. It was looking for the necklace, but then it saw you and screamed so loud that the sound made my bones ache. Other black spirits heard the cry and came, but from far away. You need to get out of there now."

The bell above the shop door opened, my stomach clenched. I felt sick. I squeezed Ramsey's hand.

"Too late." I turned to Ramsey. "Please, look at the counter, don't look around the room, don't make eye contact with anyone."

His brow furrowed and his lips tightened, but he nodded and looked at the display of ancient coins.

"Listen he can't see you, do you understand. You can't let him see you. He isn't that strong, and he's there for the necklace, get out of there as soon as you can. If he sees you he will call for backup, and that was bad in my dream, very bad."

Not good, not good. I blinked willing myself to feel the spelled contacts, the one that hid the flames that danced in my eyes, marking me as a Child of Fire. A walk-in—one of the Sons of Belial's henchmen—are spirits their leader Cartazonon sends into people who owe him a favor. They weren't strong, and as long as they couldn't see the fire in my eyes they couldn't track me beyond their human host's ability.

"Sasha," I began rubbing the hand print scar on my wrist where Cartazonon had grabbed me in a dream. Miu had stopped the pain but couldn't help the scarring.

"No listen, keep your head down, he is focused on his search. Right now he assumes the object is powerful, which is why he's not looking for you. Get out of there as soon as possible."

The bell rang again. A chatty group came in. Yes, they would confuse the walk-in.

"Okay, yes I'll be right there," I said signing the receipt. "I am so sorry I forgot."

"Call me when you get away." Sasha hung up.

"Have a good day," said the sales clerk.

Turning to Ramsey, I stood on tip toe and hugged him and looked over his shoulder. I found the walk-in, a plump middle-aged man with thinning mouse-brown hair, on the other side of the store his head jerking as he looked each item over. "Do you know what a walk-in is?"

"Do you mean a hunter, a ghost that steals people for the Sons of Belial?"

Okay, good description.

"There is one in the store. We need to leave, but not let him see us," I said.

"Oh, Gerald, come and look at this," called out a woman. The walk-in scurried to the back of the store where the woman went.

I tugged on Ramsey's hand. Once outside Ramsey took the lead, weaving us through the crowd. My skin felt dirty, but the persistent itching faded.

"Ramsey, I don't feel it as strongly. Let's stop so I can focus better." I wanted a shower. It took water, or Phoenix fire, to cleanse the gross feeling of having been close to something so warped and evil off of my skin and empathic bubble.

Ramsey ducked into an alley. I leaned against the side of a building, took a deep breath, and reached out with my empathy. "Found him, he's frantic and searching but doesn't know which way to go. The ambient magic in London is confusing him, plus the magical creatures scattered about."

"What creatures?" asked Ramsey.

"Little pixies, fairies, and brownies that live in the nooks and crannies of the buildings."

Ramsey smiled. "Do you mean broonies?" A lovely rolled r and drawn out oo sound sent a shiver down my spine. Down, hormones, down, now is not the time.

"I've always heard it pronounced brownies, but it *is* a Scottish word so you would know," I said trying for casual. Judging by his grin I failed. "Anyway there is also a lot of magical blood in the human population too, apparently there was a lot of free love at some point."

"Well," said Ramsey. "We *are* irresistible. Should we go ahead and go? Is there any way to insure it won't follow us?"

"Purrrhaps I can help."

I jumped and looked up. Okay it had happened, I went insane. It is official.

"Bloody hell," Ramsey said. "You scared us."

"You see it too?"

"Actually it is a she, and yes, you both can see me." The cat grinned. I blinked, nope it was still there, an orange striped cat. The different shades of orange in the cat's fur made my head swim.

"Have you never seen a witch's cat before?" Ramsey asked.

"No. It reminds me of the Cheshire cat." Okay mythical creatures being real is one thing, supposedly made up creatures in stories was a bit hard to take. Focus, Sapphire, focus. "You said you could help us?"

"Hummm, yes. I have nothing else to do today, so it would amuse me to lead your evil spirit away. The church grim two streets over is bored. I'll take him there."

"That is very kind of you," Ramsey said. "What do you want in return?"

The cat chuckled, a cold shiver ran through me. "A chance to help Phoenix royalty is enough." The cat stood, stretching every muscle in a slow arch until the tip of her tail gave a little shake. "Okay, time to play. Take care, Jewel of the Phoenix King and Queen."

The cat jumped to the sidewalk and faded inch by inch as she walked towards the walk-in.

"Jewel?" Ramsey asked.

Chapter Nine

I pulled out my phone. "It's nothing important. I have to call Sasha. Which way should we go?" I tried not to flinch as Ramsey's irritation scraped across my shields.

"Fine, there is a bench over here."

I twisted my mom's ring on my finger. Should I tell him the truth about being the Jewel? Maybe he wouldn't treat me differently. I mean he didn't know about the Jewel legend, so he might not care so much. My stomach gurgled a mix of fear and hunger.

Ramsey sat on the bench. "Hey, Murdock, are you still at the flat?"

I guess we weren't going to talk about it right now. I called Sasha and sat down with a sigh.

"Are you okay?"

Wincing, I held the phone away. "Yes, we're fine. A few magical beings decided to help us out and are leading the walk-in away."

"Good, I was worried. From now on I shall tell you my Dreams right away," Sasha said.

"This isn't your fault. Like you said earlier, this is the first time you've gotten a Dream that happened so quickly." I moved the boxes from the antique store into the bag from the dress shop and threw away the antique store bag, just in case. "Do you remember anything else?"

"Two, the walk-in has to leave at two. I'm not sure why—I think it's something to do with the host." Sasha sighed. "I'm sorry. I wish I knew more."

"Sasha, you did great. Thank you. If you hadn't warned me, who knows what would have happened. I guess I'll stay out until two, I don't want to lead them back to all of you."

"You should call Nyota, she can help," Sasha said.

I relaxed a little. "Great idea thanks."

"Take care, and let everyone know what's going on." Sasha hung up.

I called Nyota first.

"Hello, Sapphire is everything okay?" she said.

I never called her so I suppose there was cause for concern.

"Not really. I just ran into a walk-in, and I have an artifact from Akasha which he was sent to get. Oh, and there is a selkie with me," I said.

"Glad one of us isn't having a boring day," Nyota laughed.

I ran my fingers through my hair they got caught on tangles. "I don't want to lead it back to the hotel or the gym, and I'm not sure what to do."

"Can you feel it now?" Her voice sounded far away—she must have put me on speaker.

"No. A few magical creatures helped us out and led it away, but Sasha said he Dreamed about it last night, and the walk-in will be active until two."

Nyota muttered, and I heard a zipper. "Is there a restaurant nearby?"

"I suppose, hold on. Ramsey, is there a restaurant close by?"

"Yes, about two blocks is the Queen Victoria Pub."

"Okay, great," Nyota said. I guess she heard him. "Go to the pub, sit, order something, and I'll catch a taxi and meet you there. I have a portable field generator. I'll bring it with me, and we can hang out until it's safe to come back," she said. The snick of a door closing echoed through the phone.

"Okay, we'll see you there," I said.

I stared at the screen for a moment before sending out a general group text. Ran into walk-in, got away, Nyota coming with field generator, will be back after two, please stay at the hotel.

"Come on," I said and explained what Nyota wanted us to do.

"So she has created a machine that sends out a vibration which masks your magical signature so the walk-ins can't find you?"

"Yes," I said focusing on keeping my energy contained but open enough to feel the walk-in and not run into anyone. The constant chirping from incoming texts was a bit distracting.

"Do you think she could make one for me? For my band?" Ramsey asked.

I shrugged. "I guess. At this point I think Nyota can do anything she wants to. You can ask when we see her."

"Cheers. We're almost there. Do you feel anything?" he asked leading me down a busy street. Christmas light twinkled as we moved through the crowd.

"No, nothing strong, but I still feel kind of gross being that close to it." I shivered.

"There." Ramsey pointed to the corner where a deep red building with gold trim stood.

Stepping inside, Ramsey turned to me.

"I don't feel anything bad," I said.

Once seated, Ramsey ordered a pint of bitter while I chose a hot chocolate. Scanning through my texts I saw that everyone was safe at the hotel. I looked around the room. It was bright and warm with light wooden tables and wallpaper that looked like a sunset, with metallic gold patterns on top of a red-orange background. The open space and natural light from the windows made it seem warm instead of gaudy.

Ramsey sipped his drink and glared at the table. I guess he was still irked about the whole Jewel thing. Should I tell him? Did I trust him enough? What if he treated me differently after he found out?

I twisted my mom's ring, the midnight blue stone sparkled like stars in the sky. "So did you still want to know about the Jewel comment?"

Ramsey frowned. "If you want, if you think you can trust me."

I rolled my eyes. "I barely know you, so getting snippy about trust is a bit much don't you think?" Hot anger flared from Ramsey. I continued. "I am sure you have plenty of secret things that you aren't ready to share with me."

Ramsey sighed and tugged on the yoga bag strap across his chest. "Okay, sorry, you're right. I would like to know, if you feel comfortable telling me."

I smiled and took a stalling sip of hot chocolate. "So you know I'm a Child of Fire, but I am the strongest Child of Fire. I am like Shamash and Aya's first children."

Ramsey frowned. "Shamash and Aya?"

"The Phoenix King and Queen."

"My gran used to tell stories about them, but she died when I was little." His brow furrowed. "Isn't there a myth about a Child of Fire being able to open a doorway or something?"

"Yes, my family and I are strong enough to open the portals to Akasha," I said.

Ramsey leaned back in his chair, away from me. His energy contained. "So you're going to send us all to Akasha?"

Rude. Did I seem like the kind of person that forces people to do something they don't want to? "No, I open the portal for beings to go through if they want to. I don't 'send' anyone."

Holding up his hands, he leaned closer to the table. "Okay, sorry. That was harsh. Bloody hell, I have never thought about going to Akasha. I didn't think it was anything more than a faerie tale."

"Like selkies?" I asked, grinning.

He laughed and warmth flowed through me. I saw Nyota's dreadlocks, damn it. I waved to her, she sat down ordered a pint.

"Nyota this is Ramsey. Ramsey, Nyota." See, I have manners.

"So it's not here," she said setting her bag on her lap and fiddling with something inside.

"No. I haven't felt anything since we called you."

She nodded. Something clicked then there was a soft hum. Smiling, she set it on the floor. "There, the pub is safe. So lunch?" She picked up the menu. Her sleeve fell back and a pink burn marred her mocha skin.

"Nyota, what happened?" I asked.

"Oh that," she said, glancing at the burn before going back to the menu. "I bumped into one of the stage lights last night."

"Did you go and see Miu?" Nyota didn't have a lot of Phoenix Magic in her but there was enough for Miu's healing powers to work with. Even if she couldn't heal things directly, Miu always had some cream, tea, or foul herbal concoction that made you feel better.

"It didn't seem that important. I'm fine," Nyota said.

"You need to see her, she can heal it."

We ordered and then handed our menus to the waitress. Nyota turned to me. "Have you told Gavin and Anali yet?"

I flinched. "I texted them along with everyone else."

"That's mental," said Ramsey. "You can't text something like this. He's your guardian right, you have to call him."

Sighing, I pulled out my phone and called Gavin while Ramsey asked Nyota about her dampening field machine.

After the fourth ring I was hoping it would go to voicemail. "Hey Sapphire, I almost missed your call. My phone is on vibrate. Anyway are you having fun?"

"Um, yes. Well, I've hit a tiny snag."

Ramsey snorted. Rude.

"Are you okay?"

"Yes, I'm fine. Nyota is here and her portable dampening field is working great, so no need to worry."

Nyota's head hit the table, her dreadlocks fanning around her and her shoulders shaking with laughter. Ramsey shook his head. I glared at him and he looked away taking a sip of his bitter.

"Sapphire," Gavin said his voice sharp. "I would like you to start from the beginning."

"There's not much to tell. I was shopping with a friend."

Ramsey mouthed "friend" miming sticking a knife into his heart. Nyota, the traitor, laughed.

"I felt something from Akasha, and bought it. There will be a big charge on my credit card, sorry," I said.

"I don't care about the card, finish your story," Gavin said.

I twisted a curl around my finger. "Well, a walk-in came into the shop. I assume for the necklace I bought. Anyway, we got away, not a single hair out of place, because Sasha warned me in the nick of time. I called Nyota because I didn't want to lead it back to you guys, and I knew she had a portable dampening field machine. So now we're going to wait at this pub and have some lunch."

"What?" he asked.

"Oh, I ordered a veggie burger and chips."

Gavin groaned. "No, Sapphire, not what did you order. What are you doing? And what pub? And are you wearing your contacts?"

"The Queen Victoria Pub and the plan is to wait until two, Sasha said it would be gone by then, and yes, I have my contacts in," I said.

"Did you tell anyone else?"

"I texted everyone."

"Ah, yes. I see a bunch of texts. I'll call and make sure everyone is okay. I want updates every ten minutes."

"Uncle Gavin, I'm fine, you don't have to ..."

"Every ten minutes," Gavin said.

I sighed and fought the urge to pout. "Okay."

"Take care and I'll see you soon."

"Bye." I tucked the phone into my pocket. Ramsey and Nyota were chatting about her field using words I didn't understand and drinking beer. I sipped my hot chocolate getting whipped cream on my nose. What was I, five? The urge to pout came back.

Instead, I used my empathy to scan the restaurant. Layers of emotions crashed over me. I filtered out the people. The transparent images of the past came into sharper focus, especially the few images of people who had died in the pub. I took a deep breath and did my best to ignore them and their stories. There was a group of brownies or 'broonies' living in the basement of the building, but other than that everyone else was human.

The waitress brought our meals. I blinked and strengthened my bubble to protect myself from the swirling emotions filling the pub.

"Sorry, Sapphire," Nyota said, as she spread cilantro chutney on her roasted eggplant and paneer wrapped in naan. "I got excited about being able to talk with someone who understood what I was saying."

"It's okay," I said with fake maturity. "I had to talk to Gavin any way."

"She's going to build us a field generator," Ramsey said cutting a piece off his fried fish and dipping it into a fancy looking tartar sauce. "Of course, I'll have to figure out how to tune it to mask our magical energy."

"Like I said, you're welcome to email me with any questions." Nyota took a big bite of her sandwich.

I took a bite of my burger. The flavors were unique with a hint of Indian spices which warmed my tongue. The rich, hot food made the residual itchy sick feeling from the walk-in fade.

"I love their chips," Ramsey said, picking up what I would call a French fry. It was crispy and flecked with spices.

I jumped when Gavin burst through the door. Okay, in reality he walked, but his energy burst through the pub. He was full of anger, worry, and fear. I could feel it when he found us—on the outside he was calm and polite but his green eyes were hard, scanning the room as he walked toward us.

"Are you okay? Have you felt anything?" He knelt in front of me and reached out to touch my face. I squeaked, his fingers cold on my cheek.

"I'm fine, Uncle Gavin, and no I haven't felt it since we came into the pub."

Squirming, I did my best to meet his gaze. "Why didn't you call me right away?"

"I knew I needed to get to a safe place, and Nyota was the one with the field generator. Are the others safe? Is it okay that you left Anali?"

"Yes, they're fine. Why didn't you call me?"

Guilt fluttered in my stomach. "I'm sorry I didn't want to call until we were safe. I didn't want to upset you and Anali."

The muscle in his jaw jumped and his anger prickled against my skin.

"Sir," said the waitress, "can I get you anything?"

Gavin stood, his body tight. "Yes, I'd like a mocha and a veggie burger please."

"Right away."

"The generator is working," Nyota said. "And I checked the one at the hotel and gym yesterday."

"Good, thanks." He sat and rubbed his face. He seemed to do that a lot around me.

Ramsey cleared his throat. I frowned. He rolled his eyes, and looked at Gavin then back to me. Oh!

"Uncle Gavin, this is my friend Ramsey McDaniel. Ramsey, this is my uncle Gavin Marsh."

"It's very nice to meet you, Mr. Marsh," Ramsey said holding out his hand.

Gavin shook his hand. "So you are the friend."

What? Gavin normally asked to be called by his first name and smiled when he met someone.

"I guess so," Ramsey said molding to the chair as he sipped his drink.

Their energy sizzled in the air. I looked at Nyota, her eyes crinkled as she ate. I didn't understand what was happening.

"He plays the cello in the band we saw the first night here, and I ran into him when I was training with Shin. He helped me get back to the hotel."

Gavin sniffed, leaned back in his chair, his eyes focused on Ramsey. Of course, the whipped cream covered drink ruined his posturing.

"Do you want to see what I got?"

"The necklace?" Gavin said, focusing on me, and his body softened a little.

I nodded and dug through the bag, shaking the boxes. I wouldn't want to pull out the wrong one.

His fingers ran over the braided silver metal. "It looks Viking, but the features of the dragon are more delicate and the blue jewels aren't something they would have had. I'm glad you found it. Was there anything else there?"

"Well," I glanced at Ramsey. He nodded. "Ramsey noticed a sporran that was made from selkie skin."

"Are you?" Gavin asked.

Ramsey nodded.

"I'm sorry."

"Who would do such a horrible thing?" Nyota asked.

"Someone could have found the skin and not known, thinking it just a seal skin. I'd like to imagine it was an accident, but our skin is our connection to our magic and the sea. If it's destroyed our magic fades away and we die," Ramsey said.

I clasped his hand under the table, his sorrow cold against my shields.

Gavin arched an eyebrow and stared at the table. I refused to let go of Ramsey's hand. "Do you want it? I wouldn't know what to do with it."

"Do you mind?" Ramsey asked. "I'll take it home and we could bury it. Maybe my family heard of this happening, so we could bury it with the person, if possible."

"Of course I don't mind," I said.

"Thanks. I can pay you back," Ramsey said.

"No, don't worry about it. It's fine, right, Uncle Gavin?" I said.

He nodded. "Yes, of course. It's part of the whole helping magical creatures gig."

"Are you sure?" Ramsey began when his phone rang. "Sorry. I should get this. Hello, Solange." He stood and stepped outside.

"You met him how?"

I sighed. "I bumped into him while doing the test for Shin. And we recognized each other. It's not a big deal."

Gavin arched an eyebrow. "It sounds suspicious to me. How did he recognize you from the pub? You didn't dance, it was dark and there was a crowd around the stage."

"Oh, well." I ate a chip and tried to think of how to say this without getting into trouble. "He's a selkie, so is his brother who plays the drums, and the flutist is one of Pan's descendants. Both the singer and violinist are sirens."

"This doesn't explain how he was able to pinpoint you," Gavin said.

"Oh, well, you know, I felt them and opened up my empathy to figure out what they were doing. The sirens draw energy from the crowd during shows."

"You mean they were feeding off the crowd," Gavin said. "Why didn't you say anything?"

"You and Anali were having fun, and they weren't feeding off of the people, more like soaking in the energy they emitted into the air. And I assumed we'd never see them again." Taking a bite, I stopped the frantic attempt to find an excuse Gavin would like. Judging by the cold sharp irritation against my shield I wasn't helping the situation.

Gavin buried his hands in the hair. "Sapphire, we need to talk." The waitress set his food down. Gavin inhaled, his chest expanding. "Oh this smells good. I've been eating bland foods to avoid upsetting Anali." He moaned in happiness at his first bite.

Nyota smiled at me. Yes, yes, I had lucked out, for now. I was sure Gavin would come out of the happy food place and remember our conversation.

"I have to go," Ramsey said eating the last of the chips off his plate. "My cousin woke up and saw my text and is freaking out."

"Be careful." I handed him the box containing the sporran.

His jaw tightened as he took it. "Thank you, I'm sorry I have to go." Reaching into his pocket, he pulled out some money. "This should cover me."

"You don't have to," I began but his dark eyes held determination. Maybe this was one of those male ego things.

"It was nice meeting you," Nyota said. "I'll have Sapphire contact you when I get your field generator ready."

"Text me to let me know you got home safe," I said.

Ramsey winked at me. He was trying to be light hearted but his worry tugged at me. "Don't worry about me, hen, I'll be fine. You take care. Nice to meet you Mr. Marsh, Nyota."

Nyota and I said "bye." Gavin snorted.

"What does hen mean?" Nyota asked.

"Not sure. I think it's like dear or honey."

"I don't like him," said Gavin. "He looks shifty."

Nyota snorted. "That's the same thing my dad said about the boy who walked me home from school in the eighth grade."

Gavin sat up straighter. "And I'm sure your father was right."

"He was the class valedictorian, in the chess club, volunteered at the animal shelter, and the old folks' home his grandparents were in."

Gavin pointed a chip at Nyota. "See he was cultivating an image of being a good person. I bet he wound up being a serial killer."

"He's at MIT studying sustainable energy and engineering."

"Nope, just wait. I'm sure your father was right. We have a sixth sense about these things."

Nyota rolled her eyes, and I laughed. Overprotective much?

"So what else did you buy today, Sapphire?" Nyota asked.

"Oh, Miu said I would need a dress to go clubbing in."

"Well show me."

I smiled at Nyota's excitement. I hadn't hung out with her much. Since she was twenty-two, I didn't think a group of teenagers would interest her. I wiped my hands on my napkin and held up the black dress.

"Oh that's so cute. Do you have shoes?"

I pulled out one of the copper Roman styled high heels.

She wiggled her eyebrows, making the silver piercings shift.

"Very sexy," she said.

"Sexy," Gavin said around bite of chips. He glared at the dress. "How low is the neckline? It looks very low."

"Uncle Gavin, it's fine. I tried it on." I put the dress back in the bag and tucked it all under the table.

"I want you to show me or Anali before you go out in it."

"Fine," I said, rolling my eyes.

"I bet the guys at the club will go nuts when they see you in that." Nyota's pale gray eyes sparkled with mischief.

I glared at her. She smiled.

"Maybe I should come to your party, too," Gavin said. "I mean—I don't want you to feel like I'm ignoring any important events."

"Hey, where are the others? They texted me saying they were fine and wanting me to be safe and such," I asked trying to distract Gavin.

"Oh, I have them all hanging out in our suite. I wanted them to be all together." Gavin sent off a text.

"Good plan," said Nyota. "Although they should be undetectable at the hotel."

Gavin's phone lit up. "They're all fine."

"So it's ten minutes to two." Nyota said. "Do you feel any walk-ins?"

I closed my eyes and let my shields down. I could feel the magical creatures and a naughty gleefulness that I assumed was the witch's cat. But nothing evil, nothing dark, and nothing that reminded me of the Sons of Belial. "Nope, nothing."

Nyota nodded. "Okay. Let's wait until two before we leave just to be on the safe side."

Gavin stood. "I'll pay the check."

"You were not helpful," I said to Nyota.

She smiled. "I'm not Anali and going to smooth everything over. Anyway it's fun to wind him up."

"You need another hobby," I said.

Nyota laughed.

Chapter Ten

Cartazonon took a deep breath of the cold Montana air. Why he allowed Lee's horse obsession to influence him, he'd never know. Lee raced across the snowy meadow on the sturdy gray Mongolian pony. His cheeks were ruddy, and the flaps from his fur hat fluttered around his face. Cartazonon was transported back to his first human life. He had spent years in his animal form, hiding, barely surviving, and then finally he was able to transform. He'd watch the Mongol warriors for years and knew their ways. Lee was a young boy, well man, back then at fourteen, and he'd been thrown from his horse and wounded. Cartazonon had rescued him, saving his life. At least Lee and his family had thought so, and they had taken him in.

Cartazonon rose to power, becoming a feared warlord with Lee by his side. More than a thousand years had passed, and Lee was the only one he truly trusted.

Which is why he was freezing his ass off in Montana in the middle of winter. He sensed a cold presence connected to him: the walk-in he'd sent to London. He sat still on his mount while the images from the walk-in played in his mind.

Damn it, he wanted that torc. Was there a chance that someone bought it? He should buy the stupid antique store. There were several antique stores that would post photos of their new merchandise but would only sell things in person. His long pale fingers engulfed the crystal around his neck. The Akashic crystal thrummed with the magic and life force he'd taken from magical beings. He followed the connection to his people and holdings in England.

At first everything seemed as it should. The web he created connected all his people and properties. He reached out to his general there, a bright glimmer. He reached deeper, under the surface—a different energy was replacing his. This wasn't an attack, but a bid for freedom.

Cartazonon clutched the crystal so hard the tip cut into his palm. After centuries of feeding energy, money, and knowledge into his general this was how she repaid him.

"Khan, is everything okay?" Lee asked, his cheeks red from the cold wind.

"We need to go to London," Cartazonon said, letting go of the crystal and healing his hand.

Lee frowned and patted the neck of his horse. "Now?"

"No, I think patience is the key. We'll wait a bit. But not too long. Someone is trying to betray me." Cartazonon looked over at the porch swing.

Sapphire held her breath, hoping he wouldn't sense her this time.

"Our mysterious visitor is here again," Cartazonon said.

Lee's thin eyes narrowed. He pulled a wicked curved blade. "I don't like it. Who dares to watch us, and how do we rid ourselves of their presence?"

Sapphire stepped away from them, grateful she didn't leave footprints in the snow. She wasn't sure what would happen if he stabbed her, but she definitely didn't want to find out.

"So about the general in London?" Lee asked.

"I'll have our people investigate. Time means nothing but timing is everything, after all." Cartazonon smiled, not willing to give too much information in front of the invisible stranger.

Lee huffed. He'd been using that line for over five hundred years since he first heard it, and now Cartazonon had appropriated it.

Is the general in London a possible ally? Sapphire wondered. Or someone who wants to be the head of his own evil empire and not a minion?

"Go and ride some more. I know you want to," Cartazonon said. "I'm going inside. It's cold, and I have a meeting over Skype in a few minutes."

Lee glared in Sapphire's direction. "What about our visitor?"

Cartazonon smiled and held up his hand drawing power to his palm.

Sapphire flinched as white energy grew, it looked like a sparkle lay on his hand.

Cartazonon looked into her eyes and smiled. "Good-bye."

He threw the energy at her.

Sapphire screamed as it hit her shields.

* * *

Panting, I scooted away from the power Cartazonon had thrown at me, and fell off the couch. I was safe. I patted my body making sure his energy hadn't touched me. Okay. Taking a shaky breath, I stood up. Well, that was new and unpleasant.

Opening my laptop, I emailed Gavin everything I remembered about my dream. Unlike Sasha the images and words from my dreams tended to fade. I wasn't sure what would be important, so I did my best to remember even the smallest detail, as the images and words began to disappear.

I knew better than to fall asleep after being close to any of the Sons of Belial. Once we'd come back to the hotel I'd been steered to Gavin and Anali's room where I was hit by a wall of emotions, fear and anger being the strongest.

They talked—well ranted—and with the way the others were going on, you'd think I had been in mortal peril or run off and done something stupid again. Thankfully, the intensity of emotions had given Anali a headache, and we'd all been sent out of their rooms.

Miu had stayed to help Anali, and I'd rushed to our room shutting the door. I had fallen asleep instead of reading as I had planned. I texted Gavin letting him know about the dream/vision and the email.

I jumped as the alarm on my phone beeped at me. I had to be ready in an hour for the stupid party. Sighing, I headed for the bathroom and a hot shower. Hopefully, the hot water would wash away the crazy from the day.

Chapter Eleven

"Let me do your hair," Miu said, her eyes shining, hands clasped to her chest, and pigtails with dark pink flower clips making her look five instead of seventeen.

I jumped, not realizing she was even in the room. I tugged on the belt for my robe. "I hadn't planned on doing anything special with it."

Miu rolled her peridot-green eyes. "Yes, I'm aware of that. Come on, you're going to a fancy party, no a GALA. Let me fix your hair."

"Okay, sure." I hadn't spent a lot of time with Miu recently, maybe this would make up for it.

"Does your dress have to go over your head?" she asked gathering up supplies.

I frowned. "No, it zips and I step into it."

"Okay then we can do your hair and makeup before you get dressed. Sit, sit."

I obeyed sitting on the vanity chair where Miu was set-up.

The hair dryer hummed, and I relaxed allowing Miu to move my head as she wanted. The smooth steady strokes of the hair brush felt very soothing. I closed my eyes. Miu was great—her touch firm yet gentle as she brushed, pulled, and twisted my hair into whatever shape she was going for.

"There." Miu clasped her hands to her chest. "Can I do your make-up?"

I laughed. "Sure. You'll do much better than I would anyway." I could do makeup for the circus performances, but for a fancy evening out, I wasn't so sure.

Miu tilted my face as she applied different smelly, sticky substances. "I wish I was going. I'm so jealous."

"Didn't you volunteer to perform?" I asked.

"Look up," she said bringing the mascara brush to my eyes. "No, there are others who want the exposure the gala will bring them. Anyway, I have a fabulous evening planned."

"Oh? What are you doing?" I blinked, my eyes watering a bit from being held open.

"Well," she grinned. "It's very fancy you see. I'm going to Skype with some friends and family in Japan, take a bath, and then watch a movie."

I closed my eyes, Miu stroked the soft wand over each lid in an interesting pattern. "Sounds like a wild night."

She chuckled. "As much as I adore all of you, it will be nice to have some time alone."

"If you ever need some space, just ask, and I'll find somewhere else to hang out," I said.

"Open your mouth." Miu applied the lip gloss, frowned, wiped it off, and dug through her makeup bag. "Different color. And don't worry, enjoying an evening alone isn't the same as being desperate for time alone. I am able to set boundaries. Don't let the pink lace and ruffles fool you, I do know what I'm doing."

I opened my mouth to reply when another brush began to paint my lips. I tried not to fidget, but I wanted to talk, to make sure she knew that I knew that she was more than her vast array of Hello Kitty clothing and accessories.

"Much better," Miu said stepping back to look at her work. "A bit of clear gloss."

I waited patiently, well kind of patiently my feet and fingers were twitching. I let her finish my lips and didn't bite her, so I was calling it good.

Turning back to the table, she hunted through the makeup. Muttering, "no, too bright, too pink, too sparkly."

"Miu, I know you are more than ruffles and pigtails. You are a strong valuable member of our group and not just because you can heal us. You are intelligent, and the Shinto ritual you lead to open portals is very valuable. I am so glad to have another girl my age here." I cleared my throat, I hadn't expected to vomit all those words out.

Miu smiled and ran a brush over my cheeks. "I think young women instead of girls."

She stepped back, and I saw myself in the mirror. I blinked, that was me? Miu had swept my hair up into a bun, but left a few inches free so black and red curls fell around the top of my head. Scattered in the hair were small bobby pins with clear crystals on them. Shiny dusty rose made my lips several shades darker than my normal color. My cheeks had a faint brush of the same shade as my lips with a tiny bit of sparkle. My eyelids were a sparkling dusty blue on the outer edges and against my black lashes, which faded into dusty white on top. The effect was kind of smoky and sexy.

"Miu, thank you. I love it. I was just going to leave my hair down and put on some lip gloss," I said.

Miu twirled one of her pony tails around a finger. "Yes, I know. You do realize that you can care about how you look and still be independent and strong. I used lip stain for the color, so you just have to take the lip gloss with you to reapply."

"Thanks," I went and got the silver beaded clutch Anali had picked out to go with my dress and put the clear lip gloss in it. "Anything else I should take?"

"Yes, your phone, key card, breath mints or gum." Miu tapped her lip an evil grin forming. "A condom?"

I turned and took the suggested items out of my regular bag and tucked them into my evening bag, careful to keep my key card away from my cell phone so it wouldn't be erased. "I seriously doubt I'll need anything like that. I'm not going on a date. It's some stuffy, boring adult charity party. I'm probably going to have to listen to old people talk about how important the charity is and all of the work they are doing."

Miu cleaned up the makeup. "Maybe, but one never knows."

I took my dress and shoes and went into the bathroom ignoring her happy humming.

I stepped into the midnight blue velvet dress. Keeping my fingers tucked together I slid my hands through the sleeves. The top of the chest, shoulders and sleeves were fine white lace with thin silver threads which sparkled in a delicate snowflake pattern. The cuff flared slightly around my hand, a disaster waiting to happen, but I would try my best to make it through dinner. More snowflake lace covered the midnight blue velvet bodice with a sweetheart neckline and ended at my waist. The full midnight blue skirt fell to my feet, which I slipped into silver pumps.

"Oh, you look so beautiful, like a winter princess," Miu cooed.

I rolled my eyes.

"Sapphire, are you ready?" Gavin called out as he knocked on the door.

"Yes," I grabbed black wool dress coat Anali had insisted on getting for me. "Thanks Miu, enjoy your quiet evening."

"I will. Tell me all about it when you get back," Miu said.

I smiled. "I'll takes notes and as many pictures as I can."

I opened the door. Gavin stood there in a black tuxedo. His flame red hair was brushed back into a ponytail with a silver Celtic knot clasp holding the wild locks into place. "Wow, you look great, Uncle Gavin."

"Yes, I do cut a rather dashing figure, don't I?" He turned, and his smile changed to open-mouth gaping. "What? Oh, you look beautiful."

"Thanks, Anali helped me pick it out."

"And you look amazing," Anali said. Her rich purple sari flowed around her as the gold beading along the edge caught the light. Her freshly painted bindi was bright against her copper skin. The paleness was gone or masked behind her red blush and lipstick.

"Would you let me write 'I'm only fifteen' on your forehead?" Gavin asked.

Anali swatted his arm. "Really, such silliness. Your niece is a beautiful young woman. And I am sure she will have many admirers this evening."

Gavin groaned. "I can still remember when she was a toddler wearing a dress with Winnie the Pooh on it." He held out both his arms. "Well I suppose I shall have to accept that the constant stares I receive tonight will be because of the beautiful women on my arms."

Anali laughed as she slid her arm through his. "Your poor ego—however will it survive?"

He grinned. "I'm sure you can make it up to me later."

Ewww, gross. Why must they flirt in front of me? "I think we should go." I placed my hand in the crook of Gavin's elbow.

"Your car is ready, sir," said the doorman. A sleek black car waited in the driveway the engine running.

The doorman opened the back door for me while Gavin opened the door for Anali. I laughed and walked to the other side of the car.

Gavin tuned the radio to holiday music while the driver pulled out into the street. Pale pinks and oranges lit the evening clouds.

"How are the others getting there?" I asked.

"They left a few hours ago to set up," Gavin said. "Michael, Taliesin, Nyota, the Russian pole group, the jugglers, the woman who does hula-hoop, and the girls who do diabolo will all be there."

Anali turned in her seat. "Apparently there will be different performances. Other than our circus, there will also be bands, singers, dancers, and performance artists. I'm so glad I'm finally feeling better, at least in the afternoon, this morning was horrid."

"I'm glad you're feeling better, too. Don't we have your cousin's wedding soon?" I asked.

Anali squealed a bit. "Yes, next week. I am so excited I haven't seen most of them since they flew to India for our wedding." She reached over and clasped Gavin's hand. "Your uncle looked so handsome. He wore a traditional Indian wedding suit. Have you seen the pictures?"

"Yes, you were both stunning."

Anali had been dressed in a bright red sari and Gavin in a gold tunic that fell below his knees with red pants underneath. Both were embroidered in red and gold almost to the point of being gaudy.

"I can't wait, and while I've had some nice Indian food if I make it or go to specific restaurants, it'll be nice to have authentic Indian food again." Anali sighed and rubbed her belly.

"Sapphire, I hear you're going to wear a sari," Gavin said.

I nodded. I would wear it if I could remember how to put it on.

"Yes, and she looks so lovely in it," Anali said. "It's the same shade of green as her eyes with gold beading. I'm going to wear dark blue with silver embroidery."

"What about you, Uncle Gavin?" I asked.

"I think I'm wearing a black tunic with gray embroidery along the front. Right dear?"

"Yes, the bride and groom are dressing in dark red and cream, so that'll be perfect." Anali turned to me. "I hope you'll have fun."

"I'm sure I will. Uncle Gavin can always entertain me while you catch up with family."

"Keep the riffraff away from her is more like it," he muttered. "Are you going to the hen party?"

"You make it sound like some party with drinking and strippers, and yes, I am going," Anali said.

"What will you do?" I asked. It was good to see Anali feeling well enough to tease and laugh.

"Oh, it'll be so much fun. We will paint my cousin's hands and feet with henna. As long as the henna stains her hands, she doesn't have to do any house work, so it's a very important ceremony."

"Then come the strippers," teased Gavin.

"Then," she said, arching a thick dark eyebrow. "Those of us who are married complain about our husband and bemoan what poor matches we made and hope the new bride has better luck."

"I'm sorry, Anali." Gavin patted her leg. "I hope you won't be too sad that you have nothing to talk about."

"You are so kind to worry about me, sweetums," she crooned. "But don't worry. I have plenty to talk about."

Gavin sniffed. "I can't imagine even one moment where I have been less than the perfect husband."

The car turned down an unmarked gravel lane. Small lanterns glowed at the base of each towering weeping willow tree. The bare gray branches swayed in the wind. "Oh, this looks like the perfect start to a horror movie," Anali said.

"Anali, knock on something," I said. "Knock on the wood paneling. Quick."

She knocked on the door her bracelets jingling. "Better?"

"Yes, thank you," I said, knocking on the side of the car. Better to be safe than sorry.

After half a mile the driveway opened up to reveal Pressyne Manor. Gray ivy covered stone walls topped with pointed spires and gargoyles loomed above us. The windows glowed yellow in the dark night. I tried to think of them as inviting, but they felt more like creepy eyes. We drove around a marble fountain in the center of the circular drive. Two beautiful mermaids stood with their backs to each other, and their arms reached to the sky. Water flowed down their marble bodies and dripped off their tails into the pool.

The car stopped, and a woman and a man in black slacks and short white coats rushed to our car to open our doors and help us out. The fabric of my dress twisted around my legs, and I held on to the woman's hand, focusing on getting out of the car without falling over. Success.

Gavin held out his arms to Anali and me, and we walked up the stairs where massive wooden doors opened before we even touched them. I let go of Gavin so he could hand the invitation to the very fancy looking bouncer.

"Welcome, Mr. and Mrs. Marsh and Miss Rayner." He handed us square booklets. "Inside you will find a list of all the items for auction along with a list of the different entertainments that have been provided for your enjoyment. If you have any questions, please ask any of the staff."

We stepped into a cavernous entrance way. Parquet floors reflected the light from a crystal chandelier. The walls were painted a pale turquoise and gold framed paintings of mythical ocean creatures hung on the walls. We gave our coats to the coat girl, and stepped to the side.

I flipped through the booklet's rich, thick pages. The first few touted the charity, The Marine Conservation Society, and all the good work they do. Then the auction items—gross who wanted to buy a chamber pot even if it was antique? Next a map of the grounds and a list of the different acts. I scanned it until I found, Cirque du Feu Magique aerial silks at 18:45. "Gavin, what time is it?"

"Six-twenty," he said.

I did a quick calculation in my head. "Okay, I should be able to find him by then."

"You've seen his act before," Anali said. "Don't you want to see something new?"

"I want to see the balloons." I looked at the map, they were at spot four which was outside in a tent. "Where are you two going?"

"I'm not sure, Anali?" Gavin asked.

"I think I would like to see the silent auction items. You have your phone on you?"

"Yes, Anali. I'll see you guys later."

"Oh, let me know if you see something you want in the auction. You have to be an adult to bid," Gavin said before I rushed off.

I had stepped into a Cinderella movie. Bejeweled women in sinfully extravagant dresses smiled at men in fitted tuxedos, chatting about a variety of boring socially acceptable subjects. The nasal British accent that flowed around me sounded all proper, but they couldn't hide their feelings from me. Lust, anger, envy, and greed slithered around my empathic bubble.

The wealthy were not any happier than any other group of people. Laughter echoed over the marble, and I turned into a room where some of the auction items were. I froze. Holy crap. The royal family, and was that—? I held in a fan-girl squee; he was even more beautiful in person. How did Gavin get invited to a party with the royal family and movie stars?

I felt dizzy from the wealth that surrounded me and famous people within it. How did I wind up here? I didn't belong here. Taking a deep breath, I straightened my shoulders and faked that I belonged here. At least my dress belonged here.

As I moved through the crowd I noticed other familiar faces. I assumed I'd seen them on TV, in movies, or the news. I did my best to not stare like some bumbling idiot. Stepping out onto the porch, I followed the lanterns to the large white tent. It was funny—we always performed inside theaters but never in a circus tent. Inside, chairs were set up in a semi-circle around a stage. Waiters in white jackets served glasses of champagne and fancy little hors d'oeuvre that looked too pretty to eat.

I smoothed the back of my skirt as I sat down— some habit an old foster mom drilled into me. The house lights dimmed as the stage lights came on. The people around me whispered, their clothes rustling as they settled in to watch. Michael walked onto the stage. "Good evening, ladies and gentleman. Thank you for allowing us to entertain you tonight. I have a treat for you, a magical creature who will amaze you with his strength and beauty, and perhaps the poetry of his motions will make you think that he is the reincarnation of his name sake. I give you Taliesin."

A sweeping bow, and Michael moved aside as the two men, who balanced the Russian poles, held ropes attached to a bunch of large silver weather balloons. Hanging beneath them looked like a white silk cocoon. Harp music and a woman's voice wordlessly singing filled the tent as the men began to release some rope and the balloons rose into the air. When had Taliesin created this piece? I held my breath along with everyone else, my excitement bubbling inside of me while the crowds bubbled along my shields. The men holding the ropes walked further away from each other as the balloons reached the ceiling of the tent.

For a moment the cocoon hung in the air. A foot emerged, then an arm and the white silk fluttered towards the floor. Taliesin's costume was bright, circles within circles and crescent moon shapes, all in purples, blues, and greens. He moved so slowly, stretching his body, curling into the silk, and floating through the air. Taliesin owned the audience. I felt it—our breath was synced to his amazing feats. The tent was filled with amazement, desire, and awe. My fingers trembled with the intensity of emotion, but I couldn't look away from Taliesin— not even to strengthen my empathic bubble and protect myself.

Taliesin fluttered in a circle, and the silk flowed behind him like wings. I am so stupid. A butterfly: the markings on this bodysuit were of a butterfly emerging from his cocoon and exploring the world.

The music forced my heart to follow it, becoming louder and faster. Taliesin twisted into the silk and spun in a circle. My heart stopped as he began to tip upside down, then fell rolling towards the floor. My hands flew to my mouth and I gasped. He stopped inches above the hard wooden stage. I had seen him do that move hundreds of times, and yet I was completely enraptured.

Taliesin bowed low. We burst into applause, standing up while he made several swooping bows.

Michael came onto the stage. "I told you, Taliesin is poetry. In ten minutes we have three jugglers who will be performing to delight and amaze you."

The stage lights dimmed and the house lights brightened. Several people pressed forward, stopping Taliesin before he escaped backstage. He smiled and answered their questions. I thought about joining his fans. I wanted to tell Taliesin how much I'd enjoyed his performance, but between the crowd leaving, new people coming in, and those gathered around Taliesin growing, I decided to slip away. Standing on tip toe, I waved hoping to catch his attention but a crowd of bejeweled elite held his focus.

* * *

I wandered through the different rooms admiring the art, outfits, and entertainment. In one of the ballrooms—seriously, I'd have to check the map they provided to figure out where I was at this point—I watched couples dancing. Not cool club dancing, or pathetic school dance dancing, but elegant, regal ballroom dancing.

Couples glided across the parquet ballroom floor. A flash of red hair caught my eye. I watched as Gavin led Anali across the parquet. Their smiles were infectious. After days of being ill, Anali's cheeks were a healthy pink, and she seemed to glow.

"Excuse me, miss," said a middle aged man. He was a little taller than me with thinning brown hair and a charming smile. I couldn't help but relax and smile back. Something about him put me at ease. "I do hope I'm not being too forward as we haven't been properly introduced. My name is Quintin Monroe. I noticed you were watching the dancers. If I'm not being too presumptuous, would you like to dance?"

He held out his hand. I smiled and placed my hand in his. "Sapphire Rayner, and I would love to dance. I have to warn you that I have never waltzed before."

"Then you are most fortunate, as I am an excellent dancer," he said as he held me out onto the floor. "Put your left hand on my shoulder and your right stays in mine." He placed his hand on my waist. "Now look at me and let me lead you."

I opened my empathy up a bit, yes I cheated so I wouldn't look like an idiot. We seemed to glide across the polished floor, my dress swirled around my legs without tripping me up.

"Are you sure you haven't waltzed before?"

"I guess, Mr. Monroe, that you are indeed a very good dancer."

He smiled, his round cheeks pinking. "That is true, but your natural grace does help."

I laughed. "I don't think I've ever thought of myself as graceful before, thank you."

"How were you forced into coming here?" Mr. Monroe asked.

"My Uncle Gavin received an invitation. And you?"

"I am on the board for the Marine Conservation Society. So I'm here to schmooze and liberate as much money as I can from this lot. You think dancing with me is fun, just wait until you hear my riveting speech during dinner."

"And here I thought the night was going to be boring."

"Oh, no. I brought pictures of baby seals."

I missed a step because I was laughing, but Mr. Monroe kept me from falling.

"So are you visiting London or did you move here?"

"Just visiting, we're leaving after the New Year," I said.

"Not the nicest time of year to come here. London is so gray and bleak in the winter."

"It's still beautiful—all the old building and the holiday lights. Anyway, I've never been here before so I don't know the difference."

"I guess ignorance really is bliss," he said with a grin.

I gasped as a couple moved past us, their hatred piercing and freezing cold. They looked lovely, but they danced without looking at each other. I shivered as Mr. Monroe moved us away from them. I tried to relax as and focus on how I needed to move for the waltz. Wait, my eyes widened. I stared into Mr. Monroe's hazel eyes. I couldn't feel him! Why couldn't I feel him?

Mr. Monroe winked at me.

My breath caught.

"There you are Quintin," said a woman in a gray-blue silk dress that moved around her like water.

"Hello, Melusine. May I introduce Miss Sapphire Rayner. Miss Rayner, our hostess, Melusine," Mr. Monroe said.

I started to move my hand to shake hers but Mr. Monroe tightened his grip.

"I am so sorry to interrupt, but I must steal Mr. Monroe. There are some people who have some questions before they loosen their grip on their wallets."

Mr. Monroe sighed, a twinkle in his eyes. "Well, my dear, it's time for me to get to work. Thank you for a lovely dance."

"Thank you, Mr. Monroe, for risking your toes. I had a lovely time." I watched them walk away. Melusine held onto Mr. Monroe's arm, and her brown hair fell over his shoulder as she looked down to talk to him.

What just happened? Who was he? I snagged a booklet as I walked out of the room flipping through it until I found Mr. Monroe's picture, and a basic bio: college, marine biologist, on the board for five years, blah blah blah. That wasn't helpful at all. I snagged some hors d'oeuvres from a passing tray. Biting into a half moon pastry, I moaned at the creamy mushroom filling. I needed a whole plate of these.

I wonder if this is how ghosts feel, wandering around people who don't see them, looking at things so odd you know you're out of place. My fingers twitched as I looked at the vibrant tapestry of mermaids and seals lying in the waves, a group of ugly hunters sneaking up behind them. I wanted to touch it but didn't, I could feel how old it was.

My shoes clicked on the wood floor, where to next? Turning a corner, I heard singing and felt a little tug of magic. I followed it, my smile broadening. A miracle might happen tonight. A smaller ballroom held a younger group of London's elite. They sat at tables chatting, and some were dancing as the Water Nymphs played.

Ramsey's wild curls fluttered around his face, but the rest of him looked respectable, his black jacket and waistcoat fit snugly around his chest and shoulders as he played his cello. His kilt looked new, the blue and green tartan with a thin line of red. His cousin Solange sang, beseeching her lover to return to her. I felt her and the violinist soaking in the energy of the crowd. The flutist danced and flirted, I could see Pan in him now. Murdock grinned the same dangerous grin that Ramsey flashed at me several times. The brothers looked a lot alike, but Murdock was stockier, kind of like a small bear.

I slid through the crowd until I was near the stage. Unlike at the club, people weren't pressed against the stage. The groups of admirers sat further back in comfort. I waited until the song ended, then stepped closer. "You wanted a miracle?"

Ramsey's head shot up and he choked on the water he was drinking.

His brother smacked him on the back. "You okay there, Runt?"

"Sapphire, what are you doing here?"

"This is the fancy party my Uncle dragged me to."

And there was the evil sexy grin. My stomach fluttered. I'm sure it was because I was hungry.

"Hen, this is brilliant."

"Time to play," Murdock said.

"Stay?" he asked, putting his bow on the strings.

I nodded as a deep note vibrated from his cello which he held between his legs. He moved and I saw that same bit of tattoo on his thigh.

I found a small table and watched Ramsey, and the others, careful to keep my shields up so the sirens couldn't feed from me.

* * *

"You look amazing. I thought the little black dress was nice, but this. . . I'm glad you sat too far away for me to see you, otherwise I would have stared at you all through the set and messed up on every song," Ramsey said, sitting down. "I still can't believe you're here."

My face was so hot. Damn him for making me blush like this. "Well, now you'll have keep me from being bored."

He looked at his watch. "I can do that for an hour. We can stay until it's time for dinner, then we'll leave by the servants' exit in the back."

"Can you leave now, or do you need to finish up?" I looked where the two sirens were talking to a group of people.

"I can go, I'm not very good at the networking thing. Anyway the Water Nymphs is their band. The other cellist left when his wife had a baby, and they asked me to join them. So I'm just along for the ride."

"Runt," Murdock said. "Are you taking off?"

"Yes. You?"

"No, I have a few lasses who want to get to know me better." He wiggled his eyebrows then turned to me. "I am sorry to leave you with Runt here when you are obviously worthy of a real man. See you back here in an hour and don't forget what you promised me."

I shook my head as he walked off to his group of admirers.

Ramsey groaned and stood up. "Ready?"

"Sure."

"Do you mind going to the auction really quick?" he asked.

"Not at all. I haven't been yet."

"Brilliant. All of my friends, and Murdock made me promise to check on their items and bid on them if no one had yet."

"Why does he call you Runt?" I asked looking up at Ramsey, he had to be close to six feet tall.

He sighed. "I'm slender like my mum and sisters, my da and brothers are broad."

"Oh. Well, you look nice enough to me and very handsome tonight."

"Such sweet words." Ramsey pointed to an open set of large dark oak doors. "It's in here."

I gasped. The map had said the auction was in the library, but I had imagined a small study with some books on the walls, not an actual library. The walls were nothing but books. Curling wrought iron staircases led to a walkway that ran along the walls and allowed access to even more books. Over the smell of food, wine, and perfumes floated the rich smell of old books. I wrapped my arms around myself to keep from rushing over and running my fingers over the cloth and leather spines.

"It's amazing, isn't it?" Ramsey said, taking my arm and leading me to the first cherry wood table. "Come on, you can leer at the books while I find my friends' pieces."

"I am not leering at the books, I am admiring them," I said, trying to focus on where I was going and not the gold lettering on the books which seemed to wink and call to me.

"Yeah, right. Sorry I don't know where their items are placed."

"I don't mind, like I said I haven't looked yet." On the tables were a variety of items, art work of all kinds, jewelry, antiques, gift baskets, and gift certificates. Below them was a piece of paper where people wrote their bids and names.

"There is Murdock's bodhran." Ramsey pointed to a beautiful round drum painted with an elaborate Celtic knot. It took a minute of staring at the brown knot work to realize it was three seals. "One person has placed a bid. If the other pieces have been bid on maybe I'll add a bid, hopefully that'll add interest, because I already have two of his drums."

"It's beautiful," I said. I started a text message to Gavin asking him to bid on it for me. I would wait to send it in case I wanted something else.

"Don't tell him you like it, he'll never stop flirting with you then."

I laughed and didn't resist as Ramsey slide his arm around my waist. Possessive much?

"The necklace made of sea glass, that's my friend Mindy's work."

Three strands of green sea glass had been strung lengthwise with small seed pearls in-between. It made me think of something a child of the ocean might make for their mother at school. "She has quite a few bids," I said. "It's a very whimsical piece."

Ramsey chuckled. "Mindy bounces between mature tortured artist and childlike creative sprite."

"Oh look," I moved ahead to look at a picture of a seal. Its large liquid black eyes stared out with such wisdom I wondered if it was a selkie.

"It's a seal," Ramsey said.

I read the description, Mr. Quintin Monroe. "I danced with the photographer earlier."

Ramsey arched an eyebrow.

I smiled and turned to look at the photographs. I didn't owe him an explanation. We weren't dating.

"Is he handsome?" Ramsey asked his voice calm but his irritation scratched across my bubble. "His photographs are okay."

"He's cute, I guess, for an old guy."

"Old?" Ramsey asked.

I wrinkled my nose. "He was like forty or something."

Ramsey relaxed. "You should be ashamed winding me up like that."

"Should I?"

He grinned and leaned in to say something when someone called his name.

"Cheers, Mindy. How are you doing?"

"Ramsey, thank you so much for coming down here," she squealed, hugging him tight in plump tan arms. "I have met so many amazing people, and Melusine said she loved my work and wants me to come by next week to talk to her."

"That's wonderful. Mindy, this is my friend Sapphire. Sapphire, this is Mindy. She made the necklace I showed you."

"Nice to meet you," I said holding out my hand. I could feel the bit of Fae in her when we touched. "It's a lovely piece."

"Thank you, I have a bracelet and earring set on another table that is being bid on." Mindy took Ramsey's hand. "Can you come and meet someone?"

He turned to me.

"Go ahead. I'm going to finish looking at these photos."

"We won't be a minute," she said to me, then turned to Ramsey. "I really like him. We've been seeing each other for a week now." I watched them walk over to a group of artists. At least I assumed they were artists because they all had a magical feel to them, and their clothing was less high fashion and more self-expression.

I admired a photograph of a humpback whale when I felt him enter the room. Smiling, I turned toward the door. Taliesin stood tall, his white hair loose around his shoulders. He wore a pearl gray tuxedo. As always, he looked like he stepped out of an issue of GQ. My heart sped up a little at the sight of him.

I waved.

He nodded and began to walk towards me. Then stopped as someone talked to him. Taliesin was a flame, and moths would be fluttering around him all night.

I turned back to the photographs. Mr. Monroe had captured an image of a mother orca nursing her baby. How did he manage to take such amazing images? Maybe next semester I'd take the photography elective through our virtual school.

Everything stopped. I could barely breathe. Something tightened around my chest. I looked. Found a chair. Focus, focus it's only a few steps away. What was happening? Sit, just sit, and then I could figure it out. Pain ripped through me. I slapped a hand over my mouth to keep from screaming. My knees buckled. Strong arms wrapped around me. Safe hands.

"Sapphire?" said Ramsey.

"Let's get her to the couch," Taliesin said.

"Sir, is everything okay?" asked a waiter.

"Yes, sorry she gets these sudden migraines sometimes. Once she takes her medication she'll be fine," Taliesin lied.

"Very good sir, I'll ask everyone to stay back."

"Thank you," Taliesin said.

Ramsey supported me to the couch. Another wave of agony, a soul screaming out for help. I whimpered, tears streaming down my face.

Ramsey sat with me half in his lap supporting me. Taliesin sat down and glared at him. I wanted to say something to introduce them but my breath was stolen and white hot pain was followed by numbness.

"Just breathe," Taliesin said as he wiped away my tears with a handkerchief. "Can you sip some water?"

I nodded and sat up.

"What happened?" Ramsey asked.

"Something drained the magic out of a creature, a gnome." My eyes fluttered, I felt the being's heart trying to beat and ache as their lungs gasped for air. "They aren't dead, whatever it was didn't take the creature's life just their magic. They are hurting so badly. I don't think they will live."

"She needs to go outside," Taliesin said. "Let me text Gavin, and then I can carry her out."

"Text him now," Ramsey said. "I can carry her."

"No, you don't understand," Taliesin began.

Ramsey scooped me up, and I was surrounded by him, physically and emotionally.

I curled up, still feeling the pain of the poor gnome, but now I could feel Ramsey, his anger, fear, and helplessness ripped at me. I tried to breathe to restore my empathic bubble. The gasping breaths I managed did nothing but increase my panic.

Ramsey stormed through the mansion, his emotions crashing and rolling like a sea during a storm.

My fingers curled into his jacket and I whimpered as we passed a crowd. Their emotions felt like hail pelting me without mercy.

"They will meet us in the front," Taliesin said. "Gavin has all the tickets and such but we have to get her outside."

What was he talking about and why did we need tickets?

Taliesin's fingers folded over mine. I shivered as I felt his moonlight cool magic touch my skin. "No, Taliesin no, not here. What if whatever it was feels you?"

He squeezed my hand. "Hurry up."

"I could run if you want," Ramsey snapped.

"You'd probably trip."

"I'll get the door sir, can we help at all?"

"No, thank you," said Taliesin. "Her Aunt and Uncle are coming."

"Very good sir, let me know if we can be of service."

I gasped as the cold air surrounded me. I wanted to burrow into Ramsey but didn't want to tap into any more of his emotions. The fact that I managed to avoid skin to skin contact was amazing.

"We can sit on this bench," Taliesin said. "Put her down."

"No, she'll get cold," Ramsey said sitting with me still in his arms.

"Idiot, she's an empath who has been over loaded. You need to stop touching her."

Ramsey growled low in his chest but set me on the freezing bench. I gasped the night air cold, sharp, and clean. I relaxed and opened my eyes. The night was black, stars glowing in the sky. I didn't know if it was a new moon or it just hadn't risen. One would think after the werewolf incident in Argentina I would be more aware of the cycles of the moon.

Taliesin and Ramsey sat on either side of me, their energy tight with restrained anger and fear. They were both trying so hard to keep their emotions to themselves. I would thank them when I could speak again. I looked over the perfect gardens, and into the looming trees in the distance.

"Everything is dead," I said.

"What?" asked Taliesin.

"Look, there is nothing, no magical creature at all on the grounds."

"Well," began Ramsey. "It is night and cold out."

I shook my head. "No, there is no magic out here, not even a glimmer of it. Even the trees and soil are devoid of magic."

"We need to get out of here," Taliesin said.

I nodded and wrapped my arms around myself, my breath visible as I spoke. "I don't feel anything evil, but then I didn't even when it was hurting that poor creature. I can still feel it. Its poor body, trying to live with such an important part of itself missing."

I felt Gavin, his emotions reached out for me even before he left the mansion. I tried to smile and stand as Gavin came down the steps.

"Sapphire, are you all right?"

"I'm okay." And then I wasn't. The creature's body shuddered. I twitched, my eyes losing focus. I saw a plain white ceiling through iron bars at the same time I could see Gavin's worried face in front of me. The gnome gasped. I gasped.

"Sapphire?"

"… get her out of here …"

The gnomes friends cried and held her hands. Their thick fingers were cold.

"… car sir."

I began to fall. Someone held me. The gnome and I took a stuttering breath.

I was passed to someone else.

"Sorry … I … warn… call…"

Thump, a heartbeat. A shallow rattling breath.

"… must drive faster."

Thump. Our eyes closed.

"…not breathing."

Moonlight surrounded me. I gasped and choked as I was cut off from the dying gnome.

"Taliesin," Anali asked, her voice thick with tears.

"I've got her."

I relaxed onto his chest, surrounded by moonlight cool magic. Tears ran down my cheeks as I surrendered to the darkness.

Chapter Twelve

"Only when we are no longer afraid do we begin to live." ~
Dorothy Thompson

Turquoise filled my vision, and a warm flower scented breeze
flowed over me, washing away the fear, anger and pain which
clung to my skin. Turning my head, the vibrant green grass
tickled my cheek. A bevy of nymphs played in the water. I sat
up as two Phoenixes flew over to me. The Phoenix King
Shamash with flame feathers of yellow, orange, and red, and
besides him Queen Aya her feather's the blues, purples, and
greens from the heart of a fire. Hovering in the air their bodies
shimmered and shifted into their human forms.

My many times great-grandparents smiled and knelt on the
grass besides me. "Sapphire, dearest, what happened?" Aya
asked, her voice laced with a musical tone that soothed me.

Their coloring reminded me so much of Anali and Gavin.
Aya's copper brown skin and black curls, and Shamash's milk
white skin and flame red hair was almost the same shades as
Anali and Gavin.

"Something sucked the magic out of a gnome, but not one of the Sons of Belial," I said.

"Tell us," Shamash said, "so we can help you."

Aya patted her thigh. I laid my head on her leg and sighed as she combed her fingers through my hair. I told them about Ramsey, the torc, and the dead gnome.

"The person must have studied Earth magic," said Shamash. I frowned.

"There are some magical beings that are unique to Earth itself," explained Aya. "And a type of magical practice that taps into the power and energy of Earth."

"I had no idea," I said.

"You'll need to be careful since you can't feel the person who did this," Shamash said. "I wish I had advice to offer, or something I could share with you to help."

"Perhaps you found the torc for a reason," Aya said. "It might be able to help you when you wear it."

"I'll try that. Oh, speaking of help—Sasha said he dreamed that I need to talk to trees. He doesn't understand what the images mean."

"Oh, the hamadryad," said Shamash. "Yes, there is one at Hampton Court."

I arched an eyebrow.

"I can't go to Earth, but that doesn't mean I don't know what is happening with my people," Shamash said.

Aya's smile lit up her face and made her even more beautiful. Shamash's eyes softened as he grinned at her. Four thousand years and they were still in love.

"What your grandfather means is he talks to different Children of Fire and magical beings when they dream and does his best to help them," Aya said.

"Oh, okay. I can ask Gavin to take me."

"You should go soon; the hamadryad will guide you to Avalon," Shamash said. "They've spent centuries guarding a portal and protecting magical beings."

"They are very clever," Aya said. "It's all tucked away, a door in a doorway."

Shamash frowned for a moment, then sighed. "Enough of this. You know what you need to do, and you know we are always here to help you. Shall we swing for a while?"

I couldn't remember the last time I swung with my grandparents on the large faerie swing made from wood, moss, and flowering vines. I stood up and held a hand out to Shamash. "Adadda," I said. 'Grandfather' in Babylonian.

Smiling, he took my hand.

"Amagal," I said, holding my hand out to Aya, my many times great-grandmother.

My stomach growled. Frowning, I tried to ignore the noise and burrow under the covers. My muscles ached and my head pounded. What was going on? My stomach growled again.

"You're going to have to get up, Sapphire," Miu said with a chuckle. "I have some breakfast waiting for you."

My stomach cheered with the idea of breakfast. "Why do I feel like death warmed over?" I asked, sitting up. Then realizing that my stomach wasn't the only organ being ignored, I stood on shaking legs and shuffled to the bathroom.

Washing my hands I looked in the mirror. Holy crap, what in the hell happened? I looked like a photo of a celebrity lying in the gutter the morning after a party. Searching the counter, I found Miu's make-up remover and scrubbed my face. My hair, stiff from gel and hairspray, wouldn't let a brush through it, but I manage to pull it into a ponytail and out of my face. I would have shower right then, but my stomach couldn't tolerate the wait.

"Better?" Miu asked.

"I will be once I eat something." I sat at the table and took a long drink of orange juice. Miu uncovered a plate of eggs, beans, toast shining with butter, cooked tomatoes and mushrooms, and fruit. "This looks amazing."

"It's the veggie version of an English fry-up."

I nodded. I was taught not to talk with my mouth full.

"I let everyone know you were awake and fine. Gavin said he'd come over as soon as possible, he's jumping between Anali and her morning sickness and you and your blatant refusal to wake up all morning."

I offered a grunt of thanks to Miu, mouth still full. Whoever added baked beans to breakfast was a genius.

"Taliesin texted your friend Ramsey back last night," Miu said. "I guess the beeping of your phone started to drive him nuts. I talked to him an hour ago when he called and let him know you were fine but still sleeping."

"Thanks," I said spreading marmalade on my toast. "Did he say if he and his friends were all right?"

Miu nodded as she began to eat her own breakfast of fish and eggs. "Yes, he said that they all got home safely."

"Good." I slowed down and started eating like a normal person when I realized my plate was already half empty. Did I even chew anything? "What time is it?"

"Almost eleven," Miu said.

"We have a show at two right?"

"Yes, then again at seven, are you up for two shows?"

I wiggled about a bit stretching my arms and legs, rolling my neck. My body felt a little stiff, probably because I slept for, what like fifteen hours? My headache already vanished. "Yes, I'll need to get a good warm up but I should be fine."

A knock, then Gavin opened the door. "Sapphire, how are you? Sorry I wasn't here."

I smiled, but kept my lips closed, just in case I had pieces of marmalade stuck in my teeth. "Anali needs you. I understand. How is she?"

Gavin frowned. "Sick, but not as bad as before. More importantly, how are you?"

"A little stiff from sleeping so long, but Shamash and Aya helped me. Oh, Hampton Court, we need to go to Hampton Court, there is a tree I need to talk to there."

Gavin raised an eyebrow. "A tree."

"Well, a hamadryad, to be exact. Apparently, the hamadryad will tell me how to find Avalon."

"The Arthurian Avalon?" Miu asked. "I love that story."

"Okay. Well we have plans for your birthday, but the next day we have off, so maybe we can go then. I'll look into it." Gavin ran a hand through his hair. "Are you sure you're all right?"

"Yes, I'm going to finish this, shower, and as long as I get a good warm-up in, I'll be ready for the show at two."

Gavin sighed, looked at the door, then back at me.

"Uncle Gavin, go back and take care of Anali. Last night wasn't a big deal. I'm fine now." Adults get so worked up sometimes.

"Sapphire, you stopped breathing, which is a very big deal." I ate some eggs. I didn't know what to say to that. And the whole not breathing thing was short-lived anyway. Gavin sighed and continued. "Did you learn anything in your dream? I asked Sasha to check, and all he remembered was magic Earth."

"Earth magic. Shamash and Aya said the person was probably using Earth-based magic, which is why I didn't sense them," I said.

He nodded. "Okay. I'll call Philip and see if he knows anything."

Grinning, I thought of Philip's salt and pepper Mohawk. A year ago when I turned fifteen, I was drawn to the San Francisco Circus Center, Philip was the first Child of Fire I met. We still kept in contact. He helped research and acted as our contact for the other Children of Fire groups. He was also Michael's brother. "Will you ask him about Avalon too?" I asked.

"Yes, of course." Gavin knelt in front of me looking me over. "Are you sure you're okay?"

"Yes, I'm sure."

Gavin hugged me, lifting me off the chair. "I was terrified. Please tell me right away if you feel even a little bit off."

"I will," I promised.

"Is everything okay?" Anali asked, standing in the doorway. Her copper skin looked chalky, but she smiled and her eyes were bright.

"Yes, I'm fine. How are you?" I asked.

"I think I'm done throwing up for the day," Anali said.

Miu walked over and touched Anali's arm. Miu's eyes fluttered and closed, and she began to glow a little. "Everything feels fine. From what my powers can tell me, you need something to eat and drink."

"Well, then, I should get you some breakfast," Gavin said, squeezing my shoulder as he stood up.

"I want samosas, and lassi, but I'm not sure if I want plain or rose, and peanut butter and chocolate fudge ice cream."

Miu and I frowned and turned to look at Gavin who stared at his wife. "Um, sure, whatever you want."

Okay, that sounded a bit odd for someone who just threw up. Shouldn't she have toast, or plain crackers or something?

"Come on, let's go back to the room and I'll call room service," Gavin said.

"Wonder what they have planned for your birthday," Miu said as we sat to finish our breakfast.

I thought for a moment. "Probably going out to dinner, if Anali is feeling well enough. I'm not holding out for anything special, they have so much going on."

Miu nodded. "I am sure they will do something fun for your birthday."

Maybe, but I wasn't counting on it. "It doesn't matter. I mean at the group homes I got a cake and a gift or two."

"Well, not this birthday," Miu said. "I have a wonderful party planned, food, decorations, the club, the whole circus will be there."

"Little Sister," Kayin said. He wrapped his arms around me. I hugged him back breathing in his spicy scent, feeling relaxed and safe.

"Hey, Big Brother. How are you doing?"

He snorted. "Better than you. Can you perform today?" He stepped back and pulled juggling balls from his pocket.

My eyes narrowed. Kayin only obsessively juggled when he felt stressed. I would have to make time to talk to him alone. "Yes. I'll need a good warm-up but I should be fine."

"And a shower," Sasha said giving his bangs a little toss. The obedient red-streaked honey blond locks fell perfectly into place.

I stuck my tongue at him. Of course I would shower.

"Is Taliesin okay?" I asked.

"Yes, he's fine. He didn't have a bad reaction to what happened," Miu said.

"He seemed fine at yoga and breakfast this morning," said Kayin.

Sasha chuckled. "Yes, we heard all about your friend, Ramsey, in great detail."

"Is he evil?" Kayin asked. "Taliesin seemed to think he's evil."

"Who?" Shin asked.

Was everyone going to invade my room while I looked like crap?

"Ramsey, apparently. Taliesin doesn't like him," Miu said.

"They didn't even really meet. They both rushed over to me when I started feeling the gnome, and then they got me out of there."

"And Ramsey wouldn't let you go," Kayin added.

"Yes," Sasha said. "Even though Taliesin knows you better."

"And obviously the one who could help you," Kayin finished.

My face burned with embarrassment. "I hate all of you."

They all smiled at me. I shifted in my seat and looked away. "Oh, Sasha," I said with a perfectly good reason to change the topic. "Hampton Court—the tree I'm supposed to talk to is a hamadryad at Hampton Court."

"Ah," Sasha nodded. "I kept seeing the image of a pig on a tennis court. I suppose that was the note I made for myself so I wouldn't forget."

"You are so weird," Miu said.

I smiled and finished my breakfast as Miu and Sasha began to bicker.

* * *

My shoulder ached. During the matinee I almost slipped and wrenched my shoulder trying to straighten up. Kayin, as always, created a steady and strong foundation, and his support helped me right myself. The crowd clapped, thinking we had performed some amazing feat of strength. When really I was lucky, very, very lucky that I didn't fall on my face. Miu left with Taliesin right after we had signed programs, and I was waiting for her to return and heal my shoulder.

"Can I help at all?" Kayin asked.

"No thanks," I said, leaning back on the old couch. "If any of the others find out I'm hurt, then I can't have Miu fix me. How could I explain my rapid healing?"

Kayin nodded. "Did you get enough to eat?"

Some of us didn't bother to go back to the hotel between matinee and evening performances, and Michael would order in food.

"I'm fine," I said. "I noticed your admirer was back."

Kayin sighed and sat next to me. "I don't like how he looks at me."

"Neither does Shin."

Warm happiness mixed with prickly anxiety washed over me. "No, he doesn't. Do you think it's okay?"

"That Shin doesn't like some guy staring at you?"

"That I like that he doesn't like some guy staring at me."

I blinked, trying sort that out. "Oh, well yes. It feels nice when people want to take care of us and keep us safe."

"I don't know what to do."

"Big Brother, you don't have to do anything. Take your time figuring things out."

Kayin sighed and lay his head on my good shoulder. "What if he moves on? What if he finds someone else?"

"Maybe that fact that you're worried about those things is the answer," I said.

Kayin's sadness took my breath away. "I fear I will lose my family if I do. How am I supposed to choose?"

"I wish I knew. But what if your father would understand? What if he accepted you? What if you could have everything you want?"

"What if I lose everything trying to find out?"

I held his hand. "I'll be here no matter what happens."

"I don't think I have ever felt so scared or confused," Kayin said. "Even when I was kicked out of my village and a few days later I was in New York, I felt more numb than scared."

"I think the scary part is before you act; before you make a choice. After that, things are in motion, and the what-ifs bopping around your head are quieter," I said. "At least that's what my mom wrote in her journal, and her advice seems to work for me."

"Tell me, what advice did your mom give you?"

"We worry about and fear what isn't happening. We fear the unknown and the possibilities more than what is happening right in front of us. We fear if we go water skiing that we'll fall. If we fall, we fear that we have broken our leg. If we break our leg, we fear we'll have to have surgery. And on, and on, and on. Live in the now and you will do away with so much fear and worry. Live with purpose, strength, and love," I recited.

"Easier said than done," Kayin said.

I laughed. "Of course. Isn't everything?"

"I am here to save the day," Miu announced as she came around the corner.

"Thank goodness," I sighed, sitting forward so she could put her hands on my shoulder.

Miu hummed and opened her connection to Akasha. Heat surrounded my shoulder. "You wrenched your shoulder pretty bad. Let's see what I can do. Even if I heal the muscles, they might be too weak to perform again today."

"I'll be fine," I said.

Kayin snorted. "You are such a brat."

"I'm not fixing you if you re-injure yourself," Miu said. She sent hot healing Phoenix energy into my shoulder, and the tension and pain melted away.

"Of course," I said knowing that when I slept I usually spent at least some time in Akasha, and my many time great grandparents would heal me.

"Forty-five minutes," Nyota called out, walking the hall backstage. "There are people in the house now."

Her field generator protected us but only when we weren't actively using our powers.

"Almost done," Miu said. A short burst of energy and she took her hands away. "Okay, there you go."

I rolled my shoulder; the pain was gone. "Awesome, thanks."

Miu stood. "Go warm up, and be honest. If the muscle isn't weak, perform. I need a quick nap and some candy before I can go on."

* * *

I watched the crowd—they didn't take their eyes from Shin and the other Chinese pole performers. The audience gasped in unison as their lust and amazement began to fill the theater. Rolling my shoulder, I tried to figure out what to do. My shoulder felt weak. I completed the warm-up but used my right arm more than my left. With focus I could use both my arms equally but there was a difference in strength. I felt pretty sure I could get through the routine, but my shoulder would hurt after. Hopefully, I would dream and my shoulder would heal.

I wish Gavin and Anali were here to talk to. I wasn't sure what to do, and my mom's journal didn't have advice for this one. I mean there's trusting your instincts, and listening to yourself, but right now my body, heart, and mind weren't agreeing.

"Ready to go on, Sapphire?"

"Of course, Michael."

"Do you know what my Phoenix gift is?" he asked.

My brow furrowed. "No, I've never thought about it."

He placed a hand on my shoulder his thumb pressing into the joint. I gasped as my arm fell limp. "I can tell when people lie."

Rude! "Okay so here's the problem, I wrenched my shoulder during the matinee, and Miu took off before I could get her help. She fixed my shoulder about an hour ago, but it's still weak. I think I can do all my parts and get through the show. But I'm not sure, and I don't know how to tell," I said in one breath.

"Sapphire, I appreciate you wanting to go on, but if your shoulder is hurt like this, statue isn't safe for you or Kayin."

Okay, using Kayin against me isn't fair. "I don't want Kayin to get hurt."

"I don't want either of you to get hurt. You can do stilts and jump rope but not statue," Michael said.

My stomach sank. "Okay I'm sorry."

Michael patting my injured shoulder. "Injuries happen. The important thing is to tell me." He sighed and stepped closer to me. "I haven't said anything but an aerial artist died yesterday while performing in Quebec. Her partner didn't tell anyone his wrist was hurt. She trusted him to hold her and he couldn't. She fell twenty feet and broke her neck. Please don't hide any injuries, weaknesses, or concerns from me. There are much more important things than performing."

"That is awful, I can't imagine. The poor man." I felt nauseated. I knew we could get hurt, but dead?

"The whole troupe is devastated, and many of them are blaming themselves for not knowing." Michael shook his head. "What's so upsetting is this accident was completely preventable. Sometimes they're not, but this one was. Go tell Kayin and the others."

"Okay. Thanks, Michael."

I found Kayin standing next to a sweaty, grinning Shin.

"Hey, Kayin. Michael said I couldn't do statue, that my shoulder is too weak. I'm sorry."

"Little Sister, don't worry." Kayin wrapped an arm around me and gave me a hug. "I'm sure you'll be fine for tomorrow."

"Can you do stilts and jump rope?" Shin asked.

I nodded. "Yes, Michael said I could."

"I guess this means everything has moved up in the schedule," Shin said.

Crap. "I'll go tell Nyota," I said.

"I saw her head stage right. I'll go stage left and tell everyone," Kayin said.

"Okay thanks," I said.

"I'll check the green room in the back," Shin offered.

I felt like I was letting everyone down. I felt even worse as people said how they understood, not to worry, and they hoped I felt better tomorrow. Cold guilt settled in my stomach at me with every word of sympathy. I knew the same injury I had would have taken them a week or more to heal.

Nyota hung by her knees from a bar rewiring something. Her dreadlocks hung down looking like Medusa's' snakes. "Nyota."

"Hey, Sapphire, what's up?"

"I can't do statute today; I tweaked my shoulder."

Nyota pulled herself up and started speaking into her walkie-talkie. "Statue has been cut, queue up lighting and sound for the clowns."

"I'm going to check this way and let people know."

Nyota gave me a thumbs up and flipped down again, talking as she worked on the wires.

I should have talked to Michael earlier. I'm such an idiot.

After confessing my failure to everyone I could find, I went over to my area and got ready for stilts.

The piano piece that signaled silks began. Using a chair I carefully heaved myself up, and checked to make sure my floor-length skirt wasn't tangled up. I slid my fingers into the poi loops and held the LED balls in my hands as I straightened the cords between them and the loops. I peeked out at the audience. Sasha and Taliesin unwrapped down the silks, then stopped, hanging inches above the floor. The audience, gasped, cheered and clapped. I smiled as the warm emotions flooded the theater.

Sharp cold anger stabbed through. I gasped at its intensity. What the hell? I scanned the audience, but couldn't see anyone glaring at the stage. Maybe what I felt was something else entirely?

Taking a deep breath I tried to filter out the positive emotions and focused on the anger. I shivered as I tapped into the anger. I followed it to the balcony. It was one person, and he was very angry. I don't think he wanted to hurt anyone. I opened my empathy up, and a small little tendril of emotion caught my attention. There was desire, but not sexual, and excitement, but there was a dark edge to it.

My eyes widened, and I stepped away from the curtain. There were people in the audience who wanted Taliesin and Sasha to fall. They saw them performing these difficult and beautiful routines and someone out there wanted them to hurt themselves. I wrapped my arms around myself. How could people think like that?

I walked over to my spot and waved at Kayin to get his attention. He was juggling off in the corner wearing the black muscle shirt for his part in the jump rope routine.

"You okay?" he asked.

"Someone in the audience is very angry. I'm not even sure if the anger is directed at Taliesin and Sasha or some other person but I felt it and ..." I shivered, the feeling of people hoping they would fall still attached to me. I couldn't say it out loud, and the anger felt more active than those jerks wanting my friends hurt.

Kayin nodded. "I'll tell Michael, Taliesin, and Sasha when they get done."

"Thank you," I said. I turned on the light in my poi, let go of them, and made sure the strings were straight as the piano piece finished up. The glowing green balls hung down by my knees. We walked in time to the beat of the drums in the piece of Afro-Caribbean music we performed to.

I walked out, looking out into the sea of faces, wondering which ones were hoping for my friends to be hurt. In fact, I was so focused on finding them I missed the cue to start spinning the poi. Damn it. Taking a breath, I focused on the other spinners and matched their movements, my poi making green circles of light in the air. Tonight was turning into a special kind of crazy.

Chapter Thirteen

I was being used as protection again. Taliesin wrapped his arm around my waist as a group of young women gushed about how fabulous he was. Lust, admiration, and desire filled the room like cloying sweet perfume. The anger and fear I felt earlier cut through the other emotions like needles being thrown at me. I searched the crowd again. A distinguished couple stood near the windows. He looked out into the night, his back straight, shoulders broad, and his long brown hair touched the top of his collar. The slender woman, her honey blond hair twisted into a tidy bun looked up. Her round gray eyes widened as she saw me looking at her. Turning, she hid from me.

Something wasn't right. Kayin, Shin, and Taliesin seemed fine. Sasha and Miu couldn't see the couple because an interesting modern sculpture blocked their view. None of the other performers seemed upset or tense. I couldn't feel anything other than anger and worry coming from them, or at least from their general direction, but nothing evil. Of course, I didn't feel anything evil last night at the gala either.

I wish I had my phone so I could text Gavin.

"Do you still feel the anger?" Taliesin asked.

I nodded. "Yes, I think it's coming from that couple, but I'm not sure."

"Don't worry, we're almost done," he said.

I didn't want to say anything about what I felt, but I had to. "I need to talk to you, in private."

Taliesin frowned. "Tonight?"

I shook my head. "No, not tonight, but tomorrow?"

"Sure, are you okay?" he asked.

"Yes, I just need to talk to you about something I felt tonight," I smiled, hoping to reassure him.

Taliesin arched an eyebrow at me then turned to sign a program.

"Ladies and gentleman," Michael called out. "I am sorry but my performers need to go. Thank you so much for coming to see us, and I hope you will visit Cirque du Feu Magique again soon."

A few people rushed to get a last autograph, while the rest left. The energy slowly died down, which made the anger even stronger.

"Madam, Sir, I'm afraid you'll need to leave now," said Michael to the couple.

"Actually," said the man, his Russian accent thick and sharp, "I would speak to my son."

"Papa," Sasha said, eyes wide as the tall man walked over in long, measured strides.

I trembled at the burst of cold fear, but Sasha quickly pulled his emotions in as his face became blank.

"Sasha." The woman rushed over and embraced him. "I have missed you so much. You've grown, you're taller than me now. You were beautiful tonight."

Sasha sighed. "Mama."

"Your babushka and I cried as we made latkes for Hanukkah when we realized you weren't going to be eating with us." She wiped a tear from her eye. "You always ate so many you gave yourself a tummy ache."

Sasha smiled. "My friends made me latkes. They weren't as good as yours, but it was very kind of them."

"Enough," snapped his father. Hot anger flared as he began to speak—his words cold and sharp in Russian. His words were vile, and if Sasha's father respected him at all, he would never speak to his son like that, let alone in front of people. I did my best to ignore what was being said.

I wanted to go to Sasha, but Taliesin held me back.

"Lev," said his mother in Russian, placing her hand on her husband's arm. "Please, he is a boy, of course he is going to want to try new things. And he looked so lovely, I could see the skills he learned in ballet during his performance. It warmed my heart."

His father ranted some more.

"No," said Sasha in English. "No, Papa, I won't stop. I do practice ballet some, but I am here touring with this circus right now, and I want to perform. I love silks and I am learning trampoline and German wheel."

I shivered at the coldness of his father's voice, as he snapped at him in Russian.

"I love this more than ballet," Sasha said.

His dad slapped him. Okay, that was it. I wrenched out of Taliesin's grip. "Leave him alone," I said.

His father sneered at me. "Or is this little tart what you love more than ballet?"

Whoa, wait a minute.

"Papa, I am not a little boy you can bully into doing what you want. This is what I want, and I'm not leaving, and I'm not stopping, and if you hit me again, I will hit you back."

I stood near Sasha supporting but not wanting to interfere. Okay, I lied. I wanted to kick his dad hard, in his stomach, but respected Sasha so I stood there being supportive, and gave his father the evil eye.

"If you don't give this up, you don't need to bother coming home when this craziness is over with," his father said.

"I'm sorry you feel that way." Sasha stood there straight and strong.

His father cursed in Russian under his breath. "Come, Alexandra."

Sasha gave his mom a soft, sad smile. He expected his mom to follow his father. My heart broke.

"No, Lev. I'll meet you back at the hotel. I'm going to take our son out to eat and catch up with him." She squeezed Sasha's arm.

I blinked to hide my tears. No crying, come on suck it up.

Lev sneered, made a dramatic turn, and stalked away. Drama queen.

I stopped myself from sticking my tongue out at his retreating back.

Miu glided forward, still dressed in her kimono for the Japanese fan dance. She reached up, and placed her hand glowed against Sasha's cheek where his father had hit him. "There—all better."

"Thank you. Miu, this is my mother, Alexandra Koen. Mother, this is Miu."

Alexandra shook Miu's hand. "You are the healer, da. Did you heal my son?"

Miu smiled. "Yes, and of course, he's my friend."

"Thank you. Sasha, introduce me to everyone."

Sasha smiled, the lightness and love coming from him made my heart ache. I hadn't realized how unhappy he'd felt. I stepped back and let the others crowd around Sasha while I tried to gather myself.

"Sapphire, come and meet my Mama."

"It's very nice to meet you," I said, holding out my hand. Her eyes widened at the spark of heat. "Sorry, I do that sometimes," I said.

"Sapphire is the Jewel, the one from Babushka's stories. Sapphire, my mama, Alexandra, one of Russia's finest prima ballerinas."

She smiled. "Oh, you. That was a long time ago. It's nice to meet you. I'm sorry about the scene."

Sasha chuckled. "At least Sapphire was the only one who could understand what Papa was saying."

"You speak Russian?" she asked.

"Um, no. I can understand any language a Child of Fire is speaking," I said.

Alexandra's eyes widened.

"I tried my best to not listen—it seemed private."

"Thank you, you're a good girl." She squeezed my hand before letting go. "Come, Sasha, I am sure you're famished, and we have so much to talk about."

* * *

I lay on a stack of mats backstage waiting for Kayin to finish getting ready. My shoulder ached a little, probably from resisting Taliesin as he held me back from kicking Sasha's father. Closing my eyes, I relaxed into the mat. All I wanted was some food and sleep. I smiled as a body hovered over mine. A spicy citrus scent tickled my nose.

"Yes, Shin," I said.

"Want to go and get some Korean food with me? There is a place only a few blocks away."

"I'm tired. You'll have to carry me."

Shin chuckled. "Of course, princess."

I opened my eyes. He held push-up position above me, as if he hadn't done two performances today. I wrapped my arms and legs around Shin. With a sigh he pushed up and stood.

"Scoot," he said.

I slid around to his back. Shin clasped his hands together under my legs to support me. I wonder how long the piggyback ride would last.

"What are you two up to?" Kayin asked wrapping his scarf around his neck.

I tightened my legs and leaned back, reaching with my hands to get my stuff. "We're going out for Korean food. Want to come?" I asked, putting on my coat, bag, hat and scarf.

"You're going to have to help," Shin said holding out his jacket.

I helped him on with his jacket and scarf on before wrapping my arms around his shoulders. I turned to Kayin, who took pictures of us with his phone. Rude! "So?"

"If it's okay with Shin, I'd love to come," Kayin said.

"Of course, it's fine with me." Shin said, placing his hands behind him again to help support me. "Someone will need to help carry the princess here."

Kayin laughed as we walked out the performers' exit. Weak circles of yellow light lit up patches of the dark narrow alley behind the theater.

Shin patted my leg. "You might have to get down."

I looked ahead. A man stood in the shadows against the wall. He walked towards us, kilt swaying around his legs, curls falling over the shoulders of his leather jacket as he adjusted his yoga bag. "It's okay. Ramsey?"

"Hey, I hoped I'd catch you," he stepped into the light. "I thought you weren't hurt?"

"She's not," Shin said. "Just lazy. Wait—did something happen last night? Is that why your shoulder is injured?"

"No, I mean I messed up during the routine at the matinee, you saw me," I said.

"Yes, but then why would Ramsey think you were hurt?" Shin asked.

"Well, I fell?" It sounded more like a question then a statement. Lying is so not my thing.

"At the gala? You?" Shin didn't sound convinced.

"It's my fault," Ramsey said. "I gave her a glass of champagne and didn't realize she hadn't eaten recently."

Thank goodness he lied so well.

"Lightweight. I'm not sharing my soju with you," Shin teased.

"Korean?" Ramsey asked.

"Yes," Kayin said. "You should come."

"Cheers, that'd be brilliant. If you two don't mind."

"Of course," I said.

Shin chuckled. "It's fine with me. The more, the merrier."

"So, Ramsey, what did you do today?" I asked, hopping down to walk.

"We opened for a bigger group at a pub. We just finished about thirty minutes ago."

"Did it go well?" I asked glaring at Shin over my shoulder, as he let us walk ahead of him and Kayin. I knew Shin was watching Ramsey's butt.

"Yeah it did, and your shows? You hurt yourself?" Ramsey asked.

I huffed. "I slipped and tweaked my shoulder a bit. It'll be fine tomorrow."

"Here we are," Shin said opening a large wooden door. Korean symbols inlaid in silver shone in the light of the streetlamp.

We were ushered into a booth. I slid in next to Ramsey, leaving Kayin and Shin to share the other bench. Shin spoke to the waitress, and she smiled and hurried off.

"It's beautiful," I said. The walls were painted a dark blue, and the benches and chairs were covered in a rich cream colored fabric. Photographs of Korea and small wooden shelves displaying statues, pottery, and dolls from Korea decorated the walls.

The waitress brought a pot of tea, and two bottles of soju, and passed out menus.

"Sorry, you two are too young to drink," Shin said opening his blue-green bottle.

"What is it?" Kayin asked.

"Rice wine. Do you want a sip?" Shin asked holding out the bottle.

Kayin took a sip, wrinkled his nose, and handed the soju back. "Sour."

Ramsey held out his bottle, but I shook my head.

"So what do you recommend?" Kayin asked.

I hid my grin behind the cup of tea as Shin leaned over Kayin's shoulder to help him pick something to eat.

"This restaurant offers a lot of vegetarian options." Shin pointed at the menu, his blue streaked black bangs hanging down over his face.

I felt Kayin's embarrassment, his ebony cheeks not betraying the heat that I was sure filled them.

"Do you like spicy food?" Shin asked.

"Yes," Kayin said.

"These are good." Shin leaned a little bit closer.

"Have you eaten Korean before?" Ramsey asked.

"Only what Shin made for us. You?"

"Yes, I usually get the grilled eel or abalone porridge. What are you thinking of getting?"

"I'm torn between the sweet potato noodles with tofu and veggies or the veggie and tofu Bibimbap," I said.

The waitress came up and took our orders. Kayin and I fumbled with our menus in order to quickly pick something and try to pronounce it. Between our mangling of the Korean and our accents, mine American and Kayin's Zimbabwean, the poor waitress looked completely lost. Shin ordered for us, his lips twitching in amusement.

"Extra tofu for me," I said to Shin who nodded and told the waitress.

"I guess you like tofu," Ramsey said.

"Protein is important," I said. "Something Anali and Gavin drilled into our heads when we first started touring."

Ramsey chuckled. "When I started touring my mum kept telling me my prick would fall off if I drank too much and slept around."

Shin chuckled. "Yes, my mom is always telling me to be careful, and to wants to know when I'll come home and settle down with a nice Korean girl."

"Doesn't seem like your thing," Ramsey said.

Shin wiggled his eyebrows. "We'll moms don't need to know everything, now, do they?"

I reached across the table and squeezed Kayin's hand. His nervousness buzzed around me.

"How.." Kayin cleared his throat. "How do you think she'll react?"

Shin frowned. "At first she'll cry, and ask if I'm sure, and wonder what I'll do with my life. Then she'll think it's all her fault and wail about how she ruined me and now I won't give her grandkids. Then she'll calm down, and tell everyone she always knew in her heart, because a mother knows these things, and then she'll start trying to set me up with a nice professional gay man who wants to have a family so she can still get grandchildren from me."

"That sounds like fun," I said, heavy on the sarcasm.

Ramsey laughed. "She sounds like my mum. My youngest sister came out last year, and that is exactly what mum did."

"That doesn't sound so bad. Why not tell her now?" Kayin asked.

"Well," Shin said. "I want to tell her in person, and if she's holding a grandchild from my older brother then she won't yell as loudly."

"What about your dad?" I asked. "Will he be okay?"

"Actually I'm pretty sure my dad is gay. He's great, and he loves my mom. But I see where his eye wanders. And I know he's had affairs; we pretend it's with women. My mom huffs and randomly starts talking about the inherent weakness of men. Then my dad starts spending more time at home and buys her stuff."

Kayin fiddled with his silverware. "So you aren't worried about losing your family?"

"Oh." Shin's smile was soft and sad as he looked at Kayin. "I see. Um, no, I'm not worried about that."

Kayin nodded. "It feels like something you can't take back, like once you admit it to yourself, or another person than that's it, your life has changed."

My heart ached for Kayin. I could sense his fear and sadness thick in the air. I wanted to reach for him, to hug him, and comfort him. But it seemed like if I did that then I was admitting his feelings for him. Acknowledging that he was gay, when he is the one who should do it. Under the table Ramsey grabbed my hand and squeezed.

"I know my sister felt scared. She told me first. I told her that I would always be her family, no matter what. I also have friends who were kicked out of homes, and they made new families," Ramsey said.

I sniffed, hoping to lighten the mood. "I've already told you, Big Brother, that you are stuck with me forever."

Kayin smiled. "I won't forget, Little Sister."

Shin shivered. "Sounds like a warning to me."

"Hey," I shouted, pretending to be offended.

The waitress came with our meals. I breathed in the spicy garlic, and tangy kimchi scents. The table was covered in food. Fried dumplings, and spring rolls, both vegetarian. Little bowls filled with kimchi, mung bean sprouts with sesame oil, marinated cucumbers, and bamboo shoots with chilies were in the center of the table for us to share.

She set a hot, black stone bowl in front of me. I warmed my hands against the rough sides of the bowl while looking at the beautiful dish. Thin slices of carrots, red bell peppers, mung bean sprouts, tofu, and spinach all lightly cooked, seasoned, and placed in individual sections on top of seasoned rice, and on top of that was an egg.

"Now," said Shin who also got Bibimbap but with spicy marinated beef. "You pour on hot sauce and stir it all up."

He handed me the bottle. I squeezed out the dark red paste. Dipping the end of my chopstick in the sauce I found it to me a medium heat and slightly sweet. I added more, then ruined the beautiful arrangement by stirring everything together with a silver long-handled spoon. My eyes closed as I took a bite, this was comfort food. Warm, flavorful, and hearty. "This is wonderful."

Kayin glared at his chopsticks and then did his best to scoop some of his Bibimbap into his mouth. I grinned as half of the food fell back into his bowl.

"Do you like it?" I asked to cover up watching him work the chopsticks.

He nodded and swallowed. "Yes, it's very good, not very spicy though."

"This will fix that," Shin said handing him a small bowl. "This is garlic chili sauce, use a little at a time until you find the right amount."

I hummed as I took another bite. This was the perfect food for such a cold night.

"How do you do that so easily?" Kayin grumbled.

Ramsey waved his spoon in front of him. "I don't bother with those bloody things."

"You don't have to use chopsticks," Shin said, pointing to his spoon. "I'd rather you are comfortable and enjoy your meal."

Kayin smiled. "I'll switch later. I need to practice if I want to get better right?"

Shin smiled back. "I'm sure you'll pick it up quickly."

So good. I was hungry. If it was just the guys, I would have been shoveling the food into my mouth, but I restrained myself in front of Ramsey. "This is so good, thanks for inviting us to dinner," I said, using my chopsticks to get a dumpling.

Shin nodded. "Their food is good, even better with company. Thanks for coming with me."

Kayin took a bite of kimchi. "This is good, but your mom's is better."

Shin grinned. "I'll tell her you said that, and she'll love you forever."

Kayin's embarrassment prickled against my shields.

"So do you have shows all week?" Ramsey asked once we made sizable dents in our meals.

"We have Tuesday and Friday off," I said. "What about you?"

"Let's see, we have gigs Tuesday, Thursday, Friday, and Saturday nights. One is a wedding, and those are usually entertaining." Ramsey said.

"What is the craziest thing you've seen at a wedding?" Shin asked.

Ramsey snickered. "Okay this one time, bloody hell it was bad, during my break I heard a noise coming from the coatroom. I thought it was Murdock with one of the bridesmaids, which was the norm. I took out my phone hoping to get a picture to use against him later, and there is the groom and the mother-of-the-bride snogging against all these fancy fur coats."

"People do that in public?" Kayin asked.

"Some people," Shin said. "But not everyone wants to."

"Anyway," Ramsey said. "As quietly as I can I back away and bump right into the father-of-the-bride. And the man, he just shrugs and says. 'At least now she won't have to make up stupid excuses to leave the house.' I about died."

"That did not happen," Shin said, his eyes sparkling.

Ramsey nodded. "It did."

"Oh my god, that's terrible," I said.

Ramsey ran his hand through his brown curls and bit his lip. "Should I have told one of the 'drunken relative falls into a cake' stories?"

"Maybe you could tell one of those so I can get that image out of my head," Kayin said, his nose wrinkling and his brow drawn down into a frown.

I smiled, poor Kayin.

"Well, the worst one…" Ramsey began.

We left the restaurant close to midnight, my belly full, my cheeks hurt from laughing, and I wanted to crawl into bed. Ramsey curled his arm around my waist as we rode in a taxi back to the hotel.

"Text me tomorrow and let me know what your plans are," Ramsey said. "Maybe we can hang out."

"Okay, sounds good," I said. The taxi pulled up to the hotel. Ramsey leaned forward, and his eyes flicked down to my lips.

"Sapphire, we need to go now," Kayin said his dark eyes focused on Ramsey.

Ramsey smiled and leaned back against the seat. "I'll talk to you tomorrow, hen."

"Good night," I said trying not to trip as I got out of the taxi.

Kayin took my arm as if he worried I would try and jump back into the taxi and go home with Ramsey.

"Have you finished all your school work?" Kayin asked as we got onto the elevator.

I glared at Shin, chuckling behind me.

"I have a French test, and a science test, then I am finished. You?" I said.

"I need to do the history paper and the math test," Kayin said. "Maybe we could do our work together tomorrow."

I rolled my eyes and squeezed Kayin's arm. "That sounds good. After yoga and breakfast?"

"Yes, that'll be good."

"Your virtue is safe for one more day," Shin teased as the doors opened and we got off on our floor.

"I'm not sure I like Ramsey," Kayin said.

"Big Brother," I said, hugging him. "Thank you for looking out for me."

Kayin hugged me tight. "Thank you for being my family, Little Sister."

"Always, no matter what."

Kayin let go of me and I hugged Shin good night before heading into my room.

"Hey Miu," I said.

Miu put down her manga. "Did you have fun?"

"Yeah, we went out for Korean food," I said getting my things ready for bed. "You and Taliesin?"

"Hmm, yes," she said before picking up her manga.

Okay, odd, normally Miu over shares. Oh well. It's not any of my business.

Chapter Fourteen

Miniature dragons ran around me under Akasha's turquoise sky. Shamash and Aya had healed my shoulder earlier, and now I played with the two small dragons while their mother hunted for fish in the river. The green-gray one ran up my back and hid in my hair. Its warm smoky breath tickled my ear. Her brother's butt and tail wagged as he stalked around me, his brown scales doing nothing to hide him in the bright grass. A cricket chirped, and he jumped into the air, his wings flapping uselessly as he fell back down emitting a puff of smoke and fire. I laughed, careful to not dislodge the baby miniature dragons.

"Sapphire," Aya said walking towards me a frown marring her face. "You need to go—he needs you."

"What? Who?" I asked settling the baby dragon on the ground before standing up.

Aya kissed my forehead, her power comforting and insistent. "Wake-up."

Gasping, I sat up in bed. Miu huffed in her sleep and sprawled out over her mattress. Red numbers glowed in the dark room: five-thirty. What kind of evil is up this early?

Climbing out of bed I went into the hallway, the carpet cool on my bare feet. I pressed my ear to Gavin and Anali's door and didn't hear anything. Walking down the hallway I passed the elevator and turned the corner. Kayin stood juggling in black cotton pajama bottoms and dark red long sleeved top.

"Kayin, what's going on?"

"Sasha, woke up at five and said he was going to the gym, and I couldn't stop thinking about … things and so I came out here so I wouldn't wake up Taliesin," he said not stopping the five balls dancing in the air.

I guess two of my guys needed help this morning. "Go get dressed. We need to go help Sasha."

Kayin caught the balls. "Five minutes?"

"We'll meet at the elevator," I said, walking back to my room.

I slept in black yoga pants and a long sleeved brown shirt with gold cheetah prints on it, good enough. I wrote Miu a note, grabbed my bag and the layers I would need for the dark, cold December morning.

Kayin waited for me. "So what's going on?"

I pushed the button for the lobby. "I don't know. I was dreaming in Akasha, and Aya told me he needed me and woke me up. You seem to need to talk, but I'm worried about Sasha, since he left the hotel. Did he say anything?"

Kayin shook his head. "No, I woke up hearing him moving around the room. He was going to the gym since he couldn't sleep."

"Feel like running?" I asked as we walked out the glass doors. The cold wet air stung my cheeks.

Kayin bounced a few times, warming up his legs. "You hate running."

"I'm worried," I said.

"Let's go."

We started to jog, I forced myself to let my muscles warm up before speeding up. It didn't take long, or more likely I was impatient. "Okay," I said and began to run.

Kayin ran beside me, our breath came out in foggy white puffs. My chest ached by the time I saw the school. The lungfuls of cold air were painful. We leapt up the stairs and burst into the gym. An early morning Zumba was starting in the dance studio to the right and on the left, Sasha.

"Oh," I gasped. "I didn't realize."

Sasha danced—no not danced—flew, leapt, and flowed across the floor with passion, power, and grace. I'd never seen him move like this. Careful to be quiet, we went in. A blaring classical piece shut out any noise or thoughts. We took off our jackets and sat in the corner and watched. Sasha's dance was filled with agony. Even without my empathy, his pain and anger were easy to recognize.

Kayin wrapped an arm around me as hot tears burned my cold cheeks.

The music faded. Sasha's labored breathing echoed across the dance hall. His arms hung at his sides and his faced turned up toward the ceiling. I held my breath. He didn't move. I stood up.

"Sasha."

He turned, his eyes red and bloodshot. He rubbed his eyes with his bruised knuckles.

"Oh," I ran over to him and hugged him. He stood still for a moment, his body tense. Sometimes you have to hold onto boys longer. Several minutes later he started to shake, and his emotions washed over me as he wrapped his arms around me. I held him, just being there, not saying anything until I felt him relax and let go of some of the anger and pain. Sasha took a deep breath.

I stepped back. "I'm sorry. Is your mom okay?"

"Da. I'm happy I got to see her. We talked for hours. He was waiting at the hotel."

"What happened?" Kayin asked.

"He thought my mother would talk some sense into me," Sasha said, his bitterness sharp. "When I was a child she always smoothed everything over."

"And this time?" I asked.

Sasha smiled, his blue-gray eyes shining with tears. "She told me I was beautiful. That she was proud of me, and I should follow my heart."

I smiled and blinked back tears. She was my new favorite person. "She's right. You're amazing at silks."

"And your father?" Kayin asked.

Sasha rubbed the back of his hand. "He disagreed."

"Are you hurt?" Kayin asked.

I took Sasha's hands and inspected them.

"No more than a hard training session with Shin," Sasha said.

"What happened?"

Sasha shrugged. "He had been drinking and tried to hit me. It didn't go well for him."

"Is your mother okay?" Kayin asked.

"Yes, he never hits her, and he never beat me or anything. He was raised being hit as punishment and continued the practice with me." Sasha shook his head. His red-streaked, honey-blond hair fell perfectly into place, of course. "Anyway, onto important things. Why are you two here so early?"

"To see you, to make sure you're okay," I said. "And I'm so glad we came. I've never seen you dance before—you're amazing."

Kayin nodded. "Yes, you should add ballet to your act."

I clapped. "I wonder if Taliesin could learn some moves?"

"What am I learning?" Taliesin said. Miu yawned and waved.

"What are you doing here?" I asked.

"We felt a disturbance in the Force," Taliesin said.

Obviously, he hadn't drunk any coffee yet.

"We both woke up and knew we needed to come here," Miu said.

Sasha rolled his eyes. "Why all this fuss? I am fine."

"You're family," I said. "We're family, and we want to be here for you."

Sasha froze for a moment. "Thank you."

"So what does this mean?" Miu asked. "Us being a family?"

They all looked at me. Why in the hell would they look at me? I know nothing about being part of a family. "Um, well, I guess it means we plan on spending time together away from the circus."

"Like going out to eat?" Kayin asked.

"Yes," I said with more enthusiasm than necessary making the others jump a bit. I had no idea what I was talking about. "Last night we went out to dinner with Shin. He took us to a Korean place, and we talked. Maybe we should do that? We can each pick a place and share food we love or want to try and tell stories." Oh god, that sounds like the dorkiest thing ever.

"I've never tasted Russian food," Miu said.

"I've eaten borscht," said Taliesin.

"London has to have a Russian restaurant," Kayin added.

Sasha smiled. "They do, I found a few close by. I figured I'd go while I was here."

"We can all go," I said. "And instead of waiting for Gavin and Anali to plan outings we can each take a turn. I mean we're here for what? Another three or four weeks? And families go on outings and stuff together right?"

Taliesin smiled at me. "Yes, they do. My mom always dragged me places."

"Mine too," said Miu.

Kayin nodded. "I went places with my dad sometimes."

Sasha grinned. "Can we go to lunch today?"

"Sounds good to me." I needed to text Ramsey and tell him I couldn't meet up.

The others all nodded.

"I need some coffee," Taliesin said.

I looked at my watch. "They should have breakfast ready."

"So," said Miu. "Now that we are talking and sharing does this mean we can ask who you've been sneaking off with?"

Everyone froze.

"I didn't realize there's anything to talk about," I said putting on my jacket.

"Stop," said Taliesin. "If she is going to be stubborn, then I need coffee before we talk."

What? Rude!

"Yes," Miu said with a grin. "Coffee is a must."

Double rude!

* * *

Four sets of eyes stared at me. I guess the coffee had kicked in, and they felt ready for an important discussion. I still didn't see the big deal. "What?" I asked taking a bite of beans on toast. So good—why didn't Americans eat this?

They all looked at each other, obviously having some kind of silent communication. Brandon came in with a tray of pastries. Yes, distraction!

"Good morning, can I get you anything else?" he asked, setting the pastries on the buffet.

I walked over and grabbed two of the chocolate almond pastries. Score! "I'm fine thanks."

Miu cleared her throat. "You should order some eggs. You have a lot of carbs going on, and you know how Anali is about our food."

I pouted, but picked up the menu.

"The chef's special is eggs Benedict, with ham or steamed asparagus," Brandon said, taking out his note pad.

"Steamed asparagus for me," I said handing him the menu.

The others ordered, and I focused on my pastry.

"My grandmother asked me to check in and find out if her reading helped," Brandon whispered as other performers came in.

"We're fine," I said. "Not sure how her reading fits into everything yet."

"I'll let her know, and thanks." Brandon went to take other orders.

"Should we tell him about whatever sucked the magic out of the gnome?" Taliesin asked.

"No, I don't think so. As far as I know he doesn't even realize he has any Fae in him. I doubt if he even believes in mythical creatures." I sighed. "How do I explain that?"

"Okay, enough of that. I want to hear about your new guy," Miu said.

Their curiosity lapped and tugged on my shields. Damn, I shouldn't have ordered eggs, now I'm forced to wait. "I'm not sure what to say. His name is Ramsey McDaniel, he plays the cello for the Water Nymphs, and he's a selkie."

"He was also nearby twice when you were in danger," Taliesin said.

"What?" Sasha asked. "When?"

"When you helped me out at the antique store," I said. "And at the gala."

"What was he doing at the gala?" Miu asked.

"Performing," I said taking a big bite of chocolate almond goodness so I wouldn't have to say more.

"With the Water Nymphs?" Taliesin's white eyebrow arched in amusement.

"It's not his band. He was asked to join when the last cellist left. Anyway I'm not sure why he's so interesting."

"Maybe," said Kayin, "because you keep going off with him and no one knows where you are."

"I always text Gavin and let him know what's going on. So what touristy things should we plan on doing?"

"The Tower of London," said Sasha.

Miu sighed. "I want to see Buckingham Palace."

"I don't know, I'll have to look at one of the guide books," Kayin said.

"I'd like to go to the National Gallery or the Tate Museum," Taliesin added.

I nodded. "Okay we should get a map and look over our schedule and make a plan."

Brandon came back with a tray loaded with plates. He set the eggs Benedict down in front of me. The pale yellow sauce glistened with butter and lemon, and bright green asparagus tips peeked out from under the egg. I cut a bite, popped it into my mouth, and moaned. So rich and creamy. I focused on my breakfast instead of the curious, worried, slightly embarrassed emotions bouncing between my friends.

"So have you guys worked out already?" Michael asked, looking at all the food we were eating.

"Sasha did," I said.

Michael ran a hand through his short brown hair as he sighed. You know the heartfelt adult sigh when faced with irritating teenagers. "By eleven, I expect to see you in the gym and doing at least an hour of yoga or strength conditioning."

"Yes, Michael," we said.

He rolled his eyes and joined his daughter at another table. Nyota waved at us.

"It's almost eight," said Sasha. "What should we do until it's time to go?"

"Let's watch a movie," I said. "We can meet in our room in thirty minutes?" I still wanted to talk with Taliesin.

"That will give me time to shower," Sasha said.

Miu grinned. "Thank goodness."

* * *

"So what's up?" Taliesin asked as we walked through Kensington Park.

I twisted my ring. How was I going to say this without sounding like an idiot? "Yesterday when I felt the anger coming from Sasha's parents during the performance I felt something else."

Taliesin frowned. "What?"

"It took a while to figure out, but I finally did. I suppose I could talk to Anali, but she's so sick. Maybe it's not a big deal, but I'd never even thought about it before."

Taliesin grabbed my hand. "Sapphire, you're babbling. Calm down and tell me what you felt."

"Okay, last night I felt a few people, not many, a few sick, evil people hoped you would fall." I shook my head. "Not just fall but fall and hurt yourselves, and after what happened to that poor performer . . ." I tightened my grip on his hand.

"Sapphire, I know."

"What do you mean you know?"

He smiled a sad smile at me. "It's part of human nature. Think of all the horrid reality shows out there where people love seeing others humiliated and watching them fail."

"But . . ." How could anyone want Taliesin hurt?

He pulled me close, and I wrapped my arms around him. His heart beat under my cheek, strong and steady. "I was ten when I realized there were people like that in the world."

"What happened?" I asked not moving.

"It was the first year I was training with the San Francisco Center for the Circus Arts. I was watching their summer show, and one of the performers fell and broke his leg." Taliesin shivered and his arms tightened around me. "My mom had me stay in the seat and ran up to help, while others got people out of the theater.

"The guy sitting next to me, there was something wrong. His eyes were glassy, and he was taking shallow breaths. I asked if he was okay and when he didn't respond I touched his hand. He was excited about the accident. The sound of the bone, the scream of the performer, the sight of the bone sticking out of his thigh, and the blood pooling onto the stage. He loved it all."

"Oh, God. Taliesin, that's horrible."

"It's okay, Sapphire. It doesn't upset me anymore."

"How can it not?" I said not ready to let go of him yet. "I want to go and hurt those people."

Taliesin chuckled. "I know what they're feeling isn't about me. Did you know my mom sews all my costumes?"

Okay, off topic. "Your mom makes all our costumes."

"No," Taliesin said running his hand over my back. "She designs them all, but she has people who work for her and do a lot of the sewing, but she sews mine. And while she sews, she pictures me safe. It might be silly but to me it feels like a layer of protection and the crowd's thoughts can't reach me."

"That's sweet," I said.

Taliesin sighed. "She started doing it when I was little and it stuck."

"I'm glad you're safe." I squeezed him and stepped back. "I still want to kick them."

Taliesin chuckled and turned to go back to the hotel. "Well since kicking people who make you mad seems to be your go-to thought, I'm not surprised by that."

"I don't—" Oh wait, yes, I kind of do. "I don't actually kick them, I just think about kicking them."

"Maybe I should get you steel-toed boots for Christmas."

I took Taliesin's arm. "That sounds like trouble."

"Probably. So I have a question for you."

"Okay," I said. I always worry when people warn me they're going to ask me a question.

"How do you feel about the baby?"

I shrugged. "Gavin and Anali are happy but worried. So I'm happy for them and hoping everything will be okay."

"Yes," said Taliesin slowly as if talking to a child. "But how do you feel about the baby?"

"I don't see how we can fit a baby into what we do," I said. "I mean when we're driving in the RV, I guess it won't be so bad, but what about when the baby starts crawling or walking around? And once Anali wants to perform again, do we pass the baby around backstage?"

"True, it'll be interesting to see how and if they can make everything work, but that doesn't tell me how you feel about it."

"How am I supposed to feel? The baby doesn't have anything to do with me?"

"Well," said Taliesin. "Some people get jealous and afraid that a new baby will take away attention and love from them."

I snorted. "It's a baby, of course it'll need more attention. That's how things work. When someone needs attention focused on them, the others have to accept it."

"What about them loving you?"

"Of course they will love the baby more. It's their baby, their child. I'm not. I never will be. Why would I expect them to love me the same?"

Taliesin looked at me his blue eyes soft. For a moment I felt a wave of sadness, then he closed off his emotion. "On a lighter note. What movie are you making us watch?"

I huffed. Making? As if he wasn't looking forward to it. "We should watch a Christmas movie."

"Like *Miracle on 34th Street* or *It's a Wonderful Life?*" Taliesin asked.

"I was thinking, *While You Were Sleeping*, or *Love, Actually.*"

* * *

I felt a hand shaking my shoulder.

"Sapphire, wake up."

I opened my eyes. Gavin knelt next to me, his pale green eyes crinkled in amusement. Credits scrolled down the TV. I stretched a bit and realized that I was surrounded. My head lay on Kayin's thigh, Miu's head lay on my stomach, and Taliesin's legs entwined with mine.

"You guys look like a pile of puppies. Why are you sleeping?" Gavin asked.

"We woke up too early, and then ate a lot. What's up?"

"Michael said you guys were working out at eleven, and Anali wants me to go and do something today."

I grinned. "She kicked you out."

"She said I was making her anxious." Gavin looked at the door towards their room.

"You guys aren't used to being cooped up in a room together twenty-four seven. And you're both normally so active, she probably needs a bit of breathing room. Maybe after lunch you could go for a walk in the park," I said. "If she's feeling well."

"She still gets sick, but most afternoons she's feeling better. Good idea. You're going to make a great big sister." Gavin clapped his hands. "Now how should we wake everyone up?"

Me? A big sister? Is that how they thought of me? Of us as a family?

"We're awake—just pretending to give you privacy." Miu sat up.

"What time is it?" asked Taliesin, stretching. I squeaked as he moved my legs.

Gavin looked at his watch. "Ten-fifteen."

"That's enough time to get ready," Kayin said, jiggling his leg.

Sighing, I sat up. "Should we meet at the elevators in ten minutes?"

"Fifteen," Sasha said. "There are three of us and only one bathroom."

"Can I wait here?" Gavin asked. "Anali is napping."

"Sure," I said. "Give me a minute." I freshened up. Seriously my breath must smell gross, and I needed to pee.

"So," Gavin asked when I came back brushing my hair. "What's new? I feel odd asking that, we haven't been apart like this since we started touring."

I started braiding my hair. "Not much, did you hear about Sasha's dad?"

"No. Did his parents get to see him perform?" Gavin smiled.

"Yep," I said and explained what happened.

Gavin's jaw clenched and his eyes narrowed, his anger burned hot and sharp against my empathic bubble. "He hurt Sasha?"

"Yes, but Sasha took care of himself. And we decided to do more family kind of things together, you know like go out to eat, watch movies, and do touristy things," I said.

"I think that's a great idea," Gavin said. "And I know Anali and I would love to join you once she's feeling better."

"Ready," Miu said. She wore lavender yoga pants with a pale gray long-sleeved tee shirt with smiling, dancing cupcakes on it.

I smiled. My gray yoga pants and dark green shirt looked depressing next to Miu's.

"Well, come on," Gavin said.

Kayin stood by the elevators. "They're just finishing."

"I'm ready," Taliesin said, walking towards us finishing his braid. "Sasha is almost ready."

"Sorry, my mama called. She and my papa are headed back home today," Sasha said.

"Is your mom okay?" I asked.

Sasha nodded. "My father is angry, but he won't hurt her."

"Are you sure?" Gavin asked. "I can help her get away from him if she needs it."

Sasha smiled, a tinge of evil to it. "My mama's brother, he is a very important person with very scary friends. Papa wouldn't dare hurt her, and in fact is probably going to try and make-up on the flight home. If my uncle finds out how he treated me..." Sasha shrugged. "Who knows what could happen?"

"Good, let me know if anything changes. Now let's go work out."

Chapter Fifteen

"Gavin must be going crazy trapped in the hotel," Taliesin said as he sat down and scooted into the booth.

Sasha groaned as he sat. "I am not sure I will recover in time for show tonight."

I sat next to Taliesin and scooted close to make room for Kayin. Miu and Sasha sat on the other side of the booth. Sasha smiled as he looked around the Russian restaurant with its rich red walls painted with black and gold patterns. The waitress set down a glass pot of tea and glass teacups with silver lace holders.

I opened the menu. "So what should we get?"

"I think we should order several dishes and share," Kayin said. "I want to try everything."

"What a great idea," Miu said.

Sasha ordered for us. "Okay," Sasha said once the appetizers arrived. "Everything but the smoked halibut and caviar is vegetarian."

"What's this?" I asked. Picking up a spoon and dipping it into the purple red pureed soup. It was sweet and warm.

"It's borscht, a beet soup. My mama said it was good for your blood and had the cook make it three times a week," Sasha said. "In summer it would be served cold."

"It's richer than the borscht I had before," said Taliesin. "It's really good."

Kayin held up a crescent moon pastry. "These are yummy, cheese and spinach I think."

"Yes, my babushka would make them for parties. I would sit at the table with her and help fill the dough with different kinds of fillings. My favorite are the potato and cheese ones. I ordered some of those for the main course."

"So is there a special way to eat these?" Miu asked pointing a platter of smoked fish and tiny pancakes.

Sasha gray eyes looked a bit sad. "My papa has a smoker; he goes fishing with friends and smokes his own fish. It's the only cooking he ever does."

We all froze for a second. Um, what am I supposed to say to that?

"Sorry, so you take an oladji," he said picking up a tiny pancake. "A bit of sour cream, add onion or a slice of egg if you like them and either a piece of smoked halibut or the caviar."

The soup reminded me of the pureed beets at the restaurant, but sweeter. I scooped a little sour cream onto my spoon then filled the rest with the thick purple red soup. "I like this."

"The smoked halibut tastes so good," Miu said spreading caviar, onions, and sour cream on the little pancake. "Yum, this is good too."

"What do you think, Sasha?" Kayin asked picking up another one of the little pastries.

Sasha nodded spooning up some of the borscht. "It's very good. But some day, I'll take you home and let my babushka cook for you."

"Well, it's unfair to compare any cooking to a grandmother's cooking," Kayin said.

"Why?" I asked.

"Grandmothers always cook the very best," Taliesin said.

Sasha smiled. "It's the love. That's what my babushka says, that because she loves me so much and wants me to be happy and healthy all her prayers and wishes for me go into her cooking, and that's what makes it taste so good."

Taliesin chuckled. "My grandma said almost the same thing when I asked why her food tasted better than anyone else."

"Grandmas don't lie," said Kayin. "And mine said the same thing."

"Well," said Miu. "My sobo, my grandmother, can burn rice, she's an awful cook. My dad says he's such a good cook because he didn't want to starve as a child."

I laughed, wondering if either of my grandmothers were good cooks.

"So what is all of this?" I asked when our main courses were delivered.

Sasha smiled. "There are bell peppers stuffed with rice, fruit, cheese and topped with tomato sauce. I would pick peppers on my grandparent's farm for this dish. Rice covered with sour cream, mushrooms, and gherkins, and dumplings filled with potatoes or cabbage and cheese."

"So what's going on with the whole portal thing?" Taliesin asked once we served ourselves.

"I've had a Dream—well several." Sasha ran a hand through his hair. "Sapphire needs to talk to a tree."

"A hamadryad, I need to talk to a hamadryad and there is one at Hampton Court. I told Gavin, and he said he would make plans to get us there," I said.

"Okay anything else?" Miu said.

"Well," began Sasha. "I keep Dreaming about a doorway. A large castle doorway, no castle, no ruins, just a doorway on top of a hill in a field."

Kayin shook his head. "I've never seen a castle doorway by itself."

"Tell them about Avalon and the Earth magic," Miu said.

"Avalon?" Taliesin asked.

"Well, Shamash said the hamadryad would tell me how to get to Avalon, where the portal is."

"And the Earth magic?" Sasha asked.

"Well apparently a village of fae got very sick and before anyone from Akasha could come and help them devas came and healed them." I explained.

"What are devas?" Taliesin asked.

"Devas are magical beings that are tied to a specific planet helping it grow."

Kayin frowned. "How did that make Earth magic or are they Earth magic?"

I tried to remember all I had seen at the museum. "They are Earth magic, and they altered the fae's magical energy when they healed them, so now the fae's magic is Earth based, and I guess there are others whose power is Earth based as well."

"How did you get all of that from a Dream?" Kayin asked.

I flushed and focused on my food. The mushroom dish reminded me of stroganoff, but I'd never eaten it with sweet pickles before.

"If Sapphire can Dream like that we don't need you anymore," Miu said.

Sasha glared at Miu, and a sharp spike of worry and anger came from him.

"No," I confessed. "It wasn't all from a Dream, but it doesn't matter."

My gut clenched at the wave of hurt and anger from Sasha.

"It does matter. We have to tell you everything, why do you get to keep secrets?"

"Sasha, I'd like to know too," said Miu. "But isn't the information what's important?"

Kayin nodded.

"So we have to tell everything, give up everything and Sapphire can do whatever she wants?" His accent thickened in his anger, hurt still swirling around the heated emotion.

I held up my hands, something more was going on here than me not telling him something. "Sasha I'm sorry you're upset, I'm not keeping anything important from you."

"Then tell us everything. We have a right to know what is happening with the Jewel since we have to stand beside you and risk our lives."

I held back my desire to defend myself, something was off with Sasha. Trying to fix things, I took a deep breath and confessed. "I might have, for a brief second, fallen into one of the pieces at the museum, a pair of brooches."

"You lied to me, Little Sister," Kayin said. The coldness in his voice made my stomach drop. "You said you were fine, you said that only stared at the piece a little too long."

"I was fine, I didn't lie I just didn't tell you everything, and I didn't want to upset Anali and Gavin, and I had it under control."

"Is there anything else we need to know? Any other secrets you're keeping?" Sasha asked his accent thicker with his anger.

"Woah, wait, what? It's not like I purposely keep secrets. I didn't say anything about at the museum, because Gavin and Anali have enough to deal with right now. And I told Gavin about the dream, Miu was in the room which is why she heard."

"Why didn't you tell the others?" asked Miu.

"I at least come and tell you when I have a Dream," Sasha said. "I share important information."

"So do I, while this information is helpful, none of it is life changing," I snapped. My calm was gone, whatever emotional crazy had set Sasha off I was done trying to be nice and fix things.

"Is that why you couldn't feel anything evil at the party because it was Earth magic?" Taliesin asked.

"Yes," I said keeping my voice calm. "Earth magic is different enough that I can't sense it."

"We should have been told that," Sasha said. "What if I had Dreamed something about Earth magic? I wouldn't understand without this information. How are we supposed to protect ourselves if we don't know things have changed?"

"How are you supposed to protect yourself from it now that you know?" I asked.

"You need to stop keeping secrets—it puts us all in danger," Miu said frowning at me.

"You're making it sound like I'm hiding things on purpose, which I'm not." I sat back against the booth and crossed my arms. What was going on?

"But you don't tend to volunteer information, either," Kayin said, his voice soft and hurt.

Sasha banged his fist on the table. "You don't think to tell us what's going on but we have to tell you."

"I think we should all calm down," Taliesin said.

I held up a hand. "You guys look to me as a leader. When things get difficult you turn and look at me to figure out what to do. So I have to know what's going on with you."

"So that means you don't have to share with us?" Sasha asked.

Hot anger flared from them and me. "Of course not."

"Then why did you keep information from us?" Kayin asked.

I exhaled slowly trying to keep my temper. "I didn't keep anything from you. I didn't think to tell you something."

"And what is the difference?" Miu asked.

"Intent, I didn't plan to keep anything from you."

"So you forgot about us? The people you are supposed to keep safe," Sasha said.

"Kayin, move," I said.

Taliesin laid a hand on my arm. "Sapphire, wait."

I shook my head. "I'll tell you what, the next time I feel the magic painfully being ripped out of a creature and connect to it while it dies, as soon as I start breathing again, I'll be sure to call you. Kayin move, I'm leaving."

Tears blurred my vision.

"Sapphire," Kayin said.

"Move now, I'm leaving."

He moved.

I found my stuff on the coat rack and put it on.

"Is everything okay?" asked the waitress.

"Everything was wonderful, I have to leave." I handed her a hundred pounds. "This is for the bill, if it's more than that the others can cover the rest."

"Thank you, have a good afternoon."

I walked down the street my eyes blurry between the tears and the sunlight. I opened up my empathy and looked up and down the street. Everything felt and looked okay.

We'd taken a taxi to get here, and I wasn't exactly sure where I was but I didn't want to wait for a taxi in front of the restaurant. I focused on walking and making sure I looked for oncoming traffic properly. According to the guide book at the hotel, many tourists are hit by walking into traffic because they forget about cars driving on the left side of the road.

My phone rang several times, I ignored each call. What were they going to say anyway? Sorry we judged you as being someone who would let us be hurt or killed? Is that what they thought of me? Or worse, is that who I am? Have I purposely kept things from them? Putting them in danger?

My phone rang again. I looked at the caller ID. "Hey, Gavin."

"Are you all right? The others came back and told me what's been going on."

"I'm going for a walk, I'm fine," I said, hoping he wasn't about to chew me out over the phone.

"You're not fine, and I'm sorry I haven't seen that. I'll come and get you, where are you?"

"I have no idea. If it's okay I'd rather walk around for a bit."

"Are you sure you're okay?" Gavin asked.

I looked around the ghostly images of trapped emotions, loops of moments in time surrounded me. My shields were low enough that I saw some Roman soldiers, that hadn't happened yet. Beyond that, the buildings and real people looked nice. I hadn't managed to wander into a dangerous part of town. "I'm safe. I need some time, it's a little after three right?"

"Yes, and you need to get to the theater by five at the very latest."

"Okay, that's fine, no problem."

"Call if you need anything, and Sapphire—"

"Yes, Gavin."

"We will talk about all the things you've not told me." His words were calm, but I heard the anger in his voice.

I sighed, tears welling in my eyes. I blinked them back. "Fine," I said.

"Sapphire."

"I have to go. I'll see you later." Hanging up, I turned off my phone and started walking. My empathic shield was crap and my emotions in chaos. I heard the voices of the dead. Felt them tugging on me as they tried to get my attention.

"Sapphire." They knew my name? This was a new crazy.

"Sapphire." Strong fingers wrapped around my arm and a sense of water washed over me.

"Ramsey." I turned. He stood next to me, his large dark eyes full of worry. My chin wobbled.

"Oh, hen, come here." He wrapped his arms around me.

I leaned in letting his emotions surround me. I fought against crying. I didn't want to sob all over him. How embarrassing would that be?

"Come on, let's get out of the street," Ramsey said. He led me to an alley where a blue van was parked the doors open. "We're setting up for an audition."

"I'm sorry. I didn't mean to interrupt. I didn't know you were here. I don't even know where I am." I pressed my lips together to keep from babbling further.

"Well, this," he said waving his arm towards the unmarked door, "is the exclusive and illustrious back entrance for the Whitechapel Club. Be careful where you step—this isn't the cleanest alley."

I smiled but knew it didn't reach my eyes.

"What happened?" he asked.

"A stupid argument, not worth mentioning," I said.

"Good," said the violinist. "Because we have to go, and this is important."

"Courtney," hissed Ramsey.

"What, she's a cute piece of ass, shag her and dump her. We have work to do."

Ramsey stood. His hot anger mixed with Courtney's sharp cold anger. Okay, time to leave.

"I'm not like your boyfriend. I don't treat women like that," Ramsey said.

I stood. "Listen, I have to go get ready for our show tonight."

"Sapphire," Ramsey began.

"Let the little tart go. There are plenty of groupies where she came from." Courtney reached out and grabbed his arm.

Ramsey's anger flared, and Courtney's jealously seeped through her icy anger. Oh, I felt nauseous.

I walked away while they argued. I didn't get far—the alley was a dead end. I hadn't noticed because of the crowd at the end. Not a real crowd, just the emotional impressions left behind from a tour. Why would a tour be down here? They stared at the ground, most were men only two women joining them. Obsession, admiration, longing, lust, and violence hung around them like a fog. Blood dripped from some of the admirers' fingers.

My panting breaths echoed in my ears. *Slow, Sapphire, you need to breathe nice and slow.* My hands shook as the crowd began to part. I didn't want to see. I knew I didn't want to see. *Walk away, walk away,* I yelled in my head, but I couldn't move. I was trapped by the energy. A woman's hand was the first thing I saw, reaching out for help even in death. She wore an old-fashioned dress, something I would expect to see in the original Sherlock Holmes movies we watched.

She'd been torn apart, blood splashed everywhere. His joy as he'd cut her up wrapped around her like a ribbon.

"No, please, no." Everything vanished, and she stood translucent but alive and a man in the long cloak came out of the darkness. The knife in his hand flashed in the lamp light.

The woman and I both screamed as his knife plunged into her the first time.

Arms wrapped around me. I flailed. Someone picked me up. "Sapphire, it's me, calm down."

I froze.

"That's it, hush, hush now. Courtney, get the fuck out of the way."

I shook as everything became cold. Jack the Ripper. I saw Jack the Ripper. "I'm going to be sick."

"Two seconds," Ramsey said, and he kicked open a door.

The harsh smell of bleach hit my nose and my stomach roiled. He set me down, removed my scarf, and held my hair as I threw up.

"Are you throwing up blood?"

I waved my hand. "Beets," I choked out before I threw up some more.

"Oh, thank god."

When I finished, I flushed the toilet and let Ramsey help me up. I rinsed my mouth and splashed water on my face. I looked pale and my whole body shook.

"What do you need? How can I help?" he asked.

"Ramsey, can I help?" Solange asked.

"Water," I said.

She snorted. "That might work in America, but here we must give you tea. I'll go get some."

I smiled. Weakly.

Ramsey wrapped his arm around my waist. "Come along, we must act properly, make you drink tea with lots of sugar and milk. Best thing for a shock of any kind. Unless you want a stiff drink—that's the second best thing."

"I think the tea will be fine," I said looking around the empty club. The smell of stale beer did nothing to help my stomach. "Did I horribly embarrass myself?"

"No, actually I think I'm the one in trouble," Ramsey said.

"What? Why?" I sat and wrapped my hands around the warm mug of tea.

"What have you done to this poor girl?" Murdock asked.

"I didn't do anything," Ramsey said.

"So," said Solange. "Did you just let an empath go down an alley where Jack the Ripper killed a woman?"

"I'm normally better at shielding, but I'm emotional from earlier." I took a sip of tea. Wow, very sweet.

Ramsey ran a hand through his curls. "I honestly didn't even think about it. I'm so sorry, Sapphire."

I patted his hand. "It's not your fault, it's mine. I should have taken better care of myself. It's not like this is the first time something like this has happened."

"So, what do you need?" Ramsey asked.

"The tea is helping a lot, then I need to rebuild my bubble."

"Bubble?" Murdock asked.

"I see my shield as a bubble that surrounds me. I know what people are feeling but the bubble keeps their emotions from invading me."

"That makes sense," Ramsey said.

"Hey, are you guys going to play or what?" asked Courtney.

"Go. I'm fine—I have tea," I said.

Ramsey smiled and kissed my forehead. "We will probably only play one song. Then I'll take you to the hotel."

"Okay, thanks," I said.

I let the music and tea fill my senses. Taking deep breaths, through the three songs they were asked to play, I managed to rebuild my bubble. My fire pendant heated up as I pulled energy from Akasha to help rebuild it.

I poured myself a second cup of tea as the club owner talked to the Water Nymphs. I chuckled at the name.

"Sorry," Ramsey said. "It won't take long to pack up."

"What time is it?"

"Ten to five," Ramsey said.

"Shit," I took out my phone, my leg bouncing as I waited for it to turn back on. I ignored all the beeping letting me know about missed texts and calls. I texted Michael letting him know I was fine and on my way. "I have to go I'm supposed to be at the theater in ten minutes."

"You're on the other side of town right now," Ramsey said.

"Maybe I should take a taxi?" I said standing up.

"I'm sorry," Ramsey said. "It'll take us fifteen minutes minimum to pack up."

"No it's fine. I should have been watching the time better." I wrapped my arms around Ramsey and hugged him tight. "Thank you for helping me."

He held me tight. "Anytime, hen. I'd come by later, but we have a gig tonight until one."

"No worries. I have to go."

"Text me to let me know you got there safely," Ramsey said.

"I will."

* * *

Never tell a cabbie you're in a hurry. I closed my eyes for the manic drive across London, but I arrived at the theater by five thirty. I ran to the door, then took a deep breath and walked in calmly. I changed into my costume, brushed my teeth, and went to go warm up before putting on my make-up.

"Sapphire," Michael called out. "Everything okay? The others have been nothing but bags of nerves."

"Yes. I'm so sorry. I won't be late again."

"Sapphire," said Michael his brown eyes calm as he looked me over. "You do remember I know when I'm being lied to."

"I'm in control, and I can perform. I'll need to warm-up and drink a protein shake while I put on my make-up. I could talk about everything thing, but then you'll lose my ability to do the show." Seriously, one or the other, people. Pick one.

Michael nodded. "But you will talk to someone once you can?"

"Yes, I will," I said doing windmills to warm up my shoulder.

"Okay, off with you then."

"Thanks." I lost myself in my warm-up routine, a mix of power yoga, conditioning exercises, and stretches. My muscles loosened and became more flexible. I felt better and began five-count breathing to strengthen my bubble before the audience came.

"We need to talk," Sasha said.

I laughed, bitter and a bit cold. I let my forehead rest on my shins. "Not right now we don't."

"You'll run off with Ramsey later and avoid us," Miu said.

"We should wait for Gavin," Taliesin said.

Enough of this crap, I was done. I stood up, and all of my 'family' stood there together. All of them as one group against me. They looked like some weird superhero team, everyone wore their costumes for the show. "Look, in less than an hour the audience is going to show up."

"So," said Miu.

"So I'm empathic. And every single show, the audience's excitement, awe, envy, desire, inspiration, and lust beat against my shields. It's even worse when I'm on stage. And if I'm not focused and centered, I can't keep my shields up, which means I can't perform. So you guys can either continue with your attack, or I can do the show."

"Hey," Gavin said, unwinding his scarf. "What's going on?"

"Sapphire was telling us that her control on her empathy is so weak we can't talk things out before the show," Sasha said.

My hands shook. Sasha's anger along with something cold and hollow slammed into my shields. What the hell was wrong with him? This needed to stop. "Did you know a girl hung herself in this room? Did you? Any of you? Because I can see the impression of her death every time I come in here." I pointed to a rafter. "She threw a rope over that beam and hung herself. Her image sways right there."

Kayin stepped forward. "Sapphire, we had no idea."

"It doesn't matter. I deal with it. I deal with it every day. Now, my shields were already ripped to pieces earlier, and that was super fun. I have them built up, but I either have to strengthen them, or I'm not performing. Please pick now, before I start to put on my make-up."

"Could we just talk about—" Miu began.

"No, I can't." I shook my head, and the images from earlier today rushed forward. "Not even a little bit."

"Stop," Gavin said his voice firm. "Even if Sapphire weren't empathic, this kind of conversation isn't appropriate to have before a performance."

Miu frowned. "Earlier you were as upset as we are."

"Anali, happened I bet. Thank goodness," Taliesin muttered, leaning against the wall away from everyone else.

"Tonight, after the show we will all meet in my suite," Gavin said, looking at everyone. "I'll order a bunch of food, and we'll talk. Sapphire, can you perform with Kayin? Or do you two need to talk first?"

"I can perform." I could feel some anger, but mostly sadness and hurt coming from him.

"Kayin?" Gavin asked.

He nodded. "I will be ready, and do my best to have my emotions tucked away."

"Thank you." I walked past them before they said any more and grabbed a protein drink before sitting at the make-up mirror.

I took sips of the sweet vanilla drink as I painted the thick red and black make-up on using the white to create highlights. With each stroke of the brush against my skin I let my day fall away and got into performance head-space.

Standing next to Kayin, I waited for our cue and took his hand. We connected, and our breathing synchronized. I could do this. Fake it until you make it.

Chapter Sixteen

Melusine clapped as the Chinese pole dancers left the stage. "Quintin, I am so glad you came with me."

"Well, you're such enchanting company."

"That silver tongue of yours is going to get me into trouble one day," Melusine said.

Quintin grinned. "If only I could be that lucky."

Three young women came onto the stage, they each held sticks with a length of rope attaching the sticks together at one end. The women moved the rope which made an hourglass figure twirl, bounce, and spin into the air. Quintin clapped as they began to toss the hourglass figure back and forth to each other. The girls bowed as the music changed, and Sapphire and a young man walked onto the stage.

"Oh," said Melusine. "They're stunning."

The male performer held his arms straight over his head and Sapphire held his hands and moved slowly until she held a handstand above him.

Quintin focused on the young woman from the party. "Yes, they are. Most extraordinary."

Melusine chanted a spell under her breath while they clapped for the statue performers. Quintin sat next to her with his plain, boring, and completely human aura around him. Scanning the crowd, she saw a few auras that sparkled with faint traces of magic, but nothing strong enough to bother with the expense of a kidnapping.

Her head began to ache as the spell faded. The hula-hooper bowed as two silks fell from the ceiling and two young men walked onto the stage. Melusine gasped at the brightness of their auras. They sparkled like sunlight on newly fallen snow. Melusine fought to hold onto the spell, but the pain became too sharp. Exhaling, she released the spell, her eyes watering after being forced to see auras.

With their magic I can be free and powerful, Melusine thought. "I must meet them," she spoke aloud to Quintin.

"If that is what you want, then that's what will happen," Quintin said.

Melusine smiled. "I'm so glad you understand how things work."

* * *

"We'll miss our reservation if we don't hurry," Quintin said, looking at his watch.

Melusine smiled. "You worry too much. Look, the crowd is thinning out." She walked to the table where the two aerial silk artists stood greeting people and avoiding the grabby hands of horny admirers. The one with the white hair kept looking at the end of the table, as if he expected help.

"You both were magnificent," Melusine said, looking over the young men for some clue as to what kind of mythical beings they were.

"Thank you," said one with a Russian accent.

"I have a gift for finding talent and helping those who are truly gifted become famous and respected in their field. You should give me a call." She handed each of them a pale turquoise business card with silver gray writing.

The pale one raised a white eyebrow, and his forehead wrinkled. "Thank you but I don't think either of us is thinking of leaving Cirque du Feu Magique."

"One never knows." She smiled and reached out to touch the pale young man.

"Melusine, would you like me to call the restaurant?"

"Oh, Quintin, you do fuss so. Okay, come along." She pulled her hand back and took his arm. "Good evening, gentleman."

"Mr. Monroe?"

"Oh, Miss Rayner, good evening, you were just lovely," Quintin said. "You remember Melusine, our hostess at the gala."

"Yes, it's very nice to see you again," Sapphire said.

"And you my dear. I'm afraid I don't recognize you with the make-up on. You must have made quite an impression on Quintin for him to remember you," Melusine said.

"Well, I didn't step on his toes when we danced."

Melusine laughed and pulled another card out of her purse. "You and your partner should come and talk to me. I could make you rich and famous."

Melusine placed the card in Sapphire's hand, her finger grazing the girl's palm. Warm fire sparked then she was pulled away.

"Quintin."

"I'm so sorry. Someone bumped into me and I was so enamored being near two such beautiful woman that I fear I lost my balance," Quintin said. "You're all right, my dear, aren't you?"

Melusine looked down at him and smiled. "I'm quite all right. Come along, we do have a reservation to keep."

Quintin looked back at Sapphire, she rubbed her hand frowning. Oh well, at least he'd tried.

Chapter Seventeen

Kayin, Sasha, and Miu sat on the couch across from me. Kayin looked uncomfortable while the other two looked ready for a fight. Trays of sandwiches, fruit, crackers, cheese, and desserts covered the large coffee table in between us.

Taliesin fixed a plate and poured a glass of juice, handing them to me before sitting down with his own on the chair closest to the door. The others got food while we waited for Gavin.

"What's going on?" Anali asked, tying the belt of her robe. Her face was pale. I wanted to leave so she could go back to sleep. Why had Gavin asked us to his room anyway?

"I told you we all needed to talk," Gavin said standing beside her, his hand on her elbow.

"Yes, I set the alarm so I'd be awake and ready," she said. "No one told me we were attacking Sapphire."

"We're not," Gavin said firmly, sitting in an overstuffed chair between us. He wore a layer of calm, trying to hide the worry and anger swirling inside him. At least he was trying.

Anali snorted and walked and sat down next to me on the loveseat. She reached out to touch me. I pulled my hand back. "I haven't showered, and I don't know what's stuck to me I don't want to risk touching you."

"What do you mean?" she asked.

I waved my hand at the others. "We had a fight at lunch, and my shields were trashed so I went for a walk. London has a rich history of violence and suffering."

"Are you okay?" Anali asked.

"I think so. I want a shower, and I'll probably have nightmares."

"Oh, sweetie, I am sorry."

"See this is what we need to talk about," Sasha said. "She's keeping secrets."

Anali sniffed. "She's allowed to have some privacy. She doesn't have to tell us everything."

I love Anali.

"She does if it affects us," Kayin said, his tone calm.

"Sapphire dear, could what happened to you this afternoon affect us in any way?" Anali asked.

"No," I wrapped my arms around myself and shivered as the feelings washed over me. "No, it was just an image from the past."

"But it upset you," Gavin said. "We should know what it was. At least I would like to know what happened."

"Well I might be willing to tell you if I didn't feel like I'm being ganged up on," I said.

"We have a right to be angry when you have been lying to us, keeping things from us that could affect our safety," Miu said.

"As I said before, I haven't been purposefully keeping things from you."

Anali held up her hand. Three mouths hung open ready to speak no words coming out. "What secrets are we talking about?"

Gavin sighed. "I talked to the others this afternoon. In the hopes of keeping this from getting out of control, I would like to be the one to ask Sapphire about your concerns."

Kayin nodded, his shoulders dropping as he relaxed against the arm of the couch. Sasha snorted and glared at the table. Miu crossed her arms but nodded. Taliesin's foot stopped shaking, not sure what that meant, and Anali smiled.

"While we were at the museum, Sapphire fell into a piece of jewelry and experienced some of its history. Is that correct?"

"Yes," I said.

"Sapphire, did you get information from that which could help protect us?" Anali asked.

"No, I don't think so. I saw devas healing a village of Fae and that changed their magic."

"To Earth magic, a magic she can't sense," Sasha said.

"What I saw didn't tell me that," I said.

"Why didn't you tell us?" Gavin asked. "We should know these things."

"I didn't say anything because I was fine. Kayin was there holding my hand and grounding me. It was Anali's first outing I didn't want to spoil it."

"Sapphire, it was very kind of you to want to protect me, but I am an adult. Even sick, it is my job to take care of you, not the other way around," Anali said. "Now, you are becoming a young woman, and you have dealt with a lot. I trust you to decide if you can handle something or not, but please don't keep from asking for help because you are worried about me."

I nodded. "Okay, and thank you for trusting me."

"That's not all she's been keeping from us," Sasha said. "She found out that whatever ate the gnome's magic uses Earth magic which is why we can't detect it."

Anali turned to me.

"After the party I dreamed in Akasha, and Shamash and Aya explained about Earth magic. And I told Gavin about it," I said.

"Yes, you did tell me, and I passed the information onto Philip. He said he'd let me know as soon as he found anything out. In the future, I will make sure everyone knows. I had assumed Sapphire would tell you," Gavin said, some of his forced calm fading.

"Okay," Anali said. "And did you tell the others about the Earth magic or the fact that none of us felt the person who attacked the gnome?"

"No, no I didn't. I didn't think about it. The night was so crazy."

Anali hummed and sat back against the couch, her posture relaxed.

"What about the guy she's been sneaking off with?" Miu asked.

"I'm not sneaking off with anyone. I have happened to run into Ramsey several times and we hung out."

"And he just happened to be there when you ran into the walk-in and at the party?" Taliesin asked as a wave of worry came from him before he shut his emotions off from me again.

"Oh," said Anali. "Is he the handsome young man in the kilt?"

"Yes," I said.

Gavin muttered, "He's not *that* handsome."

"He has a Scottish accent, right. I love those, they sound all sexy," Anali said. "Is he nice?"

"I think so. He's been nice to me."

Anali smiled. "You'll have to tell me more about him later. So anything else?"

The others looked at the floor, the wall, their hands, but said nothing. I hope Anali gets better soon—obviously, we can't function without her.

"Oh, wait," I said. "Melusine, the women who hosted the party, was at the show tonight. She gave me her card."

"Sasha and I got one too," Taliesin interrupted.

"Did she touch you?" I asked. "Because when she touched me, it felt odd. And I could tell that she felt something too."

"Odd how?" Gavin asked.

I shook my head. "The touch was really quick. I didn't have time to figure it out. Mr. Monroe was there, he tripped and she moved."

"Mr. Monroe?" Miu asked.

"I met him at the party. He asked me to dance," I said.

"Another man," Taliesin said.

"Sapphire is a lovely young lady," said Anali. "I'm not surprised she has men taking notice. If it bothers you, maybe you should do something about it."

Taliesin's cheeks turned pink but his sky blue eyes darkened and narrowed. Guess he didn't like that idea.

"Well I'm not sure what has all of you in such a snit. I don't feel like Sapphire kept anything from anyone on purpose. Now that she knows that we would all like to be informed of any magical information, I'm sure she'll be more conscientious of passing information onto everyone," Anali smiled.

"I don't like that you lied to me, Little Sister," Kayin said. "I understand why, but I wish you would have told me."

"I'm sorry I hurt you." I said. "Honestly, I didn't think it was a big deal at the time."

Kayin gave me a small smile. We would be okay.

"I would like to know what happened today," Gavin said.

I snorted. I was so not telling them about running into Ramsey and then seeing a Jack the Ripper killing. "It wasn't anything magical. Can I please go and take a shower now?"

"I would like to speak with you alone for a minute first," Gavin said.

The others filled up their plates before leaving.

"Good night, Little Sister."

"Sleep well, Big Brother."

"Good night."

"Night, Taliesin."

Anali yawned. "I'm headed to bed, too. Once I'm feeling better, the two of us will go out so you can tell me all about your handsome Scotsman," Anali said.

"I can't wait. I guess I'll have to do something exciting with him so I have something interesting to tell you."

Anali giggled. Gavin growled.

"So what did you want to talk about?" I set my plate down. There was no way I could have this conversation and eat at the same time.

Gavin frowned and looked at the floor. "I believed them at first, well, until Anali calmed me down. I was scared you were in trouble and angry at you for not telling me."

"But I was telling you the important things, like the walk-in and about the Dream."

"I guess I thought this was how you were acting out."

Acting out? What new crazy is this? "Why would I act out?"

Gavin paced, his hands joining into the conversation. "Because of the new baby?"

"That doesn't even make sense. What does the baby have to do with all of you assuming I'm such a horrible person that I would keep secrets that would threaten your safety?" My voice cracked.

"No," Gavin knelt in front of me. "No, I never thought that, and neither did Kayin or Taliesin. You're not the type of person who would do that!"

"Then why do they think I would? Why did you?"

Gavin rubbed his face. "I don't know about Miu or Sasha. Maybe they are lashing out because of the holidays and being separated from family."

I nodded. At the group home, kids always had a difficult time at the holidays and would emotionally vomit all over you for the slightest thing. I'd learned not to take it personally.

"As for me," Gavin continued, "I don't think you're a bad person. I thought you were acting out, because of the baby."

"Why?"

"You aren't coming to me, or asking for help, or demanding I spend time with you," Gavin said. "So, I thought you were keeping secrets to see if I would notice."

I blinked. What? Adults were so confusing. "Okay. After my dream I did tell you what I needed help with. If I needed you I would speak up. And why would you want me to act like a brat demanding your attention while Anali is sick?"

Gavin sighed and sat next to me on the couch. "I guess I was expecting it. Once Anali told me she wanted to have a baby, we read books on how older kids can feel when there is a new baby on the way. We wanted to make sure we could understand anything you might be going through becoming a big sister."

Laughing, I shook my head. "Okay, but you realize kids have always come and gone in my life. Older, bigger, scarier kids, and younger, cuter, sweeter kids. I usually step back and wait to see what the new dynamic is, or at least I used to. After my second year at Hope House, I stepped up and took charge."

Gavin tilted his head to the side. "Why, what changed?"

"Well it was my home, and I wanted the new kids to fit into what we had, not try to change it."

"So, we don't have a strong enough dynamic for you to try and keep in place?"

Guh, more adult gibberish. "Gavin, we don't have a set routine. Anali is pregnant. A baby changes things, we will all have to adapt."

Gavin held up a hand. "How do you know so much about all of this?"

"In an effort to reduce teen pregnancy and stop the cycles of abuse, Four ..."

"Your caseworker before David?" Gavin asked.

Well, since David was Five, then yes, Four would be the one before him. "Yes. Anyway, she sent me to this family/parenting/pregnancy/anti-drug class. We learned about birth control, sexually transmitted illnesses, how a normal family is supposed to work, read parenting books, learned how to budget and balance a checkbook. All that grown-up life stuff."

"How old were you?"

"Thirteen."

"That's young," Gavin said with a frown.

Gavin was so naive. "Gavin, most of the girls in the group home weren't even virgins at thirteen."

"Are you?" Gavin blurted out then turned bright red.

I raised an eyebrow. "Does it matter?"

Gavin closed and opened his mouth several times. Poor man, he didn't know what to say.

"Because it seems to be important to you, even though it's not any of your business, I will tell you. Yes, I am still a virgin."

Gavin exhaled and relaxed. "Thank you, and I want you to be safe, so when you're ready Anali or I will take you to the doctor and make sure you have whatever kind of birth control you need."

"Thanks, but I already have an IUD."

"What!"

"After the class, I was taken to the gynecologist, examined, and offered birth control. I choose the IUD." Gavin turned a bit green and started to pant. "Relax, I'm not making any plans to have sex."

Gavin snorted. "No, but someone else might have different ideas."

I smiled. "If you're talking about Ramsey, he might. I'm going to go and take a shower."

Gavin pressed his lip together, and his emotions swirled around him. I expected him to say something else. Instead, he looked at the bedroom door and nodded. "Okay, if you need anything let me or Anali know. No matter what is going on, we are here for you and want to help."

I smiled. "I know, Uncle Gavin. Sleep well."

* * *

Gasping, I sat up in bed. Miu murmured but didn't wake. After three nights of nightmares, I had finally stopped screaming and waking her up. The clock's red numbers glowed 5:15. Guh, that is disgustingly early, but I wasn't going to go back to sleep. I got dressed, grabbed my laptop and phone, and went to the lounge on the second floor.

I settled down with a cup of tea and looked out the windows. They faced the east so I could watch the sun rise again.

—*Good morning, can you get away today?* I texted Ramsey. I set my phone down and opened my computer. One last bit of homework to finish, then I could catch up with friends. I hadn't seen Ramsey in a few days. He had been busy, or avoiding me after my crazy freak-out on Monday, which was fine. I'd been napping in the afternoons.

My phone chimed.

—*Why are you up so early?*

—*I'm sorry I didn't think you'd wake up. Go back to sleep.*

—*Sapphire, are you okay?*

—*Yes, I just couldn't sleep.*

He didn't text back. I smiled. He must have fallen back asleep.

I finished my homework when my phone chimed again.

—*I'm here at the hotel, where are you?*

I frowned down at my baggy yoga pants and sweater. Oh, well, too late now.

—*I'm on the second floor in the lounge.*

—*Ok.*

The elevator chimed. Ramsey's curls were wild, and his cheeks flushed from the cold. I blushed as he turned to get a cup of tea, his worn blue jeans fitting very snugly. He sat next to me on the couch setting his yoga bag next to him. "Morning, hen."

"Morning. I'm sorry about waking you up. I didn't think my texts woke you up."

"I changed the setting."

I bit my lip and looked up at him through my lashes. "I was a bit worried I'd freaked you out the other day."

"Seems like you're the one who was freaked out," Ramsey laid his arm over my shoulders and I snuggled in close. "Why are you up so early, again?"

I fiddled with the edge of his scarf. "I keep dreaming about what I saw, in the alley."

"And what did you see? Have you talked about it at all?" Ramsey propped his booted feet onto the coffee table.

"No. I got into this big fight with the others about keeping secrets and I didn't want to tell them. Anyway it doesn't affect them."

"So tell me. Maybe it'll help if you aren't keeping it hidden."

I shrugged and Ramsey started rubbing my arm. "At first I didn't realize it was a vision because the people had recently been there to see where he killed his victims. Not just tourists, but those who admired him, wanted to be like him, the sickos. Some of them had blood dripping on their fingers. And then they moved, and I saw her—the woman Jack the Ripper had killed. She was lying on the ground with her hand reaching out and what he'd done to her."

Ramsey pulled me closer as I choked back a sob.

"Then I saw her standing alive in the alley. The man wearing black walking towards her, and his knife flashing before he drove it into her. We both screamed, and you pulled me away before I could see any more."

"Bloody hell, no wonder you've been having nightmares." Ramsey pressed a kiss to the top of my head. "I'm so sorry, is there anything you can do?"

"This helps." Guh, that sounded stupid.

"I'm glad."

The black sky began to lighten and the stars faded.

"I can't remember the last time I saw the sun rise. Sure I must have been on the way home at the time." Ramsey yawned.

"I should let you go so you can get some more sleep." I started to sit up but Ramsey held me tight.

"You're fine. If I wanted to be in bed sleeping, that's where I'd be."

I grinned and rested my head on his chest, watching as the clouds turned pink and orange.

* * *

My neck ached and my pillow moved. Groaning, I opened my eyes. Light blue sky peeked through the gray winter clouds.

"What time is it?"

"Hmm, what?" muttered Ramsey.

"It's eight," snapped Gavin. He sat in one of the chairs, his face a mask of contained anger. And the day had started so nicely.

"Mr. Marsh," Ramsey said, as he shifted, putting his feet on the floor and stretching his back. "Oh, I'm going to need a hot shower."

"I know my neck is stiff," I said, rolling my shoulders trying to get the muscles to loosen.

"What exactly is going on here?" Gavin asked.

"I texted Ramsey when I woke up, he came over, and we fell asleep watching the sunrise." I said. "Oh, and I finished my school work."

"Why did you leave your room?" Gavin asked.

"I couldn't sleep and didn't want to wake Miu up again," I said. "I didn't realize that I wasn't allowed to leave my room."

"It sounds like I should go," Ramsey said.

"Good idea," said Gavin.

I laid my hand on his arm. "Wait. What are you doing today?"

Ramsey looked at Gavin, then at me. "Nothing."

"I need to go to Hampton Court, will you come with me?"

"I said I would set that up."

"Uncle Gavin, I need to go. I need to talk to the hamadryad. And Anali isn't feeling well enough to go yet."

"Well, why don't you go with the others?" Gavin asked.

I crossed my arms. "Kayin could come with us, but I'm still not talking to the others."

"Why?" Gavin asked frowning.

"He's the only one who's tried to talk to me."

"Maybe you should talk to them first."

I glared at Gavin. "No. I didn't start the argument. Not one of you asked me nicely or tried to understand. They will have to come to me." I turned to Ramsey. "So Hampton Court?"

"Sure, sounds like fun."

"Not just the two of you," Gavin said.

I rolled my eyes but texted Kayin and Shin. "There. I asked Kayin and Shin if they want to go. Gavin, do you know where Miu is?"

"Yes, she called to let me know you were missing when she got to the gym this morning," Gavin answered.

"Okay." I stood up and held out my hand to Ramsey. "Come on up to my room. I need to change and grab my stuff."

Ramsey slid his yoga bag over his head, took my hand, but kept his eyes on Gavin.

Gavin stood and followed us to the elevator. "I'm not sure about this."

"Gavin, he can sit on the couch and I'll change in the bathroom." My phone chimed. "They can both come. They just got done working out and will meet us for breakfast. How's Anali?"

"Okay. She woke up earlier and was sick but kept down some crackers and tea and went back to sleep. I was planning a trip to Hampton Court."

"We can go again, but I know I have to talk to the hamadryad," I said.

"I'm sorry," Gavin said.

"It's fine. Anali needs you right now." Why did we have to keep going over this?

"I can be here for you and Anali at the same time," Gavin snapped.

I opened the door to my room, and Ramsey darted inside.

"Uncle Gavin, I'm not questioning that."

"It seems like you are."

"I can feel that I need to go now. I know it needs to be now. I'm not upset, or angry, or anything."

Gavin sighed and looked at the door. "Don't let him pressure you into anything. Boys can be very persuasive, so make sure he's not pushing you into anything you don't want or aren't ready for."

"I won't, and he's not like that anyway. I'll tell you everything when we get back." I went into my room and shut the door.

Ramsey looked relaxed lounging in a chair but I felt his tension. "So," he said.

I rolled my eyes. "You heard everything."

"Yes."

"So blunt or embarrassed silence, which do you want?"

His brow furrowed. "Blunt?"

"I'm not ready to have sex. Is that a deal breaker for you?"

He blinked. "I don't think I've ever met someone so calm and casual when talking about sex."

"My mom said that if you aren't capable of talking about sex and birth control with someone, then you aren't ready to have sex with them."

"How old were you when your mum died?"

"Five."

"And she told you that and you remembered it?" Ramsey squeaked.

I chuckled. "No, sorry. According to Gavin, my mom panicked while pregnant, worrying she wouldn't be a good mom. She started a journal with her favorite quotes and what she'd learned from them. So you didn't answer me. Is the fact I'm not ready to have sex a deal breaker?"

Ramsey stood up. "No, I don't ... I'm not ..."

I raised an eyebrow.

He groaned. "What Courtney said about having sex and ditching you, that's not who I am."

"I know that. I wouldn't be with you at all if you were a slime-ball."

Ramsey ran the back of his fingers along my cheek. "Is it okay if I try to seduce you?"

I blushed. "As long as you act like a gentleman."

He grinned, that evil 'I'm in trouble' grin. "Well, I can't be a perfect gentleman now, can I?"

My cheeks heated up, and I held my breath as he moved closer.

I jumped as someone knocked on the door. "Sapphire," Kayin called out. "Are you ready?"

Ramsey kissed my forehead. "I think it's cute that you can calmly talk about sex but blush when I do anything."

Heat rushed to my face, again. "Well, they are different things." I opened the door. "Morning Kayin, Shin. Come on in. I need to change."

Shin grinned at me and handed me his phone to show a text from Gavin on the screen.

—*I'm counting on you to keep Sapphire safe today. Call if you need anything, and keep an eye on Ramsey. I don't trust him.*

I sighed and gathered my clothes. I was going to have to speak to Anali about her husband.

Chapter Eighteen

I needed a flowing dress, a white horse, and a tiara. Definitely needed a tiara. Maybe the gift shop sold them. Massive walls and towers of red brick and windows painted in white trim stood proudly against the gray sky. "Hampton Court is a castle. A real castle like in the movies." I have never wanted to be a princess so bad in my life.

Ramsey chuckled. "Didn't you know that?"

"Even I knew that," Kayin said. "I Googled it."

"Why did you want to come here if you didn't know what it was?" asked Shin as we walked under a large gate with a gold clock set into the top.

"Oh, it was on some blog that everyone who comes to London has to go here, and I wanted a day away from everyone," I said.

Ramsey arched an eyebrow at me.

"He doesn't know," I mouthed soundlessly.

Ramsey rolled his eyes. "Come on, the entrance is over here."

Art—the whole building was art. Gilt-framed paintings of long dead royalty and mythical stories covered the walls, unless the walls themselves were painted in murals of Roman gods and goddesses who looked down on us. Statues, suits of armor, even the furniture was art. My fingers twitched, and I took a stuttering breath. Emotions had seeped into this palace. I grabbed Ramsey's hand to ground myself.

"Are you okay?" he asked.

"Yes, it's just a lot." My wet tennis shoes squeaked on the polished wood floors.

"This is amazing," Shin said. "Look at the ceiling. Who bothers to make a ceiling so ornate?"

I looked up at the intricately carved wooden arches along the hallway. "Who dusts them?" I muttered.

Kayin laughed. "They do look very clean from down here."

Ramsey tugged on my hand. "You're such a romantic."

Kayin and Shin walked next to each other pointing out things which caught their attention. Their hands brushed as they walked. Their fingers would twitch sometimes, reaching like they were going to hold hands and then curling in away from the other. The sparks of longing, fear, sadness, and confusion were going to make me cry soon.

"They're driving me nuts," Ramsey whispered in my ear. His hot breath made me shiver. "I want to grab them and make them hold hands."

That was one way to go about it. "We shouldn't interfere, but I agree."

"Wow, that's some bed," Ramsey said.

Rich cream velvet hung down from the ceiling, framing the back. The fabric was gathered on the sides. The duvet was the same rich cream with a white leaf pattern, and plump white pillows covered the top. It stood in the middle of a dark green, paneled wall. This room was less cluttered—I guess to show what it originally looked like. It was so big it seemed empty. But I supposed if it was a woman's room she'd need the floor space to get around in those big poofy dresses.

Sighing, I watched as Shin and Kayin's hands continued to accidentally bump against each other. Then Shin changed the game. He turned his hand so Kayin's hand bumped into his open palm. I squeezed Ramsey's hand and held my breath. Kayin didn't move his hand for a second, then he turned, and their fingers curled around each other. Yes! Internal squee and happy dance.

Kayin looked back at me. I grinned so big it hurt my cheeks. He shook his head, and I bet he was blushing.

"Where should we go next?" Shin asked.

I looked at the map. There was still a lot I hadn't seen yet, but I needed an excuse to get outside. Seeing the gardens in winter wasn't going to be believable. "They have a maze."

"Where?" Shin asked, stopping to look at my map. I guess he didn't want to let go of Kayin's hand to look at his.

"It's outside past The Wilderness." I pointed at the map. "Can we go?"

"Sounds like fun to me." Ramsey adjusted the strap on his yoga bag.

"If that is what you want, Little Sister," Kayin said.

"Well, let's go," Shin said, walking towards the exit. "After we get all cold we can have tea, then tour the rest of the house."

Orderly. The gardens were the most controlled and precise gardens I'd ever seen. They were beautiful, but the forced control on the plants didn't appeal to me. Many of the trees were naked for the winter, but some were still green, their boughs shaped into rounded cones. The trees seemed embarrassed like toddlers dressed in sailor outfits by their parents.

The gravel crunched under our feet as we walked through the trees of The Wilderness to get to the maze. A cold wind blew around us and something reached out to me. A stag stood amongst the trees. He snorted and turned. I had to follow him, but I needed to do it alone. How? Shin would follow if I just started walking off into the woods, and there wasn't a way to ask Kayin for help.

If only I could go all Jedi on Shin and have him wait here. I touched my throat. I could, but on Shin for something like this? There had to be a better way. I wracked my brain but couldn't think of anything else. The stag followed us, and I felt his irritation.

I let go of Ramsey's hand and took a deep breath letting my necklace connect me to Akasha. Power flowed into me and I concentrated it all in my throat. Shin stiffened and looked around.

"Bathroom," I gasped, letting the power go. "I have to go to the bathroom. There's a bench right there, you guys sit and I'll be right back."

"You couldn't have thought of this when we passed them?" Shin teased.

I sniffed. "I didn't have to go then."

"I'll walk with you," Ramsey said. "You two have fun; we'll be right back."

Shin grinned and tugged Kayin towards the bench. A bench which faced the opposite direction, yes! We walked a ways down the path then headed into the trees. "Did you see the stag?" I asked.

"It's not just a stag, it's one of Cernunnos' stags. One of his messengers."

"What? Who?" I said and focused on the ground so I wouldn't trip.

"He's a god of the forest, and protects the animals and beings living there. Well, as best as he can these days," Ramsey said.

"How can you tell?" I hadn't felt anything magical coming from the stag.

"He's marked. The ring of white fur around his neck is a torc."

"Oh." I'd thought it was a natural marking.

The stag stopped in front of a large tree. Its leaves were long gone, so I had no idea what kind it was. The gray-brown bark was decorated with pale, dusty-green lichen. I let go of Ramsey's hand and opened the connection to Akasha. I took a deep breath then exhaled and placed my hands on the rough bark.

"Hello, Phoenix sapling," a voice echoed in my head, it was slow and thick like the cold sap creeping through the tree. "I'm so glad you've come. I'm Oak."

"Hello. Shamash and Aya said I needed to speak to you. That you could help me find Avalon," I said. Focusing on the words and not the images and memories of the past five hundred years. My head throbbed at the amount of information flowing into me.

A face slowly formed in the bark, round plump cheeks, small kind eyes, a large hooked nose, and thin smiling lips. I couldn't tell if Oak was old or young because of the bark. Ramsey gasped. I guess he saw the face too.

"Avalon sunk down into Earth, little sapling, allowing our mother to protect those who honor her and those of Akasha. Only those of magic who seek to help Avalon can enter." Oak laughed as a squirrel ran up its trunk and ducked into its nest. "The doorway is in the Tor."

"Okay." I would need to write this down. Right now it didn't make much sense.

Oak sighed. "I will tell the trees to let all the magical creatures know to go to Avalon. They will be there when you are ready."

"How will you know? I don't even know when I'll be there."

"Because timing is everything." Oak yawned. "Come visit me in the summer one day when I have the energy to talk. I would love to hear about all your adventures."

Oak's face sank back into the tree. I blinked as the connection faded. "I will, Oak, and thank you." As I stepped back my knees buckled and Ramsey caught me.

"Are you okay? You were—well, whatever you were doing, took almost thirty minutes."

"Crap, how are we going to explain that?" I said, standing up and shaking the pins and needles out of my legs.

He grinned.

I smiled and stepped back, it was his evil "but it'll be so much fun" grin.

"I have an idea." He scooped me up and placed me on the ground.

"I'll get leaves and grass in my hair," I said.

"Yes, we both will." He lay next to me and ran his fingers over my cheek. I held my breath. Leaning over, he pressed his lips to mine. They were warm and slightly chapped. Then they were gone. I opened my eyes, when had I closed them?

"Okay, hen?"

I looked into his warm black eyes and nodded, then looked back at his mouth.

He smiled and kissed me again. His fingers threaded into my hair. He shifted, making the kiss deeper. His tongue slid across my bottom lip, and then he sucked my lower lip. Oh. I pressed my hand against his cheek, his stubble was rough under my palm. Ramsey slid his tongue between my lips. My tongue met his, and Ramsey's arm slid behind me. He rolled us over so he lay on the grass.

The kiss ended. I leaned up and looked down at him.

He smiled. "Now, you have a good excuse for why we were gone so long. In fact, I doubt they'll even ask once they see you."

"Is that why you kissed me?"

"Well, it was the first gentlemanly reason I could find to snog you."

I blushed. "Oh."

That wicked grin was back as Ramsey buried his fingers in my hair. "I think I'll have to kiss you at least one more time, if they are going to believe that's why we were gone."

"As long as you're being a gentleman, I suppose it's fine," I teased.

"Of course," he said pressing his lips to mine.

* * *

"We thought we'd have to send out a search party," Shin said, pulling a leaf from my hair.

My face was so hot I was afraid my brain would fry.

Kayin glared at Ramsey and took my arm. "Come with me, Little Sister, we need to talk. Shin keep an eye on him."

Shin laughed. "Whatever you want."

Kayin ducked his head and led me down the path. "Are you okay? Did he force you to do anything? Do you want Shin and me to deal with him?"

"Big Brother, calm down." I whispered. "I went to speak to the hamadrayad. We took so long Ramsey decided to use kissing as an excuse for being gone so long."

"So he didn't kiss you?"

"No, he did, but only twice, well three times." I blushed and looked at the ground. "It was really nice."

"And he behaved himself?" Kayin asked.

"Yes, he didn't try to put his hands anywhere he shouldn't have."

Kayin sniffed and looked back at Ramsey with a glare. "Good."

"What about Shin? Was he a gentleman?" I asked.

Kayin looked at the ground and I swear his cheeks were darker. "We talked and held hands. I don't ... I don't know what to do."

His emotions itched against my skin, anxiety, confusion, a bit of fear. "What do you mean? Do about what?"

"I don't know how to act. Do I let him lead, am I supposed to lead? I've only seen male/female relationships, and there were clear boundaries, roles, and rituals in place. We're both men—I don't know what to do."

"Oh." Wow. Okay, how to help with this? "Well, every relationship is unique. Having grown up in San Francisco I've seen all kinds of gay men. I've seen skinny young men, big hairy men wearing leather, feminine fashion gods, drag queens, and business men in suits. They dated men different from them and men like them. Shin likes you, just as you are. You don't have to change, and you two will figure it out."

"I'm still not sure, that's what we talked about. That I like him, but I still have to choose between risking losing my family and him," Kayin said.

I took Kayin's hand. "Not just him, but being true to yourself. Shin and you might be together forever, or you might date for a few months and realize it doesn't work between the two of you. You're choosing between possibly losing your family and being true to who you really are."

Kayin sighed.

"What did Shin say?" I asked.

"He was kind," Kayin said. "He said he understood that this was a difficult decision, and he would be here to help me as a friend or more." Kayin bit his lip. "Are you sure I wouldn't have to change if we dated?"

"Big Brother, Shin likes you. I think the only thing he wants to change is how much to two of you touch."

"You are naughty," Kayin said.

I grinned. "Maybe, but it's the truth."

"So have I passed?" Ramsey asked. "May I walk with Sapphire through the maze?"

"Walk in front of us, so we can make sure you're being a gentleman," Kayin said.

I laughed and held my hand out for Ramsey as we walked into the maze. Bushes had been shaped and grown until they were well above our heads.

He took my hand and winked at Kayin. "You just want to check out my arse."

Kayin's mouth fell open, and an odd squeak was the only noise he made.

Shin grabbed Kayin's hand. "Well, it is worth looking at."

"Cheers, mate."

"Hey, could you move your yoga bag it's blocking the view?" Shin asked.

Ramsey chuckled and moved his bag.

"Yes, quite nice," said Shin.

"You're so bad," I said. Poor Kayin was flustered and confused.

"So," I said turning to Ramsey. "What are you doing Tuesday night?"

"I have a gig until eleven. Why?"

"Miu organized a party for my birthday, and I was hoping you could come. It doesn't start until ten because we have a show at seven, so maybe you can come after your gig?"

Ramsey squeezed my hand. "Of course I'll be there. Where is it?"

"It's a club called Enchanted."

Ramsey smiled. "Perfect. It'll take only seconds for me to get there."

"Oh, are you playing close by?"

"Yep, fate must want to keep us together."

I blushed. It did seem that way.

* * *

We ran laughing into the theater, bursting through the doors at four-fifty-nine. The other performers were walking around settling into their pre-performance routine. The stale scent of popcorn, sweat, and make-up hung heavy in the air. Guh, I wanted to open all the doors and windows.

"Have a fun day?" Michael asked.

"Yes, it was great," I said, hanging up my things.

Michael smiled. "Good. Now all of you get ready."

"See you guys later," Shin said.

"Bye," Kayin said.

—*Back at the theater. Things went well. Will tell you all about it after the show. I'll text when I'm back at the hotel. Nothing urgent or dangerous,* I texted to Gavin.

I shivered at the memory of the others accusing me of lying and putting them in danger, so I sent the text to everyone. There, that should keep them happy. I still wasn't sure what I had done to have them think so badly of me. I gathered up my things and changed into my costume and went to warm up.

Kayin and Shin weren't there yet, but the others were. I went to a corner by myself, no point in getting into another argument.

"Sapphire, can I talk to you?" Miu asked.

I reached out and clasped my hands under my feet. "Sure what's up?"

"I want to apologize. I thought about what was said the other day. We did start out worried, with the baby coming, and what happened at the party, and then I don't know we started talking and then thought that maybe you were keeping things from us. Then we got angry that you were keeping things from us." Miu sighed. "We should have—no, *I* should have talked to you. We share a room. I had plenty of chances to talk to you. I'm sorry I let myself get carried away and didn't trust you."

I forced back tears and fought to keep my face and breathing normal. They had all sat down and talked about me and decided I was risking their safety and lying to them. That is who they thought I was?

Kayin had been hurt that I had lied to him at the museum. We had talked that out, but the others thought the worst about me. "It's okay, sometimes people get carried away. I understand."

But I didn't understand. My heart ached and my eyes burned. I thought we were becoming a family. I had been stupid enough to think this once before. I'd been with my second foster mom for two years. She bought me all sorts of stuff, let me paint my room purple, and even bought me a kitten. There were two of us girls living with her, and we were treated like princesses. Then she chose to adopt the other girl, and I was put into a group home. I gave up the dream of having a family and refused to go to another foster home after that.

"And we're still on for Tuesday before your party at the club right?" Miu asked.

"Lunch and some mystery event before the show," I said plastering on a smile and dredging up enthusiasm.

"I'm so glad," she said blinking rapidly. Her eyes shone with tears. "We're going to have so much fun. I found a Japanese restaurant to go to. And then for the surprise."

"Do I need to wear anything specific for this surprise?" I asked.

"Nope, jeans are fine. I have to go, my makeup takes forever. I'll see you later. I can't wait to hear about what happened with hamadryad."

"Bye Miu."

Pretending to be okay takes a lot of energy. I exhaled and began to move into my warm up routine, letting the familiar movements relax me.

"So you and Miu are all happy happy again," Sasha said.

What had crawled up his ass and died? "What do you need?"

"I'm not going to apologize," Sasha blurted out.

"Okay." Like I cared.

Taliesin came over. His worry danced around me, but my own anger blocked it from reaching me.

"So I assume I can't come to hear what happened if I don't do what you want," Sasha said.

"Yes, that's right," I snapped. "I don't even know why you're asking. I feel like I've shown myself to be such a selfish, cruel, egomaniac that if you aren't behaving exactly as I want, then I'll shun you and treat you like crap. That is my normal behavior, but I'm positive that if you get to Gavin and Anali first, they'll make sure you can stay despite the huge fit I'm likely to have."

I stood up. Taliesin and Sasha's mouths hung open. What were they expecting? Exactly how much do they think I can take? Anger—no, fury—pulsed through me like bolts of lightning. "I don't want you to apologize. Do you think it will do any good? You showed me exactly what you think of me and some stupid words said out of guilt won't fix anything."

"Sapphire," Taliesin said. "Your hand is on fire."

I clenched my fists, then exhaled and opened my fingers wide shoving everything down as much as possible. The fire faded, thankfully before anyone saw anything.

"Is everything okay?" Shin asked from the other side of the room.

"Yes," I said. "It's all good."

I turned and grabbed my towel and water bottle. Empty red-rimmed eyes stared at me from the mirror. Thank goodness for makeup.

"What about Miu?" Sasha asked.

I shrugged. "What about her? I have no intention of saying anything to her. Why hurt her like that?"

"So you can work it out," Taliesin said.

I snorted. God, they were stupid. "Work what out? That you all think I'm a selfish bitch who puts you in danger and doesn't support you in any way? How does that get fixed? Not by talking. I have to go and do my make-up."

"Sapphire," Shin said pulling me into a hug. "You're the worst liar ever."

"Not here," I said, my face buried in his chest and tears burning my eyes.

Shin lifted me off the floor and started walking. Somehow he found a dark, quiet corner and sat. "We're alone."

I curled into him and began to cry.

He didn't say anything, just held me and let me cry, and held me some more.

"I'm sorry," I muttered.

"For what?"

I sat up and wiped my face on my towel then tried to dry him off.

"Sapphire, don't worry about it. I don't wear this for the show," Shin said. "Do you want to tell me what happened, or is this about the secret you all are keeping?"

I stiffened. *Crap, oh crap. What was I supposed to say now?*

"Relax," Shin said. "You don't have to tell me."

"How did you know?" I asked.

Shin chuckled. "Because I see with my eyes open. So do you want to talk about it in obtuse vague terms?"

I laughed. "It's not a big deal. I just thought that we were becoming a family, and that they trusted me, but they don't and we aren't."

"What happened?"

"Basically, they were worried I was keeping secrets from them. Instead of asking, or considering that I had simply forgotten, they thought I was keeping secrets on purpose. And not little things, either, but keeping things from them that could keep them safe."

"But that's not who you are," Shin said. "Maybe they're stressed out. People do say things they don't mean when angry."

"Things they don't mean or things they didn't mean to say?" I asked.

Shin sighed. "Things that are only a part of what they think. You are the leader, and they are worried that you will keep something from them. They're afraid that if you don't care enough about them, they might not get important information. But they also trust you, they look to you when things happen. They became afraid, which turned into anger, and they lashed out with their fears, not their hopes."

"But I've never done anything like that before. I don't purposefully keep important information from them."

"No, but if you did, they'd be in trouble," Shin said. "And in the eight months we've traveled together, this is the first time you've done things without them. You guys are always together. Either in small groups or as a whole. Maybe they are feeling insecure about how important they are to you. Maybe they're wondering if they're replaceable?"

"I suppose, but they have made friends and gone off to do things with them." People are too confusing, I liked being a recluse better.

"They make friends with other people in the circus, people who are already part of our family," Shin said.

I rubbed my face. "So what do I do?"

"I don't know. Could you give them the benefit of the doubt, the way you hope they will give you? Assume they are speaking out of fear and anger instead of hope and love."

"Maybe," I said, but did not pout.

Shin laughed. "You don't have to decide tonight, but we do have to get ready for the show."

"Thank you, for helping me. I didn't even realize how upset I was."

Shin wrapped an arm around my shoulders. "Of course. And if you want to tell me your secret, I'll listen."

* * *

This time everyone was spread out around the coffee table in Gavin and Anali's room, eating the food that had been ordered and badly faking being relaxed.

Kayin sat on the arm of the chair I was curled up on. I took a huge bite of raspberry brownie. At least being here wasn't a total waste.

"So," Gavin began, sitting next to Anali who looked alert and had pink cheeks. Her hands were decorated with red-brown mehendi patterns. "I don't need to be an empath to know something is wrong."

I shrugged. "We can't get along all the time."

"Well, I hope you all sort it out before your birthday party," Anali said. "I'd hate for this misunderstanding to ruin your special day."

"I'm sure it'll be fine. So about the hamadryad," I said. It wasn't the smoothest segue, but I wasn't interested in having an intense, touchy-feely talk.

"Wait," Kayin said when I finished telling what had happened. "You were gone for forty-five minutes, and that's all that happened?"

I felt my face heat up. "Well, it's winter, and the hamadryad had to work to stay awake and focused. Anyway, I think trees probably talk more slowly when they are dormant."

Anali leaned forward. "I hope touching Oak for that long didn't cause any problems."

"No, not really. I mean I saw a lot. It's funny how people seemed to know that tree was special. They would come and talk to it all through the centuries that it grew there. Children and adults would come and talk to Oak." I picked up an egg salad sandwich, the sugar from the brownies was started to buzz in my head—I needed some protein. "Oh, also Shin knows we're keeping some kind of a secret. He doesn't know what, and he didn't pressure me to tell him, but he knows something is up."

Sasha huffed and waved his hands in the air. "See, this is what we're talking about. You're just telling us now?"

"Well, since I found out right before the show tonight, and since this is the first chance I've had to talk to all of you, telling you now seemed like the right thing to do," I snapped.

"Did he figure it out today?" Gavin asked.

"No, I don't think. He sounded like he'd known something was up for a while."

"Sapphire and Ramsey did have a good excuse as to why they took so long," Kayin said.

Taliesin raised an eyebrow. "Really, because you don't lie well."

"True, but I didn't have to lie."

Everyone looked at me. I ignored them.

"What she means is that they came back with grass and leaves in their hair, and Shin didn't even ask what they had been doing," Kayin said.

"And what had you been doing?" Gavin asked.

"That," said Anali, "Is none of our business. So what do we do about Shin?"

"Stay away from him," Miu suggested.

Kayin tensed up.

"No," I said. "I don't think he's a threat."

"But he could figure it out," said Sasha.

"That won't put him or us in danger," said Gavin. "I trust Shin. I'm not ready to tell him everything, but I don't feel the need for us to hide from him."

"Good. I like him too," said Anali. "So what about this Tor?"

"Well a Tor is a hill or an outcropping of rocks," said Gavin, while looking up something on his phone. "But the most famous Tor is Glastonbury Tor which is said to have been where Avalon once was. Here."

Gavin held up his phone and a picture of what looking like a stone gateway for a castle standing on a hill.

Sasha pointed at the phone. "That is what I saw! That is the image from my Dream."

"So when do we go?" Taliesin asked.

We all looked around the room trying to find the person with the answer.

"Well," began Gavin. "Oak needs time to let beings know, so not in the next few days. Sasha, could you ask in your Dreams, see if you can find any information?"

He nodded. "Da."

"Okay, anything else?" No one said anything. Gavin clapped his hands. "All right. Well, have a good night then. Sapphire, can you stay for a bit?"

My foot twitched as I waited for everyone to leave. Was I in trouble? Were we going to have another talk about sex? Or Ramsey? I yawned. I hoped this won't take long.

"How was the party?" I asked Anali.

"Oh, I had so much fun. We ate so much, and talked, and painted henna on each other." She held up her hands, her palms looked like mandalas. She smiled so bright and looked healthy again, my heart relaxed. "I can't wait for you to meet everyone tomorrow."

"I'm looking forward to it too. I've never been to a wedding before. What time should I be ready?"

"The ceremony starts at two, so one-thirty?" Anali looked at Gavin.

"One-fifteen in case traffic is bad."

"Okay, great. That'll give me time to sleep in, and I can train in the morning before getting ready." Uncomfortable silence. "Anything else?"

Gavin cleared his throat. "I'm sorry about the other day. When the others told me you were keeping secrets, I got scared that you were in danger. I reacted when I should have talked to you. I wish I had remembered how level headed you are most of the time, and that I do trust you."

I sniffed but wouldn't argue with the 'most of the time' comment. "It's okay, I understand."

"Do you?" Anali asked.

"Well, Shin explained it to me, and I'm trying. But..." I exhaled and curled up, wrapping my arms around my legs. "Do you guys really think that about me? I mean that I'm that bad of a person?"

"No." Gavin jumped up and sat next to me. "No, not at all. I was worried, and angry at myself for not noticing you needed help, which I guess I didn't need to do. I'm sorry." Gavin kissed my head.

"It's okay. I can see how your worry would make you overreact." I could understand Gavin, but I wasn't convinced about the others.

Chapter Nineteen

A sari makes normal women look like royalty. The bright jewel colors, the way you have to hold yourself so it will stay up, and the movement of the fabric. I did my best to act like I fit in, but I felt awkward in the silky fabric and kept checking to make sure it wasn't about to fall off my shoulder. Most of the translucent peridot green sari was wrapped around my waist with the weight settled on my hips. The end crossed over my chest and fell halfway down my back. Anali said the gold beads on the edge would help keep it in place. The matching green silk top was small with buttons down the back, covering my breasts and tops of my arms. I fluctuated between feeling feminine and beautiful to clumsy and wondering if everyone could tell I'd never worn a sari before.

The bride wore a dark red sari with so much gold and crystal beading that it looked uncomfortably heavy. The groom wore a rich cream coat which fell to his knees, with gold elephants embroidered along the edges. Their happiness filled the room as they made their vows.

I looked around the Orangery and its bright, white, wood-framed glass panels. At one time this was a greenhouse specifically for oranges and other citrus. Garlands of marigolds were draped over every available surface, their bitter scent filling the room. I'd have to ask Anali about the importance marigolds because even the bride and groom had necklaces made from them.

Cheers filled the air as the newly married couple kissed. They walked back down the aisle receiving hugs and kisses and offered blessings of a good life and many children. I stepped out of the way. I didn't want to get caught up in that.

Anali wiped her eyes and adjusted her dark blue sari. The silver paisleys caught the light as they moved. "Wasn't that lovely? They look so happy."

"They do look happy," Gavin said, taking her arm. He wore black slacks and a tunic jacket which fell to his knees. Gray tigers were embroidered on the front along the buttons on his chest.

We followed the bride and groom to a different hall. My stomach churned, and my heart beat frantically. Now I would meet Anali's family for the first time. Gavin didn't have any more family left, but Anali had tons, and I couldn't help but worry about what they would think of me. Would they pity me and praise Anali for taking me in? Would they dismiss me because I wasn't really family?

The cold gray day didn't dim the brightness of the reception room. A clear glass ceiling and white walls made more of glass than wood seemed to coax the sun into to room, giving everything a warm glow. Orange and red marigold garlands hung from the walls. Centerpieces with pink-tipped lotus blossoms floating in crystal bowls sparkled on the white table clothes.

"Anali, my darling, I am so pleased you could come," said an older woman. Her black hair had a single silver streak in it and was pulled back into a bun.

"Auntie," said Anali kissing her cheeks. "I'm so happy to be here. You remember my husband Gavin, and this is Sapphire."

Anali's aunt kissed Gavin's checks, then grasped my upper arms to hold me still while she looked me over. "Oh, you're as beautiful as Anali said. Welcome to the family, little niece." She pulled me into a hug, then pushed me back enough to kiss my checks. "I must go and mingle but I'll be back."

I stared after her, wide eyed.

Gavin chuckled. "She is still a force of nature. I'm so glad she likes me."

Anali laughed.

Names, faces, and saris blurred into a swirl of colorful chaos in my head as I was introduced to at least half of the two hundred guests which filled the hall. All of them greeted me with the warmth that Anali's aunt had, and they all called me little cousin, little niece, or little auntie. Whatever Anali was to them, I was that with little in front of it. I blushed every time and wished we lived around Anali's family all the time.

"So my dear niece, how are you?" asked her aunt, who returned as we were served the soup course. The spicy smells of the Indian meal blended with the bitter floral smell of the marigolds. She glared at Gavin. "It must be so hard for you to travel all the time and not have a proper home."

I put a spoonful of soup in my mouth to keep from grinning. My eyes fluttered in pleasure at the taste of creamy lentil dal.

"I love traveling. We have seen so many wonderful places and met such delightful people. When we're done, we have the house in New York waiting for us," Anali said.

"And when is he going to give you a baby?" Auntie sniffed.

"Well," said Anali with a smile, "I only have to wait about eight more months."

Auntie squealed something in Hindi and squeezed Anali tight. "You naughty child, why didn't you tell me yesterday?"

"After what happened last time, I wasn't sure I wanted to tell anyone until I was at least three months along," Anali said.

"Of course you need to tell us, we're family. Now we can give you and the baby our blessings and pray for you both." Auntie kissed her cheeks again.

Gavin handed Anali a handkerchief as she started to tear up.

"Thank you, Auntie."

"Of course, child. This is such exciting news, such a blessing that you will be adding to your lovely little family." Auntie smiled at me. "And you I can tell you are going to make a wonderful big sister."

"I hope so. I've never been around a baby before."

Auntie waved her hand as if banishing my concerns. "You have a good heart—that will guide you."

"Baby?" asked the bride. She and her husband were traveling from table to table, making sure to greet everyone.

"Yes, I'm due in early August," Anali said.

The bride rushed over to Anali, the stacks of bangles on her wrists jingling. She hugged her and kissed her forehead and said a blessing in Hindi. Then she did the same for Gavin, and then for me. I have no idea what was said, but her happiness for us and her affection were real.

This act started an avalanche. Soon even the groom's family and friends we didn't know at all were coming up and offering 'our little family' blessing on the new baby. It was overwhelming, but Anali was glowing, and I swear getting stronger with each heartfelt prayer for her and the baby. I tried to think of a way to escape, but nothing polite came to me. So I breathed and strengthen my shield and waited.

Apparently the signal to stop, or at least wait until later, was the arrival of small pyramids of golden fried samosas brought out on white platters. I didn't blame anyone, these were one of my favorites too.

I wish I had chosen to follow Anali's example and taken small portions of each dish, but it was all so good. When they cut the cake, I was stuffed but I had to eat a piece. I mean who refuses red velvet with cream cheese icing? I'd never eaten it before, but now it was one of my favorites. I sat off to the side watching people dance, sleepy from too much food and buzzing from how welcome and part of the family I felt. Maybe when we were done traveling the world we could live in London and be near Anali's family. I'd ask them later.

* * *

Barely managing to escape, I wound my way through the crowd. I need to get something to drink. Thirty minutes into the dancing, my new 'cousins' coaxed me, rather forcefully, onto the dance floor. After the first few waltzes, the DJ played a mix of pop and Bollywood music. My cousins had far too much fun teaching me Bollywood moves, or at least they had fun watching me trying to learn them.

After downing a glass of water, I found the bathroom. Taking a deep breath and saying a prayer, I went into one of the large stalls.

Happy dance! I managed to finish without unwinding the sari or dropping it into the toilet. Reaching for the stall door handle, I stopped as a group of giggling women came in. "It's so good to see Anali again."

"Yes, and that husband of hers. She married well. Too bad he doesn't have any brothers."

They giggled again. I was going to leave. Right now the embarrassment would be minimal.

"I'm so excited that Anali and Gavin are going to have a baby, now they can be a real family."

A real family. The three of them would be a real family.

"Don't forget Sapphire."

One of them snorted. "Please. I mean Anali obviously cares about her, but it's not like she's a real part of their family. They're taking care of her because her parents died. Once she's eighteen they can be done with her. I mean she didn't even grow up with them. My mom says she grew up in an orphanage. Who knows how she'll act around the baby? I'd be worried if I was Anali."

My hands shook as I pressed them against my chest.

"Come on, let's go back. I think Jai might ask me to dance."

"You say that every time we see him."

I pressed my forehead against the stall door, my breath coming in shallow pants. Did they all feel that way? Were they pretending to make Anali happy? I waited until I was sure they were gone and my eyes no longer burned with tears I refused to shed. I opened the door and washed my hands, because even in times of emotional distress hygiene is important, then slid into the hallway. To the right the party, to the left a long hallway and a door to the outside.

Gasping at the cold wet air, I followed the path a bit. I could hear the music from another wedding. I sat on a stone bench and began five-count breathing. Inhale: one, two, three, four, five. Hold: one, two three, four five. Exhale: one, two, three, four, five. Hold: one, two, three, four five. My heart calmed, and I began to tuck my emotions away. I still had a few hours to get through before Anali would want to leave.

Gravel crunched. I looked up and saw a man in a kilt. I sat up and smiled. How in the world was Ramsey here?

"Seth, wait up," said a woman in a small tight dress.

I shook my head. God, I was pathetic. I couldn't stay out here much longer with the temperature dropping by the minute. Okay, if I go back inside and sit at the little table by the plants, no one will see me.

Gravel crunched again, I didn't bother to look up this time.

"Here I thought I was going to have to sneak into the room, and I think I'd stand out at an Indian wedding."

"Ramsey." I leapt at him wrapping my arms around him and knocking him off balance. He stayed on his feet, swaying just a little. "What are you doing here?"

"We played at the other wedding. What are you doing out here in the cold?" he asked.

I stepped away to admire him in his formal kilt, waistcoat, and jacket. "I needed a break."

"You look lovely." Ramsey leaned down and kissed me. His lips were warm and soft. I sighed placing my hands on his chest.

"Sapphire," Gavin called.

"Here, Uncle Gavin." I stepped back and took Ramsey's hand. "Come with me?"

"Sure."

"What are you doing out here?" Gavin asked then saw Ramsey. "This is quite the coincidence."

Ramsey cleared his throat. "I was playing at the wedding at the other side of the hall."

"And you just happened to find my niece?" Gavin arched an eyebrow.

"Uncle Gavin, I told Ramsey that we were going to the wedding. He came to find me after his gig." I shivered.

"Cold," Ramsey asked wrapping an arm around my shoulders.

"Let's go inside," Gavin said. "Your cousins have been asking for you."

I managed not to snort or say anything rude as I followed Gavin back inside. I should get a gold star.

"Wow," Ramsey said. The dance floor was packed. The variety of colors of the bright saris and men's tunic length jackets with metallic embroidery gave an overwhelming visual impression of movement. All those colors and flashing decorations turning and spinning together looked lovely.

"It's beautiful, isn't it?" I said.

"I don't think I've appreciated saris properly until tonight," Ramsey said looking down at me.

I blushed. "They're beautiful, aren't they?"

"Well, you certainly look beautiful."

It couldn't be good for me to have this much blood racing to my face.

"Why don't you join us?" Gavin said.

We followed Gavin to a table where Anali was sitting, her cheeks flush and her eyes bright with happiness. "Anali, this is my ... friend Ramsey McDaniel. Ramsey, this is my aunt, Anali Marsh."

"Good evening, Mrs. Marsh."

"Oh please call me, Anali. How did you wind up here?" she asked.

"I was playing at another wedding and decided to see if I could sneak in and find Sapphire," Ramsey said.

"Oh, that is so sweet. Isn't it, Gavin? But I think you would have had a bit of a hard time sneaking in," Anali said smiling.

"Aye," Ramsey said deliberately thickening his accent, "Lass, just what do you think would give me away?"

Anali laughed. Gavin glared at him.

"Sapphire, come and dance with us," said one of my 'cousins'.

"Yes," said another. "We were looking for you. Where did you go?"

I smiled for Anali, and stood up. "I needed some air. Ramsey, would you like to dance?"

"Of course," he said taking my hand.

"Be warned, they keep trying to teach me Bollywood moves," I said.

Ramsey chuckled. "My sister had a friend who introduced us to Bollywood. They would learn all the dances and force me and my brother to do the guys' parts."

"I have learned something new about you."

Ramsey arched an eyebrow "Ach, aye, I'm full of mystery."

Chapter Twenty

Melusine rubbed the tip of her finger, the finger that had touched a Child of Fire. She was sure of it. She looked up at the painting of Glastonbury Tor. Those stupid druids banished her from her home, cutting her off from the magic her mother taught her how to use. Closing her eyes, she tried to remember the feeling of Earth magic flowing through her body but it had been too long.

Cartazonon had found her dying, gasping for life, much like the last gnome shaking in the cage behind her. Cartazonon had talked to her for a while then offered to help. She shivered. She still remembered the bitter, icy feel of his foreign magic invading her. Earth magic pulsed with warmth, but the girl she'd touched at the circus—she felt hot.

Half of her library lay strewn about the room as she researched the descendants of the Phoenix King and Queen. Their powers were formidable, and she needed one of them. They would open the door to Avalon, and she would have access to enough power to make Cartazonon unnecessary.

Three sharp knocks.

"Come in Miss Thurston."

"The thugs you hired called in. They say they have found the weakest of the group. So far the others haven't left her alone. But they will grab her as soon as they're able to."

Melusine smiled. "Perfect. Make sure they know I'm not worried about getting it done quickly. I want it done right. We'll only have one shot at this."

"Of course," said Miss Thurston. "I already made sure they understood."

"You're such a treasure," Melusine said. *I'm going to have to find a way to keep her with me.*

* * *

"Now, Lee, don't pout," Cartazonon said. "We can come back soon."

Lee's scarred face frowned. "I'm not pouting. I don't think they're caring for the horses properly."

"I have yet to find anyone that meets your standards in the past three hundred years." Cartazonon picked up his phone.

Lee grunted. "I have a new report. Melusine seems to be watching some circus people. But the walk-ins can't figure out why, they don't feel anything. So it's possible she wants them for their talent."

"She's such a collector."

"Speaking of which, I won the auction for the unicorn figure carved out of ivory."

"Lee, I can always count on you."

"I live to serve."

Cartazonon chuckled. "So when do we arrive in London?"

"On the twenty-first, sir."

"The darkest night of the year—that goes well with my evil plans."

Lee smirked. "Better than the handlebar mustache you used to spend so much time waxing."

"I looked good in that mustache."

Lee chose to keep silent.

"Who is Peterson? He's quitting due to family problems," Cartazonon said reading his email.

"He works in the Chicago office. His wife has cancer and needs care. He is in R and D."

"Wait, is he the one working on the Tesla coil project?"

Lee nodded. "Yes."

"Oh, no. That's not going to happen. Send someone from HR to find out what he needs and give it to him. He can work half days, get him a nurse, increase his salary, set him up to work from home, whatever. And then have HR go over our insurance and benefits and find out how this happened and fix it for everyone."

"It will be done," Lee said.

Chapter Twenty-One

"Go for it now. The future is promised to no one." ~ Dr.
Wayne W. Dyer

My breath fogged up the hotel window. Miu got in the shower,
and I waited to go out on my 'birthday adventure.'

"Come in," I called to the knock at the door.

"Anali, is everything okay? Do you need Miu?"

She smiled. "I'm fine. I wanted to talk to you."

"Okay. Well, sit down. Do you need anything?"

"My goodness, you fuss as much as your uncle."

Rude!

"Did Miu just get into the shower?"

Japanese pop covered the sound of the running water. "Yes,
why?"

"I wanted to talk to you alone," Anali said, relaxing into the
couch.

My stomach tightened. Talk to me about what? The
wedding last night? The argument? Ramsey? The baby? What?
"Okay."

Anali arched an eyebrow and gave me the 'mom' look.

I squirmed the tiniest of bits.

"My goodness, I have been out of the loop. I don't think you've reacted that strongly to me wanting to talk since the first month you lived with us." Anali stared at me for a moment as if she could see all the different thoughts and worries bouncing through me. "Well, what I want to talk to you about is your outing with Miu."

"Has something come up? Do we need to do it another day?" I said.

Anali wagged her finger at me. "This is what I'm talking about. You're not excited. You're not looking forward to this at all."

I turned and looked at the bathroom door, music and steam escaped under the bottom. Leaning forward, I whispered. "Miu doesn't need to know that."

"Don't you think you should be honest with your friends?"

"No."

Level four mom glare. Rude.

"Sapphire, you and Miu have been getting closer. She's growing up, you're relaxing a bit and allowing yourself to try new things."

"Yes, and this is important to Miu. Once she saw my new clothes and the fact that I'm willing to wear them, she got this manic look in her eyes and asked if she could take me out for my birthday gift."

"So you care enough about Miu to want to keep her happy but not enough to talk to her and try to work this out?"

I looked at the bathroom door again. "Look, I haven't quite got this whole thing figured out."

"Kids didn't overreact, say things they didn't mean, or lash out at the group homes?" Anali placed her hand on her belly, as if protecting the baby.

I snorted. "Of course they did, but there was always a reason. They couldn't cope with the transition from a visit to back at the home. A visit was canceled. They got in trouble at school. Someone forgot to give them a med. There was always a clear cause for their lashing out. And anyway their emotional cups were so full, that anything that upset them caused things to overflow."

Anali held up a hand. "What?"

I sighed. "I always imagined emotions as a cup which is full of all this old yuck, so when something happened it was like dropping a rock into the cup and all this emotion would come spilling out."

"How interesting."

"My houseparent Melanie called it emotional vomiting."

Anali wrinkled her nose and smiled.

"Anyway, these guys don't have any excuses. They got together, talked, and decided I was a bad person who lies to them and puts them in danger." I said, glancing at the bathroom door again.

"So the fact that the holidays are coming and they won't be with their families couldn't be putting them on edge?" Anali asked. "Or the fact that you're their leader, you keep them together, and you've found someone else to spend your time with? Not that I blame you. Sasha lost his father, perhaps forever, and only got to see his mother for one night. And Miu wants to be your best friend so badly, it hurts her when you leave her out of things."

Frowning, I looked out the window. "Yeah, okay. I can see how they could have been emotionally venting and didn't completely mean the things they said."

"They told me about your idea to be more like a family."

"Yeah, that worked out well," I muttered.

Anali laughed. "It did actually. Other than the fight, they felt like you cared about them. They felt listened to."

The steam stopped flooding from under the bathroom door. "So what do you want me to do?"

Anali reached out and took my hand. "I want you to have fun today. I want you to know that they're truly sorry and feel guilty for how they handled things. I want you to know they feel stressed out and are missing their families."

"How do you know this and I don't?"

"I've been empathic longer than you and I know how to read the emotion under what they are projecting. I wasn't upset, so my own emotions didn't get in the way. You work very hard to block out other people's emotions, because you feel them more intensely than I do."

I nodded. Most of the time I only felt what skimmed across my empathic bubble. Rarely did I search beneath the surface of what people felt. "Wouldn't it be wrong of me to read people's emotions at that level? I mean it seems like it would be invading their privacy."

"You have to figure that out for yourself. I am able to sense the layers of emotions and when needed, I look deeper. You are their friend, but also their leader," Anali said.

"I don't want to become overwhelmed by their emotions. I'm not sure how to sense theirs and not everyone else's, and I don't want them mad at me because I'm invading their privacy."

Anali squeezed my hand. "We can talk about this more later, and I am willing to help you. For today try to have a good time. Families fight, then they forgive each other."

"Okay, I'll try, but I reserve the right to fake it to keep Miu happy."

Anali kissed the top of my head. "Okay Sapphire, have a good day."

The front door shut as Miu opened the bathroom door. "I'll be ready in five minutes."

I shook my head—that meant ten minutes. It didn't matter, I was ready. "Hurry up. I want my surprise."

Miu's smile was worth exaggerating the truth.

* * *

Something was wrong. I rode the elevator up, stopping at every floor hoping to get an idea of where to go. I wanted to nap. My day with Miu had worn me out.

The door opened to the tenth floor. A soft cry. A gasp for air. Walking towards the sounds, I lowered my shield a little. Sorrow, guilt, and an odd sense of peace floated on the air like a fog. Looking into all the shadowy places, I walked down the hallway. Around the corner, Taliesin knelt on the floor holding the hand of a woman who was gasping for breath, her lips blue and her eyes wide.

"Taliesin, have you called for help?" How did he always find these people? First Argentina, the guy in Mexico, and now here.

He shook his head, his white hair swaying.

I knelt next to him. A silver blue star glowed on his forehead where his horn would be in unicorn form. Tears filled his eyes, and his jaw was clenched tight.

"Taliesin?"

"You can go and get help, but she'll probably be gone by then," he whispered his voice rough.

"Should we try CPR?" I asked. Michael had made the whole troupe take First Aid/CPR when we started touring. I remembered hoping I'd never have to use it.

Taliesin tightened his grip as she convulsed. "No, this is what she wants."

"Okay." I took his free hand. His magic felt fierce and demanding.

The woman's eyes seemed to focus on the ceiling, but I doubted that's what she was seeing. I gasped at the burst of shame and guilt coming from her. Her breath came in short rattling pants. The space between them grew longer with each one. When the next one didn't come, I held my breath. The life faded from her body. Everything went limp. And the emotions faded like smoke in the wind.

"Oh," I said, wiping tears from my eyes. "She just ...oh."

Taliesin lay the woman's hand on her stomach. "Thank you for staying with me."

"Of course, you needed me," I said. "But what happened? Is it a unicorn thing to know when someone is going to die? When they need comfort?"

Taliesin's laugh sent a shiver along my spine. "No, nothing quite so noble. We should probably tell someone."

"I'll go to the front desk and let them know."

He nodded.

As I rode the elevator, I sent Philip a text, asking him for the book he wrote on royal magical creatures. It was time I studied unicorns.

* * *

"Are you sure?" I asked, pushing the button for the elevator with my manicured and polished fingernail. Miu had taken me to get our fingernails and toenails done as one of my gifts. Miu's nails were done in a powder pink glitter polish with rhinestone tips and Hello Kitty painted onto each ring finger. Mine were classic red, a much brighter color than I normally do.

Taliesin rolled his eyes. "Yes. I'm ignoring it for tonight. We got through all the questions from the manager, and then the show, and now it's time to go to your party."

"If you're sure. Because we can cancel it or go later if you need to talk?" Taliesin felt like he'd surrounded himself in glass with his emotions locked away.

"If you don't want to go, that's fine. But I'm going, and I'm going to have fun and relax and pretend none of this happened." He smoothed his wrinkle-free royal blue shirt. He had left the first few buttons undone. His milk white skin glowed against the vibrant silk, and you could see the curve of his muscular chest. Charcoal gray slacks were fitted tight and made his ass look rather spectacular. "Anyway, you dressed nice enough that I'm willing to be seen with you in public. You don't want to waste that rare opportunity."

I shoved him. "You're such a brat."

He chuckled.

"Are we ready?" asked Kayin. Shin was going to drool. Kayin wore black jeans that showed his muscles moving under the fabric, and a fitted, cream silk shirt that clung to his body. I hoped he knew what he was getting himself into.

Sasha followed behind him, black slacks molded to his thighs and probably butt. I'd check later. The thin plum cashmere sweater did nothing to hide the muscle underneath. "Where's Miu?"

"She went ahead to make sure everything was perfect," I said. "I think she took the hula hoop and the diabolo girls with her. You both look lovely."

"I can't believe Gavin is letting you out in that dress," Kayin said. "You look sexy."

"Well, Anali might have seen me first then pretended to feel sick before Gavin saw me."

"That explains it," Sasha said, looking me over. "There is no way he'd let you leave looking like that."

I was going to take that as a compliment. The elevator doors opened.

"So Gavin rented us a car?" Kayin asked.

Taliesin snorted. "He rented limos."

"What?" Why would he do something that extravagant? "A limo really?"

"Several," Sasha said. "Enough for the whole troupe so that everyone would get back to the hotel safely."

"Oh, well. That was thoughtful." I put on my coat as the elevator door opened and we walked into the cold night. Squeezing into the limo, I wound up sitting on Kayin's lap with my legs over Taliesin so we could all squeeze in with the acrobats.

We heard the music from the club before we even opened the door. The bouncer, a stocky muscular man with tattoos decorating his deep brown skin, pointed up to the metal spiral staircase. This took us to a loft space where we could look onto the rest of the club. There was a long table covered in food and pitchers of drinks. On a smaller table were gifts and cards. Miu had decorated the whole place in purple and green streamers and balloons. There was even a banner that said *Happy 16th Birthday Sapphire!* When did she have time to make a banner?

"Happy birthday," Miu said, her arms wide.

"Thank you. This is amazing, and you look wonderful."

Miu twirled. She wore a golden yellow silk dress with a black patent leather belt and Mary Jane pumps with rhinestone Hello Kitty buckles.

"Thank you. So come on and enjoy yourself. We have food, drinks, a space for dancing, and plenty of tables and chairs to relax." Miu grabbed my arm. "You look hot in that dress. Are you hungry?"

I laughed. "Starving."

"When is Ramsey getting here?"

"I don't know. He has a gig, then he'll come afterward." I filled up a plate with french fries—chips here, I suppose—egg rolls, mac 'n' cheese, mini mushroom and cheese pies, and some sandwiches. There was more to choose from but my plate was full. "So, is there a master plan or wild unorganized fun?"

"I figure two hours for people to eat, dance, and socialize, then presents and cake."

I sat at a table overlooking the dance floor and stage. "Sounds good, although aren't people always hungry for cake?"

Miu chuckled. "Probably. Looks like they are setting up for a band. I didn't know there would be live music. I hope they're good."

"Looking at the crowd gathering near the stage I'd say they are. Good food," I said biting into a pie.

"Brandon's aunt was so helpful." Miu bit her bottom lip. "You really like it?"

"I think it's great. I never imagined it would be this big. Look at everyone—they're having so much fun." The whole troupe was there, filling their plates, toes tapping, and shoulders bopping. As soon as bellies were full, the dance floor would be full of gyrating bodies. "And what is with that pile of gifts? I thought I said no gifts."

Miu raised her hands. "I said no gifts. It's not my fault no one listens to me."

I sniffed but grinned. "It's very sweet of everyone, but what could they have gotten me?"

"Aren't gift supposed to be a surprise?" Kayin asked as he sat.

"That is the way normal people go about it," added Sasha.

"Well," I said, before Taliesin could add to the supposedly funny comments. "For the past few years I've always known what my gifts were going to be. It's been years since I was surprised by a birthday gift."

"Tonight that changes," said Miu.

"Good evening, ladies and gentleman. Before I introduce the band, I want to say happy sixteenth birthday to Sapphire."

The crowd and all my friends cheered. My cheeks heated up to the point I was worried I'd be red all night.

"And now tonight's band: the Water Nymphs."

"What?" My gasp was drown out under the crowds cheering. I glared at Ramsey, and, even though I doubted he could see me, he grinned up where I was.

"Isn't that Ramsey?" Shin asked as he sat next to Kayin, stealing an egg roll from his plate.

"He said he was performing close by, not that he was performing here," I said.

"Hurry up and eat," Shin said. "Those of us who don't take as much time to look stunning are ready to dance."

"Are you saying I wasn't worth waiting for?"

Shin grinned at me. "Honey, you look so lovely I almost wish I was straight."

* * *

Women don't sweat, we glisten. After dancing pressed against every member of the circus at least once, I was glistening a lot. It had started out as a big friendly dance fest. Now people were started to pair off or trying to pair off. I moved between people to grab a cup of water from the table. I watched my friends dancing. Several of the guys took off their shirts and were dancing in muscle shirts which clung to their bodies. I leaned on the railing and watched the band—well, okay Ramsey—play. I wasn't the only one watch him in his kilt and black tee shirt.

There were many people in the crowd focused not on the band, but on us dancing. I wondered how many of the troupe would decide to go on to the main dance floor and pick someone up. I hoped the wave of anger from the men at the bar who were glaring at us wouldn't cause trouble for anyone later. They looked nice enough from up here, but they were normal guys and for lustful club thoughts and hopes, our muscular circus bodies caught more attention.

"Having fun?" Kayin asked, his chest heaving.

"Yes, you?"

"I am. Dancing is fun."

"I saw you and Shin dancing earlier." I smiled as he looked away.

"Well, we were dancing close but not together, we were part of a group." His nervousness prickled against me.

I sighed, poor Kayin he was still confused about what to do. Then I saw something that might help him make up his mind. I pointed to the dance floor. "Looks like you won't have to worry about it anymore."

Hot jealousy flared from Kayin as he watched Shin dancing with one of the Russian pole performers, Derrik. Their bodies were pressed together and Derrik's hand was on Shin's butt. "He shouldn't dance with him like that."

"Why not?" I asked. Kayin stood taller as his jaw clenched. "Is he yours? Because if he's not yours, he can dance with whoever he wants to."

I gripped the railing as the mad swirl of Kayin's emotions made me dizzy.

"I just don't know."

"You can waste your life waiting to know for sure. Waiting for a sign, or to know without a doubt." I said, repeating the words my mother wrote in my journal. "There is no certainty in life. Weigh the pros and cons, make lists, listen to your mind, your heart, and your gut. But in the end you have to act, you have to do something. You have to make a decision and move forward in your life. For good or bad, you must choose."

"Your mother?" Kayin asked his eyes still fixed on Shin.

"Yes."

"I'm scared."

I held his hand. "Of course you are, Big Brother. That's normal, that's life. Are you going to let it stop you?"

Kayin took a deep breath, squeezed my hand and walked over to Shin. He tapped Derrik on the shoulder, cutting in a like a gentleman. Those BBC period dramas taught him proper manners. Derrik left, and Shin stood there. Kayin moved closer and slid his arms around Shin's shoulders, his hands shaking. Shin moved closer and started to dance. It wasn't as raunchy as with the other guy, but a hundred times sexier.

"Thank god that worked," Miu said.

"What? Did you set that up?" I didn't think Shin would play with Kayin like that.

"Just Derrik hitting on Shin."

"What if Kayin hadn't reacted?" I asked.

"Derrik is easy. He wouldn't have cared how it worked out."

I wrinkled my nose.

"Yeah, not my thing either. And I didn't think Shin would go off with him even if Kayin chickened out. But I had to do something. The longing looks and sad sighs, I couldn't take any more of it." Miu grinned.

A slow song began. Kayin and Shin curled around each other swaying to the melody of Ramsey's cello.

"Did they finally get everything figured out?" Nyota asked.

"With some help from Miu," I said. "You look hot."

Nyota wore a pair of red satin pants and a lacy black bustier. I don't think I've actually ever seen a heaving bosom before.

Red and black beads were draped over her creamy brown skin drawing even more attention to the heaving. Her dreadlocks wove a complicated braid which fell down her back.

"Thanks. My poor dad took a moment before he relaxed and remembered I'm twenty-four and not fourteen."

"He looks like he's having fun."

Michael was dancing with a group.

"Your dad is a good dancer," Miu said as he broke out some disco moves.

"Well," I said laughing. "At least he does those moves well."

Nyota shook her head. "Oh well, he wouldn't be a dad if he didn't embarrass me sometimes."

"You've been a great audience," said Solange. "Thank you for coming out tonight, we'll be selling CDs for a bit at the back table."

"Okay, everyone," Miu called out while the club was—well, not silent but there was no music blaring. "Let's do cake and presents."

She made it sound like I was five. I hope people didn't fight over the icing roses.

The staff brought out a cake that looked like it belonged on one of those cooking shows. It was three tiers covered in bright blue icing with purple irises. They looked so real that it took me a minute to realize they were made of icing. There were sparkling rhinestones that I assumed we could eat, because they were scattered all over the cake.

Miu lit the candles, my face heated up, and I wondered how Miu knew irises were my favorite flower? I couldn't remember ever talking about it. I blew out the candles, and my wish was that someone else would cut the cake as I didn't even know where to start. Wish answered. The server came back and handed me a slice with a large purple iris on top. Inside it was chocolate with a dark shiny chocolate filling that tasted like soft fudge. My eyes fluttered as I took a bite.

"Lucky cake."

I opened my eyes to see Ramsey standing in front of me.

263

"You are in trouble."

He placed his hand on his chest and fluttered his own eyelashes.

"Me, whatever did I do?"

"You didn't tell me your gig was here," I said, trying to glare. I couldn't help but smile, a closed-lip smile in case I had chocolate in my teeth.

He flashed his evil grin.

"Happy birthday." And kissed my cheek.

"Cake?" Kayin held out a plate.

"Cheers. Looks like a smashing party," Ramsey said. "Great cake."

"It's wonderful. Everyone seems to be having a great time," I said taking a small bite of the icing. It was creamy, rich, and sweet but not teeth-achingly sweet. Best cake ever.

"You look so sexy by the way," Ramsey said. "I know I saw you in this dress before, but my memory must be faulty because you look even better than I remembered."

"She does look great," Shin said, his arm touching Kayin's as he ate his cake.

I blushed again.

"You sounded wonderful tonight, and seem to have drawn quite the group of fangirls."

Ramsey chuckled.

"Since I'm the most handsome man in the group, the others were happy to see me go so they could have all the female attention. But I also noticed a lot of the women looking up here, not that I blame them." Ramsey looked at Shin arms.

Shin grinned and shifted the muscles moving under his amber colored skin. "Poor ladies, and guys. I guess we are irresistible."

I rolled my eyes, but couldn't disagree.

I put the last bit of cake in my mouth, savoring the flavor and sad that it was all gone at the same time.

"Are you done?" Miu asked. "Let's open presents."

"I thought there weren't supposed to be presents," I said, again, as my plate was taken away and I was led to a table.

Miu sniffed. "I can't control people."

There were only a few packages and the rest were cards. That was okay. We celebrated everyone's birthday in the troupe, but never with parties this big. I felt bad being treated differently from everyone else. I opened the cards reading the birthday wishes. A few people included gift cards, and more told me to expect an email from Amazon. Because we traveled so much the majority of gifts we gave each other went right into our computers, tablets, MP3 players, and cell phones. I liked gift cards, but getting a specific book, movie, or CD was a little more personal. I thanked each person, or group, and most wandered off to get more food or go back to dancing.

Miu pushed the packages at me. "I can't wait to see what is in them."

The first was from Michael and Nyota. "It's beautiful."

"Dad, got the yarn, and I crocheted it," she said.

Bright red yarn, almost the same shade as my nail polish, had been crocheted into a lacy sweater. "I love the collar and hem, they remind me of poinsettias."

Nyota smiled. "I thought so too. Dad thought they looked like pinwheels."

I laughed. "I can see that."

Two other packages looked soft and squishy. Many of the performers did some kind of handcraft, partly because they're simply creative people and partly because they're ADD and need something to do all the time. I got a pair of knitted fingerless gloves in multiple shades of blue from some of the acrobats. Now I could stay warm but still work touch screens. There was a knitted cowl in a pale gray that was big enough to wrap around my neck three times. The yarn was so soft I wanted to bury my face in it like one would with a kitten.

Kayin set a coin on the table in front of me.

"Thank you." Um, what?

Kayin smiled. "Give it to Shin after you get your gift."

Shin held out a package wrapped in black rice paper flecked with rainbow-colored pieces of paper. Under the paper was a polished wooden box. "Oh, shiny." A knife, the silver blade recently oiled, and the dark wooden handle with the silhouette of a tiger carved into it, lay in the box. "You're going to teach me how to use this right?"

"Yes, there is a rubber practice knife in the box too. We'll start with that," Shin said. "Now give me some money."

"Why the money?" I asked, handing him the coin and putting the knife away.

"You can't give a knife as a gift, it could cut your friendship, so you always give a coin in exchange to pay for it."

Ramsey laughed. "We have the same tradition."

"Da, in Russia too," said Sasha. "Here, mine is the last gift."

I peeled back the metallic blue paper. "Oh they're … magical." I wrinkled my nose at my very poor save in front of Shin and the others. A pair of earrings with Akashic energy lay on a square of white cotton. Each earring had seven silver spiderweb thin chains of graduating lengths. At the end of each chain hung a teardrop shaped stone, one for each color of the rainbow. I took out my simple gold hoops and put these in. "Where did you find them?"

"In a dream."

"Someone called their store, In a Dream?" Shin asked.

Sasha nodded. "Yes, I thought it was silly, but these were in the window."

"Well I love them, thank you."

Sasha bowed his head.

"Don't forget we're going out on Wednesday," Kayin said.

I stood up and hugged him. "Big Brother, how could I forget that?" He'd planned something super-secret, like Miu had. I doubt we'd get our nails done, however.

"So," said Ramsey. "Do I get to dance with you now?"

"Of course." The club DJ was playing standard thumping dance music. "Unfortunately, the music isn't as good now."

Ramsey smiled and wrapped an arm around my waist. "Oh, you know how to warm a man's heart."

I slid my arms around his shoulders as our bodies began to move to the music. All night I had danced with people, but this was different. There was an intensity that made me blush. His desire and happiness wrapped around my own. My head swam with emotion.

Ramsey found a way to pull me closer as a slow song came on. His nose tickled my ear as he kissed my neck. "You smell like jasmine."

"Hmmm, oh yes. Miu took me to LUSH, and I bought a Godiva shampoo bar," I said.

Ramsey kissed my neck again "Whatever it is, it's a very enticing scent on you."

"I'm glad you like it."

I squeaked.

"Sorry," said Kayin. "Didn't mean to bump into you."

Shin rolled his eyes, as Kayin moved to face us and started dancing.

Ramsey smiled, winked at me and backed up so we could all dance together.

The joy of Big Brothers.

Chapter Twenty-Two

"Happy sixteenth birthday," Ramsey said and bent down to kiss me.

Do I even need to say that I blushed, just assume if Ramsey is kissing me, then my cheeks are bright red.

"Thank you."

He shifted his yoga bag before taking my hand. His other held a large red gift bag with tissue paper sticking out the top. What had he gotten me? I wanted to grab it but resisted. "Have you eaten yet?"

"No, I haven't been awake that long." Truthfully, I only got out of bed because Ramsey texted me to let me know he was awake. I had an hour to get ready and meet him at the cafe. Looking like you didn't put any effort into looking good takes more time than one would imagine.

"So tell me all about your birthday fun," Ramsey said after we ordered and had a cups of hot tea in front of us.

"Well, yesterday I went out with Miu." I began adding milk and sugar to my tea. "She took me out for Japanese noodles and dumplings. Then we went shopping. According to Miu a woman should use quality beauty products, so she took me to LUSH, Ulta, and Sephora."

"That sounds like fun," Ramsey said. "Did you get a lot?"

"Well, I got a ton of LUSH, different soaps, shampoo bars, bath bombs, and other essentials."

"Bath bombs are essential?"

I chose to ignore him. "I got some makeup and nail polish at the other stores, and you were at the party."

Ramsey smiled. "Sounds like a fun day."

"It was." I ran a hand through my hair. It was still a little damp from my shower. "Of course, I'm sure today will be pretty great too."

"I hope so. I brought you something." He handed me the bag.

"You didn't have too," I said, while removing the tissue paper. "Oh, Ramsey, it's beautiful. Did your brother make it?" I ran a finger along the edge of the drum. Green and blue knotwork decorated the edge. In the center, a knot-work unicorn and phoenix were entwined.

"Yeah, I told him how much you liked the other one. He woke up the next day and started painting this one."

I looked in the bag and smiled, pulling out two CDs from Ramsey's band and a stuffed seal. "It's so cute."

"I know you're kind of old for a plushie, but I wanted you to have something to remember me by," Ramsey said with a grin.

"I love it," I said, giving the toy a squeeze.

We stopped talking while the waitress set down our plates. Ramsey sprinkled salt and pepper on his scrambled eggs and salmon. I poured maple syrup over my French toast and scrambled eggs.

"That is gross," Ramsey said staring at my syrup covered eggs.

I laughed. "It grosses Taliesin out too. So what do you have planned for today?"

"Well, I was planning on taking you shopping for makeup, but since Miu beat me to it, I'll have to think of something else," Ramsey said a small version of his evil/fun grin.

I shook my head. "You are trouble."

Ramsey's response was a full evil/fun grin.

"Thank you for breakfast," I said swirling the last piece of French toast in the syrup.

"You're welcome. Are you ready to have fun?" Ramsey jumped. "Hold on."

I finished my tea while he read over an apparently long text.

"I'm sorry, it's my friend Mindy. She's freaking out. I mean she does this every few months, but this time is kind of weird." Ramsey slipped his yoga bag over his chest.

I smiled trying to hide my disappointment and picked up my gifts. "I understand."

"Can we meet up later?" he asked as we walked into the damp cold morning.

"Maybe. I have plans with my aunt and uncle at five. Of course, if Anali is sick that might fall through."

"I'm sorry, Sapphire," he said, his hand cupping the back of my head and his forehead pressed to mine.

I placed my hands on his chest, gathered my courage and kissed him, sucking on his lower lip gently.

Ramsey groaned and wrapped his other arm around my waist, pulling me close.

Yay, I must have done it right! I wrapped my arms around him as he kissed me back.

"You know . . ." His breath was warm against my lips. "She gets like this all the time. I can check on her later. I bet one of her other friends is already over there anyway."

"Are you sure?"

I took his kiss as a yes.

* * *

"A carnival?" I asked, looking at the booths, rides, and attraction decked out in holiday decorations.

"Yes, Hyde Park looks even better at night with all the lights turned on, but I figured this would still be a fun way to spend the day," Ramsey said.

"I think it looks wonderful. What should we do first?"

"Well, they have rides, a market, an ice kingdom, and ice skating." Ramsey pointed at the wooden map where each activity was marked.

I didn't know how to ice skate, so we would be avoiding that, hopefully without having to admit that I'd only done it once and ended up with a broken wrist. "What's the ice kingdom?"

Ramsey held out his hand. "Let's go find out."

I slid my hand into his.

"Wow, this is all ice?" I looked up at a castle with turrets and a drawbridge large enough to walk through.

"Yes, I guess they truck in huge ice blocks and snow," Ramsey said.

"It reminds me of the Snow Queen fairy tale." I said, as we walked around and through the ice sculptures.

"I think," said Ramsey, "she's right over there."

"Oh," I gasped. Sitting on an ornate throne was a queen made of ice. She stared down at her court. The lords and ladies were dancing. "It's beautiful. Thank you for bringing me here, I've never seen anything like it."

Ramsey smiled, his black eyes shining. "You're welcome."

He moved closer. I started to close my eyes. A group of laughing children ran by.

"Come on," he said. "We have more to see."

My butt was freezing, but I sat in the carriage carved from ice long enough to get a picture with Ramsey and a quick, well maybe not quick, but very nice kiss.

A carved bear stood at the exit holding out a paw as if waving goodbye.

"Do you want to do some rides?" Ramsey asked.

"Yes. I think the last time I went to a carnival I was too short to go on any of the big rides," I said, adjusting my cowl.

"That long ago?" Ramsey asked. "Do they not have fun fairs where you grew up?"

I laughed. "No they had them, but well, they can be expensive to take a bunch of kids to. And sometimes there would be kids in the house who weren't safe to take. I was too short until I turned thirteen, and then I caught up with the other girls. I probably wouldn't have been able to go on a lot of the rides anyway."

"Well, then, scary rides it is, but you'll have to hold my hand." Ramsey winked at me.

A little while later, I held my breath as the roller coaster climbed to the top. What in the hell was I thinking—this was bad, so bad. And Ramsey, who obviously wanted me to die a painful death, had insisted we go in the very front car. I was pressed against the seat with my hands gripping the so-called safety bar close to me. In front of me nothing but sky. I closed my eyes and tried to figure out which god or goddess to pray to.

"Don't close your eyes, it'll make it worse." Ramsey said. "Are you going to be okay?"

I opened my eyes and nodded. The car stopped. I gasped. Ramsey put an arm around my shoulders. How long were these sadists going to make us stay up here? The wheels squealed as it began to move forward and we went down, straight down.

I screamed and clung to Ramsey.

"That was so fun!" I said, holding onto Ramsey's arm. The adrenalin made my knees weak. "Can we go again?"

Ramsey chuckled and kissed my cheek. "As many times as you want."

* * *

"Okay we have to stop, no more rides," Ramsey said, looking at me. A breeze picked up and blew curls across his face. Reaching up, he tucked the dark brown strands behind his ear.

I took a deep breath to try and keep my teeth from chattering. "I'm fine."

He raised an eyebrow. "Your lips are blue." Wrapping an arm around my waist he guided me towards the tents. "Come on, let's get you warmed up. We still have two hours before I have to have you back at the hotel. We can go on more rides later."

I snuggled into him, maybe I was a little cold. "I like the rides."

"You are a closet adrenalin junkie," Ramsey said with a chuckle. "And since we've gone on almost every ride three times, I kind of reckon you enjoyed them."

Ramsey wove through the tables. "Here, this spot is close to a heater. You sit here, and I'll bring you something hot."

I sighed as heat enveloped me. I wasn't going anywhere. I held my hands out towards the glowing red coils. Heat is good.

"Here we go." Ramsey set down a tray. "Feeling better?"

"Yes, much. Thank you." I took the cup of hot cider. Yum.

"So I have two bread bowls: one cream of broccoli and the other potato, leek, and Stilton cheese. They were the only two vegetarian options."

How sweet. "Thank you. They both look great. I don't know which one to choose."

Ramsey relaxed and sat back in his chair. "Well, I don't mind sharing if you don't."

"Sounds perfect," I said, accepting a spoon and napkin.

"I also have a selection of Christmas biscuits and minced pies," Ramsey said setting a pink cardboard box on the table.

"Bread bowls are very popular in San Francisco," I said taking a bite of soup. Oh, Stilton is like blue cheese, the tangy flavor perfect with the potatoes and leeks.

"You grew up there, right?"

I nodded. "Yes, they put clam chowder in them, plus other soups and salads."

"I like the bread once the soup is gone," Ramsey said.

My stomach rumbled. "I guess I'm hungrier than I thought."

Ramsey grinned. "It's one of the things I like about you."

I frowned at him, my mouth full of soup.

"That you actually eat. I've dated girls who always seem to be on diet, or don't eat in front of guys."

"Oh, well. Anali, Gavin, and Michael would freak if I were dieting. They watch all the performers carefully and notice any changes in what we eat. We had a girl pass out a few months ago, turned out she had an eating disorder. She was sent home to get help."

"I'm sorry."

"She's doing well, she's in treatment and getting better. Anyway, as for not doing something in front of a guy, I never understood it. No guy is worth my pretending to be something other than what I am. And why would I want to date a guy who wanted me to be stupider, or eat less, or not be good at something to make him feel better about himself?"

"It's very true. Only a weak man would want the woman he's with to be less than she is. I'm comfortable with the fact that you're stronger than I am."

I raised an eyebrow.

"And," Ramsey added his eyes sparkling. "That you can eat as much as I can."

"You're a brat," I said pointing my spoon at him. "I can eat as much as you, and I suppose that depends on how you define strength. I have no idea if I could beat you arm wrestling, but I can do handstand push-ups."

"I would pay to see you do those," he said. "And I'm not going to risk my manly dignity by challenging you to an arm wrestling contest."

I laughed and tore off a piece of the bread bowl. The soup was almost all gone, so it was fair game. "Oh, hey, do you have any special powers or gifts, as a selkie?" I probably should have read up on them in Philip's book on magical creatures but I've been busy and distracted, and honestly, it seemed a bit rude.

"Not really. We metabolize fat better than regular people. But in the water, then we are brilliant." Ramsey's eyes lost focus as if he was looking back at a memory. "In school my siblings and I were on the swim team and we always came in first. Well, unless there was a selkie on the other team. Then there was real competition. The coaches wanted us to try to go to college on scholarships or join teams that competed nationally, but they do blood tests looking for drugs at that level and our blood would come up looking different."

"I'm sorry. That sucks."

He tore off some bread. "I can always slip into my skin and race other seals or whales."

"That must be amazing."

"I love the ocean, and I love the city. I think I'd go crazy if I couldn't have them both."

I leaned back, sat up and pulled my braid in front of me, and relaxed again into the chair. I twirled the black and red end of my braid around my finger. "So when do you leave? I mean I assume you'll be going home for Christmas."

"Hen, are you trying to get rid of me?"

I rolled my eyes.

Ramsey gathered up the empty plates, set them aside, and picked up the pastry box. "Dessert?"

"Of course." I moved so I could see what he'd brought.

"I wasn't sure what you like, so I got a variety of Christmas biscuits, and a mince pie for each of us."

"They all look wonderful." I picked a shiny dark brown sphere.

"That's a rum ball. Be careful, they can be potent."

I smelled the rum, and a sweet warmth filled my mouth. "Yum, but I don't think I should eat more than one."

Ramsey ate the other, and his eyes widened. "These are stronger than my Grandfather's, and I didn't think anyone would dare make them stronger than that."

"You have a big family—that must be nice," I said.

"Aye. Of course sometimes it feels overwhelming when you're related to half the village you grow-up in." Ramsey grinned. "Of course when I was in trouble there were plenty of places to run away to."

"I grew up alone, there was no one to run to. Who I lived with changed all the time. I can't even imagine having the security of being surrounded by family," I said, picking a round white cookie out of the box. It was so pretty. The image of a snowman stood out on the top of the light cookie. I bit into it and wrinkled my nose. The pretty cookie was a trap. What was this? Licorice? What kind of person makes licorice cookies?

Ramsey laughed.

I glared at him.

"I'm sorry," he said clutching his side. "It's just you looked so betrayed. Some people like springerle biscuits."

I washed the bite down with the last of my apple cider. "Normal people?"

Ramsey shook his head, trying and failing to contain his laughter. "Yes, normal people. Oh, God, that was brilliant."

I looked at the other cookies, lying in the box all innocent and delicious looking. I didn't trust them. "Are there any other surprise cookies in there?"

"No, I don't think so. All normal respectable, wholesome Christmas biscuits," he said.

I picked a shortbread cookie, something I was sure would be safe. I mean how could you mess up butter and sugar?

"Good choice, always go Scottish."

"Maybe I want to get it out of the way," I said biting the cookie in half. Perfect.

"Your face gives you away, you're either very expressive or completely blank when you're hiding something." Ramsey stared at me, making me blush.

I ignored him. "So what's in a mince pie?"

He grinned. "Dried fruit, sugar, spices, probably brandy. I did ask to make sure they are vegetarian."

That sounded safe. I picked up one of the little pies, the top of the crust glazed with white icing. Sweetened spices flooded my mouth, followed by a tang of alcohol. "These are good. You might even be forgiven for the evil cookie."

Ramsey shook his head and grabbed a pie for himself.

Once the pastry box was empty I patted my now rounded stomach. "I don't think I can go on any more of the rides."

"Come on," Ramsey said gathering up the trash. "I have the perfect thing."

* * *

"It's beautiful." The carnival was below us. Beyond that, modern buildings mixed with old, as cars darted down busy streets. The gray gloom was broken by colorful Christmas lights. I gasped and scooted closer to Ramsey when the Ferris wheel stopped.

He chuckled. "You loved the roller coasters, but stopping as they let people on the observation wheel scares you?"

"I can't think on a roller coaster—it goes too fast," I said, trying to sit still so the carriage wouldn't swing.

"Oh well, I haven't told you the best part about this ride yet." Ramsey's rough hand cupped my cheek and guided my face to his. He leaned close, his lips almost touching mine. "Snogging you senseless."

My eyes fluttered closed as his lips caressed mine. I parted my lips and his tongue slid along mine. My hands tangled into his curls, and I relaxed into him. I squeaked as we began to move.

"See, best part of this ride," Ramsey said.

I bit my lip and looked up at him through my lashes. "I don't feel senseless."

Ramsey evil grinned. "I didn't say I was finished."

Chapter Twenty-Three

Fastest shower ever. My skin still tingled from where the hot water warmed up my cold fingers and toes. Wrapping my wet hair in a towel, I texted Anali.

—*How do I need to dress for tonight?*

Breathing in the gentle scent of lavender from my LUSH face moisturizer, I applied it as the sales lady taught me. Thanks to my Buffy Body Butter Bar I didn't have to worry about lotion, and according to Ramsey, my skin felt soft and smelled lovely, so I'm calling both keepers. I'd have to thank Miu again for taking me there.

—*Nice but not super dressy. Can you be ready in fifteen minutes?*

I sighed.

—*Sure, no problem.*

Throwing on a new pair of jeans and a purple blouse, I shoved my feet into black ankle high boots and turned the blow dryer on to high. It would take until it was time to leave to get my hair even partially dry.

"Sapphire," called Anali. "Are you ready?"

"Sure, let me grab my stuff. Are you sure you're feeling well enough?" It's not that I didn't want to go, but I was honestly shocked that we were.

"Yes, I've been feeling much better. The midwife came by and checked me again earlier today. The baby and I are fine. And as she said, the less stressed I am the better I feel." Anali wore a golden yellow salwar kameez and a fuzzy gray shawl that looked big enough to be a small blanket. "Well, come on. We have a sixteenth birthday to celebrate!"

"Okay, okay. I'm coming." I slid my coat on and grabbed my cowl and bag. "So where are we going?"

"No spoilers," Gavin said. "There's a car waiting for us downstairs."

"Tell us all about your day," Anali said, once we were driving to the mysterious place.

"Well, Ramsey took me out to breakfast and then to Hyde Park for their Winter Wonderland Carnival." I focused on the view outside trying to ignore my hot cheeks.

"Oh, how fun!" Anali said. "We are going to go right?" she asked Gavin.

"Yes, I was planning on going Thursday night, since we have it off," Gavin said. "I thought we could all go."

"Oh, I can't wait to see it lit up at night," I said, turning to Anali and Gavin. "I mean it was super cute today with all the decorations and such, but I bet it's lovely at night."

"Well," said Anali. "If Ramsey isn't doing anything maybe he'd like to join us."

"Really?" I looked at Gavin who sighed, and I was pretty sure he wanted to object but nodded instead. "I'll ask him. Thanks."

The car slowed in front of a row of houses and stopped in front of one painted a soft sky blue with white trim.

"Go on," said Gavin.

I got out of the car. Filling the front two windows on the bottom floor was a tree decked out with white lights and white, glass, and silver ornaments. On the front door hung a wreath of fresh pine boughs. Gavin helped Anali up the steps and rang the bell.

A moment later the large white door opened and a man stood in the doorway, his bald head glowing in the bright light. "Good evening Mr. Marsh, Mrs. Marsh. Everything is as you requested."

"Thank you, Simmons. Sapphire, this is Eric Simmons, the butler."

I held out my hand. "It's very nice to meet you, Mr. Simmons."

"Miss Rayner, it is a delight to meet you again. You were six months old when your parents brought you to see Mr. and Mrs. Rayner." Simmons let go of my hand and stepped back, letting us in. "I took care of your father when he was a boy. He was a fine young man. And while I only met your mother a few times, I could tell she was a lovely lady."

I blinked back tears. "Thank you. So, wait, did my dad grow up here?"

"Certainty Miss, may I welcome you to Rayner House."

I stepped inside. My boots echoed on the cream-colored marble tiles. The walls were painted a deep burgundy, and paintings hung on the walls. A few feet down, a staircase started. The hallway in front of us showed more art and doors, and to the right a room with a fire crackling merrily beckoned us to enter and admire even more pictures on the mantelpiece.

"Normally the family photos are carefully stored when the house is being let, but I brought them out for you," Simmons said.

The tree filled the window. Several chairs and loveseats, covered in beige fabric with pink and white flowers, were set in a circle around a coffee table facing the fireplace. I slid between them to look at the pictures. My grandparents, lines and gray hair marking their age, sat with bright smiles holding a fat baby boy. Pictures from my dad's school, birthday parties, family trips, and more family portraits filled every available space. On the end, my grandparents, now with white and silver hair, held a fat baby with brown hair that stuck up. On either side of them sat my parents. I picked up the photo. "This was me?"

"Yes, Miss," said Simmons. "Mrs. Rayner called the photographer the minute she knew your parents were bringing you to visit. Mr. Rayner was having heart problems and couldn't travel to visit you, I'm afraid."

I set the photo down and wiped away my tears.

"I'll go check on dinner." Simmons left, shutting the door without a sound.

"I didn't even know my dad was English," I whispered.

"I know," Gavin said standing next to me. "We never really talk about your parents. The books all said to let you ask first, so I've been waiting. I hope this isn't a bad surprise. Once I realized we'd be here for your birthday, it seemed perfect."

"No, it's great, I'm just a bit surprised. How long are the renters going to be gone? I'd love to look around."

"This is a vacation rental only. No one lives here full time except for Simmons and Parker, the cook. I have it for the rest of the time we are here. We can even stay here if you want," Gavin said.

"Oh. Can I think about it?"

"Of course you can, and while you're doing that, we do have one other surprise for you," Anali said.

Gavin grinned. "I'll be right back."

"Sapphire!" My vision was filled with pink lace and dark brown curls.

"Shante?" I held her tight. "When? How?"

"We came yesterday, and we spent the night in this fancy house, and I wanted to see you, but they said I was your birthday surprise, and I had to wait, and mommy made me a new dress for tonight," she said in one breath.

"I'm so glad you're here. I missed you so much." I buried my face in her hair, trying to hide my tears. I was so sure I'd never see her again once I left the group home. "Let me see your new dress."

Shante grinned, showing her missing top teeth, and twirled. She looked like cotton candy.

"It's a beautiful dress," I said taking her hand. Her skin was darker than mine, a mix of African-American and Mexican, which is also where her thin sausage curls came from.

"Happy birthday, Sapphire," Cordelia said, dabbing at her eyes with a handkerchief. Her skin was pale and sun kissed, her hair golden blond, and she wore a lavender dress. She looked warm and inviting and everything I'd hoped for Shante.

"Thank you, and thank you for coming here and bringing Shante," I said.

"You're welcome, but I must admit it wasn't entirely selfless. I'm so happy to be able to spend Christmas with both of my children." Cordelia held out her hand and Taliesin came in from the hallway. He took his mother's hand, his milk white skin and hair looking icy next to her warmth.

"I have a Big Brother now," Shante said and ran over to him. Taliesin scooped her up. She wrapped her arms around his neck and kissed him on the cheek.

Taliesin smiled. "The best Big Brother ever."

Shante rolled her eyes.

"What," he said. "You don't think I'm going to be the best Big Brother ever?" Holding up his free hand Taliesin began to wiggle his long fingers then attacked.

Shante squealed with laughter.

"Tell me I'm the best Big Brother ever," Taliesin said his loose white hair falling onto Shante's face making her giggle ever more.

"You're an okay, Big Brother," she said, breathless.

"What? Just okay?" He tickled her tummy.

"Okay, I give. You're the best Big Brother ever."

"I knew you'd see things my way." Taliesin adjusted Shante so she was upright. "Happy birthday, Sapphire."

They looked so cute together, like a prince and princess of a royal family in a fantasy/ sci-fy novel where one would rule the night and the other the day. "Thanks. Have you spent the day here?"

He nodded and Cordelia reached out and rubbed his arm, her warm blue eyes soft and watery as she looked at her children.

"Dinner is ready sir," Simmons said.

I jumped. Where had he come from?

"Great." Gavin held his arm out for Anali and Cordelia. "Taliesin, will you please escort Shante and Sapphire?"

Taliesin held out an arm for me to take. Shante wrapped her arms around Taliesin's neck.

"The food here is so yummy!" Shante said. "And Mr. Parker, the cook, is super nice."

"You like him because he keeps giving you cookies," Taliesin said.

Shante sniffed. "Biscuits—they call them biscuits here."

"You are so clever," said a middle-aged Chinese man. His short hair was covered by a white cook's hat and his white cook's uniform was spotless. I doubted he actually cooked in it. I bet he changed before bringing up the food. "Come and sit. I have dinner ready."

Shante clapped as Taliesin set her down and helped her into her booster seat. A year ago, I would have been the one helping her. Taliesin sat her right next to his mother. "Sapphire sit here," Shante said patting the chair on the left.

I sat down, laying the white cloth napkin across my lap.

"Tonight I have prepared a salad of mixed baby greens, candied walnuts, dried cranberries, and raspberry vinaigrette," Parker began as he and Simmons set the salads in front of us. "The main course is fettuccine alfredo, garlic bread, and steamed broccoli with lemon butter."

"Thank you," said Gavin.

"It looks lovely," Anali said.

The rest of us agreed and began to eat.

"I like salad," Shante said, her mouth full. She held her hand up trying to cover it. I guess Cordelia was teaching her some manners.

"Me too. How was your flight over?" I asked.

"It was scary at first, 'cause I never been in a plane before," said Shante. "But Mommy brought lots for me to do, and I slept for a while."

Cordelia smiled at Shante. "I'm glad that's how you remember it. It was long, good overall, but very, very long."

"How long are you visiting?" I asked.

"We'll be here until New Year's," Cordelia said. "I brought all the new costumes, so I'll be doing fittings and making adjustments."

"And we get to go to the ballet," Shante said. "We're going to see the Nutcracker. I got to be a super plum fairy when my ballet school did the Nutcracker. Mommy said I was the best one."

"Well," Cordelia said with a smile, "it was true you were the best one, but you were a sugar plum fairy, not a super plum fairy."

I smiled. It was obvious they loved each other.

Anali placed her hand on her stomach while gazing at Cordelia and Shante. Gavin wrapped an arm around her shoulder.

"It's true," Taliesin said. "I saw the video, and you were definitely the best sugar plum fairy."

I looked away from the two happy families. Is there anything more lonely than feeling alone in a room full of people?

"We all get to go see the Nutcracker," Anali said. Her eyes found mine and crinkled as she frowned. "We're going to day after Christmas."

Simmons took away our empty salad plates while Mr. Parker set out dinner plates. My mouth watered at the smell of garlic, butter, and cheese. Focus on the food.

"And we get to be here for Christmas," Shante said. "I left a note for Santa at our house, because I told him my new address before I knew we were coming here. You don't think he'll forget me again, do you?"

"Of course not," I said quickly, feeling sadness emanating from the others. "I bet one of Santa's elves made a mistake that year."

Shante giggled. "I remember you said an elf must have eaten too many cookies and was in bed with a tummy ache and it was his job to put my gifts in the sleigh and that's why Santa forgot me. But he came last year."

"And he'll come this year," Taliesin said. "I wrote him and told him where you would be as soon as mom said you were coming to visit."

Wow, he was quick. He would be a good brother for Shante.

"Thank you," Shante squealed, hugging his arm and getting sauce on his blue cashmere sweater.

"Of course," he said, waiting until she was focused on her meal to clean off his sleeve. "So, Mom, how are they going to survive the holiday season without you?"

"Oh, my assistants will be fine. All of them have been with me for years," Cordelia began.

I listened, laughing when appropriate, but I felt disconnected. Looking around the room, I tried to imagine my parents having dinner here. The dark oak table was covered with a white lace table cloth. A matching cabinet with glass doors showed china with translucent edges and cut crystal stemware. I was glad we weren't eating off those. The walls were painted dark green, and paintings of the current Queen and her predecessors hung on the walls.

"Sapphire," said Cordelia in a tone which meant she'd called my name a few times. "Is that okay?"

I had two choices, admit I wasn't listening and ask her to repeat the question, or I could agree and hope it wasn't anything too awful.

"Of course it's okay, right?" Shante said. "Kayin said it would be fine."

Saved. "Of course you can come with us tomorrow."

"Is anyone else going?" Gavin asked. Was I imagining things or did his voice seem a bit cold?

"No, I don't think so. Kayin said he wanted to take me out for my birthday, and he planned a surprise," I said.

"I can't wait." Shante did a happy dance in her seat.

"Calm down," Cordelia said. "I don't want you to choke."

"Okay, Mommy."

* * *

Gavin and Anali sat on the couch cuddling, their hands clasped on her stomach. They were gazing at each other and smiling. It was sickeningly sweet. I set down the bag I had brought to clean up the wrapping paper scattered on the floor and backed away. Tiptoeing, I climbed the stairs. Maybe I could read Shante a bedtime story.

"Please, please, please," Shante said.

Taliesin chuckled. "Okay I'll read you a story, which one?"

"Angelina Ballerina. You read it the bestest of anybody ever."

I reached up, placing my hand on my chest where my breath seemed to be caught. I guess I wasn't needed. No, this was good. They're family, and she should have her new brother reading her favorite Christmas story to her. Praying none of the boards creaked, I went up to the third floor. Simmons had told me that was where my grandparents' and dad's rooms were.

The first three rooms I opened were small and nothing personal was in them, so just guest rooms. The next door opened into a sitting room with a cream settee with dark mahogany frame and carved legs. A mahogany vanity laid out for my grandmother sat frozen in time. I picked up a crystal perfume bottle and pulled the stopper. Roses. A silver brush and comb, gleaming as if they had been just polished, lay next to a jewelry box. I opened it, a little dancer popped up as music played. Inside was empty. I guess the jewelry had been locked away.

Near the window a dark brown leather chair sat next to a bookshelf. On the other side, a small table with a crystal decanter, glass, and a pipe and ashtray all waited for my grandfather.

I sat in the chair that was turned to face the vanity. Was this where my grandfather read or watched his wife getting ready for bed?

The bookshelf held mysteries, thrillers, and spy novels. The books downstairs were leather bound classics, proper books. These were paperbacks, the spines creased from use. I trailed my finger over the books organized by genre and alphabetized by author.

Their four-poster bed was hung with white gauzy curtains and a white duvet with purple hydrangeas. A little table set on each side with lamps with frosted glass shades. I opened the drawers. They had papers, letters, all sorts of little personal things. I shut them again. It felt invasive to hunt through their things. They might have been my grandparents, but in reality they were strangers.

My dad's room was felt the same. It was smaller, and the chair next to the bookcase looked out the window. He liked to read biographies and historical fiction. Next to his mahogany four-poster bed with its navy blue duvet was a cradle. I walked over and touched the tiny white lace coverlet. The mahogany cradle rocked without squeaking. I had been here. I had slept in this matching, expensive little bed. I opened his closet, but like my grandparents it was empty.

This was all that was left of my family—cold, sterile, memories of dead people. I ran my finger along the silver frame of my parents' wedding portrait. At least I had this, right? I mean, when all of this Akasha saving magical creatures thing was done, I would come and live here. Gavin had given me the house for my birthday. I could come here and sit in their preserved rooms, and read the books that they had read. I could get everything from storage, all the valuable family heirlooms, and live here and get to know my family as best as I could.

My hands shook as I stopped the cradle.

I left and sat in the window seat in the hall between their two rooms and stared out into the dark night. Small lights on the ground lit the backyard and the gate. The shadowy shapes of trees loomed in the night. Wrapping my arms around my knees, I tucked myself up into the corner and leaned my head against the sill. My breath fogged the glass. Faint whispers of old emotions floated around me, letting me know that in two hundred and fifty years I wasn't the only Rayner to sit here staring out the window at nothing.

* * *

"Sapphire."

I blinked. Taliesin sat next to me on the window seat.

"Hey, are you okay?" he asked.

I opened my mouth to say I was fine, but he'd be able to tell if I was lying. "What's up?" I sat up my muscles stiff, how long had I been here?

"You've been gone for a while, we were starting to get worried." Taliesin held out a small black box. "And I wanted to give you your birthday gift."

"Oh, you didn't have to. I mean I know you don't..." Breathe, Sapphire and stop mumbling like an idiot. "Thanks. You didn't have to get me anything."

Taliesin's white eyebrows pulled in as he frowned at me. "If I had to do it, it wouldn't be a gift."

I took the box and opened it. "Are you sure?"

"Yes," Taliesin said his voice soft. "I made it for you. You're not okay are you?"

I avoided answering his question.

"It's beautiful." I took the bracelet made of braided unicorn mane out of the box, the clasp was a simple loop of the braided mane which fit snuggly over a cut crystal bead. "When did you change into a unicorn and how did you change back?"

"Miu's been helping me." He took the bracelet and fastened it around my wrist. His fingers ran over the smooth finger-shaped scars Cartazonon had left on me. "She figured out how to channel enough Akashic energy to help me shift between forms. I can do it now on my own if I focus."

"That's wonderful, congratulations." I held my wrist up, admiring the silvery white braid against my copper skin. "So what does it do?"

"What makes you think it does anything?" Taliesin asked.

I rolled my eyes. "Because I know you, and you wouldn't give me this just because it's beautiful."

"It'll tell you how dark someone is without your having to touch them. The crystal will change colors depending on how untrustworthy, dark, or evil the person is," Taliesin said.

"So like a mood ring, but for other people?"

"I guess. At least that will be a good explanation if someone sees it changing colors. I figured it could help with the whole Earth magic and regular people issue."

"So it will mimic how you see auras?" I asked. "That you can see how unbalanced, or dark, or bad the person is but you don't know why?"

Taliesin nodded.

I covered the bracelet with my hand. His moonlight cool energy caressed my skin. "Thank you, it's wonderful."

"You're welcome. Can I help you?"

I smiled—well, I tried to smile. "Do I look that bad? I mean can you tell by looking at me that something is wrong?"

Taliesin waved a long finger at my face. "It looks like you were crying."

"Damn it." I got up and headed for the bathroom in my dad's room. At least it was just dried tear tracks and not red, puffy eyes. I washed up and pulled up some enthusiasm. Tomorrow I was going on an adventure with Kayin and Shante, I had some lovely birthday gifts, and I bet if I asked, Simmons would let me take a piece of the caramel cheesecake Mr. Parker made for my birthday with me. Okay, sad emotions tucked down under those to deal with later, or not, and happy emotions on top. Any leftover moody can be explained by the house and being tired. Okay, good enough.

Taliesin stood in the doorway. "Sapphire?"

I patted his arm as I walked by him. "It doesn't matter. Come on, I bet Anali is tired and ready to go."

"I know things have been rough. We haven't hung out much lately, but I'm your friend, and I want to help," he said, grabbing my arm.

The crystal on the bracelet he made me turned purple. I was too numb to feel anything from him. "Taliesin, it doesn't matter. It's nothing important, and there's no fixing it anyway."

"You matter, you're important," he said.

I shook my head and walked down the stairs. Not here, not really.

* * *

"Sapphire, are you ready?" Shante asked running around my room checking everything out.

"Yes, I just need to tie my shoes."

"I have Velcro so I don't need to tie my shoes." Shante put her foot an inch from my face so I could see.

"Very nice. Okay, ready." I grabbed my things and headed for the door. Kayin and Taliesin waited for us by the elevators.

"Are you sure it's okay that I come along?" Taliesin asked.

"Of course it's okay," Shante said. "Sapphire says family that loves you is important, and she doesn't lie. Right?" She turned to me, her big brown eyes demanding I agree with her.

I smiled and rubbed her cheek. "Yes, of course you should spend time with your brother. You two are family now."

Shante's grin was triumphant as she grabbed hold of Taliesin's arm. "See, told you so, we're family now." Their happiness bubbled around me. I focused on their feelings instead of my own.

The elevator door opened. Kayin clasped my hand as we headed to the lobby. "I thought it would be fun to take the bus. I was told the one we need is a few blocks away."

"Do you think it'll be one of those pretty red double-deckers?"

"Shante, wait," I said, kneeling down to fasten her coat and adjust her scarf. "Maybe we'll get lucky and be able to ride a double-decker bus."

"Sorry," Taliesin said. "I guess you have a lot to teach me."

I shook my head. "I'm sure you would have done up her coat once we got outside. You would have noticed, or she would have complained."

Shante grabbed Taliesin's hand. "Come on."

I looked down at the bracelet Taliesin had given me—the crystal was a soft purple. It seemed this was the color for people who cared about me. "So where's Shin today?" I asked.

Kayin smiled, then looked away. "He said he had stuff to do. I felt kind of bad leaving him behind, but he said he understood, and he wouldn't want to come between us."

I followed him onto the bus, my heart light and full of joy. He hadn't wanted to bring Shin along—he wanted to go out with just me. We walked up to the second floor. Taliesin and Shante found seats near the front and she was already pointing out all the interesting things she saw.

"Here." Kayin reached back and grabbed my hand. We sat as the bus began to move. "So did you have a nice birthday yesterday?"

"Yes. I spent the day with Ramsey. Oh, you and Shin should go to Hyde Park. They have this wonderful carnival there right now."

Kayin smiled. "He took me there last night. We went on all the rides, and …"

"Yes," I said, when he didn't finish his sentence.

Kayin leaned towards me. "He kissed me when we were on the Ferris wheel."

I grabbed his arm and squealed. "Like a kiss on the cheek?"

Kayin shook his head, a smile tugging on his lips.

"And is he a good kisser?"

"I don't know I've never kissed anyone before, but," he paused to leaned closer. "He made my toes curl."

I squealed again. "Oh, my God, Kayin that's so romantic! Your first kiss, and he made your toes curl." I sighed.

"Does Ramsey make you your toes curl?" he asked.

I shook my head. "He makes me feel all hot and tingly, but no toe-curling kisses yet."

"Our stop is next," Kayin said.

We got off and walked along the Thames, past the London Eye, next to a gray stone building six stories tall with tall columns and pale gray chimneys rising out of the brown tiled roof. We walked about half a block and were at the midpoint of the building which curved inward. Above the gray gate gold letters said AQUARIUM.

"I thought it would be fun," Kayin said.

"It's great. Remember the first thing we ever did together was go to the Monterey Bay Aquarium? This is a perfect birthday present."

Kayin smiled.

"I want to see the sharks," Shante said, as we walked passed the column.

"I'm sure we'll see everything," Taliesin said.

I wasn't sure, this place was massive.

Shante screeched and buried her head in Taliesin's shoulder as we walked through the tunnel that was surrounded by the shark aquarium. She was peeking out from under his hair. "Are you sure it's safe?"

"Perfectly safe," Taliesin assured her.

She looked at me, white-blond hair covering half of her brown face. "Really safe?"

"Yes, perfectly safe. Taliesin wouldn't bring you anywhere unsafe," I said.

"Hey," said Kayin.

"Neither would Kayin or I."

"Okay," she sat up. "But don't put me down, just in case things go wrong."

Taliesin chuckled, but held onto her.

The sharks swam around us, slightly curious and content. I guess they weren't about to rampage. Deep calm radiated ahead of us. A giant sea turtle swam above us. His Zen-like calm washed over me, I rolled my shoulders as tension faded from my body. "I want a turtle."

"I don't think we can travel with one," Kayin said.

"Someday," I said as we walked to the next section. The turtle winked at me before swimming away.

* * *

"This has been the best day ever," Shante said, holding onto the stuffed hammer head shark she'd begged Taliesin to buy her.

"I agree." I leaned against Kayin as the taxi darted between cars. "It's been a wonderful day, thank you."

"You're welcome, Little Sister, and happy birthday," Kayin said.

My stomach lurched, and an oily itchy feeling slid over me. "Shit." I sat up and looked around. The feeling was gone.

"Oooo, that's a bad word," Shante said pointing at me.

Kayin frowned and rubbed his stomach.

"Sorry, baby." I looked out the back window. A silver Rolls Royce caught my eye. A face hidden in the shadows was turned towards us. I got out my phone and sent everyone, including Ramsey, a text.

—*Just passed a Son of Belial, not a walk-in. Felt like one of his generals or maybe Cartazonon himself. He's headed away from the hotel right now in a silver Rolls Royce.*

My unicorn hair bracelet glowed black against the handprint on my wrist then slowly faded to gray.

The guys' phones chimed.

"Are you sure?" Taliesin asked.

I nodded and leaned on Kayin again. What were they doing in London? Did they know about us? Would we have to leave?

My phone chirped all the way home as everyone checked in and Gavin insisted that everyone get to the hotel.

Chapter Twenty-Four

Cartazonon watched the taxi disappear down the busy London street. "Well at least one Child of Fire is here."

"I wonder why Melusine didn't say anything about it," Lee said, turning the page of his newspaper.

"Oh, I'm sure sweet little Melusine didn't know," Cartazonon said, relaxing onto the beige leather seats. "She has so many projects going on right now."

Lee shrugged. "Or she thinks she can steal their magic to help free herself from you."

"Perhaps. I have a few questions to ask her assistant. I'm supposed to meet with her tonight." London had grown so much over the centuries. It made him nostalgic for the old days. Especially corsets, he missed the corsets. "Do you remember Rome?"

Lee smiled, how could he forget Rome? "Good times. Should I get your gladius sent over?"

Cartazonon shook his head. "No, we don't solve problems with swords and lions anymore."

"Unfortunate," Lee sighed. The lions had been a lot of fun.

"Yes, well. Melusine might wish for lions once we find out what's going on."

"How are you going to get her assistant to talk? You know Melusine spells them safe with Earth magic, so we can't hurt them."

Cartazonon waved his hand. "I have her younger brother in the trunk. It shouldn't be that difficult."

Lee frowned. "I bet she'll be so upset just seeing her brother that we won't even get to torture him."

"Don't worry, Lee, I'll make sure you'll get to torture someone. It's Christmas after all—a time when wishes come true."

Lee grinned. "Speaking of wishes, should I have our London men gear up? You said you wanted a Child of Fire."

"Yes, have them ready themselves." Cartazonon opened the door as the car pulled in front of his office, thirty-eight floors of gleaming metal and glass reflected the weak sunlight. The original building had been destroyed during the blitz. He had found the brass plaque engraved with his name amongst the exploded bricks. Now it hung in his office. He'd built an ugly concrete building to replace it, knowing that once money and resources were replenished after the war, he would rebuild his London stronghold to a glory worthy of being one of his centers of power. The ancient catacombs underneath the building protected a key energy point in his web.

He'd thought of moving the stone table inlaid with metal from Akasha. It was the first one he'd ever built, but he liked the centuries old stone arches and walls. They felt homey, especially in the firelight.

"Mr. Cartazonon, welcome back sir," the doorman said, bowing his head as he walked by.

Cartazonon grunted, taking off his coat as the artificially heated and dried air hit him. "Are there any problems we need to take care of while we're here?"

"Aren't there always?" Lee said, taking his coat. He smiled inside as the secretary heard them, her eyes widening in fear.

Her manicured nails clicked against her phone, a sure sign she would text as soon as they got in the elevator.

"You are so mean," Lee said as the elevator door shut.

Cartazonon's lips twitched. "I like seeing how hard my people will work to prove themselves to me when I visit."

"You could let them be self-motivated."

The elevator opened onto the thirty-seventh floor. Cartazonon pushed open the six foot high polished stainless steel doors. Floor to ceiling windows showed the heart of London, including the Eye and the Thames. His lion-footed mahogany desk gleamed. Stacks of folders sat on the left side of his desk set. Above the set lay invitations. The envelopes appeared tasteful, yet screamed expensive.

Sitting, Cartazonon flipped through the invitations, while Lee used the intercom to ask his assistant for tea, Darjeeling.

"Lee, we were invited to a gala Melusine gave to support a marine charity."

"Interesting that she should send it here instead of to your email. One would think she didn't want you to attend."

Cartazonon said. "I have ignored her for far too long. Obviously, Melusine is more of a problem than we anticipated."

Lee raised a scar-bisected eyebrow. "If you recall, I wanted to kill her the second I saw her."

"I need a connection to Earth magic, and so far she's the only one who's willing, or was willing to work with me. Maybe it's time to work more closely with those Zuni witches I helped in New York." Cartazonon flipped through the other invitations. "The Equestrian Society is holding a gala and show tomorrow night, shall we attend?"

"Sure. Will I have to wear a tux?"

"You look very scary in a tux."

A bookcase swung open, and his assistant backed into the room bringing a tea cart with him. Cartazonon's eye twitched as one of the wheels squeaked with every turn. He opened his mouth to fire the boy, but Lee placed a large hand on his shoulder. Yes, better to demand he fix it. After all, Bradley had been with him for fifteen years, his loyalty proven through several emergencies and government inquiries.

"Send our RSVP to this event," Cartazonon said holding the invitation out for the boy to take.

"Yes, sir. Shall I have your tuxes readied?"

"Yes, and then see to that wheel."

"Of course, sir."

"What is he again?" Cartazonon asked as the bookcase shut.

Lee sighed, why must they go through this every time? "He's of Cerridwen's line, about four generations removed."

"Hmm, barely a snack, I suppose he is more useful as an assistant then."

"At least for now," Lee muttered under his breath.

Cartazonon opened the top folder. "At least for now."

Chapter Twenty-Five

Checking my phone, I wiped the sweat off my face. Gavin led the morning conditioning class and his excitement was infectious. My body buzzed from the workout and the energy of everyone in the room.

—Can you meet me this morning? Ramsey texted.

I looked around the room—ah, there he is.

"Gavin, Ramsey texted me asking if we could meet this morning."

Gavin frowned. "We talked about this last night, I don't want anyone going anywhere that there isn't a protective shield until we know why the Sons of Belial are here. I'm not sure if we can even stay here through the holiday like I'd planned."

Mental eye roll. I could feel if the Sons of Belial were close. I could feel them stronger than anyone else. This made me safer than anyone else, but arguing with Gavin's protective instincts without Anali around was an exercise in futility.

"What if I meet him in the hotel?"

Gavin's green eyes widened. "Not in your room."

I held my hands up. Wow, overprotective much?

"Okay. I'll meet him in the restaurant, not a big deal."

Gavin's jaw clenched, and he looked like he wanted to say no but couldn't come up with a good reason to refuse. "Fine, but stay at the hotel, and he can't come to your room for any reason. Are there other people going back? I don't want you walking on your own."

"We're headed back," Kayin said. Shin stood next to him.

"Perfect."

Gavin sighed and nodded his head. "Okay then, but be careful and let me know if anything unusual happens."

"I will, promise." I sent Ramsey a message and grabbed my coat.

"So," said Shin as we walked into the cold gray morning air. "What's going on? Gavin is really tense. He asked me to teach you guys a martial arts class before lunch, which is fine, but it seemed extremely important to him."

Kayin bit his lip and looked away, a fog of guilt floated around him. I guess he didn't want to lie to his boyfriend. Understandable, but lying and telling certain parts of the truth are different. No, they are. I swear.

"A kidnapping threat," I said. After all that's what he told Shin when he asked him to train us. "I guess he got a note and saw some suspicious guys hanging around."

Shin frowned holding Kayin's hand, tugging him closer. "You should tell me when stuff like this happens. I'll make sure I'm watching people more carefully."

"Well, I'm telling you now," I said. "And we're not sure if there is a real threat. Gavin's people are looking into it."

"You should sit with us during breakfast," Shin said.

"We'll see, Ramsey is meeting me."

"Apparently he's anxious to see you," Shin said, a grin on his face.

Ramsey stood in front of the building. The breeze fluttered his kilt around his thighs. He didn't feel excited to see me. Sadness, anger, guilt, and a cold suffocating helplessness emanated from him. Red-rimmed eyes looked at me through windblown curls.

I ran over to him. "Ramsey, what's happened?" I asked as I wrapped my arms around his neck.

He gasped, his body shaking as he wrapped his arms around me. "Mindy, you met her at the party, she...she killed herself."

"What? Oh, my god, I'm so sorry." I held him tighter. I remembered Mindy smiling at the gala, showing me her necklaces for the silent auction. The mix of stones and sea glass was as whimsical and beautiful as she was. What had happened to make her so depressed so quickly?

"She," he gasped. "She didn't contact anyone else, just me, and I didn't go over, and later when I texted and called she didn't answer me but I thought ... I thought she was okay, you know, wrapped up in a new project or busy with friends."

Guilt pierced my heart and clung to me like weighted chains. This was my fault. If I had said goodbye to him . . . If I hadn't kissed him . . . he could have saved her. "Ramsey, I'm so sorry. I ..." I choked on the inadequacy of what to say. A breeze whipped around us. "Come on let's go inside and get warm."

He nodded and let me go.

I clasped his hand our fingers entwining. "Are you hungry?"

He shook his head.

Stupid question. "When was the last time you ate?"

"I don't know—a day or so ago." The fingers of his free hand wrapped around the strap on his yoga bag.

"Let's go and get some breakfast, or at least some hot tea," I said as he began to protest at the idea of food.

I guided him to a small table in the back. "I'll get us some food and be right back."

"Is everything okay?" Kayin asked as I filled two plates at the buffet.

I shook my head and forced back tears. "His friend killed herself." And if I'd let him go instead of tricking him into spending the day with me, she'd still be alive.

Warm compassion flowed over me. "I'm sorry. If I can help at all, let me know."

I nodded. "Thanks."

"Where's Shin?"

Kayin grinned. "He saw someone suspicious and went to follow them."

"I'm sorry I lied to him."

"No, don't worry. Go back to Ramsey, he needs you right now."

"Thanks, Big Brother."

I set down two mugs of tea and two plates. I pushed the one with the kippers in front of Ramsey.

"It's my fault." Ramsey said, wrapping his hands around the mug but not drinking. "They all said it wasn't, but not only was I not there for her—everyone who is depressed, they all went to that party and met with Melusine. That can't be a coincidence. I mean I know artists can be moody, but more than half of my friends feel depressed right now."

My brow furrowed. "Were they all magical?"

"Not like me, not full, but yeah they all had at least a little magical being in them. Their magic is what made them such good artists. They possessed this interesting connection and view of the world that came through in their art."

"At the party the gnome had his magic sucked from him. Not his life just his magic, and he died, but …"

"What if they were mostly human, what if she took the magic part of them?" Ramsey groaned. "Bloody hell! They all said they couldn't do their art. The technique was still there, but their passion their muse, gone. And I fed them to her. She wouldn't have even known about them if I hadn't sent them to her."

I grabbed his hands hoping to calm him down. "You didn't know. I didn't know anything was wrong with Melusine until she touched me, and even then I wasn't sure she was the one. We'll sort it out. We can talk to my uncle and see what can be done. Maybe Miu can help heal them?"

Tears flooded his black eyes and fell down his pale cheeks.

I sat in his lap and wrapped my arms around him. A low moan rumbled in his chest as his shoulders shook. His arms wrapped around me. His fingers dug into my sides as he clung to me. I did my best to push aside my own guilt and breathe, sending calm energy to surround him. His breath began to return to normal, and his body calmed. I rubbed his back and his arms relaxed

"I'm sorry I must look a right wanker," Ramsey muttered into my shoulder.

"No, you're fine." This was after all one of the few emotional things I was good at.

A storm of rage and fear crashed into the room. Gavin burst in like lightning.

"Uncle Gavin," I said. I stood up, and my hand gripped Ramsey's shoulder.

His red-rimmed eyes scanned the room not seeming to see anything.

I choked on his fear. "Uncle Gavin."

He focused on me and rushed forward, his fingers digging into my shoulders. "They took her. I can't believe they took her. Did you feel anything? Do you know which way they went, because she gone and she can't be gone. She just can't."

My vision faded, and my body went cold. "No, Gavin, no. There has to be some mistake. Anali was in her room. She was feeling better, we were going to go out to lunch today."

"They," Gavin voice cracked. I swayed as his fear and pain crashed into me. "They took her from the room. Shin he tried, I mean I know he must have done his best, but …damn it, they never should have gotten her. I should have …"

"Uncle Gavin," I interrupted. Ramsey stood behind me holding my hand. He was trying to ground my emotions but his own sorrow was too raw and sharp. My head began to throb. I had to do something. "Where is everyone else right now?"

Tears filled his eyes. "She's gone. And the baby. Oh, God, the baby. I couldn't keep them safe."

I placed my hands on Gavin's face and tilted his head down so I could meet his eyes. "Uncle Gavin, where are the others?"

"Upstairs in our room."

"Let's go." I grabbed Gavin's hand and pulled them upstairs. Gavin bounced on the balls of his feet the whole elevator ride up. His deep breaths seem to shove down his fear, and the rage became stronger with each floor.

Gavin strode from the elevator, his hands clenching into fists as he walked. His jaw clenched, and his red-rimmed eyes were hard. "I will get her back and kill everyone who touched her."

"Do you feel them? Can you follow them?" Miu asked as soon as I walked into the door.

"Why would you feel them or be able to follow them?" Shin asked. His wrists were raw, the skin around his mouth red, and several bruises began forming on his face and arms.

"Good going," Sasha muttered.

"No, I didn't feel anything." I led Gavin and Ramsey to the couch and made them both sit. Taking a few steps back, I tried to center myself. "Okay, this is chaos. We need to figure out what to do next. Shin, what happened?"

Shin raised an eyebrow and looked at Gavin, who was staring at the floor, then turned back to me. "I followed these two men in suits, they didn't seem right. Too hard, too aware. I followed them up here. They took the stairs, and I stayed back so they wouldn't see me. They knocked on the door, and Anali opened it before I could stop her. They injected her with something and shoved her into a laundry hamper. I tried to stop them." He rubbed his purpling jaw. "They were good, professional. Under their suit jackets they wore hotel uniforms. Within a few minutes they had me bound and gagged."

I stiffened as sharp anger came off of him. "Okay, anyone else see or know anything?"

"Da, but I'm not sure I should say right now." He looked at Shin.

"Okay, so not the time and we need him." I looked at Gavin and he nodded. I knelt in front of Shin and held my hand up drawing on Kayin's power. I surrounded my hand in flames. "So, five-second explanation of our secret. We are magical beings who are hunted by the Sons of Belial so they can steal our power."

Shin nodded, his eyes fixed on my hand. He reached out stopping before he touched the flames. "It's hot."

"Fire tends to be. Kayin can tell you more later." I let the flames go and stood. "It could also be Melusine, the woman who put together the gala. Ramsey and I think she took the magic from his friends. One became so depressed she killed herself. Sasha, what did you Dream?"

"A mermaid is trying to get into Avalon," he said, his gray eyes hard.

"Melusine," Ramsey said. "Legend tells of a woman and her sisters, mermaids, cast out of Avalon because of their cruelty towards their human father."

"We have to go to Glastonbury Tor." Gavin stood and grabbed his jacket.

I shivered at the coldness of his voice. "Yes, but not yet. They can't get in. I bet they're hoping Anali can open the doorway for them."

"Can she?" Gavin asked twisting his jacket so tight the leather creaked.

I had no idea. "Do we know anything more about Avalon?"

Gavin shook his head. "Philip sent me a bunch of links to different myths and stories, but nothing that would help me save Anali."

Miu waved her phone. "The Tor closes at sunset, which is four o'clock this time of year."

"They won't go while people are there," Shin said. "Not with how professional they seemed."

I nodded. "Uncle Gavin, do you know if the Children of Fire know about the Tor being special? Do we have anyone watching it?"

Gavin looked at his watch, the muscle in his jaw twitched as his fear spiked. "Eight hours. I'm supposed to wait for eight hours? I have to know she's safe. I need to go and get her now."

"Uncle Gavin. I understand. I do, and if you know where she is we'll go right now, but otherwise we'll have to wait," I said, holding his hands before he tore at his hair. "Now do you know if there are any Children of Fire watching Glastonbury Tor?"

Gavin fell into a chair shaking his head. "I don't know."

I opened my phone and called Philip. He smiled at me from the picture I'd taken of him, his salt and pepper mohawk standing straight and his skin crinkling around his blue eyes. "Hello," he said his voice thick with sleep.

"Philip, we have an emergency," I said. "I'll explain later. Do we have anyone watching Glastonbury Tor?"

"Yes, several people work there."

"We need to have access to the Tor tonight after closing," I said.

Philip cleared his throat. "It'll happen."

"Let them know it's not the Sons of Belial but a woman with Earth magic. Her name is Melusine," I said.

"The mermaid?" Philip asked.

"Yes, we think so."

"She's a bitch, be careful of her. I'll let you know once I have everything sorted." Philip hung up the phone.

"Now what?" Miu asked.

I had no idea. "How long does it take to get to Glastonbury Tor?"

"From here," Ramsey said, "about three hours."

Shin stood. His blue streaked black bangs covered half his face. "So we get ready, shower, eat, rest, and gather supplies for this afternoon."

"I can't eat." Miu twisted her pony tails. "I'm too upset."

"If you don't eat you can't come," Shin said. "You'll be a liability."

"Hey," Sasha began.

"He's right," Gavin said. "We need to be ready to fight and open a portal and you can't do that when fainting from hunger. Go get ready, pack a bag for cold weather, and meet back here as soon as you're ready, and no one is alone from this moment on."

Ramsey touched my arm. "I'll be back. I need to let the others know what's going on. I'll be back in an hour."

"Okay. Stay safe." I wanted to kiss him goodbye, but the others stared at me.

He squeezed my hand and left.

"Come on," Miu said, tugging my arm. "Let's get ready."

I nodded. My fingers wrapped around my fire pendant. Its warmth increased under my touch. *Anali, please stay safe. We're coming.*

* * *

"You're all set," Philip said. Gavin put the call on speaker phone as he drove the van down the M4. "We have several people working for the National Trust. I've told them all to stay back, but are you sure you don't want any help?"

Gavin gripped the steering wheel hard enough to turn his knuckles white as the car in front of us slowed. "No, they need to be gone. I'm not trusting strangers. We don't know what to expect, and I need to get Anali back."

Philip sighed. "Okay. I'll text all of you a number you can call if you do need help. Call me once you have her safe."

Gavin cleared his throat. "I will. Thanks, Philip."

"Anytime. Call me when you have her back, no matter what time it is."

Silence fell, and tension buzzed through the van. They say anticipation is usually worse than whatever is waiting for you. I would agree. Fear, anger, and helplessness surrounded me. I rubbed my arms in an attempt to stop the feeling of ants crawling over my skin. Ramsey laid his arm over my shoulders. I leaned into him, but it was weak comfort as his anxiety coursed through me.

"Finally," Gavin muttered turning off onto a smaller road.

The tension rose as adrenaline began to increase and people prepared to battle. I needed to get out of this van. The GPS gave mechanical directions as we sat in silence.

We drove to the gate where a man stood waiting. Gavin rolled down the window. The faint hum of Akasha came from him.

"If you need anything, ring. We're set up in different places and will keep an eye on things." His accent so thick I could barely understand him. "Two women and five armed men are already up there."

"Two women," Gavin said. "Was one of them Indian? Did she look okay?"

He nodded. "Yes. She looked upset but walked fine."

"Thanks." The roughness of Gavin's voice brought tears to my eyes.

"There's no way to sneak up on them," Shin said. "Glastonbury is on a hill in the middle of a field, even with careful planning and time I probably couldn't figure out how to sneak up there."

Gavin nodded. "Then I guess we'll walk up there."

The moonlight showed the Tor standing tall at the top of the hill. The gray stones looked ghostly in the pale light. I was glad the moonlight was bright enough to not need a flashlight. They made the darkness scarier, because they only showed you a small bit of the world. Anything could lurk along the edges of the light.

Taliesin pulled the hood of his coat up, trying to hide from the moonlight so his skin wouldn't glow.

Pebbles and dirt crunched under our feet. We sounded like a herd of cattle. No chance of having an element of surprise.

"I'm going to teach you all how to walk quietly," Shin whispered.

"I want the door open." Melusine's voice carried on the wind.

"I can't. I don't know how," Anali said.

We walked faster.

Gavin stopped as they came into view. Anali leaned against the thick stone walls of the Tor, surrounded by men in black. Melusine stood to the side in a long blue coat which flowed around her legs in the breeze.

"Now what?" I whispered.

Gavin and Shin moved further along the path, whispering as they tried to plan.

"If you can't open the door then you're no use to me," Melusine said. "Well, except for your power."

We needed to get Anali out of there. She and the baby must be kept safe. After that something can be worked out. Kneeling, I laid my hands on the ground. My eyelids fluttered at the power hidden underground. The bead on my bracelet glowed a pale blue. I hoped that was a friendly color.

"Taliesin," I whispered.

He knelt next to me. "Yes."

"Can you speak telepathically to the creatures underground?" I asked.

He closed his eyes.

I waited.

"Yes." He opened his eyes, which looked clear in the moonlight.

"Tell them what is happening, who we are, why we are here, and about them." I nodded to Melusine and her group.

"Okay. And what are you going to do?"

I stood. "Get Gavin's family back."

I walked over to Gavin and Shin. "I can get Anali back. I can trade myself for her with the promise of being able to open the door."

"What? No," Gavin hissed.

I held up a hand. "Listen. We have to get Anali and the baby back—that is the most important thing right now. Melusine wants the door open. Once inside, I'm hoping the magical creatures Taliesin is communicating with will help me, and you guys can come rushing in after us. This will buy us time."

Gavin looked between me and Anali, his emotions so intense and confusing they made me queasy.

"Okay," Shin said. "But be careful, and remember what I taught you. We'll be right behind you."

I looked at Gavin.

He sighed and nodded.

I brought my hands to my face and removed my contacts.

"What are you doing?" Gavin asked.

"She needs to see my power, or she'll never let Anali go." Taking a deep breath, I opened my connection to Akasha. My fire pendant warmed and I shivered as hot Phoenix magic flowed through me. I walked to the Tor.

"What are you doing?" asked Ramsey.

"Getting Anali back."

"Gavin, what's going on?" Miu asked.

"I can open the door," I said. The men turned to look at me, their bodies tense and ready to fight. I ignored them and looked at Melusine.

She gasped. I guess the fire dancing in my eyes was visible.

I walked forward. "If you let her go, I'll open the door to Avalon for you."

"Maybe I should take both of you?" Melusine said. "I'm sure my men wouldn't have any problem acquiring you."

I shook my head, letting my power flow. Melusine shivered. "I won't help you until Anali is safe."

"Sapphire," Anali said, moving towards me. "Stop this right now. Go back to the others and get out of here."

One of the men grabbed her arm and yanked her back. Anali cried.

"Get your hands off my wife," Gavin yelled. I heard a scuffle. Turning, I saw Shin and Kayin holding Gavin back. I needed to fix this. I sent out my power and intentions. Please work, please work.

Stones screeched as they grated against each other. I smirked. "Oh look, I opened the door a tiny bit. Not enough to find it, I bet."

"Go and get her and let that one go. She is useless." Melusine said.

The man who held Anali came towards me. I swallowed and forced myself to hold my ground. He looked like a muscle-covered refrigerator. With his free hand, he grabbed my hair at the base of my braid and pulled.

I stood on my tip toes. "Let her go."

Fridge smiled and threw Anali to the ground. She whimpered and scurried back from him, her hands on her belly.

"Anali," Gavin cried. I heard him run to her. She started crying as he soothed her. They were safe. Now, could I get myself out of trouble?

He pulled and walked me over to Melusine.

"Open the door," she said.

"Let go of my hair," I said with more confidence then I felt. In fact, I was pretty sure I was close to throwing up and peeing myself.

Melusine nodded.

Fridge grunted and released my hair.

I walked over to the wall and placed my hands on the smooth stone, the door pushed out only a quarter of an inch but its magic called to me. I sent Akashic energy into the stone and to Avalon so they would know we were coming. The stone groaned as it opened.

Stone steps led into the Earth.

"Yes." Melusine's happiness bubbled around her. "Oh, I'm finally home."

The men didn't move.

"You two with us," Melusine said. "And you three kill them, then join us."

I turned, and Fridge grabbed my hair again. "Three of them are coming for you," I screamed. "Get out of here."

The other one hit me. Blood ran down my cheek and my head buzzed unpleasantly. Fridge shook me and we went down the stairs. Flashlights illuminated small sections of the stairs and created deep creepy shadows along the walls.

A primal yell, no a battle cry, filled the air, then screams from outside echoed around us, too faint for me to tell who was yelling. My stomach clenched. Oh, God, what was happening? Had I kept them safe at all?

Fridge yanked on my hair again as we turned to go down another set of stairs.

The air became moist, and a gentle warm thrum of energy emanated from the walls around us. I breathed in the energy trying to calm myself as I was forced to go deeper into the Earth.

The stairs ended at a small room with more cave openings. Some were pitch black and others held flickering lights deep within them.

Melusine closed her eyes and took a deep breath. "This way." She pointed to a cave with a faint light flickering somewhere within it. Footsteps echoed above us. "Oh, good. Sounds like your friends have been dealt with." She draped her scarf on the cave floor showing which one we went into.

Something watched us. I felt magic and emotions. Whatever lurked in the shadows was wasn't happy about us being down there and was getting ready to fight to protect its home. I hoped the being understood that I wasn't the enemy. The energy built as it—no they—prepared to attack.

I pretended to slip. Fridge jerked me back and wrapped his arms around me in a bear hug. Yes!

"You had best behave," he growled in my ear. "Not all of my associates are as gentlemanly as I am. You don't want me to get tired of you and give you to one of them."

I threw my head back. His nose crunched and he yelled. Hot sticky drops of blood fell on my neck as I brought my legs up and shoved them to the ground. His arms loosened enough to thrust my arms forward and my elbow back into his rock hard stomach. Ouch, my elbow.

"You little bitch." He backhanded me and I hit the ground.

Growls echoed against the rock walls.

A pasty white hand reached out and grabbed Fridge by the top of his head, yanking him into the darkness.

Melusine ran, chanting something under her breath. The other guy pulled his knife and stood still. His eyes darted at each sound he heard.

A wail started. I slapped my hands over my ears as the wail became a high-pitched scream. A ghostly woman with white hair and a torn black dress soared towards the other man. He struck at her, but she didn't stop. Grabbing his face, she kissed him. His body shook as she lifted him into the air. His life flowed into her. A bright white light reflected a rainbow of colors.

"Are you okay?"

I turned and gasped. A man in a blue jeans and a cable knit sweater held out his hand. The same hand that grabbed Fridge. He smiled, his full lips bright pink.

I took his hand and shivered. Death and stolen life, no not life, blood. The crystal on Taliesin's bracelet glowed blue, please be a good sign.

"Thank you for helping me." Polite is always a good choice.

He inclined his head, his dark hair falling over his brown eyes. His features seemed fine like what one thinks of when they imagine old-fashioned royalty. "But of course, welcome little Phoenix. Avalon awaits you."

He led me through the tunnel, which opened into a massive cave. "Did Jules Verne ever come here?"

The vampire laughed. "Yes, actually he did. We tried to wipe his memory but he must have had some magical blood in him. He remembered quite a bit."

A meadow, lake, trees, and cottages stood before me, not clumped together, but a large thriving village. Large clusters of crystals dotted the landscape, clear quartz, cubes of green and purple fluorite, and pale yellow calcite were the only ones I recognized. Moonlight glowed above us lighting the valley where bonfires and torches didn't reach. This wasn't just a cave where they hid, but their sanctuary, and safe haven where they lived. I couldn't see the other end of the cave. I jumped as something emerged from the water.

"Don't worry it's just Nessy," the vampire said.

"Miss Rayner, I do hope you're quite all right."

"Mr. Monroe! What are you doing here?" He seemed more out of place than the Loch Ness Monster.

He wore a brown monk's robe. More men in brown robes followed with women in white robes after them. Several of them had long ash-blond hair. Were they the Fae I saw from the memories of the dragonesque brooches?

He smiled. "I'm a Druid priest—one of the protectors of Avalon."

"Oh." I wasn't expecting that. "I thought you were friends with Melusine."

"You know what they say, keep your friends close and your enemies closer." He reached into his pocket and brought out a jar. "Let me tend to your wound."

He smeared a thick green paste that smelled of beeswax and bitter herbs, onto my cheek. I winced but didn't move. "The others."

"I fear we were too late to help them."

My heart sank. No, oh please, no.

"They dispatched her henchmen rather efficiently by themselves."

The sound of footsteps preceded them, then Gavin exited the tunnel first. His hair was wild as he looked around. The knife in his hand dripped with blood. A slash on his jaw was already healing. Taliesin, Shin and Kayin followed him. All of them were bruised, and their clothes torn and dirty.

"Sapphire," Gavin called when he saw me.

"Is she okay?" Anali said. I couldn't see her yet.

"Stay with Miu, Sasha, and Ramsey," Gavin said, his eyes focused on Mr. Monroe. "Sapphire, come here."

I walked towards him. "Everything is okay. This is Mr. Monroe, he's a protector of Avalon. They helped me get away."

His hand reached out yanking me into his arms. "I'm so sorry. I got to you as quickly as I could. Are you okay? Did they hurt you? Where are they? Never again, you're never again risking yourself like that."

I tried to breathe as Gavin's arms tightened around me, his fear twining around us both like a boa constrictor. "I didn't want anything to happen to Anali and the baby—they're your family."

Gavin pushed me away, his pale green eyes hard. "Sapphire, you're part of our family and the thought of losing you . . ." He closed his eyes. Tears clung to his lashes when he opened them. "You are as precious to me, to us, as this baby is."

"Let me go," Anali said. "I want to see her."

"Gavin," Sasha called. "Can I let Anali go before she kicks me again?"

"Yes, everything seems safe enough for now."

Anali flew at us. I stepped back so she could reach Gavin. Gasping, I jerked as she flung her arms around me. "Are you all right? Don't you ever trade yourself for me again! You were so brave! But you're grounded for being reckless."

"I'm fine," I said, smiling as she ignored me and began to check me over. Her eyes welled with tears as she touched my cheek. I held her hand. "I'm fine. It's just a scratch."

The others moved into Avalon, each touching me as they came close.

"Little Sister," Kayin said as he wrapped his arms around me.

"I'm fine," I said, hugging him back.

He let me go and Ramsey moved in, wrapping me in his arms and burying his face in my neck. "My heart almost failed me when I saw him grab you."

"I hate to interrupt, but are you opening the portal tonight?" Mr. Monroe asked.

Ramsey let me go. I turned to Gavin.

He nodded. "We can. Now that it's safe."

"I don't know where Melusine is," I said. "She ran off chanting something."

Mr. Monroe sighed. "Probably a cloaking spell so we can't find her. We do have people looking for her."

The vampire snorted at 'people'.

"Can we get you anything?" asked one of the priestesses.

"I'd love a glass of wine."

I turned quickly and my braid smacked into someone behind me. "Cartazonon."

I rubbed the scars on my arm from where he touched me in a dream and froze my skin.

Cartazonon stood at the tunnel entrance, a smile on his thin lips. He looked out of place. His black hair was cut short on the sides with the top left long in a trendy style. He wore a three-piece dove-gray suit with a mint-green tie, and his polished black shoes looked perfect despite the walk to get here. Why didn't I feel sick?

Melusine stumbled next to him. Lee's hand wrapped around her neck, his fingers touching at the front of her throat as she chanted.

"You can stop, my dear," Cartazonon said.

Melusine stopped.

I stumbled as the itchy, oily, unnatural feeling swept over me. My skin felt like bugs crawled under it. My stomach clenched in fear and tried to roll with nausea at the same time.

"So. This is very exciting." Cartazonon walked towards us, revealing several mercenaries and walk-ins. "Melusine, you were going to keep all of this from me? The one who saved your pathetic life and sustained your for centuries."

"No," she whispered. "Of course not. I wanted to make sure Avalon was here before telling you. I didn't want to waste your time."

He smiled. "Give us a kiss so we can make up and put this all behind us."

Melusine walked to Cartazonon. Her body trembled, but she held herself tall and proud. Smiling, she wrapped her arms around his neck and tilted her head up to him.

I whimpered and backed up, my hand frantically reaching behind me. Her revulsion and his triumph slithered around me. Cool moonlight energy grounded me. Taliesin.

Melusine started to push at his shoulders fighting to get away. Cartazonon's arms tightened as he pulled his power from her. He lifted his head, and a black worm of smoke slid into his mouth. Melusine dropped to the floor. She screamed, looking at her withered hands.

"Get her out of my sight," Cartazonon said, stepping over her before a black gloved hand pulled her into the tunnel. Her cries echoed on the stone walls as she begged for forgiveness and pledged her loyalty.

Taliesin pulled me back as Cartazonon walked towards us. "We have to get to the other side of the lake, where the gateway stone is." He whispered, his hood rubbing against my cheek.

"Do we run?" I asked, watching as Cartazonon's people advanced behind him. I wasn't sure I could outrun them.

"On the count of three apparently," Taliesin said.

Cartazonon grinned. "Going to try running, little one? I know you, you've visited me. Invisible. In my rooms. Watching me."

"One," Taliesin said. I tightened my fingers around his. "Two, three."

A jet of fire burst between us.

Taliesin yanked my arm and we started running past a huge brown and copper dragon. His sharp teeth were masked by the fire he was breathing for us.

Miu's eyes grew wide. "Not good, not good."

I looked back. The flames spread, arching up to the ceiling instead of going into the tunnel. Cartazonon blocked the flames, protecting his people. Miu was right, this wasn't good.

Ramsey grabbed my other hand. "Come on."

We ran.

Cartazonon bellowed.

Heat exploded around us. Lifting us up. I screamed, trying and failing to hold onto Taliesin and Ramsey. I hit the ground rolling until I slammed into a boulder. My breath left my body. My chest burned. I smelled burnt hair and resisted the urge to check if the smell came from me. Reaching out I grasped on to the smooth stone. Warm Earth magic flowed into my hands. Unfortunately, the magic did nothing to help the sharp hot pains shooting in my ribs and back.

Chaos. The protectors of Avalon ran to hide. To fight. To protect.

The Sons of Belial swarmed. Stun guns erupted like lighting as they hit humans and magical creatures alike.

I turned, seeing a flash of red. Gavin carried Anali into a circle of oak trees. I could feel the hum of the gateway stone. Priests and priestesses held hands. A pale green wall of Earth magic shimmered as they chanted their prayers. A walk-in ran to them and screamed as he hit the barrier.

A mercenary grinned and charged. A scream caught in my throat as Gavin jumped over the clasped hands of the druids, his knife in one hand, to attack the mercenary. Their arms moved in a blur of motion, with the occasional silver flash as they struck at each other with knives. Oh God, this couldn't be happening.

My stomach clenched. I stumbled. Unnatural magic slithered through the air.

Cartazonon held his hands up. Thick oily power emanated from them.

"You don't have to hide," Cartazonon called. "Come, my dark ones. Come and join me, and we shall rule."

The shadows began to move. Black dogs crept from hidden caves, growling. Dark ghost-like wraiths floated above us, their red eyes fixed on Cartazonon. A wyvern slid by me her fangs dripping poison which hit the ground with a hiss.

"Yes, come into the light where you belong," he kept chanting like some evil Pied Piper.

"No."

I turned, my vision swimming at the sudden movement. Taliesin winced as he took off his jacket. The underground moonlight, caressed him and made him glow. His white hair looked silver, and a blue star shone on his forehead. He was a beacon of light in the chaos. I wanted to run to him and hide until this was all over.

"Stop. We're here to send you home. To help you get back to Akasha. Back to where you will be free to roam. Back to your own kind." His voice carried his moonlight cool magic. Every magical creature stopped and looked at him. "Come to me. I will keep you safe and we will open the portal to Akasha, to your home."

Taliesin walked to edge of the circle. The magical beings following him.

Cartazonon lowered his hands, his dark eyes wide. He said something but I couldn't hear him. His eyes never left Taliesin.

I screamed as a hand clamped on my shoulder. "The boss will be so pleased to get to meet you."

Shining black skin covered hard muscle. The woman smiled at me, small braids of black hair falling over her face. These weren't weak walk-ins, these were powerful people who owed him a huge debt. I broke out in goose-bumps as the walk-in's energy surrounded me.

I grabbed her hand and twisted her arm forcing her to bend over. I kicked her stomach as hard as I could, then pushed her away. I couldn't pin her to the ground—more were coming. Turning, I saw a handle of a sword or knife on the other side of the boulder. Oh, you have got to be kidding me.

"I'm going to make you pay you little bitch," the walk-in said.

I grabbed the silver and gold handle and pulled. A glowing sword slid free from the rock. I held the sword front of me and pretended I knew how to use it. She lunged and I swung the sword hitting her in the arm with the flat side. She screamed, falling to her knees. The walk-in left her body. Its gray form hovered above her for a moment before it vanished.

"Do you even know how to use that?" Shin asked, taking the sword from my hands.

"No, no idea."

"They don't seem to like touching the sword much. I'll do my best to not kill any of us." He looked at the circle. "Go, you have a job to do."

"I can't leave you alone. Come with me," I said, tugging on his arm.

"He's not alone." Ramsey held a knife in one hand. The other held tight onto the strap of his yoga bag. Half his face showed scratches and bruises. "Go on. I have the feeling that opening the portal will change things."

"Stay safe." I kissed his cheek, squeezed Shin's arm, and ran to the circle.

"Let go!"

Lee dragged Miu by her arm. She looked like a toddler as she hit and kicked at him.

I opened my connection to Akasha and ran, engulfed my hand in flames and grabbed his arm.

He dropped Miu and grabbed the front of my shirt, throwing me to the ground. He held up his injured arm. My hand print was burned into his skin—skin that now looked old and wrinkled. His thick fingers became bony and crooked.

His thin eyes stared at me. I couldn't move as he drew a wicked curved blade.

Chapter Twenty-Six

"Sapphire, duck," Kayin yelled as a fireball flew over my head, hitting Lee in the center of his chest.

Lee roared and stumbled backwards. His shirt burned and his chest underneath became bright pink. The muscles sagged, and the skin looked wrinkled and old.

"Lee," Cartazonon called. His fury made me shiver. I scrambled to my feet, clasping hands with Kayin and Miu.

A hoard of magical creatures screeched their defiance. Surrounding Taliesin, creatures both light and dark sent out a wave of fierce protection. Thank goodness he was safe.

"Come on." Kayin helped me up and pulled me forward. A mercenary screamed as the vampire who helped me earlier tore open his throat. The man gurgled and twitched as his blood poured onto the floor.

"Oh, gross," Miu said. Her pale skin turned green as she covered her nose against the copper scent.

Cold hard arms wrapped around me. I opened my mouth to scream, but fear froze me. Miu and Kayin's hands were ripped from mine.

"You hurt one of the few people I care about. I will drain your magic and life from you slowly, causing you as much pain as possible," Cartazonon hissed in my ear.

Kayin and Miu stopped running. "Get to the circle," I yelled.

Miu ran.

Kayin's hands burst into flames. "I'm not leaving you."

Cartazonon started to walk backwards.

His energy made focus impossible, and my powers sputtered as I pulled Phoenix fire into my hands. Nothing. I reached behind me trying to fight back. Cartazonon hissed and moved so all I got were a few strands of hair.

"I have been fighting for centuries. You are nothing compared to me, and you're certainly not going to get away."

My breath caught in my throat. I believed him.

The chanting grew. The lyrical words broke through my terror. The wall of Earth magic sparkled with copper in the rich transparent grass green. Earth magic reached a foot or two above their heads. The amount of power they raised was impressive, but it wasn't going to stop Cartazonon.

Mr. Monroe smiled at me, then winked as he raised his arms. Power swirled around him, black as midnight and sparkling with rainbow flecks.

The other priests and priestesses followed his lead. Their power grew, the wall of Earth magic grew a few inches taller, the color deepened to a bright emerald green, and more copper flecks appeared.

"What is a god doing here?" Cartazonon whispered.

What? The power grew, forming a large sphere. Tendrils of Earth magic began to join the black power.

"We need to leave," Cartazonon yelled, pulling me backwards.

I grabbed his hand and raked my knuckle hard over the tendons on the back of his hand. His grip loosened, and I dropped to the ground letting my full weight fall and pull against his grasp.

A battle cry. A flash of silver.

I hit the floor and my battered ribs found another rock. Blood dripped from Cartazonon's arm. Dark red drops fell onto me. Gross. I scooted away. A hand grabbed my shoulder and yanked me up.

"You okay?" Shin asked.

I nodded.

"Sapphire," Ramsey called, running towards me. He scooped me up and turned. I screamed as I saw the knife flying towards us. Ramsey's body stiffened and began to shake.

Pain racked my body, sharp heat from the knife and cold evil as Ramsey's power drained from him. I looked up. Cartazonon held out his hand. He had used the crystals and Akashic metal in the knife as a conduit for him.

"I'm sorry," I said reaching over and grabbed the knife. The hilt burned ice cold. I bit back a cry and yanked. Ramsey screamed then collapsed. Blood gushed from the wound.

"Oh shit." Shin took off his shirt and pressed it against Ramsey's wound.

Close your eyes. A man's voice echoed in my head.

I looked up. Mr. Monroe grinned, making me shiver. He brought his arms back, the ball of power and magic moved.

I grabbed Shin. "Close your eyes."

He dropped next to me. I covered Ramsey's head, and Shin covered mine.

Power and light exploded.

Men screamed.

Warmth, strength, comfort—this wasn't going to hurt us.

Minutes passed. The magic swirled, protecting us all. The light dimmed, and I opened my eyes. The moonlight illuminated the cave. Confused people looked around, some crying. The walk-ins, pulled out of the bodies, leaving their hosts lost without direction.

A wheezing gasp.

I turned. Lee and Cartazonon supported each other. Their bodies shook, eyes clouded over, skin wrinkled and hung loose as the life and power they stole was removed from them. Cartazonon snarled at me as they turned and hobbled out of Avalon.

"Ramsey," called a woman. She and two younger women rushed towards us. His mom and sisters, judging by the dark brown curls and black eyes.

Miu ran right behind them. "Let me heal him." She placed her hands on his back and opened her connection to Akasha. Power flowed into him. The bleeding slowed but didn't stop. Miu shook her head. "I can't do more than that. Too much of his own magic is gone."

"He needs to go to Akasha," Mr. Monroe said. "You must open the portal now. Some of us will follow them in case he tries to send more men."

I nodded as he and several of the guardians of Avalon left.

Ramsey's family picked him up. "We only came to see what was happening, none of us planned to go to Akasha," his mother said, tears dripping down her cheeks. "Murdock isn't even here, he can't say goodbye to his brother."

"Can I heal you?" Miu asked reaching for me.

I shook my head. "No, it's too draining. Let's get this portal open." I gritted my teeth. Pain shot through my body as I stood. "We don't have time for any kind of ceremony. We'll all touch each other's shoulders, breathe, and connect to Akasha."

"Will that be enough?" Kayin asked.

I looked at Ramsey's ashen face. I had no choice—it needed to be enough. It was all I could do. Wait. "Where's his yoga bag? It's a long black yoga bag."

"Here," Sasha said. "He tucked his bag under the boulder that held the sword. Do you think he'll be doing yoga in Akasha?"

"His seal skin is in it." I handed the bag to his sister.

"He told you that?" she asked her eyes wide.

"No, but it wasn't that hard to figure out once I knew what he was." I groaned, my body shaking. I was in so much pain. *Too bad, you have to get that portal open right now,* I said to myself.

Anali's eyes filled with tears as she saw me. She cupped my bruised face and kissed my cheeks. "I'm so sorry, my darling."

"I can still save him," I said. I wanted to fall into her arms and cry, but not yet. I stood a few feet from the gateway stone. It started in the center of the oak tree ring and reached into the lake. Kayin and Anali placed a hand on my shoulders.

"There are only six of us," Gavin said. "We normally have seven."

"Hold on," Taliesin said. "I've got them all settled down. They will behave and go through the portal without fuss."

Kayin moved his hand to my neck and Taliesin placed his hand on my shoulder.

"Okay, follow my breath and connect to Akasha." I closed my eyes and focused on the warm energy as I tapped into Akasha. One by one the others opened their connection. The heat made beads of perspiration dot my forehead, then Taliesin added his cool unicorn energy. I sighed as I felt the energy balance within me. I held my hands out and sent everything I had into the gateway stone. Bright purple light arched into a giant doorway. White light filled it, then we could see beyond. A lake, next to ours, with soft white sand and wild flowers, beckoned.

"I don't know what to do," Ramsey's mom said tears running down her cheeks. "We weren't going to go. I have my life here—but my son . . ."

My heart ached. I had no answers for her.

"Welcome my friends," Shamash said, stepping through the portal. He invited the magical beings in. Grims, fairies, gnomes, and Nessy all headed home. Shamash's smile faded as he saw the state we were in. "What has happened?"

"Big battle. I'll tell you later, but Ramsey needs help."

Shamash knelt next to Ramsey and his crying family. A large silvery tear filled his eye. He caught the tear on his finger and dropped it into the wound.

"He will have to come to Akasha for his magic to heal completely," Shamash said.

His family sobbed.

"Hush," Shamash said stroking their hair. "He will be gone only a year or two, and there are several large pods of selkies for him to stay with. What did this?"

"Cartazonon," I said, trying to stay focused on the portal when all I wanted was to sit next to Ramsey.

Shamash nodded. "He needs to heal in selkie form."

His mom took off his clothes and lay the dark brown seal skin over his naked body. Shamash set his hands on him and Ramsey shifted, into a fat round seal. Large black eyes blinked and he let out a loud growly bark.

His mother hugged him and began explaining what happened. I chuckled as she answered his barked questions.

A wet nose pressed against my leg. I looked down, and Ramsey looked up at me. "I'd hug you goodbye but I can't stop. I'm sorry this happened. Thank you for saving me."

Ramsey huffed and rubbed his face against my leg before shuffling off to the water and swimming into Akasha.

Shamash stood in front of me and placed a silver tear on my forehead. He stepped into the portal, but paused to speak one more time. "You had a trace on you. I am sorry for everything that happened. Aya and I look forward to hearing your story. Before I forget, Anali, relax. Your baby is fine."

* * *

We all sagged as we released our powers, and the portal closed. Anali turned and buried her face in Gavin's chest as he held her tight. I smiled and started to walk past them when hands grabbed me and pulled me into a group hug.

"Sapphire, I was so scared for you," Anali said.

Gavin squeezed me tighter. "Never again. I'm never allowing you to be in that kind of danger ever again."

A sweet idea, but both of us knew it wasn't realistic. This life was dangerous.

"Does anyone need to be healed?" Miu asked, her soft voice filled with guilt.

"Nothing small or that can wait without causing more damage or significant pain," Gavin said, squeezing us both then stepping back. "We're all tired. And healing drains you. We can do more in the van or at the hotel."

My ribs throbbed with pain, but I didn't ask for help. Miu looked tired. I didn't want to add to her burden.

"They've left," Mr. Monroe said. "Apparently, they had a helicopter waiting for them."

"He'll be back," I said.

Mr. Monroe smiled. "I'm sure he will, but he can't get in. We'll make sure of that. Do you need any help?"

"I think we're fine," Gavin said. "I'm surprised by the amount of power you were able to create. Thank you for helping us."

"We live to serve. We'll come along to help you back to your vehicle."

I watched Ramsey's family gather his kilt and sporran. His mother wept as she held them against her chest. His sisters held her and gave what comfort they could.

"I'm sorry about Ramsey," Taliesin said. "I didn't care for him, but he saved you. I saw that knife. He saved your life, and for that I'm thankful."

"Thank you." I took Taliesin's hand. "You don't look too banged up."

He rolled his eyes. "Once they surrounded me, I couldn't get out to help fight. They insisted on protecting me."

"Your mom will be pleased. She must be frantic right now," I said as we walked up the stairs.

"I'll text her as soon as we get out," Taliesin said.

I didn't remember this many stairs on the way down. I panted, and every step jolted my ribs. The pain made me lightheaded. Why did there have to be so many damn stairs!

Taliesin let go of my hand and wrapped his arm around my waist, supporting me as we climbed even more stairs.

"Sapphire, you're panting," Miu said, looking me over as we stepped outside.

I tried to take a deep breath of the fresh air, groaning as my ribs protested the movement.

Her small hands touched me. I gasped as she pressed on my side. Why was she being so mean? What had I done to her?

"Your ribs are cracked. I should have healed them before we walked up all those stairs," she said.

"I didn't want you to become drained," I said.

"And I don't want you to injure yourself worse than you already have. Or be in pain."

"But …"

Miu glared at me. "Yes, I would have been tired, but one of the others could have helped me walk. I would have done that for you, for any of you. That's what families do for each other." She shook her head, her ponytail swinging behind her. "I'm sorry I couldn't heal Ramsey, I wanted to. I tried, but without magic of their own my powers can't help some beings."

"I know you tried, I felt you." My gift for languages only worked on those with magic in them too.

She nodded. "I did, I really did. I mean I know it's my job to heal, that's the reason I'm here."

I looked at Miu, where was all of this self-doubt coming from? I felt way too tired and in too much pain to deal with this right now. "I'm hoping you will heal me on the ride home, but only if you're feeling up to it."

Miu smiled. "Of course, I'd be happy to help."

"Sapphire," Mr. Monroe said holding out a bag. "This is for you."

"What is it?" I asked as I opened the bag. "Chocolate bars?"

Mr. Monroe grinned. "Haven't you read Harry Potter? Chocolate fixes everything. Drive safe and thank you."

I watched him disappear into Glastonbury Tor. Wind whipped around me. Shivering, I limped to the van.

"Miu is going to heal you right?" Gavin asked as he helped me into the van.

"Yes, and Mr. Monroe gave me chocolates to pass around." I groaned and sat carefully on the seat. I handed Gavin two of the organic dark chocolate bars.

"Thanks, hopefully this will keep me awake long enough to get coffee."

I passed around the rest of the chocolate. Shin smiled. The thick green ointment on his wounds made the van smell like bitter herbs.

"Looks like Miu got to you," I said.

Shin unwrapped the chocolate bar. "I'm the only one her gift doesn't work on so she wanted to do what she could. That's a pretty awesome first aid kit she's put together."

We have a first aid kit? "Miu's very thorough so I'm not surprised. Are you okay?"

Shin nodded, leaned back against the seat as he laid his arm around Kayin's shoulder and pulled him into his side. "I am now. I had no idea what you guys did was so dangerous."

"It's not normally," I said my voice trailing off.

Shin arched an eyebrow.

"It's not," Kayin said. "Sometimes it's dangerous, but most of the time we're able to open a portal without any trouble."

"Tell me more about what you do," Shin said.

I passed Taliesin and Sasha bars of chocolate while Kayin told Shin stories about our adventures. Kayin told a great story. Even I sounded heroic. I handed Miu a bar once she finished healing Anali.

"Eat first," I said pulling out the last bar, an envelope was taped to it. Damn it, wasn't the weirdness done for the night? "There's a letter."

"What?" Sasha asked.

I waved the letter. "This letter was taped to the last chocolate bar."

"Is it addressed to anyone?" Anali asked.

"Not on the outside," I said.

"Well, open it," Gavin said. "And read it out loud."

Dear Sapphire,

It was so good to see you again. You have been doing an outstanding job. I've always known you would be an amazing Jewel. I bet Shamash and Aya are so proud of you. And while you have been doing a good job, I thought I would give you some help. Listed below are the portals closest to magical beings that Cartazonon keeps tabs on. This should make your job easier. I'll be checking in on you. Good luck and stay safe.

Love,

Quintin Monroe

"The rest are GPS coordinates," I said.

"Who is this guy?" Taliesin asked.

"I have no idea," I said. "He is very strong, his power stopped Cartazonon and the others. In fact, Cartazonon said he was a god."

"Do you think he's one of Shamash's brothers?" Gavin asked.

"No idea," I muttered around a piece of chocolate. The smooth creamy rich chocolate melted, the sugar and innate goodness that is chocolate seemed to go directly to my bloodstream.

"Done," said Miu as she placed her hands on my side.

I winced, but stayed still. Warm Akashic energy flowed from Miu's hands into my body. I gasped as my ribs heated and healed. As the pain faded, my eyes grew heavy. I closed my eyes, just for a moment while Miu was healing me, I told myself. Then I would finish eating my chocolate and feel all better. I shouldn't sleep not after being touched by Cartazonon. I was sure to dream of him. I fought to keep my eyes open, but a burst of healing energy relaxed my aching muscles and sleep won.

Chapter Twenty-Seven

"I can feel you," Cartazonon said. "I didn't expect you to fall asleep so soon. Or I would have freshened the place up."

Three bodies were shoved into a corner and Cartazonon leaned over a fourth. I turned away and looked around the plane. Private of course. Leather seats, thick carpet, and wooden tables made the room look more like a living room than an airplane. There was even a TV.

A thick sucking sound filled the room. I slapped my hand over my mouth.

"How do you like my knife?" he asked. "I can't get quite as much power from them as I like but it's more than enough and very efficient."

I shivered, glad I couldn't feel the emotions haunting the plane.

"I can feel you, but I can't see you, not yet at least," he said. I moved as he walked past me to sit in a black leather chair. "And I wonder if I can hear you. Would you speak now so I can find out?"

I stayed silent.

Cartazonon chuckled. "I bet you're not saying anything just to defy me. Do so while you can. I have so many questions. Why was there a god helping you? How long can you keep the portal open? Who is the unicorn? Does he know who his father is?"

Frowning, I turned to look at him. Why does he care about Taliesin's father?

Cartazonon sipped single-malt scotch from a square glass, relaxing against the chair. His long white fingers were stained with blood, the knuckles swollen and the wrinkled skin tight against the tendons. I guess four people wasn't enough to heal him fully. His legs crossed, the top leg swung slightly, showing brightly striped socks. Even without my empathy I knew he faked the pose. The tightness around his mouth and eyes gave away his pain and fatigue, and highlighted his new wrinkles.

"You see, only one unicorn, that I know of, has walked on Earth for the past thousand years, give or take a century or two. Please tell the young man I have answers about his father if he wants them."

The plane began to move.

"You know I don't have to kill any of these beings," Cartazonon said. "You have the power to stop all of this. If you open the portal to Akasha, I could…" He twirled his hand around as if gathering up his thoughts, "plug into that world. For lack of a better word. I could, I'm sure, get all of the power I need through the portal and never harm another creature again."

I shook my head, I didn't believe him.

"Think," he continued. "No more fighting with my men. No friends hurt, ever again. You can stop it all. I'm sure we'll talk again, think on my offer."

The plane started to rise. I held onto a chair to keep from tipping over.

Cartazonon chuckled. "I'll have to look into this connection we have."

Something cold hit my foot. A hand, lifeless and tinged blue-gray. I wish I could have looked away, but instinct betrayed me and I looked at the face. Oh god no Ramsey's brother, Murdock. In the corner the other bodies moved, revealing the rest of the Water Nymphs.

Wake up, wake up, wake up, wake up. WAKE UP!

Screaming, I arched against the seat belt. Murdock's lifeless eyes filled my vision. The door opened. I gasped at the icy air, my tears freezing as they fell. Someone undid my seatbelt, and I collapsed onto the side of the road throwing up. Cartazonon's offers echoed in my head. Taliesin's father. I can end all the killing. I thought about dealing with Cartazonon and threw up again. Then a vision of Ramsey, his shirt bloody, a knife sticking out of his back brought on another round of vomiting.

"It'll be okay," Anali said, her hand moving in smooth circles on my back. "Try and let go of your thoughts and focus on your breath. We'll sort everything out later."

I nodded and took the bottle of water Gavin handed me, and rinsed my mouth.

"Do you want to talk about the dream?" Gavin asked.

I shook my head. "No, not right now."

"Okay, that's fine. Let me know when you're ready."

I rinsed my mouth out one more time and stood. "I'm good." I needed a shower. I would force my stomach to calm in order to get a shower. I climbed into the van. Shin sat against the window, and Kayin was next to him with his arms open. I buckled in and curled into my Big Brothers arms. My eyes burned, but I wouldn't allow myself to cry, not yet. Shin's arms curled around me and Kayin. Shin's fingers gripped mine. Surrounded by strong arms, I felt the cold fear inside me began to fade, but it didn't go away.

* * *

Warm in my flannel penguin pajamas, I combed my wet hair. Simmons had set me up in my dad's old room. It felt strange, like the ghosts of my family might come through the wall to haunt me while I slept. Sighing, I stood up and headed to the parlor. Gavin and Anali insisted I meet with them before going to bed. I probably wouldn't be able to sleep if I didn't talk about the dream anyway, so I might as well deal with it.

The door was open. I slid inside. The room was empty. On the table was a tea service and platters of sandwiches and cakes. Parker had taken one look at us and rushed to the kitchen to make us something to eat. At the time I couldn't imagine eating anything, but now I was grateful.

I finished my second sandwich when Gavin and Anali came into the room. Their cheeks were pink and their hair damp.

Wow, they had showered fast. Or maybe they showered together. Eewww gross!

"How are you feeling?" Anali asked, looking over the sandwiches and taking the cucumber ones.

"My muscles are a little sore, but Miu healed all the injuries."

Anali stared at me and raised an eyebrow.

I wiped my shaking hands on my pajama pants. "Cartazonon knew I was there, he could sense me. He can't see me, and I didn't say anything so I don't know if he can hear me."

Gavin leaned forward sitting on the edge of the couch. "What did he do? Did he touch you again?"

"No, he talked to me."

"What did he say?" Gavin asked, taking the sandwich Anali handed him.

"He said that I can stop all of this." I choked as the tears I had been holding back started to fall. "He said that if I open the portal to Akasha for him he can get all the energy he needs from there and he won't have to kill anyone else. We won't have to fight anymore."

"Sapphire," Gavin said holding my hand. "This isn't your fault, and giving in to this man isn't the answer."

"But he killed them all, and if I could stop it . . ."

"Killed who sweetheart?" Anali asked.

"Ramsey's ..." I took a deep breath and closed my eyes as if to hide from my own words. "His band, the Water Nymphs, their bodies were on his plane. He'd drained them to repair the damage he suffered during the fight."

"Oh, honey," Anali came over and hugged me.

"But if I open the portal for him," I started.

"No, then you're trapped with him and that's not okay," Gavin said. "He is choosing to kill, he is choosing to fight. You are choosing to open the portals, we are choosing to help."

I nodded, but still knowing I could protect everyone if I agreed to help left a cold spot in my heart.

"Did he say anything else?" Anali asked as she moved back to the couch.

I drank some tea, the warm liquid soothing my throat. "Yes, he said he would be willing to tell Taliesin about his father."

"Did he say who his father is?" Anali asked.

"No, just that there has only been one unicorn on Earth for the past thousand years, and he knows about him," I said.

"Well," Gavin began, "while I hope Taliesin chooses to ignore Cartazonon's offer, he needs to be told."

"I agree," said Anali. "It's not fair to keep this from him. Do you want us to tell him?"

"No, I'll tell Taliesin, but could you tell the others about the deal he offered me? I mean what if they want me to take it? Even for a moment, before they think it through, I don't want to know. I don't want to constantly wonder if they were wishing I was choosing to work with Cartazonon and not continuing to risk their lives."

"If that's what you want," said Gavin. "But I doubt any of them will want you to go to him."

I picked a cheese and pickle sandwich. Why wouldn't they? I thought about joining Cartazonon to save everyone.

"When are you going to tell Taliesin?" Anali asked.

"I'll text him and see if he's still awake. I won't sleep if I'm stressing out about telling him."

"Good plan," Gavin said.

I pulled out my phone.

—*Are you still awake?*

—*Yes, why?* Taliesin texted back within a minute.

—*Can we talk? In person?* I asked. I looked at my purple flannel penguin pajamas, good enough.

—*Sure, where?*

"Gavin, where can Taliesin and I go to talk?"

Anali yawned. "I'm going to bed. Why don't you two talk here? There's plenty of food still, and that way should you need us, you can call."

"Yes, should you need us, we'll be available," Gavin said.

"Okay thanks." I texted Taliesin. "He's on his way."

Gavin stood and offered Anali his hand. "Good night, Sapphire."

They both hugged me and kissed me on the forehead before heading to their bedroom.

I started tidying Gavin and Anali's dishes and set clean ones out for Taliesin. Nervous energy can get a lot of cleaning done.

"What's up?" Taliesin said, his hair was wet and he looked almost translucent.

"Tea?" I held the pot.

Taliesin nodded and arched an eyebrow. "Sure."

"There are sandwiches, if you're hungry."

"Okay, now you're scaring me. What's with all the social niceties?"

Rude. I could be nice. "I dreamed of Cartazonon."

Taliesin grabbed a cucumber sandwich. "Yes, the vomiting gave that away."

Rolling my eyes, I continued. "Anyway um … well you see … he saw you … but I'm not even sure if I should say anything …"

"Sapphire, say it."

I closed my eyes. "He says he knows who your father is."

His tea cup clinked as he set on the table. "What?"

I took a deep breath. "Cartazonon says that there has only been one unicorn on Earth for at least a thousand years. He said that he is willing to tell you about your father."

"That's interesting," Taliesin picked a watercress sandwich. "Anything else?"

"No. Should I not have told you? Everyone was upset about my keeping secrets earlier, and I didn't want you to think I was keeping things from you, and I know how important family can be to people, but I certainly don't think it's smart to deal with him, but Gavin and Anali agreed that you needed to know—"

Taliesin's hand covered my mouth. "First, stop tapping your fingers, it's driving me nuts. Second, breathe. Third, thank you for telling me. All I know about my dad is my mom met him in

Chicago while at a wedding. They met in the hotel bar, had an amazing night," Taliesin made his voice high pitched and fluttered his lashes mimicking his mom. "My mom told me she dreamed about meeting him, and having me."

"Did she tell you anything about him?" I asked.

Taliesin shook his head. "Not a lot. He was dressed nice, wore expensive cologne, seemed intelligent, and was kind to her."

"Are you curious about him?" I took a bite of sandwich.

Shrugging, Taliesin leaned back in the chair. "A little, I guess. My mom has a little bit of magic in her, a touch of something, I'm not sure what. Anyway, she has the occasional dream and for some reason she was able to carry his child. A unicorn child. Maybe unicorn dads aren't that attentive, so I'm genetically not programmed to be interested in him. Maybe I'm still in shock from the evening. I've never believed I'd meet my father, so who knows how I'll feel in a few days?"

"When I was young I dreamed about my parents coming and rescuing me. Then I dreamed of a new people becoming my parents—or, well, parent—I had two different foster moms. After the second one gave me back, I stopped dreaming of having a family." I laughed. "I didn't even dream of getting married and having kids someday. I dreamed of having a cat, but not people in my life."

"I'm sorry. I can't imagine anyone giving you back," Taliesin said.

"I wasn't a very cute kid. I went through a long 'awkward phase.'" I wiggled my fingers to make air quotes. "Anyway, it doesn't matter now. So next time I see Cartazonon, should I tell him you're not interested?"

"Yes, please. I don't want to have anything to do with him." Taliesin froze then looked up at the ceiling. "Wait, do you think he knows who my mom is? I mean, she always told me they only exchanged first names, which is why I never expected to meet him. How could he even find her? But what about Cartazonon?"

"I don't know, he didn't say anything about your mom to me. And he didn't use the word 'parents' just 'father'."

"We know he wants a unicorn, badly, we learned that in Argentina." Taliesin stood and began to pace. "And now he's seen us. He's going to trace us, eventually he'll find my bio and my last name, my mom's last name, and that I grew up in San Francisco."

Crap, crap, crap. "Wait here." I ran upstairs and knocked on the bedroom door. Gavin answered squinting in the light. "We have a problem."

Gavin yawned. "What's up?"

"Our bios for Cirque du Feu Magique, has last names and where we grew up," I said.

Gavin frowned. "Yes."

"And now he's seen us and we've hurt him, and he wants a unicorn. Not to mention he has Melusine," I added. "And she knows we're with the circus."

"Shit," he turned and went to get his phone. Anali followed him out of the room.

"Philip, sorry, but we have another situation I need your help with," Gavin explained everything that happened as we walked back to the parlor.

"Are you okay?" Taliesin placed his hand on my shoulder. The heat went right through my pajama top. "Sapphire, you're shaking."

"I'm cold." Why was I cold? The room wasn't cold—Gavin and Taliesin both wore tee shirts and pajama bottoms. I looked at Taliesin. "Why am I so cold?"

Taliesin scooped me up and sat on the couch keeping me on his lap with his arms wrapped around me. "She needs a blanket."

I hadn't meant to cause a fuss. "Sorry, I'm so sorry," I whispered.

"Hush, you're fine. Everything is fine," Taliesin said. "I think she's in shock."

A spoon clinked. "Here, sweetheart, I want you to drink this."

Anali pressed a warm cup of tea against my lips. I took a sip. Oh, God, too sweet. I turned my head and hid my face against Taliesin's chest.

Anali tucked the blanket under my feet. At least I assume it was Anali as Taliesin still held me and Gavin was on the other side of the room talking to Philip trying to fix this mess. The mess I caused. The mess I could stop from ever happening again. I began to shake and grabbed onto Taliesin shirt as tears poured from my eyes. Images from the fight flashed through my head. My friends being grabbed and hit, magical creatures being hurt. The bodies lying on the ground. I didn't even check to see if they needed help or if it was too late.

Shouldn't I have checked on them? Isn't that part of my job, my destiny?

Murdock's lifeless face would haunt me forever. His dead black eyes seemed to accuse me of failing him, of not saving him. My body shuddered as I sobbed.

"That's right," Anali said rubbing my leg. "Let it go. Don't hold onto all of this."

Taliesin lay his cheek on top of my head and tightened his arms around me as I cried—okay, sobbed hysterically.

Once I calmed down, my breath fell in sync with Taliesin's as he exhaled and surrounded me with his energy. Cool moonlight flowed around me, and forgave me. Forgave me for all the things I had no control over and forgave me for the things that were in my control. I wasn't sure I deserved forgiveness, but I breathed it in allowing his energy to sooth my heart.

"Go ahead and go to sleep. Everything is fine," Taliesin whispered.

"Hmmm," I answered as relaxed into his arms and faded into sleep.

* * *

I scrunched my toes in the cold sand, and looked around. I'd never visited this part of Akasha in my dreams. I turned as something barked at me. A dark brown seal bobbed in the blue gray sea. "Ramsey?"

The seal nodded and swam towards the beach.

"Ramsey," I yelled running into the cold water. I fell to my knees and wrapped my arms around him. "Thank goodness you're alright. I am so sorry."

He snorted.

"I should have known, I should have stopped it. It's all my fault. I hurt Cartazonon and he needed to steal more power to heal himself and Lee. I didn't even think about checking in with your brother."

Ramsey whined.

God, I suck at this. Tears filled my eyes. "Cartazonon killed your brother and the rest of the band, in order to heal after the fight."

Ramsey howled. Magic shifted around him.

"No, you can't shift yet. There's nothing you can do anyway," I said tears running down my cheeks.

Ramsey snapped at me, then barked and whined as he swam away. Guilt, anger, and sorrow surrounded him.

"I'm sorry," I said as a group of seals surrounded him, offering comfort.

"It wasn't your fault, and Ramsey knows that. He's just upset right now," Shamash said, standing next to me.

I watched Ramsey swim away. Maybe I could visit him in another dream and he'd forgive me, or at least realize I wasn't able to do anything to save his brother. Sighing, I turned to my many times great grandparents.

"He looks better. Thank you for taking care of him," I said.

"Of course. He saved you. He has earned the best treatment, and in a year or so, once his body has been able to transmute the Akashic magic into his own selkie magic, he can go home."

I wrapped my arms around myself. "Good. I'm glad he'll get to go back to his mom and sisters."

Aya hugged me. "I'm sorry. It breaks my heart you must deal with so much."

"How are the others?" I asked relaxing into her warmth.

"Fine, a few injuries, but they are all healed now," Aya said. "And your family?"

"Miu healed everyone." I stepped back. "Cartazonon says he can tap into the energy of Akasha through the portal and then he won't hurt anyone else."

Shamash took my hand. "Sapphire, you are not responsible for his choices. Beings who are willing to warp their nature to such an extent certainty will go back on their word. He isn't safe. And…" He looked at our clasped hands, then at me, his gold eyes serious. "I won't allow him to take energy from here. I will stop him, and I always know when and where you open a portal."

I nodded. Of course Shamash would defend his world and his people.

Aya cupped her hand along my jaw. "We will do what we can to help you. You're one of ours, and we will protect you and your family to the best of our ability."

"Thank you," I said as Nessy jumped out of the sea splashing us with cold water.

I woke gasping for air, dry and warm in my own bed. I slid my feet into slippers and walked to the window and looked at the rows of white Georgian houses that lined the street. Christmas lights glowed in the fog.

I walked down the stairs, running my hand over the polished wood banister. The lights on the tree were left on so Santa could find his way, and apparently to help me too. The living room glowed under the white fairy lights. Shante left a plate of cookies and a glass of milk on the table. She had added carrots for the reindeer, too. Once she went to bed, Gavin ate several cookies leaving crumbs all over the plate and table.

Cordelia made Taliesin bite each of the carrots. He pouted. She demanded. He turned into his unicorn form to make realistic teeth marks. I smiled at the memory. Cordelia had teared up at the sight of her son and petted him the whole time.

Shante had left her program from the circus on the couch. A year ago, when I lived in the group home, I followed Shante around the theater lobby as she got autographs from the San Francisco Center for the Circus Arts Christmas Eve performance. This year Cordelia followed her around, and I signed programs.

Michael and Gavin gave tickets to the Christmas Eve show away to group homes and foster families around London. The joy and excitement the kids felt from the show and the sadness at not being at home with their families mingled, giving me a headache. I'd held Kayin's hand to ground me.

Flipping through the program, I smiled at all of the notes the performers left for Shante. I had no idea how Gavin and Philip had managed to change the programs in less than twenty-four hours, but all our bios had been changed. Last names and where we grew up and studied were gone. Michael told the group that here had been some stalker behavior and threats so this was done for everyone's protection.

I tiptoed past the tree. The presents 'Santa' brought spilled out from under the evergreen branches. Gavin, Anali, and Cordelia made sure to use a different wrapping paper for Santa gifts. I wonder if my parents wrapped gifts in Santa paper when I was little.

Grabbing the throw off the back of a chair, I curled up and stared at the picture-perfect living room. My first family Christmas, at least the first I would remember. Would we have to eat before we opened gifts? Could we wake the adults early, or would they send us away saying we should open our stockings and to be quiet until they came down? I looked at the stockings, each one a different color of satin with our names embroidered across the top.

The only little imperfection in the picture was no roaring fire. The fireplace was prepped and ready to go—too bad I didn't know where they kept the matches. Sighing, I looked longingly at the cold fireplace. *Sapphire, you are such a dork.* I tapped into Kayin's energy. Deep asleep, I tugged enough of the gift of fire to light the tip of my finger, careful not to wake him. The old newspapers and kindling started to crackle and burn. I watched as the flames teased the larger logs until they began to consume them. There, a roaring fire—now the image was perfect.

The room, the house looked beautiful, perfect, and cold except for the fire. I wish we had decorated. Last year I helped Shante and the other little girls make paper chains which we draped over the tree and ornaments the girls coated in glitter sparkled in the multicolored lights. My first family Christmas but I didn't feel at home. Not that I knew what home felt like.

The fire made half of the ornaments glow a golden yellow. The white, crystal, and silver decoration seemed warmer now that the fire lit the room, there were crystal snowflakes, silver balls, and porcelain bells that chimed when I touched them. A small faerie danced through the branches. I smiled at him. I'd felt the brownies living in the walls, but not the fairies, although I hadn't gone out to the garden yet.

"Hey little one, you look like a frost faerie. What are you doing inside?"

Pale blue lips curled into a smile. He fluttered his crystal clear wings and landed on a round ornament, tiny veins of frost emanating from where his feet touched the silver.

"What is this?" I turned the ornament. A silver holly wreath framed a photograph. Engraved on the bottom were the words "Sapphire's First Christmas." Tears blurred the picture of my smiling parents holding me. Warmth radiated from the ornament. Every year Simmons and Mr. Parker would decorate the tree and hang this ornament. They would pray for my parents, grandparents, and for me, hoping that someday I would come home.

The faerie kissed my cheek, turning one of my tears into ice.

"Thank you, little one, this is a lovely Christmas gift. May I give you something?"

He squealed and a vision of a plate of cookies and a bowl of warm milk being left outside slid into my head.

"That I can do." I went to the kitchen, only getting lost once, well okay, twice, but the second time the faerie led me astray. I let him pick from the platter of cookies Mr. Parker baked for us while I warmed up some milk on the stove. Faeries don't like microwaves. Shivering, I opened the back door and set the treats on the steps.

The faerie whistled and dozens of delicate blue and white faeries flew over on their crystal clear wings. They devoured the milk and cookies and then began to glow. They flew and danced, leaving beautiful frost patterns on everything they touched.

I shivered again and closed the door. The boy faerie waved at me through the window and then danced along the edges leaving frost leaves to mark his path.

I didn't get lost on my way back to the living room, and curled in the window seat to watch the faeries at work in the front yard. A shadow flowed over the ground. Looking up I saw a dragon, a large white and ice blue dragon. The faeries cheered and grasped hands dancing in joyous circles. I smiled and watched the dragon fly through the clouds, which got bigger and puffier with every flap of his wings.

The dragon stopped.

The faeries stopped.

I held my breath.

The dragon blew a white mist into the clouds. Snow began to fall. I almost joined the faeries in their loud cries of joy, but I didn't want to wake anyone. Fat snowflakes landed on the ground, and stuck without melting. A white Christmas.

The grandfather clock chimed five times. Upstairs my family slept—Miu, Sasha, Taliesin, Kayin, Gavin, Anali, Cordelia,

Shante, and now Shin. Shante would wake up within an hour I'd bet, what with the time difference. The stairs creaked.

Smiling, I turned to watch the doorway. My first family Christmas was about to begin.

A Dragon's Clutch

Book four in the Children of Fire series

Chapter One

The ancestral guardian of the Ryokan did not like me and didn't want me to enter. Truthfully, he hadn't liked any of us with Phoenix ancestry, but the others weren't strong enough for him to speak to. Stepping through the torii gate and into the front garden I let the other performers of Cirque du Magique Fue pass me and go into the traditional Japanese hotel. Leaning against the garden wall I checked the color of the crystal bead on my bracelet, it glowed the color of a sword's blade, protective and strong.

Taliesin gave me this bracelet three months ago for my sixteenth birthday. He used hair from the mane of his Unicorn form. It showed people's energy, the way he saw them, kind of like a mood ring for those around me. I'd never seen silver before.

"Who are you? Why do you come to this home?" said a voice in my head.

I froze and looked around me. I didn't see anyone or anything. Wait, one of the stone guardians near the door, it looked kind of like a lion, was staring at me. I focused on the statue. *"My name is Sapphire Rayner. My friend's family owns this inn and has allowed me to stay here."*

"I allow people to stay here," the voice roared. *"And few magical beings are ever allowed past these gates. Your family have already entered, but I couldn't communicate with any of them."*

"There is a unicorn, has he come, he can talk with you too."

"I let the unicorn enter, he has my blessing, you do not. I ask again, who are you?"

Power surged around me, hot and thick. *"I am a Child of Fire, a descendant of the Phoenix King Shamash and his Queen Aya."*

"And why are you here?"

"My family and I are here to open a portal to Akasha so magical beings can return home, if they wish too."

The power eased. *"I will see. But know if I deem you and your family unworthy I shall cast you out."*

"There will be no need. If you do not want us here simply tell me and we will leave peacefully."

"For now, since the Muta family has offered their hospitality I shall grant you permission to enter."

"Thank you."

"I am watching, Child of Fire."

The energy faded and the crystal became a soft periwinkle color, that meant peace and contentment, with a tiny silver flecks letting me know the guardian was still present. Well, that was a lovely welcome to Tokyo.

Looking up at the inn I sighed. Yeah, me in a building over five hundred years old that was magically protected, not a good plan. The front porch was covered in shoes, a testament to the uniqueness of our troupe. Doc Martins, Birkenstocks, Converse, sequins ballet slippers, penny loafers, neon bright

Nikes, and more where heaped together. One of the staff was straightening them into pairs and lining them up neatly.

Stepping onto the gray stone path, I strengthened my protective shield, in my mind it looked like a big soap bubble, and hoping I could block out all the emotions the building had stored, I stepped forward. Being empathic had its up and downs, and I feared their centuries old hotel would be a major down.

"Sapphire," Miu said standing on the porch her hands on her hips. Her peridot green eyes were narrowed. "Come on, I promise it'll be okay."

"I'm just admiring their garden," I said not wanting to offend Miu. Even with several of the large trees bare the garden was lovely. Dark green pine trees with long needles curved in windswept shapes. Boulders covered in fuzzy moss and stone lanterns had been placed with care. While I didn't understand the how or the why, I could feel the deliberate intentions left behind by the gardeners.

Toeing off my Keds, I placed them neatly along the wall so the staff wouldn't have to. I wiggled my toes to loosen my socks then slipped on the fancy wooden flip flop style sandals provided by the inn. Taking a breath, I stepped onto the polished wood floor.

"I am Muto, welcome to my inn." An older Japanese woman bowed, her black hair done up in a bun and she wore a light blue kimono with white and silver cranes on it.

I bowed as Mui had taught me and prayed my pronunciation would be all right. "Arigato Gozaimasu Muto-san, your Ryokan is lovely. I know I will enjoy my stay here."

"My niece speaks so fondly of all of you. I am honored to meet you and be able to provide a place for you to stay during your visit. Come, I will show you to your room."

I followed Muto down the hall, our wooden sandals echoing with each step. The outside walls were beige with sections of shoji screens which opened letting in light and fresh air and allowing people to take in the beauty of the grounds. We climbed the narrow worn stairs to the fourth floor.

"Auntie has put you in the smallest room since you're the only one staying alone. Normally, they don't allow single guests but since the circus has rented the entire Ryokan, she's making an exception for you," Miu said.

"Where are you staying?" We always roomed together. True Miu was a messy roommate, but she kept her clutter to her side.

Miu tilted her head forward her two high ponytails falling over her shoulders in a shiny black cascade she's recently streaked with pink. "I'm staying at my house with my family."

"Oh, of course. I'll miss you."

Slipping her arm through mine, she squeezed. "Please you'll love the time alone. Anyway we'll hang out every day. I can't wait to introduce you to my friends and show you Tokyo."

Muto pulled open a shoji screen and stepped back.

I stepped forward but Miu held my arm and pointed to the sandals I was wearing. Yes, no sandals on the tatami mats. I slipped off the sandals and walked into the room, the mats were smooth and a little soft under my feet. In the center of the room was a small table low to the ground. Against one wall was a twin futon on the floor, covered with a thick white comforter and in the middle a circle of an embroidered crane flying into the sunset.

On the wall opposite the futon was a small television and shoji which opened to a closet. To the left of the bed was a shelf set into the wall that held an ikebana arrangement. A pale green vase which held a twisting branch with small tight buds. I opened the shoji on the outside wall. Miu said I had to carefully look over the room before thanking my hostess for it. I stepped out onto a small balcony screened on both side for privacy and looked down onto the garden. Right below was a bare tree, small buds just starting to form on its pale gray branches. Gold, white, and red koi fish swam in the gardens pond. Dark green moss covered rocks, lanterns, and grew between the flat black stones which paved a path that wondered between the sculpted trees.

I turned and bowed. "It is beautiful, Arigato Gozaimasu Muto-san. I will be so happy here I won't want to leave."

"I hope so, Rayner-san. My daughter shall be up with tea shortly."

"The room is cute," Miu said. "And I told you it would be all right, you don't feel anything do you?"

I closed my eyes and dropped my shield a bit. Peace, tranquility, strict repression, and protection all hummed about me as faint as a bee. No strong emotions. No love, anger, death, sex, nothing that I would normally feel, and sometimes see the emotional imprints that had been left behind. "Is it because of the wood and paper?" Stone held emotions and impressions for centuries, but wood being lighter and more porous didn't hold emotions the same way.

"Partly I'm sure, but my family is Shinto. When they clean the rooms they also cleanse the room of energy and emotions." Miu smiled and moved to stand next to me.

"This is amazing. I never thought I'd be able to stay in a building this old." I sighed, not wanting to spoil the mood but she needed to know. "The guardian might not let us stay, well me and the other Children of Fire."

"What are you talking about?" Miu asked.

"Your family has a spirit or being of some kind that guards the Ryokan and all who stay here. It's very powerful. For now we have been given permission to stay, but the guardian is watching us and if it doesn't want us here we will be kicked out."

"It's that powerful?" Miu asked.

"Oh yes."

"When I was a child I was told stories about the guardians, and my brother and I would leave offerings, not only at the family shrine but also for the stone lions, but I didn't think they were real or that powerful."

I raised an eyebrow. After all we had seen why would she doubt anything at this point? Personally, I kept waiting to run into Count Dracula any day now.

"All right yes, I should be more open minded at this point." Miu leaned against the balcony. "In a few weeks the cherry tree will bloom and you'll have such an amazing view, and the scent is very soft but beautiful."

"I can't wait to see the cherry blossoms." I watched several of the performers bowing to a male staff as they passed. They didn't seem to know when to stop and the poor man's arms were full but he kept bowing. "I hope I did okay. There are so many rules and rituals in Japan. Thanks for trying to teach me."

"You did just fine, and being a foreigner no one actually expects you to do the right thing," Miu said. "It's funny we study English and American culture looking for the same structure and rules. Most of you know very little of the grammar we are forced to learn, and most of the time there are so many exceptions to the rules, it makes us afraid of English. There is no order. Did you know I took classes on how to eat like an American? The proper degree with which to hold your soup bowl when getting the last of the soup out, and the precise angle with which to place your knife and fork on the plate."

"Really? That's crazy. Were you disappointed to realize that none of us do it exactly the same way?"

"No, relieved. Once I realized American's and especially our circus troupe didn't really care about the angle of my ponytail, or if I cut my noodles or not, it was freeing. I tried a bit of everything until I found what I liked and made me happy." Miu sighed and wrinkled her nose. "Of course now that I'm back home I'll have to be all proper and polite all the time."

"Sit next to me. I'm likely to forget all the rules so you'll look perfect next to me." I pointed at a cluster of buds on the cherry tree. "Look, it's a faerie. Even they are proper in Japan."

A tiny delicate fairy with porcelain skin, wide brown almond eyes, pointed ears, and green hair swept up in the chignon with a small silver comb in it was singing to the buds. She held an odd looking harp and wore a pretty kimono made from iris petals. Her clear iridescent wings fluttered behind her as she sang. I looked around the garden and saw several more faeries in traditional dress working with the plants, their movements precise and purposeful. Their different shades of green hair and clothes made of leaves and petals were the only things that seemed to hint at a wild earthy magic.

"I hope all the magical creatures here are this kind and calm. Opening the portal to Akasha will be easy."

"You wish," Miu said. "Do you not remember all the Japanese horror movies we watched? We'll need Taliesin and his Unicorn powers to get those that want to go home to Akasha through the portal safety."

I shivered. "True, I've never seen so many scary movies where the evil wins."

"I bring tea," said a young woman in a simple brown kimono with white flowers.

"Arigato Gozaimasu," I said.

She set it on the table, backed out of the room then knelt and kowtowed before exiting the room.

"Will they do that all the time?" That just felt wrong. I am so not that special or important or conceited to need someone to kowtow to me.

"Yep, it's a sign of respect just go with it. If they think you're upset or uncomfortable it'll just get worse. I'll come by and get you guys tonight for dinner. My mom and I are making a big feast."

"Oh wait, I'm almost out of the spray you made me. It really helps protect me from other people's emotions."

Miu smiled. "I'm so glad it's helping. I'm also glad to be using my Phoenix gift of healing to prevent problems instead of patching you guys up. I'm going to tweak the recipe a bit, the books you gave me on aromatherapy for Christmas are so interesting."

"Anali said you helped ease her morning sickness, and Kayin loves the body oil you made for him."

Blushing, Miu slipped on her sandals. "I'm glad. See you tonight."

"Bye Miu." I smiled as her sandals echoed down the hall and stairs. I poured myself some tea and looked out the window. Beyond the garden were shingled roof tops then tall shining skyscrapers.

A faerie fluttered in front of me. Her white hair was streaked with pale green and her nails were long and sharp. "You feel like a Child of Fire, a powerful one. The guardian asked me to speak with you."

You mean come check me out. "Yes, I am."

"There are other's here, who also feel of Phoenix energy, but we see no fire," she said. Her voice sounded like the wind whistling through the trees.

I took out the protective contacts, showing her the Phoenix fire which danced in my eyes.

"Why do you hide?"

"Because the Sons of Belial can't track us if they can't see the fire in our eyes." No point in making things easy for the bad guys.

"Are you the child of the prophecy? The Jewel who will open the doorway to Akasha so we can go home?"

"I am."

She nodded. "Good. I have waited more than two thousand years for someone to come and open the portals again. I should like to see Akasha again."

"The portal is in the north in Hokkaido, I can't remember the specific place."

She held up a tiny hand. "Hush, child. I remember crossing the portal four thousand years ago to bless the Phoenix King and his human bride's first child. They also had onyx black hair streaked ruby red, eyes of peridot flecked with gold, and skin that looked kissed by pearl and copper. Their Jewels, they called them, just like you are their Jewel now."

"Yes," I nodded.

She looked me over and sniffed. I guess gray yoga pants and a cable knit sweater didn't impress her.

"I shall tell the others so those who wish to leave will be ready and by the portal waiting for you." She flew out over the balcony. "And I will tell the guardian you are who you claim to be, but you will still be watched. We do not allow strangers with such powers in our home lightly."

"Of course, I understand, and thank you for giving us a chance." Yay, I passed the first level of inspection. I sipped my jasmine tea. I loved the slightly bitter flora taste. Watching the sky, faeries fluttered up to see the prophesied Jewel of the Phoenix King and Queen. None of them seem impressed.

* * *

Bodies lay around me. I couldn't open the portal to Akasha. No help was coming. I couldn't save anyone. Laughter echoed along the cave walls. Icy fear filled me. The vision swirled, the screams and cries for help faded.

The sky was the wrong color. I wasn't dreaming in Akasha, but this wasn't a normal dream either. It looked fake, like a badly colorized black and white movie. Sitting on the grass I opened up my empathy. A desire to connect, and a wrongness was all I felt. A snake slithered over my leg. It didn't do anything so I ignored it. Then another came winding around my wrist. I'd been seeing snakes in my dreams lately, but this is the first time they touched me. Was some snake being trying to reach out to me for help?

"Is anyone here?" I called out my voice echoing as if I was in a bare room and not outside in the grass. "I'll try and help you if I can."

Another snake came up. It coiled, began to rattle, and lunged.

Knocking pulled me out of my dream.

"Come in," I said reaching down to rub my leg where the snake almost bit me.

"We are headed out to lunch, want to come?" My aunt Anali asked. Her shoulder length dark brown hair framed her round face. Her aqua blue sari shone in the neutral colored room.

It sounded like a request, but it wasn't. I looked at my laptop, I had a lot I needed to work on, but it would have to wait until I had soothed my aunt and uncle's worries. "Just let me freshen up and I'll meet you guys in the front."

"Okay, but hurry your uncle is sure he can remember exactly where he and your mother ate the very best soba noodles when they visited here twenty years ago." Her hand rested on her belly, which was beginning to round with the baby. Her first three months had been really difficult but now in her fourth month she was feeling much better.

"I'll be quick." Uncle Gavin made sure to take me to all the places he and my mom had gone whenever we were close enough to them. My mom had died, well she was murdered, when I was five. She hid me in the foster care system in San Francisco and my uncle found me last year when I turned fifteen and my Phoenix powers emerged. He felt guilty for the time we were apart. Some days he gets this sad look in his peridot green eyes, and I'm sure I could get him to buy me diamonds he is so consumed with guilt.

I washed my hands and dried them on a soft white towel. I didn't blame Gavin. After all my mom had changed my name and given me a fake birth certificate in order to protect me from the Sons of Belial. And we were finally figuring out how to be a family. I was even excited about the baby and becoming a sister-slash-cousin. Walking down the stairs, I wondered how many feet had helped wear down the center of each step into a soft curve. I ran my hand along the railing and didn't feel much of anything, whispers of serenity and happiness. This was the best hotel ever. What if all of Japan was this emotionally clean?

"Are you ready?" Gavin asked putting on a beanie, his bright red hair sticking out and falling over his shoulders. "I know exactly where I'm going, it'll be so much fun."

"Yeah right," I said. "That's what you said in Munich. If it hadn't been for the Askafroa we ran into we would have never found our way."

"Oh ye of little faith. I have an address." Gavin waved a piece of paper.

"Well get in the taxi," said Anali wrapping her gray shall around her shoulders. "I'm hungry."

"Here please," Gavin said handing the driver the piece of paper.

"Hai," the man said then placed his white gloved hands on the wheel and drove, calmly into traffic using his turn signals and stopping at yellow lights.

"We're in the twilight zone." I've been all over North and South America and a lot of Europe, but never had I been in such a clean polite taxi. There were white lace doilies on the backs of the seats and a vase of flowers on the dashboard.

"The Japanese are very polite people," Gavin said. "I'm hoping you kids soak some of it up while you're here."

"Gavin," said Anali. "It isn't the kids' fault you got into and lost a prank war with them."

"Yeah, and I wasn't even part of it." 'Cause I'm not stupid enough to get involved in a prank war. "Is that why the boys aren't coming with us? Are you still upset that you and Michael lost?"

"First we didn't lose, we decided to stop the war," Gavin said. "Michael is very busy as the manager of our troupe, he has too many responsibilities to have his time occupied by pranks."

"Oh yes, of course," I said.

"And I thought it would nice to have lunch with just the three of us. The boys can take of themselves. And we could have won, if we had been willing to crush their delicate egos."

The boys—Taliesin, Kayin, Sasha, and Shin—were all circus performers with fans who gave them their numbers after shows and even followed them on Facebook. They were stared at as they walked down the street. Their beauty and muscular form attracting every eye. It would take a lot to damage their egos.

"So tell me about when you came here with my mom," I said, changing the subject. The memories I had of my mom and dad were faint, only the journal of quotes and life lessons my mom left for me connected me to her. Gavin had given me my dad's family home in London for my sixteenth birthday. We had spent several days going through family photos and listening to the butler and cook tell stories about my dad when he was little and my grandparents. Gavin was the only blood family I had left, well until their baby was born. Thankfully, Anali had welcomed me into her heart as well as her life, and with the boys and the circus I was creating my own unique family. Of course, being raised in the foster care system, I wasn't sure what a real family was supposed to be, so that made things extra fun sometimes.

"We came the summer before she went to college. All I wanted to do was go to the arcades and the manga stores. Gabrielle and my parents made me go to museums and temples and other cultural stuff." Gavin smiled. "I think the only thing we both agreed on was sumo wrestling was oddly fascinating and this soba noodle place was amazing, our parents hated both."

"So other than the noodle place what was your favorite part?" Anali asked.

"I got Gabrielle to go with me to an arcade after she made me spend the morning at the Hello Kitty store. Anyway we spent hours on one of those dancing games. We hadn't seen one before. Our legs ached the next day we'd payed so long, and our face hurt from all the smiling and laughing we did."

"Here," said the driver with a bow of his head.

"Arigato," Anali and I said as we slid out of the taxi.

"It looks just the same." Gavin took Anali's hand and led us to a small door. We all had to duck to enter.

"Konnichiwa." A small women waved us to a table.

We sat on the floor and looked at the menu, all in Japanese, Anali and I both turned to Gavin.

"When I was here last time we relied on your mom's Phoenix gift of languages. This time I had Miu write it down for me." Gavin handed the paper to the waitress who bowed and went to the kitchen, returning a moment later with hot tea for each of us.

"Sometimes I wish I could understand all languages." One of my Phoenix gifts is being able to understand other languages, but only if a being from Akasha is speaking, or wrote it down. My powers all revolve around connection, and the magic connects us enough so I can understand them, but it always gives me a headache if I translate for too long.

Gavin leaned over the table. "Your mom used to pretend she couldn't understand what was being said because she thought it funny to listen to people talk about us. Well most of the time, some people got rude and she would turn bright red."

"Eavesdroppers never hear any good of themselves," I said. "It is important to respect people's privacy. That even if they are speaking about you, that doesn't mean it's mean or intended to be cruel, but maybe they are confused or venting, or trying to sort out how they feel. So even if you can listen into a conversation or read a private journal, it is best to respect other people's privacy."

"I haven't heard you quote your mom's journal in a while," Gavin said.

I shrugged. "You told me that my mom wrote the journal while she was pregnant."

"Yeah, she was scared she'd be a horrible parent and forget to teach you important things." Gavin shook his head and laughed. "She was frantic to get all the quotes and her thoughts on them written down before you were born."

"And it helped in a lot. In the past everything that came up in my life seemed to be helped by my mom's journal, but now," I shrugged. "Life just seems a lot more complicated and things have come up that mom didn't prepare me for."

Anali reached out and squeezed my hand. "I'm sorry, Sapphire. Your life has gotten a lot more complicated than any of us had planned. And while I don't have answers for everything, I am happy to listen and try our best to help."

"Both of us will," Gavin added.

"Thank you, that means a lot." I blushed and felt grateful. After the Avalon… had it been a fight, battle, skirmish, altercation? I didn't know what to call it. All I knew is I was the leader and I had failed. So many people got hurt. Some died. Visions of lifeless eyes filled my mind. Everyone said it wasn't my fault but they were wrong. Ramsey, a selkie and my first boyfriend, lost so much that day. A knife to his back, which pulled out his magic and life-force sending it to Cartazonon, forced him to go to Akasha to heal. His brother and band mates had been killed later by Cartazonon so he could heal from the fight. If I had been a better leader, a strong leader, none of this would have happened.

"So how are things? You seem to be doing well," Anali asked.

Translate into, I haven't seen any more signs of depression that the books told me to look out for but I'm still worried. "Good, I finished the English, World Government, and World Religions classes on the plane."

"You've been doing a lot of school work," Gavin said.

I sipped some tea and shrugged. "It goes really quickly when I don't have classroom lectures to sit through and students goofing off to slow everything down."

"Well, you're grades are wonderful, and I'm glad to see you focused on your education." Anali smiled at me.

"Thank you." I really just wanted school done with. It didn't help my destiny, well, except for my newest class.

"How are you liking the leadership class?" Gavin asked.

"It's very interesting. Right now I'm reading about how to support people by understanding their strengths and weaknesses."

"Since you just finished a bunch of classes what's next?" Anali asked.

"Well, the next is Shakespeare, Economics, and Photography. I'm halfway done with Chemistry and just started the next semester of French."

"That's wonderful." Anali sipped her tea and rubbed her belly. Did all pregnant women do that?

Gavin frowned. "It still seems like a lot of school work."

"Is that a bad thing?" Right after the battle of Avalon I'd wallowed in depression. I'd allowed it to affect my day to day life. First it had been Gavin and Anali always there, always checking up on me, then the others started in. How are you? Have you eaten? Are you sleeping well? Falling back on what I'd learned in group homes, I forced myself to meet the basic requirements eat, sleep, show interest in a few activities, and do well in school. Add in not self-harming or thinking of killing myself and I was left alone. Until now.

"Of course it's not a bad thing." Anali assured me then glared at Gavin.

"No, but you don't seem to get out and do much," Gavin said.

"I'm out now. And I do go out. But Kayin and Shin are dating so they need time alone. Miu has other friends. Taliesin likes spending time alone." I shrugged trying for teenage nonchalance, but fearing yet another hurdle would be set up in proving I was okay every day.

The waitress brought our meal. It felt like a blessing.

"This looks great, what is everything?" I asked hoping Gavin would be his easily distractable self.

"Okay," Gavin said with a smile. "In the small bowls is fresh grated ginger, green onions, and shiso leaves. Put whatever you like into the sauce. Then you dip the cold noodles into the sauce, just a quick dip and slurp them up."

"This looks so lovely," Anali said as she added ginger to her sauce.

I picked up the white porcelain bowl of shiso, a diced green leaf that smelled slightly citrusy. I added some to my sauce then put in ginger and green onion. The purple-gray soba noodles sat on a bamboo mat in cone shape topped with fine strips of nori seaweed and sesame seeds. Using my chopsticks I grabbed some noodles, dunked them in the sauce and slurped them up. "These are delicious," I said picking up some more noodles.

"Yes, very good," said Anali adding more ginger to her sauce.

"They taste exactly as I remember them." Gavin smiled sadly. "Your mom searched all over New York for noodles that tasted like these, as far as I know she never found any."

"Thank you for bringing me here," I said before taking another bite. I'd have to bring the boys, they'd love these.

"Of course," Gavin said.

We ate for a while, watching people walking past. Kids holding their mom's hand, groups of teen girls and boys in stylish clothes always separated by gender, workers, business people, older couples with silver hair, and occasionally a monk and people dressed in kimonos would wonder by.

"So, have you had any dreams lately?" Anali asked when we had finished eating and were sipping tea.

I shrugged. "None since we ran into the Sons of Belial in Austria. And that one was short. Ever since Cartazonon figured out who I was, he watches for me and sends me away from him. I know he's plotting something, I'm just not sure what."

"I'm sure you're right, but I've enjoyed not having Cartazonon trying to capture us and suck out our magic," Gavin said.

"They don't seem to be hunting magical creatures hardly at all either," Anali said. "At least not for a while."

I shuddered remembering the last time I saw Cartazonon suck the magic and life out of someone. I should be happy I hadn't had to see it in months, but I knew he was plotting, he wanted me to join him. And he desperately wanted Taliesin. I played with the bracelet Taliesin gave me, the crystal bead clasp glowed a soft lavender-blue color.

"I have been dreaming about snakes. It's not every night and sometimes it happens when I nap. Anali woke me up just in time today, one was coiled and read to bite me. It's very weird."

Gavin frowned. "That is odd. We'll have to look into it. Thank you for telling us."

"Course." I had learned my lesson, full disclosure of anything that could affect the group. And if I wasn't sure and it seemed private I went to Anali to see what she thought. She always respected my privacy, and was the groups' peace keeper. No one but Gavin argued with her and I don't think he ever won.

"Try not to worry too much, it could simply be a reaction to all the horror movies you watch," Anali said.

"True," I said. "We did just watch Slither and Anaconda a few weeks ago."

Gavin grunted. "That could be it, and you didn't seem to like the cruise very much."

We'd done a river cruise in Germany to open a portal. Gavin thought it would be a fun, scenic way to travel. I spent most of my time in the bathroom. "I don't like the being on the water like that. Maybe if I could swim."

"Wait, you can't swim?" Gavin asked.

I shook my head.

"We should teach you how," Anali said. "It could be an important skill. I'll ask Miu to help me find classes for you since we'll be in Tokyo for a while."

"Do I have to? I'm not sure Phoenixes are supposed to like the water."

Gavin frowned. "It doesn't bother the rest of us, and you seem to like the water just fine."

"Kayin doesn't know how to swim very well either."

"Then we'll get him lessons too," Anali said in a voice that let me know she was done discussing the subject.

"Fine," I sighed and looked out the window. I hoped Kayin wouldn't be mad at me for ratting him out.

"We do need to discuss something else," Anali said. Her voice soft and apologetic. Their nervousness bounced against my shields whatever was coming they didn't think I'd like it.

"Okay."

Gavin cleared his throat. "You know that we've been planning to stop traveling in a few months. The doctors all said it would be best for Anali to be settled by the time she's six to seven months along."

"Yes." I nodded. "The cirque will take a break and we'll all go to India."

"Yes, well, things have changed." Anali sighed then looked at me. He amber brown eyes sad. "My empathy is getting all tangled up in the baby. I'm having difficulty protecting myself from other people's emotions."

"That's not safe." I knew how it felt to be overwhelmed by emotions that weren't your own.

"No," said Gavin, "it's not. It looks like we're going to have to leave sooner. We were planning on staying in Japan with you then going to India."

"Okay."

"We don't want you to feel abandoned," Anali assured me. "And you all can come with us."

"Except, Michael has us scheduled to perform. And that would take away several acts," I said. "No, we'll be fine. You need to protect the baby."

"Philip is going to come here to watch over you and the others," Gavin said.

I smiled. I'd met Philip over a year ago right after I came into my Phoenix powers and started taking classes at the San Francisco Center for the Circus Arts. I still talked to him, as he did research for us and had written several books on magical creatures. "Cool, I like Philip."

"I dislike leaving you and not being able to protect all of you," Gavin said. "I'm not one hundred percent sure we won't be taking you with us."

"Uncle Gavin, I'll be fine." He might not be sure but I was. I had a destiny to fulfill, magical beings counting on me, and I was the leader of our group of Children of Fire. I couldn't let them down and I wouldn't abandon them.

A Dragon's Clutch can be found here-
http://alicamckennajohnson.com/books/a-dragons-clutch/

To find out when the next Children of Fire book will be published, learn more about my "eccentric artistic process", or to ask me questions, or send comments you can find me on-

Twitter
https://twitter.com/AMckennaJohnson

Facebook
https://www.facebook.com/AlicaMckennaJohnsonAuthor

Goodreads
http://www.goodreads.com/author/show/5755438.Alica_Mck
enna_Johnson

My website/blog
www.alicamckennajohnson.com

AND to get information about my upcoming books, book signings, and talks subscribe to my newsletter. It only goes out when I have something of value to share. Cross my heart!
http://eepurl.com/bc5bzn

FREE DOWNLOAD

Get your free copy of
KAYIN'S FIRE when you
sign up for the author's
VIP mailing list.
Get started here:
http://eepurl.com/bc5bzn

ABOUT THE AUTHOR

Being told she was a horrible speller and would never learn to use a comma correctly, Alica never thought to write down the stories she constantly had running through her head. Doesn't everyone daydream about flying on a spaceship while walking to school?

Not until she was thirty did Alica dare to write down any of the people living exciting lives in her head. The relief was instantaneous. By giving them life on the page they could be released from her mind and given greater adventures.

As her books grew in size and the voices in her head learned to wait their turn, Alica found a loyal group to journey with. Women who would help her slay her commas, and use their magical gifts to traverse plot holes, transform words into their proper spelling, and release characters from any Mary Sue spells they might be under.

In-between magical adventures, Alica is mom to two personal kids, five foster kids, has one exceptional hubby, a bunny she knows is plotting her death, and some fish, aka her daughter's minions.

Made in the USA
Middletown, DE
24 April 2017